BREATHLESS
TO CASABLANCA

BREATHLESS TO CASABLANCA

A NOVEL

JAMES DOUGLAS

Welcome Rain
New York

BREATHLESS TO CASABLANCA
Copyright © 2000, 2002 by James Douglas.
All rights reserved.

Library of Congress CIP data available from the publisher.

Direct any inquiries to
Welcome Rain Publishers LLC.

ISBN 1-56649-260-2

First U.S. Edition: October 2002
1 3 5 7 9 10 8 6 4 2

PART ONE

1.

The Armory is quite a conspicuous building. Strolling downtown Manhattan, one can hardly miss those red walls, even though the surrounding skyscrapers dwarf its modest five-floors. Stretching the full length of a block, on 67th Street between Lexington and Park, the old arsenal houses, among other tenants, an Army Club.

Among other tenants! Like invisible ivy, legends and rumors have grown up around the windowless rooms of the heavy-stoned building. Insiders would be happy to confirm with a nostalgic sigh, that the FBI once used these premises to eavesdrop on the nearby Soviet Mission at the United Nations. And today? Well, they might say, not all that much has changed, except for the cutting-edge millennial technology of the equipment that is being used up there. The Armory's upper floors harbor one of the finest, most efficient Intercept and Monitor (I&M) centers of the Joint Intelligence Agencies (JIG) of the United States.

The question is, whether the NYPD's 19th Precinct station house being located no more than a block away can be ascribed to mere coincidence. At that venue, solid twin rows of police cruisers did their unsubtle best to festoon this massive hulk of a building. And, on the smooth walkway to the entrance, small clusters of New York's finest, garbed in workaday blue, were in the process of taking five, nursing a regular stick of tobacco or a cup of coffee.

Upstairs on the second floor of the Armory young Rick, a graduate of Quantico Academy, the FBI talent tank, sat at his desk. He had spent the first years of service in Counterterrorism, then was transferred to Communications at the Armory. Thick, heavy curls of blond hair framed a handsome face that propped up a set of rather dainty glasses – Rick Norris, boy next door.

Motes of dust swirled through stray beams of late-afternoon sunlight, gilding the telephone and computers, the encryption and monitoring devices that surrounded Rick's work space. This afternoon, as so many afternoons of late, Rick was fighting boredom. Gazing at those dust-speckled sunbeams, he created sudden turbulence by blowing out minor tornadoes of air. Turning and twisting, the tiny motes flashed in the light, reminding him of fireflies on balmy evenings, with an ominously blue-black thunderhead piling up beyond the river. Back home.

The fax machine started purring. Rick's head came up from routinely checking his watch.

Hermetically shielded from any and all outside interference, the communications center occupied the fourth floor. Rick's workspace, wedged in between other computer desks, was part of the administrative section. The low-priority messages that came in on his fax usually did little more than perpetuate in-house red tape. Not so this time. Not by a *long* shot!

Still caught up in the laziness of the afternoon and

humming an old country tune, Rick Norris absently picked the single sheet off the tray. His gaze focused. As he began to read, he stopped breathing. His eyes darted from word to word, scanning the text. *No, sir, this ain't no administrative mumbo jumbo. This is action!* Young Mr. Norris was looking at a message, automatically decrypted, from 853, station chief, Tashkent, capital city of Uzbekistan.

Start. FROM 853. TODAY 18.00 HRS EST
BOMB ATTACK ISL. FUND. TERRORISTS
ON GREAT CENTRAL STATION NYC. Stop.

GREAT Central Station? Huh? Must've been in a real hurry, that 853! As he automatically crossed out *GREAT*, jotted in *GRAND* above it, Rick Norris noted with a certain professional detachment that his hands were trembling. It was 5:35 p.m. on his digital wristwatch. He marked the time in the lower left-hand corner of the sheet as goosebumps started creeping up his arms. He froze, as if he were sitting in an icy tomb somewhere in Alaska.

Crisis management had been an integral part of his training at Quantico, but this type of intelligence message packed enough of a punch to make even a seasoned operative bristle. Rick took a deep breath, and with his right middle finger pressed the safe-line key to the Chief of Operations (COP) Counter-terrorism, New York Police Department. Meanwhile, his left tapped the big computer through ID and password into a search mode. While calmly passing on the Red-Alert message to the COP, he watched the response to his identity search for 853 materialize on the screen. Benjamin 'Benn' Sweeney, Operation Poppy, deep cover, inside Islamic terrorist leader Yussef bin Golem's organization somewhere in the far wastes of Afghanistan.

At this point in time, only Rick Norris might guess that field agent Sweeney put his life on the line when he inserted such an obvious error.

As for agent Benn Sweeney himself, he had initially viewed this move as a calculated risk. Should someone in terrorist bin Golem's crew challenge him by claiming to know the proper term *Grand* Central Station, Sweeney would counter with a fit of anger. *Are you who's never got further than the outskirts of fuckin' Kabul gonna stand there and tell me a New Yorker don't know whether it's Grand or Great Central Station, you sumfabitchin' camel driver...* That ought to teach them!

Still, the moment the message with the telltale glitch went through, a sinking feeling in the pit of his stomach must have told Agent Sweeney this was one stupid thing to have done. All it would accomplish was to confuse people like Nick Norris, by multiplying the number of scenarios. Certainly, they would understand that Agent Sweeney was in a jam, yes, but what did it mean? Did it make the warning a fake or should it nevertheless be taken seriously? Of course, the operatives would think of a so-called AIO, an as-if-option. That was standard procedure for this type of thing. They would act as if the message was authentic.

Agent Sweeney soon had realized that he had blundered. *They'll know I got cold feet, caved in,* he mused. *Did something highly unprofessional. Went and put a personal problem above precise message content. They'll know I almost copped out. Hell, I did cop out!*

4

2.

It was rush hour in Grand Central Station when Yassir arrived. He was on time, right on schedule, ready for the next blow. At 5:45 p.m. he moved his black Range Rover up on Lexington Avenue to the lane reserved for buses and cabs between 42nd and 43rd Streets. He ignored the yellow cab honking behind him. Police cruisers and EMS van sirens were wailing everywhere in the highly congested six-block radius around Grand Central. His black shining eyes stared to the right, at the row of double doors where commuters were squeezing their way in and out of Grand Central Station.

The young Jihad warrior clenched his lips as he sat behind the wheel. The sudden police activity hit him unexpectedly. And he noticed two cops leaning against the station wall looking at him. He ignored them uneasily, trying to be as indifferent to them as to the legions of burnout commuters going in and out of the terminal doors. Crowds and noise were a normal part of the everyday reality of New York. Masses of people were on the way home, rushing to their trains that awaited them in a maze of underground platforms.

Young Yassir knew that most of the doors into Grand Central were surrounded with heavy steel frames – but the ones in front of him were being replaced, and their temporary frame was made of fragile wood. He had checked out all the entrances to Grand Central, and it hadn't taken him long to identify the weak link on Lexington Avenue that he sat in front of now.

A heavy red truck drove up on the tail of the Range Rover and honked his horn in frustration. Some people turned their heads for a second, but then apathetically went on their way. After all, this was Manhattan, the center of the world! Or at least the center of the world that smelled like fame and riches.

Immediately after receiving Rick's warning, the head of NYPD's Counter-terrorism Unit put their well-rehearsed defensive measures into action. On the west side of the station, patrol cars cordoned off Vanderbilt Avenue between 42nd and 44th Streets. Black police vans pulled up, and SWAT teams in combat fatigues leapt out and scattered. Mounted officers trotted up on horseback. A helicopter thumped above the terminal roof. Megaphones blared at the commuters, telling them not to enter Grand Central.

But there hadn't been enough time to secure the doorways. People stopped walking on the busy streets to watch the police. Heads turned everywhere, trying to find out what was going on. Many ignored the warnings, swarming into the main concourse of Grand Central where the high domed ceiling resounded with the sounds of chatter and the megaphones like the battle noise of ancient armies. Hundreds of travelers and terminal employees were trapped inside arcade shops and restaurants. A bomb attack would wreak havoc among them and all the commuters still pushing their way in and out of the buildings many doors. Meanwhile hordes of reporters have gathered in the narrow space of Vanderbilt Avenue.

In the passage between Lexington Avenue and the main concourse, NYPD Officer Phillips felt sick to his stomach. He had just heard about the threatened bombing over his police radio. What should he do? He wasn't used to this. He saw two detectives from the train-station detail, which is only a small-crimes unit. Nothing even close to dealing with a bomb threat. Phillip's normal routine was to patrol the station at rush hour. He had started his duty less than an hour ago. This was kind of fun shit. Hadn't even had his coffee and doughnut. Usually he found himself giving directions to lost tourists – or at worst helping a sick commuter. Where was his partner? She should have been over by the newsstand. His wandering eyes suddenly caught sight of the black Range Rover parked out on Lexington Avenue. He stood staring at it, uneasily, his mouth gaping, as if his broad nose wasn't letting in enough air. His wide shoulders and thick bull neck started to tremble, making the three medal stripes over his badge shake. His eyes widened, the whites contrasting sharply against his coal black skin.

Outside in the Range Rover, Yassir sees the two officers suddenly come toward him. This is his moment; he knows what he must do. He whirls the steering wheel and floors the gas pedal. The roaring engine of the lurching SUV suddenly changes the apathetic pedestrians in front of him as they dodge his rush toward the temporary doorframe. Yassir sees only contours and flying shapes as bodies are bouncing off his hood. Wood and glass shatter and splinter as he smashes into the passageway. Clutching the wheel with glowing eyes, he screams as the Rover gains speed. The V-8's roar sounds like a battle cry in his ears.

His instructions had been precise. Just before 6 p.m. he was to crash through the doors and drive right into the round information booth in the center of the concourse. There, six of his allies disguised as commuters would pull out their guns and start spraying the crowd. In the confusion Yassir was told he could make his getaway. His mission was more than important. And if everything went right, he was sure he would be accepted into the much sought-after Dynamite Club – an honor given only to those who had placed and detonated an explosive charge at the risk of their own lives. This was absolutely, positively his best mission – he had been dreaming of this moment for years. It was his day.

Crazed and determined, Yassir guides the Range Rover over the smooth marble floor of the newly renovated station concourse. White knuckles showing on his clenched hands at the wheel. His eyes search frantically for his compatriots with their blazing guns. In front of him the crowd scatters like gazelles before a hungry lion. It never dawns on him that his allies are nowhere to be found – that he was lied to – that he is completely on his own.

He roars past the arched passages to the train platforms, seeing a mob of travelers pushed back by policemen beneath the flipping numbers of the Train Departures board. The round clock on the information booth reads 5:58. Officer Phillips does, as he will later say, what any New York City cop would do. He steps in front of the black Rover. Sweat is pouring down his face. He lifts his Glock and steadies it with both hands, aims at the driver. Yassir's mind races. Success is assured. He sees the tall black cop between him and his goal. *What a hulk of a man! Goodbye Hulk!*

But Phillips keeps his cool and pulls the trigger again and again. The 9mm bullets shatter the windshield, and then Yassir's face. Phillips leaps to safety just before the Rover smashes into the information booth. The crash is followed by a silence as eerie as a grave as the Rover's engine stalls. The hands of the round brass clock read 5:59.

The shots from Phillips' gun and the raging crash leave only the most hardboiled city rubbernecks in the concourse. Phillips rushes to the Rover, joined by a SWAT team with machine guns at the ready. He opens the driver's side door, and the terrorist's body slides gently down to the marble floor – the face mangled beyond recognition, like a piece of meat on a butcher's hook. A square box dangles from the dead man's belt.

"The detonator!" Phillips screams. The red numbers count down...14, 13, 12... He pulls it from Yassir's belt – stares at the display... 5,4,3. *Kingdom come* rings in his ears.

A hand reaches over his shoulder and pushes a button – someone on the SWAT team. "You all right?" ask the uniform.

The red numbers disappear. Shaking, Phillips reads the display: CANCEL. As simple as that! The huge hulk of a cop exhales audibly, and feels ready to tumble. He looks around the station – the beautifully painted ceiling, the elegant marble stairways – all of it still there. With another sigh of relief he makes way for the paramedics who kneel next to the horribly disfigured corpse. Someone looking like a doctor pronounces him dead, writing down the time: 6:03 p.m.

3.

Visitors to the red-walled Armory can walk through doors on either Park or Lexington Avenue, but the only driveway is on Lex. Normally, like on this peaceful April evening, the driveway is open to the public. No barriers requiring proper I.D. No guards checking the cars that might have wandered in by mistake.

Muzhir wipes his sweaty brow as he carefully maneuvers his van over the sidewalk and into the Armory driveway and parking lot. His watch reads 5:47 p.m. The doorman notices the van with trained eyes, distracted as they were by a woman dressed to the nines who commandingly shoves a box at him over the counter of his station. He records the name, LENOX HILL FLORIST, painted in red letters on the van as it turns into a parking place near the door.

The slender, dark-skinned Muzhir practically leaps out of the van, running his fingers through his black curly hair. He goes to the back and opens the doors, pausing to light a cigarette. He peers sideways at the doorman, who seems to be weighing the box in his hands given him by the pushy woman who for some reason won't shut up.

Muzhir pulls a bushy shrink-wrapped potted plant from the back of the van, places it on the asphalt, and shuts the doors. His heart thumps as he looks around him. He takes a huge drag from his cigarette and blows the smoke into the air, trying to look cool.

He had parked next to a Hummer, one of several Army vehicles in the lot. He looks at this monster of a Jeep-successor with a mix of awe and longing. Deep down he wants such a car. He could put a bed in the back, and travel all over the States. Surely he would find a girl on the road to keep him company if he had such a car, someone to make his wildest fantasies come true. An *American* woman, an unashamed American woman, the kind he knew from porno tapes. One who will open her legs whenever he wants. One who will drop to her knees whenever he tells her to and give him the blowjob he deserves. Suddenly he turns away.

The doorman is surprised to see the van's driver lope over to the exit waving his palm at him, signaling *I'll be right back!* Noticing the plant outside the van's back doors, the doorman shakes his head. "Moron", he swears, " does he think I'm gonna watch his stupid shrub for him? When he's back, I'll show him who he's dealing with."

But then a bike messenger zooms into the parking lot right up to the door and tosses a pack of letters to him over the counter of his station. He forgets the van driver for a minute as he signs the receipt. The wall clock behind him reads 5:53.

Under the floor mats in the front of the van, the digital readout of the detonator moves to 5:54. Several colored wires lead from its terminals through a tiny hole to the back of the van. If the doorman or anyone else had by chance opened the back doors, he would never notice the four canisters among the boxes of plants, clay pots, and bags of fertilizer. And even if he had, the canisters had labels glued onto them that read "Weed Killer."

Meanwhile, Muzhir rushes up Lexington Avenue, heart pumping, adrenaline surging. He sees his safe harbor up ahead: a black limousine parked three blocks north. He feels relieved.

It had been a tense day: driving the van loaded with canisters of nitroglycerine from Queens to Manhattan, was rather nerve racking, even though his people had assured him the charge wouldn't detonate, unless he totaled the vehicle. Being free from his rolling bomb makes him realize he's starving. Allah's young warrior buys a hot dog smothered with mustard and kraut, and stuffs it into his mouth as he moves toward the limo. Its dashboard clock reads 5:59. The door opens, and Muzhir slips in the back next to Khalid. Chewing his hot dog, he reports: "Everything okay Boss."

Meanwhile, the doorman at the Armory is visibly annoyed. *Where the hell is that van driver? I'm not his plant sitter.* He forces his bloated body out of his chair and moves around the counter toward the van. And that is as far as he gets. A scorching red fireball flattens him – not even time to scream.

On the Armory's second floor Rick Norris had been watching the TV and just hung up the phone. The scene at Grand Central from the network's helicopter showed the SWAT teams' siege of the terminal. Police cars, fire engines, flashing lights, and searchlights, people rushing all over.

And then it hit him. The incredible force of the explosion hurled him up to the ceiling and back down to the floor. Agonizing pain ran through his body. The taste of death filled his mouth. With his last look up Rick saw in horror the ceiling collapse on him like a landslide.

The explosion shook the Manhattan canyons for blocks around the Armory. The ancient heavy-stoned building collapsed like a house of cards, burying the driveway in rubble.

On its west side the walls burst, catapulting rock, glass, computer cases, metal, and bloody human body parts all over Park Avenue. People were lying in the streets, screaming in agony, or silent in their own blood. Cars crashed into each other. A bus swerved and tipped on its side, sliding over the sidewalk. A gasoline tank truck rammed through the windows of a boutique, exploding into a gusher of flames.

In the station house of the 19th Precinct the windows burst. Shards of glass sprayed the bodies of the police officers like shrapnel. The shock wave blew computers from their desks as if they were paper cups. Telephones went dead.

But at a safe distance away, the black limousine cruised up Madison and turned left toward Central Park. Behind the darkened windows the Boss praised Muzhir: "Well done."

The young terrorist took the last bite of his hotdog and smiled. He had done it! Now he would surely be part of the Dynamite Club! Since the failed attempt on the World Trade Center a few years ago the organization had learnt a lot. Back then, when Muzhir had been initiated, the fighters of the Holy War against America had used too little explosives for the massive twin towers. It was a mistake they would never repeat. Today, the *Qaeda* had access to the most powerful weapons and the best explosive devices world's high-tech laboratories had to offer.

Fantastic! Muzhir smiled at his boss. But then froze. Khalid's hand surfaced from under the newspaper on his lap. He held a ten-inch knife in an elaborately adorned golden sheath pressed against his knee. It had a black handle edged with gleaming silver decorations. Khalid drew it. A tight serpentine blade flashed. It was a gift from a Syrian arms dealer in Damascus who had praised it as an *ornate tool to kill in style.*

"You did a fine job my son. Allah will reward you," Khalid said. He drove the knife blade forward, felt it sink into flesh. The young warrior saw the knife plunge near his heart. A bewildered, frightened look crossed his face. The driver swallowed dryly, focusing on the traffic. Tasting his kill, Khalid looked into Muzhir's pleading eyes, perversely enjoying the slow fading of his flame of life. No witnesses as bin Golem had commanded. The boy slumped sideward on the seat cold dead. The killer felt strong, in better spirits than ever before. The distraction at Grand Central had worked like a charm. *My idea! I am the greatest! Master of life and death.*

His boss, the great Islamic leader bin Golem would have every reason to be pleased with Khalid. The double attack on Manhattan, the nation's nerve center, had proved to be an ingenious blow. Thanks to Benn Sweeney's intimate knowledge of American intelligence operations, they had been able to level a major strategic target. Of course, the red-walled Armory was not Langley, the CIA headquarters. But it was a shock that would run deep, close to the enemy's heart! And the casualties were something to be proud of – 81 people killed, right in the middle of Manhattan.

Yet, the Arab was a realist. He knew his attack would prompt retaliation from the U.S. Anticipating massive attacks on the Taliban bases in Afghanistan, he had transferred his headquarters to the mountains, where his loyal followers had prepared new hideouts.

The Tomahawk cruise missiles might wreak havoc on the deserted villages – but they would not kill even one Jihad warrior. Their blows would hit nothing but thin air and unpopulated ground!

4.

A blistering sun baked down on the small tent city on a river-bank deep in the Afghan highlands. Yussef bin Golem sat on a dark blue cushion of the finest silk, tapping a large map with a beautifully ornamented ebony walking stick. On this unbearably hot and muggy afternoon, he faced two minor problems: his embarrassment of getting seasick and the fact that he had a corrupt American in his ranks.

"New York, my friends, was only the prelude. The true decisive battle will take place here!" Poking the Straight of Gibraltar with the tip of his stick, Yussef looked deeply into the eyes of his men – slowly, one by one. He had personally selected them all, and had made them his most intimate confidants. They knew it, and paid him back with blind obedience and total devotion to the death, as well as with all their special skills that had made them the inner circle of the Qaeda. Bin Golem's stare into each man's eyes was ecstatic as well as withering. Only the most hardened men were chosen to sit in the Qaeda, and to participate in this great operation named after Israel's apocalyptic battlefield *Megiddo.* And there was not one among these toughest of the tough who would have been able to withstand or even brave the gaze of the great leader.

"Tomorrow afternoon," he began, addressing them as a group; "the *Shiraz* will set sail from the port of Lagos in Nigeria on schedule." His deep-set eyes sparkled underneath his wide forehead as he smiled and went on, "I already have a supply of our medicine man's wonder cure," reaching into his pocket and shaking a small gilded pillbox. "I can't afford to be seasick when the great battle begins."

His men grinned politely and spoke animatedly among themselves. Bin Golem's stocky private physician stuck his white head and beard through the curtains and railed at them. "Keep laughing. See if I care. When you're puking your guts out over the railing of the *Shiraz*, you'll beg for my medicine."

"You can keep that crap for yourself," replied Khalid, whose tall thin body and thick shock of black curls contrasted sharply with the whiteness of the physician. He turned away with his much-practiced pose of the macho hit man.

"Any suggestions about what to eat before we get on board?" asked the Treasurer, a confirmed landlubber, with a frown.

"Bananas," replied the white-haired physician.

"Bananas? Why? The potassium?"

"No, because they taste better on the way up than they did on the way down," the doctor answered, triggering laughter from everyone but Khalid.

But then bin Golem tapped his stick on a wooden rifle chest, commanding silence. All laughter instantly stopped.

"Men, everything is at stake now. We cannot afford the slightest risk. Even a single leak could ruin us."

The men looked up at him, each one frowning.

"I know, I know," bin Golem went on. "I can trust each and every one of you as much as I trust myself. When the right moment comes, all of you will know our plan's full details. And rest assured this strike will change everything. Future generations will divide the calendar by before and after Operation *Megiddo*." The charismatic leader's speech and reference to the biblical battle was not exaggerated in his followers' minds. It alluded to a great historic parallel. If they did actually succeed in sinking an American aircraft carrier with all hands onboard, the loss to the U.S would be devastating. The destruction of such a proud and untouchable symbol of the world superpower would shock the American people deeper than had the surprise attack on Pearl Harbor. And Yussef bin Golem's place in the history of Islam would be forever secured. He would be the greatest hero of all time.

The gentle, pensive face of the Islamic leader contrasted sharply with the terrors promised by his warlike speech. Clad in white from head to foot, the 48-year-old Saudi Arabian looked more like a prophet predicting seven rich years than the wrathful Qaeda ruler. His men sat around a table made up of several layers of precious carpets, nodding at their chief's remarks, lost in thought and in Yussef's dark eyes, which promised honor, salvation, and martyrdom. Yet each of the four men felt anxiety and fear. Sitting cross-legged between Khalid and the Treasurer was Riaz, the Information Officer, who stared disdainfully at Sweeney, the American renegade, who avoided his piercing glare.

Everyone thinks I'm a traitor. But Sweeney did not consider himself such. He had come to Pakistan in 1988 as a young CIA officer. His first assignment had been carrying out interrogations in the refugee camps along the Afghan border. The Afghan refugees had called those camps *Madrasa* or seminars – and themselves *Taliban* or students. Sweeney questioned them about Soviet arms, troop movements, morale among the Soviet soldiers, the names of commanding officers. And he sent his reports to the head of his department, who in turn passed them on to CIA headquarters in Langley, Virginia.

The CIA had been in Afghanistan as early as 1980, fighting against the Soviet invasion. Working with Pakistan's secret service, Washington wanted to expand the Holy War of the Afghan people into a worldwide battle of all Muslim nations against the Soviet Union.

And the plan had worked: between 1982 and 1992, more than 35,000 radical Muslims from 40 different countries were fighting in Afghanistan against the Russians. Among them no less a person than Yussef bin Golem. Yes, world's most feared terrorist leader had been a highly regarded CIA trainee, who supported the Americans in their secret and most successful operations against Soviet occupation. Remember the *Stinger*? Bin Golem helped supply them to the rebels who then shot the Russian attack helicopters down like sitting ducks. In 1996 bin Golem thought better about it and defected. He set up shop in the terror business and declared the *Jihad* against Saudi Arabia's royal family and all of the United States of America. All of that, compressed into a millisecond, blipped through his mind in this moment, too,

Tens of thousands studied in the *Madrasa* where, as time passed, Sweeney came to learn about the *Taliban* and their strict religious beliefs.

Benn Sweeney never saw himself as a traitor. He was doing now what America had officially done since 1989 – he supported the Afghan freedom fighters. And he and his country had been successful. In 1989, the last of the Soviet troops withdrew from Afghanistan. The students of the Islamic *Madrasa* returned home from Pakistan to bring law and order to their country. They disarmed the people and introduced the *Sharia*, the Islamic code of law – and brought with them the fanaticism of holy warriors, now turning against the Americans.

The spirits I called forth are suddenly not so easy to dismiss. The old saying resonated bitterly in Sweeney's mind.

Of all the places on earth to fall in love, the refugee camp would have ranked last in Sweeney's mind. But that is where he did, with the passionate young Farah. He had never met a woman so charming, so completely lovable – the exact opposite of his image of himself as the classic secret agent: egotistical, ruthless, tough. *Les extrèmes se touchent!*

Farah was from Harat in northern Afghanistan, a city founded by Alexander the Great in 330 B.C., with an imposing citadel still sitting today atop a heap of rubble that was once an ancient fort. Farah was able to give Sweeney all kinds of information about Soviet supply routes in and around her strategically significant home city. She also told him about the opium fields, and he promptly reacted as his trainers at Langley had drilled him to– dismissive and appalled, while pondering how to destroy the plantations described to him.

And as she gave Sweeney the kinds of information he needed to do his job, Farah also introduced him in a charming off-the-cuff way to her culture and traditions. And over time, Sweeney's thickheaded western way of thinking burst like an overheated earthenware pot. She explained Deobandi to him. *Deobandi? Deo... Deobandits? God's bandits?*

Deobandism had originally been an Islamic reform movement aimed at renewing Muslim society under British colonial rule. Farah explained it to Benn: "we have derived our strict teaching of Islam from the interpretation of Deobandism." But what she didn't tell him was that the Mullahs at the camps practiced an extremely perverted reformist Muslim doctrine, while the students came primarily for education, food, protection, and military training.

Shortly before the Soviet withdrawal, Farah gave birth to Benn's son, whom they named Ahmed. And when the war ended, they moved to a village close to Kandahar in southern Afghanistan that had been spared from heavy fights. But peace was not to be theirs. The *Taliban* had radicalized the country. They banned television, and reintroduced grim *Sharia* punishments like amputation and stoning. They murdered devout Shiites and forced women to submit to the strict traditional dress code.

Suddenly, Sweeney had fallen from grace. Being a nonbeliever who had impregnated a Taliban woman, he was now marked as a mortal sinner. Hotheads made sure they had a short trial. Judge and jury consisted of a hastily scratched together assembly of villagers who decided exactly what the ringleaders suggested. The sentence was death by stoning.

5.

While bin Golem was in his tent being updated on the state of preparations for his great scheme, veterans of the Afghan war secured the camp. The radar dishes of six batteries of anti-aircraft guided missiles sat on a hilltop across the river. Their silent rotation protected a four-mile circle against ever-expected American air raids.

"We have the most sophisticated rockets available in the world today. But what we don't have are the codes to knock out the American anti-ship-rocket defense system, they call *Aegis*, named after the shield Zeus gave to Athena," bin Golem said gently, yet lifting his stick as if to strike this shield. Sweeney felt stabbed by the leader's steady gaze and licked his lips nervously. He knew what was coming.

The Sheik was alluding to Nadine Moran, as dangerous as she was mysterious. She was the queen in bin Golem's crazy game of chess, while Sweeney was haunted by the premonition that he was the sacrificed pawn.

"You know whom I'm thinking of," he went on, staring at Sweeney. "This intelligent woman, this dynamic woman."

Bin Golem was an excellent judge of character; and even though he had never met Nadine Moran, he had pegged her exactly from a dossier, a photograph, and a hazy surveillance video. As he spoke of her animatedly, his black hair fell from his turban and merged with his thick beard.

Nadine Moran was a top-level computer scientist working at the research labs in Los Alamos. That was precisely why the notoriously distrustful Americans kept her under surveillance. After all, she was French and therefore an alien - and a beautiful one on top of that. And in no way did she live up to the usual image of the disheveled, sloppy hacker with myopic vision. And three words from her mouth destroyed the idea that she might be a beautiful dumb blond bombshell. This combined with the subliminal atmosphere of suspicion in the National Laboratory of Los Alamos created the perfect breeding-ground for the Qaeda to make Nadine Moran become a real suspect. Part of bin Golem's plan was to compromise the French woman at her workplace using double agent Sweeney, this wretched creature of an American defector, to plant a few seeds of disinformation with the CIA... yeah, a hot tip coming deep from Afghanistan... *And the only way she would be able to free herself from a desperate situation would be to escape into Yussef's open arms!*

Sweeney cleared his throat nervously. "The net has been cast, sir, with tempting bait inside. The woman *will* take it. She won't be able to help herself. It's in her nature."

This made the white-robed leader's eyes shine in their deep sockets. He squeezed the rhino-horn knob of his stick so hard his knuckles turned white.

"The more intelligent, the more motivated, and the more beautiful a woman is, the more unpredictable she is," he said, without being able to hide a twinkle in his eye.

"Igor the Russian has been in contact with her. Everything is moving as planned, sir," Sweeney replied, fidgeting and swallowing nervously. "The bait is her long lost father, presumed dead or cast away somewhere in Africa, Sir!"

Bin Golem stared at him mercilessly, but not in an unfriendly way. It made Sweeney feel like a cricket in a box, held in the hand of a powerful potentate who was amused by its chirping.

'Your life is hanging by a silken thread, Yank. And you know it. If this plan does not succeed, we will skin you and throw you to the wolves, just like your depraved cavalry soldiers did to the Indians."

Sweeney bit his tongue and looked down. *This dog saved Farah's life and yours. Don't ever forget that!* And never in his life could he forget the sight of bin Golem stepping out of a Land Rover when the first rocks came flying. Suddenly the hail of stones stopped and immediate silence spread among the hostile mob. The crowd parted for the gentle looking man with the long beard as blood dripped from Sweeney's head onto Farah's white Chador. A few short words from him to the executioners, and Sweeney was dragged away.

To be shot instead of stoned to death? Was this man tempering justice with mercy? But when Farah joined him in the back of the vehicle, he suddenly realized that he had been miraculously rescued. And the price?

"I am the law. We are the Qaeda. The base. You will supply me with information from the CIA. You will do counterespionage. You will keep me informed of Washington's plans. And you will send your people whatever we give you to send them, so they will not be suspicious. And if you can't be a double agent, you will turn to dust."

Classical recruitment through blackmail.

"Farah and Ahmed will be fine as long as they obey," he added condescendingly.

Sweeney knew he was completely at his mercy.

"And bear in mind my American friend, that I not only spare your life but plan to pay you well."

To the bleeding American agent, bin Golem had appeared like a judge from the Old Testament, calmly meting out life and death without a thought for either.

"Well, *I* won't pay you well," he had gone on. "The drug dealers will. You will warn them in time and help them against the American military."

And the catch to all this?

"I will hold your wife and son in pledge of the fulfillment of your tasks. They are my live collateral."

Hostages would be more like it, you bastard!

"You would not risk the life of your son, would you?"

It had not been a question, not a threat, not even a statement. It had been a *damn* sentence! This bastard had looked him over then just as he did now in the tent – studying him with searching eyes.

Only resist his gaze! You can do it, can't you! Sweeney nodded and repeated: "If the plan doesn't work, Sir, throw me to the wolves."

Yussef bin Golem made a slight movement with his head, and immediately his men knelt down and kissed the ground before him.

"You shall fight the pagans all together as they fight you all together. Fight them until there is no more tumult or oppression, and there prevail justice and faith in God, and Almighty God will help us launch a raid on Satan's U.S. troops and the devil's supporters allying with them."

Mumbling assent, the men bowed again, joined by Sweeney, whose thoughts were scarcely touched with devotion.

He thought of Nadine Moran, and of the night he had seen her in Los Alamos as he looked up at her window hidden in the garden, videotaping her gracefully combing her hair completely undressed. Bin Golem really had no idea how hot-blooded she was. And the way Benn Sweeney saw her, he was sure she would risk a hell of a lot to get in touch with the *Qaeda*, to go any place to find her lost father... The trap was set.

What about him? Was he doomed? Sweeney asked himself. *Well, the coded message to the I&M center in the Armory had worked. Grand Great Central was still intact... and he was at least above suspicion with the people in Langley ...*

Before the meeting could end, the six-foot-five Riaz stood up and up-dated them with his intelligence reports. His wild gaze under bushy brows animated his detailing on the positions of American military facilities that were part of their selected objectives. Most of his data came straight from Teheran, where Riaz was able to log into the Iranian Ministry of Information computers. Much of it was pieced together from calls and emails of enlisted Army personnel and the Navy and Air Force crews. Their uninhibited chatter made it easy to learn about the deployment of American troops and formations.

While Riaz was talking, bin Golem's eyes were nearly closed, almost as if he were sleeping. But when the Information Officer finished, the Sheik jumped up so swiftly that all his men froze as if a viper had risen among them. His gentle yet penetrating gaze stayed on Khalid.

"You still have a lot to take care of my son. You know I'm counting on you."

Without a word, the hit man nodded twice. He

thought of the retired general in Zurich who kept a few secrets the *Qaeda* might want him to give away. But Khalid knew that there was a lot more to do than to find this old spymaster and kill him after he has talked. Casablanca was the name of the game! His mind wandered: *In Casablanca I will pull off a coup that will make them mention my name in one breath with Humphrey Bogart!*

The hollow thumping of a helicopter could be heard in the background. "Ah, my ride is here," said bin Golem.

Benn Sweeney knew nothing about Operation Casablanca, nor of what Khalid wanted to accomplish in Zurich. The strict secrecy of the Taliban went deeper than any inner circle – it was a part of every consciousness. No one was ever told more than he absolutely had to know.

Stepping out of the tent, bin Golem surveyed the red and white blossoms of the green poppy fields that swayed all the way to the horizon. They were part of the model farm where the Taliban had taught Afghan farmers the most efficient modes of poppy cultivation. According to the U.N., Afghanistan added 4,600 tons of opium to the world market in 1999 – twice the amount of the year before.

He considered this a tremendous achievement – and reveled like a child in the trouble it gave the Americans. He picked a poppy from its stem and kissed it to the skies. *I kiss you sweet death! Death to the Great Satan!"*

Today, Afghanistan produced three times more opium than the rest of the world combined. And almost all of it came from Taliban-controlled territories – essentially making them the largest manufacturers of heroin in the world. Apart from that, they pocketed 20 percent taxes from drug dealers and traffickers – money rolling straight into their war chest. Moreover, the drug barons maintained the one and only credit system of the country themselves, offering loans to farmers with opium harvests as collateral.

As a consequence, bin Golem would in no way be restricted by the way the U.S. had blocked his bank accounts in the West. Drug billions had financed operation *Megiddo*. Not to mention the money he made from smuggling consumer goods, cigarettes, fuel, and food: into Russian, into the Caucasus Mountains, into Central Asia, Iran, and Pakistan. The World Bank had estimated his smuggling operations alone to be worth over five billion dollars a year.

And all while the West sleeps... He smiled and tossed the poppy aside. *God is great! The Jihad justifies any and all means to success!*

Tarps and sheets bulged, and dust and leaves swirled as the Mi-26 helicopter landed near the tents. Bin Golem waved goodbye to his followers.

In his thoughts he was already on board the *Shiraz* in the port of Lagos, Nigeria's capital on Africa's West Coast...

His great *Shiraz* had cleared the Iranian port *Bandar Khomeiny* three months ago. As Iran ranked third among the world's oil-exporting countries, with a daily output of almost 4 million barrels, boasting 11 supertankers and nine freighters in its fleet, no one paid any particular attention when another tanker left the oil loading port on the northern tip of the Persian Gulf.

...Or perhaps he was musing over Nadine Moran, stretching naked on her bed in distant Los Alamos in the early morning hours of a new day. He would get his hands on this woman, this Nedella, as he had already secretly named her. He would break her spirit – of that he was certain.

6.

I, Stan Polinsky, knew I had a problem that Friday in Zurich – even before I had a second drink. Steinlin, my attorney, sat next to me, staring gloomily into his glass of cheap white wine. For the third time I heard the bartender tell the guy sitting on my other side "no hay problemas," while a baby-faced Brit drinking espresso at a table yelled into his cell phone "No problem!"

Apparently I was the only one in the joint with a problem – which normally I wouldn't have minded at all. Normally.

Monday-Bar started to get crowded as the regulars from the courthouse and neighboring law firms drifted in. We had just come from court, where Steinlin had convinced Judge Righetti to give us a trial adjournment until a week after next Thursday, when we were supposed to come up with a new piece of evidence that would get me off the hook in the Diesbach murder case.

But it wasn't enough time. Steinlin looked as if he had just taken a bite out of a lime. And I didn't feel very well either. A court clerk came through the door, laughing it up with some secretaries. The adjournment wasn't long enough, and our case was as good as lost.

I barked at the bartender. "Give me another one, subito!"

"Coming up, no hay problemas," he answered with a dull stare.

In the old days I might have given him a problem, I thought – but let it go.

29

"Drinking won't help," Steinlin muttered.

On the contrary, I thought. Gin calms you down, opens prospects. It was the only help at hand. Once the shit hits the fan, nobody could care less about what you've done for them in the past. Nothing left but the here and now. Can't rest on your laurels Polinsky, I muttered to myself. Polinsky, that's me. Everybody calls me by my last name.

Steinlin interrupted my brooding.

"Do you think you'll be able to find anything in two weeks?" turning his glass in his hand.

Before I could answer I saw the news crew rush through the door. Focker (yeah, the reporter's real name) homed in on Steinlin and the cameraman turned on his lights.

Time to go?

"Check" I shouted to the bartender, who actually did speed up as he replied with his usual "no hay…"

Behind me I heard Focker's braying voice.

"How do you intend to prove your theory about the third man?"

Steinlin turned around slowly and looked right into the camera.

"Whoever misses the first button will never button up straight."

"What does that supposed to mean," asked Focker, bewildered.

"Goethe," my enigmatic lawyer replied.

"Goethe? What does Goethe have to do with Diesbach's murder? Do you have any real evidence? Or are you just stalling?"

"Well, if the district attorney starts off wrong, as he did today, he'll never be able to straighten things out later. All he'll end up doing is trying to patch-up a basically flawed theory."

Focker looked as if he had just swallowed a goldfish.

"Do you have any idea who the third man could be?" he asked finally.

"The third man is the culprit. We will find him, you can bet on that, Mister..." Steinlin turned away shrugging, not giving anyone the pleasure of hearing him say the paparazzo's so appropriate name.

Steinlin, as usual, was correct. The DA's accusations were totally false. Of course it *seemed* that my uncle, Corps Commander Edouard Diesbach, former Chief of the Air Force, had been violently murdered. But I was certainly not the murderer. The problem was how to prove it – which right now was a complete mystery to me.

Steinlin told me quite simply that my only chance was to find this mystery man, whom I had literally collided with on the night of my uncle's death right outside the apartment house. My dramatic and capable attorney had played up the role of this third man in the courtroom – but I had no idea who he was or how I might find him. I could just imagine Judge Righetti's angry face if I came back to court two weeks from now with nothing to show for the extension he had granted us.

"Polinsky, wasn't your uncle connected to the Secret Service? Perhaps his murder was a belated day of reckoning?"

Focker pushed the microphone at me, and the cameraman moved closer.

I wasn't really thrilled with the idea of my scowling mug showing up in every living room in the city, so I turned away and muttered, "If you count the Holy Spirit in with French Intelligence, perhaps you're right."

"But if you say it wasn't murder Mr. Polinsky, how do you explain the fact that the Corps Commander's apartment was totally ransacked?"

I didn't feel like explaining anything. Fortunately, Steinlin never backed down from a question.

"Excuse me Mr. Sucker" (which he knew would get on Focker's nerves), "but it is not my client's job to comment on clues at a crime scene. That is the job of the police."

He turned away indignantly and pushed me out the door. The cool fresh air bathed my flushed face lovingly.

"This case causes quite a stir," Steinlin remarked.

I nodded silently.

"Not only here in Switzerland, but abroad as well," he went on. "Especially in France, and in Italy, where your uncle had many influential friends. If we lose, Polinsky…"

"Yes?"

"We'll let a lot of people down."

"Is that what you're worried about?"

"Did you notice Colossimo's thugs in the courtroom?"

"Of course," I moaned.

"The Mafioso sent his top capos."

"You seem more worried about your reputation with Colossimo & Co. than you do about me going to jail – or about my reputation," I said bitterly. Steinlin stopped in front of the parking lot and looked at me.

"Let me put it this way. I would suffer because I don't like losing a case. But you, Polinsky, will suffer more than even jail time. We're not talking about games here. There are lives at stake. This is where the serious side of life starts, as I think you already know."

He waved goodbye and walked away quickly.

"Then let's hope for a miracle," I muttered.

But Steinlin was already out of earshot.

I walked over to the taxi stand. My soul craved nature – any kind of nature – something beyond the foul taste of courtrooms and lawyers. Trees, water, or passionate lovemaking. Thinking of this, I seemed to sense a slight itch down below. Probably an illusion. For the last couple of weeks my love life, like everything else, had gone down the drain. Oh well.

"To the lake!" I told the cabdriver as I climbed in.

He looked at me in the rearview mirror.

"Hey! You're the guy from the Diesbach trial? Just got out of court?" he asked, shifting gears and smiling. In Zurich cabs cost a fortune even before they've gone ten feet.

He babbled on. I paid no attention to him, staring out the window as if the answer to my problem was somewhere out there on the streets.

As I would learn later, my thinking was not that far off. The solution was actually just two cars ahead of us tailing the streetcar. The dark green van with tinted windows and small antennas was obviously a task force unit of the security police. But I had no idea then how it might solve my problems. I was just hoping for some kind of miracle to save my sorry ass.

Somebody had left a newspaper in the back seat. An Arab's bearded face looked up at me from the front page. I looked closer. It was Yussef bin Golem, the terrorist. *The Manhattan Bomber!* Did I sense mockery in his eyes? *See you soon, Polinsky?* Something about him was bugging me. *Don't mess with him!* I looked outside again. The dark green van turned right, heading for the bridge. I urged myself to live up to my reputation as a cool customer. Relax, Polinsky, I told myself. Only calmness will do the trick. But I caught myself sighing as the cab accelerated.

"Everybody knows you now," the cabby continued. And after a pause, "Smart lawyer you've got there. Getting you out on bail. I mean, that's fine with me. Getting any fan mail yet?"

"Me? Who would send me fan mail?" But then I remembered one piece. "Oh yeah, some nut sent me a bullet – no return address."

The cabby's jaw dropped.

"Let me out here. Now!"

He slammed on the brakes and almost skidded into a bus. Annoyed, I paid the astronomical fare, wondering how many homeless people I could feed with it.

I started to walk home. Nature starts in your feet. Who said that? Goethe? Surely, Steinlin would have loved that answer. Where was Steinlin? I suddenly missed him, wondering where he might be now. But a better question was where was I right now? As they like to put it overseas, up shit's creek without a paddle.

7.

All of my problems started six days ago, on a Saturday. I was about to take a shower when the phone rang. For some reason I thought it was Focker over at the TV station, looking for some kind of hot tip. So I picked up the phone and yelled, "Shit Focker, what do you want now?"

"Mr. Polinsky, it's your uncle," came the shy voice of the housekeeper. "You should come now. He is not well."

I could see the thin old lady trembling with the phone in her hand, staring at the old man who soon would be no more.

"I'll be right over. Stay calm. And don't let anybody into the house. No one, do you understand? And wait there for me."

I slammed the receiver down and pulled on some jeans and a shirt left over from the night before. Grabbing my windbreaker from the hook by the door, I rushed out into a very nasty April day. It had been snowing in the mountains, but, being on the lake, Zurich was gray and wet, with just a hint in the west that the sun might pop through.

My old Alfa Romeo was parked down the street. I ripped the parking ticket from under the wiper and zoomed off. Exactly 17 minutes later I walked into the light-green apartment building where my uncle had lived for years in a very comfortable penthouse.

In the overgrown park next to his building an old wooden house with two small towers slowly crumbled away.

Across the street, however, modern times had moved in with a brand new glass and steel high-rise.

8.

The walls of my uncle's apartment were stacked with books: about avionics, weaponry, the Agency, wars and of course the literature one would expect to find in the library of an educated aristocrat – an enviable collection.

I entered his bedroom and was immediately struck with how pale he looked – even in his declining years he had always managed to have a tan. I sat next to his night table, covered with newspapers and books with colorful dust jackets.

"How are you uncle Edouard?"

He groped for his walking stick and pushed himself up with it to a sitting position – and then tremblingly but accurately poked it right into the middle of my chest.

"Take the file," he croaked, sinking back exhausted.

I thought, "Uh oh, this is it". But his eyes lit up again, and he pointed to something behind me.

"There. In my trousers. The little key. Behind Nabokov, the secret drawer. Open it. Take the file. It's my last will. Help me…"

He stared at me, and his eyes started to fade again.

"Uncle Edouard, wait!" I glanced nervously around the room. We were alone. "What about the file?" I bent over him and put my ear next to his trembling lips.

"I see blood… lots of blood. Thousands dead… He will strike… This time he will strike."

"Who will strike?! Who are you talking about? Uncle Edouard?"

His trembling hand found a cigar on the night table

but dropped it to the floor. He started to pant, his eyes half closed. I bent forward again, trying to grasp what he was saying.

"Don't let her down... Help the girl. This assignment is important... Don't let her out of your sight. She has the key."

"Who is she? What's her name?"

"Nadine, the beautiful... she's part of our family," he babbled. But I had never known anyone in our family named Nadine.

Just as I was about to say that, he raised his voice. "Promise you will be there Polinsky! Give me your word of honor!"

"Of course. You have my word. Her name is Nadine? Where is she from? Uncle Edouard??"

The old man sank back into his pillows, staring at me, even now with an impish sparkle in his eye.

"She is beautiful, Polinsky. Très, très belle."

Then he breathed one more word to me, against my cheek, as if he were giving up his ghost. But I had no idea what it meant.

Just three syllables, whispered from the mouth of this dying lion. "Kon-kor-ski." The rest was silence.

9.

I watched his face for a long time. An impish gentleness overcame his wrinkled features, his eyes staring.

Konkorski? Nadine? The key?

I closed his eyes and sighed, looking around the room. Finally, I reached with reluctance for his trousers and searched the pockets – and found a small golden key hanging from a thin golden chain. I removed the key and went into the living room to look for Nabokov.

Someone knocked on the door and I opened it. The housekeeper stared at me wide-eyed. I nodded to her gravely, looking down. She let out a whining sob, and then hid her face in her trembling hands. Putting my arm around her shoulder, I led her to the kitchen.

"He passed away peacefully. Call the doctor. And please, put on some water for tea."

She sobbingly reached for the kettle, and I returned to the living room to look for Nabokov. Dozens of books bound in brown morocco dominated the bookshelf like a rampart. Above them were smaller books, poetry, Balzac, Voltaire, Hugo, even erotic literature. They all looked as if they were read. Even after death the old war-horse didn't cease to amaze me.

I could hear the housekeeper on the kitchen phone.

"Doctor Gemperli? Please, could you come at once? The Corps Commander has passed away… the Commander is dead," she sobbed.

Everyone around him had always addressed him with

his military title. When he retired from the service he had been a three-star general.

Bingo! I found Nabokov. Right behind *Lolita, Pale Fire, and Speak, Memory!* I saw a small gray steel door. The tiny key fit. Deep in the narrow compartment was a manila envelope. I pulled it out, and ran my hand around inside the little safe to make sure it was empty. Without bothering to close it I put the books back as I had found them.

The housekeeper returned with a tray and put tea and cups on the coffee table. This accustomed task seemed to have calmed her down. She saw the envelope in my hand.

"Mr. Polinsky, what are you doing there?" she asked, startled.

"It's uncle Edouard's last will," I replied, holding up the envelope. "Would you like to see Mr. Diesbach now?" I asked, pointing to the bedroom. Just as she started to sob again, the doorbell rang.

"That must be the Doctor," she said, regaining her composure and hurrying to the hallway.

Aside from some loose pages, the envelope contained a fat red file, secured with a flat combination lock. I started playing with the numbers when the doctor passed me with a nod and went directly into the bedroom. I stuffed the file under my jacket and followed.

"Exitus. The Corps Commander is dead," Gemperli declared with official detachment, taking his stethoscope from his neck. "He endured a lot, for a long time. A real tough guy. Are you his son?"

Still shaking my head in agreement of his assessment, the housekeeper who had quietly snuck in answered for me.

"Mr. Polinsky is the Commander's only nephew."

Gemperli looked around the room as if calculating my inheritance.

"Nice apartment. Lots of books. What are you going to do with them?"

Shrugging my shoulders nonchalantly, I said "There are too many books in the world. Maybe I'll feed the fireplace with them. At least they'll heat up the room a bit."

Gemperli shook his head in disapproval as he filled out the death certificate – which was really what we had called him for. Under cause of death he wrote heart failure. He left, and I followed hard on his heels, slipping the housekeeper a few bills on my way out.

As I passed through the building entrance, some guy in a blue work coat saw me and followed.

"Hey, you. Is that your piece of junk parked right in front of the steps?"

He was at least a head taller than I was, which in my judgment was a good enough reason to walk right past him. But he followed me again. I opened the door of my Alfa as if he wasn't even there. But he put his huge meat hook hand on the door as well.

"Listen you. There's no parking here. Especially for a piece of shit crate like this."

"Take it easy, man. Don't make a fuss."

"*You're* making the fuss," he went on, still holding the door open.

"Hey, look pal, I don't have to explain anything to you. My car's parked on public property."

"Oh yeah smart ass?"

"I just want to leave. Let me get into my car."

"You'd like that, wouldn't you? Tell me what you're doing parked here."

And he grabbed me by the collar. I tore myself away, and the envelope tumbled from under my jacket. The locked red file slid out. He put his huge foot on it.

"And what do we have here?" he asked triumphantly.

Well, that just about did it for me. My fuse is pretty short anyway, and this clown had lit it the minute he put his claw on my car. So I slammed the Alfa's door shut, with his stupid pudgy fingers in it. As he roared in pain I brought my knee up into his groin, and then punched him in his fat gut. Moaning and groaning on the ground, he sucked his smashed fingers and held his balls, looking like the idiot he truly was.

I picked up the file and envelope, got into my car, and drove off. As I pulled away I noticed a dark-skinned man walking up the street. He stopped and looked around. Shadowy cheeks, black eyes, big nose. As I drove away I could see him in my rear-view mirror walking towards my uncle's building.

10.

What I didn't stay long enough to see was Khalid entering my uncle's building unseen by the doorman and slipping into the elevator unperceived. He went up to the top floor and found the door with *Diesbach* engraved on a brass plate.

He rang the bell but no one answered. Pushing the door he realized it was open, and slipped inside. *My lucky day*, he thought to himself as he noiselessly crossed the apartment and entered the bedroom. And there on the bed was his designated victim, very clearly already dead.

"Are you from the funeral home?" came a meek voice behind him.

Khalid turned to see the fragile housekeeper. He could see his own reflection in her small round glasses, as he put on his friendliest voice.

"Funeral home? Yes, of course. And you are?"

He moved behind her and blocked her exit.

"I... I am the Corps Commander's housekeeper. I must have been in the pantry when you rang."

"Anyone else here?" he snapped.

"No... I mean, *yes*. The doctor is still here... Doctor Gemperli."

Khalid grabbed her arm roughly. "Anybody else?"

"Mr. Polinsky was here... His nephew... He..." She pointed toward the bookshelf.

"*Polinsky?* Good." He moved her toward the hall. "Wait in the kitchen!"

She did as she was ordered, and when Khalid heard her

rattling the dishes he went over to the bookshelves. Hastily sweeping books to the floor, he located the small safe and reached in through its open door. Nothing there. *Polinsky, that son of a bitch! He snatched it right from under my nose!*

He heard a gargling flush and a door slamming shut. A man entered the room behind him, walking heavily.

"What the hell do you think you're doing here?" Gemperli asked indignantly, walking right up to him.

Khalid barely noticed his brazen attitude. He reached into his jacket pocket and wrapped his fingers around the cold metal that was so familiar to him. He pulled out the automatic with its mounted silencer, and pointed it right at the doctor's chest.

"You wouldn't dare, you impertinent..." Gemperli said.

But he said no more. The bullet penetrated his heart with a soft *plop,* throwing him backwards. Moaning, the doctor swayed for a second, and then fell crashing onto the glass table that shattered under his weight.

Furious at having lost his treasure to Polinsky, Khalid grabbed a bottle of cognac from the bar and threw it against the bookshelves, where it shattered into a million pieces. The brandy dripped all over the books on the floor. He tossed a bottle of vodka after it, with similar results. Then he opened some gin, and poured it over Gemperli's dead body; and broke a vintage 1961 Armagnac against the doorframe. Finally he poured kirsch over the silk curtains and lit a match. Tossing it onto the liquor-soaked books, he watched as flames flickered over Nabokov's *Pale Fire* and spread rapidly over the fallen books and newspapers.

In seconds the room was engulfed in flames, and Khalid had to leap over them to reach the hallway as the fire rose up the walls and engulfed the kitchen door. Coldly ignoring the housekeeper's cries from the kitchen, he pulled the key from the deadbolt lock inside the front door, let himself out, and then locked it from the outside, pocketing the key.

When he reached the cool air outside the building, he tossed the key in a high arch into the overgrown park next door, where an old wooden house was rattled by harsh spring winds.

11.

After I'd left that stupid janitor moaning on the ground, so shortly after my uncle had died, I felt a bit upset – or at least in need of a stiff drink. I saw a small parking space and drove the Alfa up over the curb to fit it in. Just down the road was a tavern, nearly hidden in the dark. I went in and sat at the bar. Nobody there but me and the bartender.

"Gin and tonic... with lemon." He spun on his heel and eventually came back with my drink.

I had a sudden impulse. "Do you know Konkorski?"

"Huh?

"*Konkorski*. Ever heard that name before?"

"Nope. Am I supposed to?" he replied with a thick Slavic accent.

My eyes automatically scanned his body, checking for maybe a knife or a gun. That, apparently, he understood.

"Man, what are you, some kind of private dick? We don't serve them here."

"Oh yeah? Guess what, you just did."

Suddenly a massive silhouette appeared in the doorway behind the bar. "What is it Slobodan?" it asked.

"This shithead here asks stupid questions. About some Kongorski."

"Konkorski," I corrected him, and sipped my drink. It was strong.

The massive bulk walked closer through the door, eyeing me up and down with his puffy face and triple chin.

"Drink up and fuck off!"

"Fat chance," I answered, casually.

"Hey, you want trouble?" He came around the bar and moved closer.

Inspired by the Nabokov title, I urged my memory to speak! Usually I would have no trouble knocking idiots like this over with some kind of witticism. But I just backed off.

"Hey, come on. I just came in here for a drink. I'm not looking for any trouble."

"He's some kind of snoop," the bartender said. "Looking for Kongorsi."

"It's Konkorski my brilliant friend. Maybe you should clean the crap out of your ears."

The huge one moved a little closer. "Pay up and fuck off."

"Okay, okay. I just need a little more jet fuel." I finished my drink and put a bill on the bar – and squeezed the lemon slice over it before pushing it at the bartender. Outside a police siren screamed by, followed by fire engines. I picked up my jacket and addressed the giant.

"Now get your fat ass out of my way before I blow your bubbly lips off your ugly face with my wonder pipe."

His eyes widened and his triple-chin dropped. But he backed away.

"All right man, take it easy. We're just joking. Don't you have a sense of humor?"

"Listen pal, humor is my middle name. Are you saying I don't even know my own middle name? Did your brain win first place in the diarrhea contest?"

And I got up and left.

I guess it wasn't my day. A couple of weeks ago, I would have charmed those two idiots and found out anything I wanted to know with ease. Quo vadis anyway, Polinsky? I drove home and parked the Alfa halfway up on the sidewalk. Heading for my front door I had a change of heart. I needed something. Maybe a nice cigar! I stuffed the envelope with the red file into my mailbox and crossed the street to Mario's cigar store.

"Hey you lazy scumbag, does the name Konkorski mean anything to you?"

I figured Mario knew a lot about politics and international affairs – certainly more than those two Slovacs.

"Nice to see you too," he answered. "But no. Here, smoke one of these," holding a box of Havanas open to me.

"Try one. Better than your usual coffin nails. First-class tobacco. Take it. It's a gift – today's my wedding anniversary."

"You have my condolences," I mocked, picking up one of the small robustos. Mario gave me a light. "Mmmm, you're right. Not bad at all." And as I puffed I paid him for two boxes worth.

"Konkord Ski? Doesn't ring a bell with me. Why don't you try the sporting goods store?"

He handed me my change and I tried to discretely look at the display of my paperbacks on the counter. It didn't look as if any had sold. I imagined myself dusting the store and finding a little spider with his web carefully built around my latest non-best-sellers. I imagined squashing the little bug between my fingers.

But then I thought of my uncle again.

"Give my that issue of *Military Aviation* over there," pointing at the rack behind him. As he got it I looked through some porno rags, picking out a *Playhouse*.

"How's the new book?" he asked, stuffing the magazines into a cardboard roll.

"That's it!" I said, realizing I had just answered my own question. "It's about the Konkorski, the Russian Tupolev that was a bad rip-off of the French Concorde. My uncle had something to do with it." I grabbed my cigars and the cardboard roll and headed out the door. "Thanks Mario."

I walked up to my apartment on the fifth floor, between the insurance agency on four and the massage parlor on six. I took off my jacket and dropped into the swivel chair behind my desk, booting up my computer. Konkorski? The smoke from the Havana rose in slow curls toward the ceiling. While the Internet search engine was looking for files, I reached into the drawer for my Sauer nine-millimeter in its shoulder holster – and put it on. I figured, on a day like this, you never know. And then the doorbell rang.

Maybe it was the mailman. I looked through the peephole and saw a big square head, a moustache, and two beady eyes. Around it were men in SWAT-team gear.

Damn! Can't even enjoy a peaceful smoke!

I knew exactly who it was, but I yelled through the door anyway.

"Who is it?" And I thought my middle name was humor. Well, maybe not.

"Polinsky, it's the police. Open up!"

"Yeah, right. Anybody can say they're the police! The

whorehouse is one flight up. Get lost!" I shouted, returning to my desk.

They must've had a battering ram, because suddenly my door buckled with a crash and they rushed in – two cops in masks and flak vests carrying machine guns and the thickhead in civilian clothes. The SWAT team guys rushed me and twisted my arm, pinning me to my desk. One pulled out a pistol and held it to my temple.

"You threatened us, you creep!" he yelled into my ear, punching me in the kidney. Ouch, that hurt!

"All right, that's enough," said the thickhead. It was Bossandey, the smart-ass examining magistrate known as "Bossi."

"He was going to pull a gun on us," whined the storm trooper who had just done his best to flatten my kidney.

"Hey, Betty Bossi," I said, in some discomfort, "Call off your Rambo dogs, will you? And then maybe you can tell me why you've decided to abuse your authority here in my peaceful home?"

His thick square head came so close to me I could smell wine and garlic on his humid breath. He hissed: "Don't call me that again, Polinsky, if you know what's good for you. Here's the search warrant."

He waved it under my nose, and suddenly about four more people came into my apartment, among them a thin policewoman in uniform. I could see one of my neighbors gaping at the crowd, hoping no doubt to see them carry my dead body out.

And then they went to work, unceremoniously opening drawers and dumping their contents on the floor, rolling up rugs, knocking here and there on the parquet floor, pulling up loose boards near the windows. They went into the bedroom and slit open my mattress, took apart the TV, smashed the VCR. The thin policewoman opened my computer and started poking around inside it like a madwoman.

My nice Havana robusto had gone out.

"Hey, Betty Bossi," I shouted, "your fucking warrant is illegal. The address is wrong. This is number 31... the warrant says 13. You're in deep shit now. And look, my name is spelled wrong too. It ends in *y*, not *i*. Nothing you find here will be admissible in court, not with this warrant. Get your ignoramuses out of here before I call my lawyer – you know Steinlin I believe? He'll make you look like an idiot."

Bossandey walked over to me slowly.

"Look, Polinsky, where's the file? Hand it over and we'll leave you alone."

I remembered that I had left Uncle Edouard's envelope in my mailbox downstairs, which turned out to be a very lucky thing.

"What file, Betty dearest? I don't know what you're talking about."

"Come on Polinsky, this is serious shit. Not even an hour ago your uncle's apartment was ransacked and burned. We know the old goat had a visitor. And now he's as dead as a doornail. In the living room there's another corpse, burned beyond recognition. Diesbach's old housekeeper is in the hospital, in a coma from smoke inhalation, probably dead by now. This is a very bad thing. The whole penthouse looks as if it were the Gulf War. We know that somebody opened the safe and removed documents. And now we're investigating a homicide. Come on, Polinsky, give it up!"

Well, at least Bossandey's ranting gave me some information. I feigned boredom and looked at my watch. If these idiots didn't get out of here fast I might miss my date.

"Look, Bossi, of course I visited my uncle. He was dying, for God's sake. I sat at his deathbed, and he passed away right in front of me. It was very sad, I tell you. And then I left and came home. I don't know anything about any files. What's it supposed to be about?"

"I'll ask the questions here," Bossi snapped. "What about the building's porter? The guy you kicked in the balls with the smashed fingers? He says you dropped some documents. Ring any bells genius?"

"Oh, yeah," I answered lightly, and walked over to my desk. All the drawers had been pulled out.

"Stop right there!" one of the storm troopers screamed as I reached for the desk. "Don't touch it!"

"Fine," I said, addressing Bossi. "Forget it."

Bossi waved his dog off and nodded to me to reach for whatever I wanted to. I picked up Mario's cardboard roll and shook out the magazines.

Bossi grabbed them.

"*Military Aviation* and... hmmm... what do we have here? Oh, so you're a little sex fiend, are you?"

He leafed through *Playhouse*, gaping at the pictures.

"Well, I guess so," I admitted weakly. "I'm guilty. I snitched the magazines from my uncle. I didn't think he'd be needing them anymore."

Bossandey glared at my suspiciously. Then he called one of his lackeys over and had a little private chat.

I snarled at the rest of the wrecking crew.

"Find anything yet? Did you stick your heads in the toilet? Don't forget that."

Bossandey made a sign for them all to leave, and they turned on their heels and marched off. He came back close to me and with a wine and garlic hiss said: "We're going to stay on your ass Polinsky."

With that he dumped the *Military Aviation* on my desk and tucked the *Playhouse* under his arm.

I gestured around the room in total chaos.

"Who's going to pay for this mess?"

I followed him, tripping over toppled furniture, glancing in the kitchen at overturned garbage and broken dishes.

"File a petition in court smart guy," Bossandey laughed. "Get Steinlin to do it for you. Maybe they'll throw you a couple of bucks."

He mocked a salute by lifting his middle finger to his temple, and paraded his thick head out the door.

12.

That Saturday of my uncle's death certainly changed my life in a hurry. I was really in a pickle this time. Well, at least Doktor Steinlin had managed to keep me out of jail. That was something, anyway – the only bright spot in my suddenly darkened life.

When I got out of the cab after leaving Steinlin outside the bar, I realized that I really didn't know how I was going to solve my problem. So I kept to my usual routine. On my way over to Mario's I caught a glimpse again of that dark green police-van pulling into a bus stop on the other side of the street. For a second I thought I'd yell something at it... but then I thought better of it, and went into the store. Mario greeted me effusively.

"Polinsky, man! How are you? Where've you been? You look good. Want some coffee?"

He realized of course that I neither looked good nor was in the mood for small talk, so he handed me my cigars and a daily paper. When I gave him the money he smiled.

"Sold two more, Mr. Successful!"

"Today?" I asked hopefully.

"Two this week," he corrected gently.

Good friend that he was, Mario kept the just-released paperback edition of my fourth novel right on the front of the counter, sitting between the crooked Brissagos and the Marlboro Lights. In spite of his efforts I knew the book was selling slowly.

I looked at myself in the small mirror above the sunglass rack and rubbed my chin, as if that might help. I looked like shit – old and gray – with a kind of hangdog expression and dark circles under my eyes.

"Man, what's wrong? The new book's not going well?"

Of course he didn't want to dive right into the fact that I was out on bail. And I thought I'd keep it on that level as long as I could.

"I don't know. I need something. Some kind of kick."

When writers like me need a kick, it usually just means they need money. If this new paperback were leaping up to number one on the bestseller list, my fat ass editor Waldo would be calling me from his old Turkish divan rocking chair twice a day – telling me to write more and to get on the TV talk shows. I could do with that kind of kick I suppose.

"What do you need, a kick in the ass?" Mario joked. "But wait, I've got a better idea. Where's Irina? Hey? That girl's one hot tomato!"

"I don't know where she is," I lied. "And I'm as horny as an old man on a roller coaster."

Mario grinned, and didn't believe me. Then, having spent enough time sensitively avoiding my real problems, he started in.

"Hey, you want to hear the latest rumor about your trial? Some people are saying Colossimo himself put up the money for your bail. That's five hundred big ones."

"Yeah, half a million mafia farts. Who cares? The only thing I care about is that I'm not in the slammer."

Mario turned away from me and walked over to the espresso machine in the corner, slowly trying to coax some coffee out of it. Despite what I had said to him, I would've given my eyeteeth to know who posted my bail. But Steinlin was silent as a sphinx on this matter, which made me think that Mario was right.

He returned, carefully carrying two demitasse cups of black coffee.

"I hope it's not all burned," wagging his head.

I didn't reply. Instead, I looked from my burning cigar tip to the hissing smoke of the coffee machine to the steaming cup of black liquid before me. I usually found it easy to turn the dissolute aspects of my life into fiction – not poetry, mind you, but fiction. But as I contemplated all this smoke and steam before me, and thought of the mess I was in, I got the feeling that I'd never be able to make sense out of it, much less get it into words. It was much too cloudy, maybe even poisonous.

Again I thought of Steinlin. Now there was a man with a penchant for titles. Maybe he should start writing paper-backs! What had he said to me? This is where the serious side of life starts? Not bad! Maybe I'll steal it for my new book: Stan Polinsky: The Serious Side of Life!

"So, you've already got a lot of stuff for your book on your uncle the Corps Commander, don't you?"

"Oh sure, I'm drowning in data, awash with facts... but I don't know..."

And I didn't get any farther than that.

The door opened with a snap and a very seductive whiff of perfume entered the store, completely vanquishing the smell of coffee and cigars. A shapely young woman stood in the doorway, her uniform jacket half opened, her red lips opened as well. Mario and I raised our eyebrows at each other.

I straightened myself up as I stood against the counter, smiled slightly. I shot for my bored-but-hot-intellectual look, which is not as easy to project as it sounds.

She came a bit closer, grabbed a magazine, and slapped it into her open palm.

"Mr. Polinsky?"

I ignored her completely.

Mario played along. "Polinsky is not available at the moment," he said.

I sipped my coffee, and saw her looking me up and down from the corner of my eye. She stared at my crotch for a minute, an area of my life where there was definitely nothing happening, and then brought her eyes to mine. Before I got too excited, her voice brayed sharply.

"Polinsky, I have a message for you."

She pulled an envelope from under her jacket and handed it to me.

Trying to find my tongue and play it relatively cool, I asked with a hint of condescension, "And to whom do I have the pleasure of speaking my Colonel?"

She smiled mockingly. "Adjutant to the Chief of Intelligence."

Mario dropped his coffee cup, which shattered all over the floor. Neither she nor I acted as if anything had happened at all.

I put the envelope to the side and said, "You will hear from me."

Mario wanted in on this some way, so he picked up a copy of my paperback from the counter and pushed it at her.

"Madame perhaps is already familiar with this hot best seller?"

"Yes, I read it in hardcover. I read everything you write Polinsky." She smiled at me seductively. "Casually put lies turn me on."

And with that she gave a military turn and paraded out of the store, swaying her ass and half-goose-stepping at the same time. Mario and I breathed in the cloud of perfume that followed her.

"Mama mia, what a wow!" Mario exclaimed, shadow boxing to work off his excitement. Sometimes I forgot that he had been national middleweight champion. He kept himself in shape, and on a good day looked like a movie star with his shiny black hair and sharp moustache.

"I don't want to hear any more about Colossimo," I said to him as I watched the nicely moving ass of the adjutant who was turned on by casually put lies strut down the street.

Pride stirred in my chest. Hey, not everybody's casually put lies can turn on a war goddess like her. I'll keep that in mind next time some green-eyed critic does a hatchet job on one of my books.

I waved goodbye to Mario and went out on the street. I could still smell her perfume. I sniffed and almost expected her to suddenly appear behind me, when I realized that the smell came from the envelope she had handed me, an odor as faint as it was compelling. What was it Polinsky? Donna Karan? Ralph Lauren? Who cares? It was the scent of a woman.

13.

On my way back to my apartment I passed the "Gottardo" – famous not only as a pass in the Alps and a symbol of resistance, but in this case for its huge wienerschnitzels.

I sat down at one of the big round tables in the front of the restaurant where the television was blasting, sitting next to a giant in blue overalls. He nodded without a word, and I murmured a hello, hoping that Irina hadn't forgotten our date and would show up soon. Everyone at the tables was watching the soccer game.

"If they don't let that Turk play forward, the rest of those sleepers will never get past midfield!" My giant roared above the blare of the TV.

I mumbled in agreement and sucked my cigar.

The Diesbach affair hadn't done much to increase my stature in the minds of Zurich's citizens – I suppose being on trial for murder rarely does. Apart from Mario, I kept my distance from most people and avoided appearing in public. I didn't mind cultivating the image of a lone wolf. After all, what writer of casually put lies wasn't? Faust, for example? Anyway, I certainly wasn't sure that my lone wolf habits were helping me – either with writing my new book or keeping myself out of jail by finding this mysterious third man.

As for the book based on my uncle's life story, well, it should have been easy and fun. The old Corps Commander Diesbach was a rather charming character in Zurich, often lighting up the city's rather dreary routine. The aging Lothario was a relic of the old-fashioned spy business, a real charmer and

59

a lady-killer as well. With my personal knowledge of his pranks during and after the Cold War I should have been able to spit out pages a day. But I was getting nowhere.

I kept to my routine, but it didn't help much. Other than writing (or trying to write), working out took up much of my day. I would jog for about 10 miles, and lift some weights. A couple of times a month I would let Li-Li beat me up with her kung fu attacks in her attempt to teach me something – or at least to keep my reflexes sharp. She was as charming as she was fast.

Oh, and of course once a week I'd go to the old fortress that had been converted to a shooting range and take some target practice with my SIG-Sauer P228 nine millimeter – and sometimes with a Glock, the preferred choice of New York City cops. But none of this was getting me any closer to solving my problems.

"Look at that! No!! This cannot be true. He missed the ball!" the giant next to me shouted and moaned, holding his bald head in despair.

I looked up from my reveries at the TV.

"Ah, they're just playing like they always do. It's our nature, see? Back passes, hold-onto-the-ball passes, ball control, back and forth." I kept giving my opinion while watching the door for Irina. "And only if it's foolproof they will, now and then, dare a little kick. See, now this idiot even passes the ball back to the keeper..."

Again I looked at the door for Irina. I had known her now for well over a year – long enough to torture myself with stupid questions like whether or not I was her only lover or whether she was just pacifying me when she said sex was better with me than with anybody else. She was a smart cookie, had studied law, and certainly had more than enough brains to deceive me on both these questions.

She often helped me with my freelance jobs in information assurance, something I did to supplement my income – after all, my books didn't sell that well. Irina's analytical mind was able to filter out important facts from seas of available information.

She spoke five languages, and thought the assignments I gave her were exciting, like secret agent work. I had seen enough of the old style secret agent work to know it was becoming obsolete – chasing diplomats and hiding transmitters in the woods. It just didn't work anymore. Information assurance was the gold mine of the future, and I wasn't opposed to mining a bit of it for myself. As for Irina, she was a natural at it – she loved to talk to people and surf the web. She was great at gathering material and turning it into reliable reports.

"You miserable cynic!" the bald headed giant yelled at me above the roar of the TV. "Why don't you just piss off?"

"Hey, I had to listen to your ranting. Don't I get a turn?"

I did a quick estimate on which was harder, my fist or his alpine cranium. Without a doubt his head won.

Luckily, this was the moment Irina chose to come in the door, rushing, late as usual. She wore loose cargo pants with pockets all over them and a white tank top four inches too short, showing off her beautifully tanned flat belly and shining navel ring. Man, was I glad to see her.

I jumped up excitedly, kissed her cheek, and patted her naked belly. She smiled indulgently at me, as if I were a silly boy, which I was with the exception of very adult stirrings in my trousers.

"Sorry I'm late. It took a bit longer than they thought."

"And what had the poor son-of-a-bitch done?"

"Same thing. Transporting drugs."

One of Irina's other jobs was to use her language skills as an interpreter at police interrogations.

"Are you hungry?" I asked, but she didn't reply. "What is it?"

"Nothing," but I could see her mind drifting.

"What? What are you thinking of?"

"Oh it's nothing. While I was at the cash machine two guys were talking about some company. I can't remember the name, but for some reason I can't stop thinking about it."

"Forget it. Then it will dawn on you unexpectedly."

"Yeah, you're right. But it was some kind of stock deal. I wish I could remember the name."

Well, stock market deals were not on my mind at the moment. My knee rubbed against her thigh, and I started to push it between her legs.

"Come on, let's get out of here," she said. "This place is a nightmare," looking at the giant next to me. Then she bent over and whispered in my ear "Uh, if you don't mind, I really want you to bang the hell out of me. Or rather vice versa."

Well, that was about all the suggestion I needed. I just hoped the mattress Mario had gotten me to replace the one the cops destroyed was up to the task.

"Hmm, let me see," I whispered back to Irina. "I think I can manage to slip you in to my busy schedule."

We left the restaurant and crossed the street to get to

my place. A young shorthaired girl walked toward us, glanced at Irina and then stared right at me, as if to say *Man, you are very cool.* For my age, I added silently, not allowing myself too much delusion. A few years ago girls like that would've considered me *fierce* rather than cool. But hell, I'll take what I can get. I flicked my cigar away and grabbed Irina's waist tightly. *Hey Polinsky, you are cool!* At least for now.

14.

My apartment had been all put back in order after Bossi's wrecking crew had ripped it apart, and as I passed my hand over the sheets anticipating Irina's arrival in the bedroom I felt something between them. Damn! The secret file! Mario, you good soul! Three letters had been written by hand on the red folder. I stared at them uncomprehendingly, shaking my head. *TCM? Well, let's see what's inside...*

But just then Irina came in and threw herself onto the bed. Or rather, in my mind, she floated down onto it in slow motion. She wore nothing now but that tiny red slip, and sprawled voluptuously on the sheets.

I lifted the file mechanically and tossed it under the bed, almost hitting my hard cock that was screaming to be released from my pants. Trying to be cool, I started to pull down my zipper that for some reason decided to put up a massive struggle.

"Hmmm," Irina whispered, "let me take care of that."

Her adept fingers vanquished the zipper's resistance. She pulled my pants down and slowly caressed me with her small red mouth. Floating on cloud nine, I closed my eyes and ran my hands through her silky black hair.

Mario's Teresa had left a basket of tomatoes and pasta on the kitchen table, which I had noticed when we came in. What would my life be without that wild resourceful Italian stallion! Mario was filled with common sense – the kind that knew what was really important in life, what really worked. He was worlds away from modern life's stereotypes. And his wife Teresa was a gem as well: lively, witty, a great cook, and equipped I'm sure to give Mario all the kids he would ever want. Now why I was thinking of them as Irina's mouth was driving me wild was beyond comprehension I didn't know. But I think the watering in my mouth had more to do with Irina than with Teresa's pasta and tomatoes.

Irina kissed me as we lay on our sides and I started to push in between her thighs. But with a throaty laugh she rolled me onto my back. She grabbed my wrists and held them down onto the pillows under my head.

"Enjoy," she whispered, rubbing herself back and forth on my hardness, her eyes closed. Gazing at her half-parted lips and at her full breasts dangling above me, it was hard to control myself. I felt myself on the verge of exploding, and to divert myself I started to think of the third man Steinlin had spoken of so eloquently in court earlier. Perhaps with too much success.

"Don't stop now," Irina purred.

I pulled her down to the bed on her side, and kissed her wild open mouth again and again. She reached for me, pressed her body onto mine, and pushed my cock into her wetness. I could feel her body tingle as I entered her, and felt her wet heat increase as waves of lust passed through my body.

While we rocked like this for a while and I felt myself floating somewhere in a warm and wet universe, she suddenly stopped and swung herself around. Then I felt her tongue on me again, literally eating me.

"This is what I like the most," she moaned in between mouthfuls. "How do you want it? Tell me."

"I want to taste you too," I moaned.

A passionate meal, I thought. No wonder French cuisine rose to such fame. I saw nothing but bright sparkling stars. I could feel Irina vibrating, and then felt everything inside her contracting – her orgasm a human-scale version of the big bang. *Dear Stephen Hawking,* flashed through my mind. *Forget all about your big bang theories.* Here is how the universe was born – here, in a volcano like this, erupting, sweating ecstasy, hot torrents of lava: mine, hers... this is how... the world comes into existence... and dissolves...

I must have dozed off, because all I remember after that is Irina kissing my cheek.

"Gotta run hon."

And then she was gone.

Exhausted but happy, I fumbled for a glass on the night table and got up, heading toward the kitchen. Sex usually gives wings to my imagination. But here I was with this great story about my uncle, and for some reason I couldn't seem to write it down. Of course I *did* have to figure out a way to stay out of jail first – which meant solving my uncle's dying riddles. A bad feeling crept over me. *Konkorski. Nadine. The mysterious third man.*

I got no peace from the hints hidden in my uncle's dying words. I sank into the dark blue sofa and let my thoughts drift back to Irina and our sweet madness.

Without thinking, I pressed the remote control, and when the TV came to life I saw myself in the endless news loop walking out of the courthouse and squeezing behind Steinlin's back past the gaping spectators as he spoke into the microphones.

My cell phone chirped its melodic electronic mating call. And just as if there had been telepathic contact, it was Steinlin.

"Put the news on," he snapped.

"I'm watching it." Grinning, I goaded him a little. "Who's that wretched creature squeezing behind you and sneaking around the corner?"

"Very funny Polinsky. Listen to me. You need a new image. Something warm and fuzzy. People should know what a nice guy you are."

I looked down at my groin where my robe cover my recently satisfied bulge, and I told Steinlin that I was in fact quite pleased with my image and that I would call him if something came up.

"I am serious Polinsky. We have to..."

"But my dear Steinlin, where is your sense of optimism? Not 'have to.' Will. We *will...*"

I laughed into the phone with tremendous self-satisfaction, pushed the hang-up button, and sprawled back on the couch.

The TV droned on. Irina's sweet smell still clung to my body, exciting me.

This was crazy. A week ago I had led a completely easygoing life. Well, not anymore. I sighed and grudgingly sat down in front of a pile of magazines and dug out some paper and my handwritten notes. Despite everything that had gone on, I simply had to push on with my research on the Corps Commander's life. Somehow I knew that the book and my life's new problems were connected.

And, if nothing else, my uncle's death had adorned my

planned biography with unexpected newsworthiness. I knew that the District Attorney believed in the third man theory, even though he apparently seemed uninterested in investigating this lead. After all, he had everything he needed to stage two press conferences a day and get all the ratings he could want from the media circus: two corpses, a brain-damaged housekeeper, and a suspect (me, Stan Polinsky) with a thin but still plausible motive.

So if anyone were going to save me it would have to be myself. But other than going on with my research, I really didn't know where to begin. That face. The face of the man I saw when I drove off. *It must have been him.*

Then I remembered the envelope that the sexy adjutant had slipped me so carelessly in Mario's store. I found in all crunched up in my back pocket, sniffed it, and imagined her eyes undressing me again. Then I opened the envelope and read it.

It was from the Chief of Intelligence, and could not have been improved upon in terms of military concision. Like marching orders, it contained only location, time, and purpose. It told me to appear early the next morning. Very nice. The same day as my uncle's funeral, which had been set for 2 p.m. at the Frauenmünster church.

I held my head and tried to think about the third man. He had obviously been after the red file – the contents of which made no sense to me at all. It was filled with encrypted text. Mumbo jumbo. Hieroglyphs. Uncle Edouard must have hidden a clue to the code somewhere. *If… wait a second! Konkorski! That had to be the key word!*

I slapped myself in the head. That must be it. But still, I knew as much about deciphering code, as an Eskimo knew about picking dates. But what had he said? *She has the key.* Uncle Edouard's last words resonated in my mind.

But I still didn't know how to go about breaking the code – or even what to do next. Finally I let my mind wander, putting off my cryptographic problems until later. At least for a little while, my uncle's secrets could rest safely in the red file in the hidden pocket of my duffel bag.

Wondering about exactly what the Chief of Intelligence might tell me the next morning my head sank slowly onto the desk. And before I knew it I was asleep.

15.

The man in the light-blue hardhat who walked toward the moored tanker along the dockyard at the port of Lagos looked just like any Nigerian longshoreman – except that his skin was lighter. His tanned face, flowing gray beard, and dark eyes belonged as much to a qualified wharf-specialist as did his blue overalls carrying the small triangle logo patch of Nigeria's largest shipyard.

A vigilant observer, however, would have noted a spring in the step of the man who appeared to be in his late 40s – something that distinguished him ever so slightly from his two companions. And something about the gaze of his bright eyes suggested he was on a mission that consumed his very soul.

Captain Souri, the tall man on his right, motioned him onto the portal crane with a polite hand gesture, and then followed him onto a small elevator. The third man looked around cautiously before joining them in the cramped space. A trained eye would have seen his tight coat betray the outline of a weapon.

The Port of Lagos has all the facilities that any modern ship terminal has. The mere size of the dry dock was astonishing, next to which the countless cranes appeared to fidget like the bent limbs of insects. These cranes discharged dry goods such as grain and fertilizer as well as general freight from ships' cargo holds that traveled there from all over the world.

Further back, giant wet dock cranes loaded logs into the deep cargo holds of freighters, while beyond them smaller boats were lined up alongside the container quays. Next to the new basins for the large terminals where oil and other fluid cargos were loaded sat the runways for the neighboring international airport. Finally, next to the storage bunkers stood the harbor's main building. On the third floor Lloyd's had set up a small office for their shipping agent.

"Ready for the big moment, sir?" asked the captain.

The man, who seemed to be accustomed to being treated with great respect, nodded with a smile. And he and his hardhat moved past the railing into the elevator car.

The CIA's Counter-terrorism Division would have gladly paid a fortune to know that this man – America's arch enemy, was at the Port of Lagos. But like any wanted man, he knew how to keep his whereabouts a mystery. Like a chameleon, he could change his appearance at will, and seamlessly blend into any environment. And just like the lizard that would effortless snatch prey with its silent tongue, this man was an expert at attacking in a flash, able to hit his enemy with utmost precision.

Yussef bin Golem was the most terrifying nightmare dreamt by all Western government leaders with their retinues of security and counter-terrorism specialists. As the elevator slowly rose, bin Golem looked down into the gigantic ship's belly with growing amazement.

Before the leader of the *Qaeda* had bought the *Shiraz* from the National Iranian Tanker Company, it had been rated as a ULCC or Ultra Large Crude Carrier. The ship onto which the elevator car now lowered was nearly 1,500 feet long, with a width of 260 feet from one scupper to the other.

Captain Souri had been commander of the *Shiraz* when

she was still regularly transporting crude oil from the Iranian oil terminal to Rotterdam. He knew his ship inside and out and had been an essential advisor to the engineers who had overseen the removal of its oil tanks and the installation of special cargo and storage holds.

The superstructure of the tanker rose four decks high into the hot and humid air.

On that afternoon in late April, the thermometer climbed to 95° F. From the main deck, which was about half-visible, all the way down to the keel, the enormous hull measured nearly 100 feet. Each of its original 60 tanks was the size of a gymnasium. Two of its mid-ship tanks had been replaced with newer equipment and remained invisible below deck.

Captain Souri reported to his passenger that last night the heavy cases had been lowered very carefully into the hydraulically operated cargo hatches by the portal crane. Bin Golem nodded composedly. He was in fact filled with pride. Every time he saw his colossus with his own eyes it took his breath away, even though he owned giant glossy photos of the *Shiraz* and had flown in several times from his secret land base to give the engineers final instructions.

In a half-hour, Captain Souri would start the 85,000 WPS engines, which would begin to turn the ship's two propellers with their 23-foot brass blades and move the giant out to sea.

"We expect to clear port in one hour. Does this schedule meet your expectations sir?" the captain asked politely as they approached the ship's bridge on upper Deck D.

Bid Golem nodded and turned to the third man.

"Khalid, have my luggage brought to my cabin."

They exited the elevator on Deck D.

"Shall we take a look at the ship's route if you don't mind sir?" the captain asked.

Deck D housed the quarters of the ship's officers. The captain's cabin was actually a suite of rooms, located traditionally on the front starboard corner of the superstructure. Adjacent to the captain's quarters on the port side was the chartroom. Through its open door they could see a large table. The captain let his guest go in first. Once inside, he pointed out the large built-in cabinets with their narrow drawers.

"We have the most detailed sea charts in the world," he boasted. "They guarantee safe passage in all seas and in every port."

It seemed as if he was going to add something, but then reconsidered. He had correctly concluded that telling bin Golem that these first-class charts had been created by the disbelieving geographers of the British Admiralty might have proved annoying to the Islamic leader.

"What route will we take, Captain?" asked bin Golem, bending over the chart table and smiling.

Souri explained that their route would take them through the Benin Bay, then south of Accra, then along the Ivory Coast before swinging off toward the northwest at the Liberian Cape Palmas towards the Cape Verde Islands.

"How long will it take us to get from Casablanca to the Strait of Gibraltar?" bin Golem asked keenly.

"Seven days and 20 hours," the captain replied, his eyes squinting over the chart.

A sudden soft vibration made the compass needle in the middle of the table tremble: in the engine rooms below the powerful steam turbines had begun to idle. A dense dark cloud of smoke belched from the *Shiraz's* giant sleek funnel, welling up into the deep blue sky – so dense that for a minute it dimmed the bright daylight in the chartroom.

"May I invite you to take over the helm once we put to sea?" Captain Souri offered, checking his watch.

The men left the chartroom and ascended the stairs to the bridge. Khalid and a steward hauled bin Golem's luggage aft, piece by piece. Khalid opened a conference room that bordered the stateroom with a key.

"Stay outside," he ordered the steward.

All of the furniture had been removed from this cabin, with the exception of a mahogany ship chest of drawers built in under the huge porthole. The floor had been decorated with precious carpets with Yussef's favorite floral designs on backgrounds of light green, violet, and red. Heavy cushions were spread about to serve as seats. Covering the wall was a brocade carpet displaying a surah from the Koran in silver writing on a black background. As per bin Golem's orders, Khalid had spread out a large sea chart, held in place with two strips of wood, on the carpet-laden floor. The quarters of the Islamic leader now looked more like the Spartan accommodations of a Bedouin tent than the luxurious cabin of a modern high-seas tanker.

On the portside, next to this cabin, was another suite, similar in furnishings to the captain's quarters. Normally it belonged to the Chief Engineer. But by Khalid's orders, the Chief Engineer had to move out of his very comfortable accommodations and take over the cabin of the third in command on the deck below. Khalid moved into the suite in order to be right next to his boss and be able to protect him at all times.

Kicking the Chief Engineer out of the quarters befitting his state in blatant disregard of the strict hierarchy that exists aboard ship caused quite a hubbub among the officers. Needless to say, none of them thought much of Khalid. Everyone bit their tongues, however, especially the Chief Engineer, who secretly seethed with rage that an arrogant landlubber bodyguard could get away with acting like the captain himself.

Deck C of the *Shiraz* was made up of the cabins of the third and fourth in command, the wardroom, and the smoking lounge adjacent to the club with its terrace and sunroom. Behind these were a large swimming pool, a Turkish bath, and a complete health club facility with gymnastics and workout equipment.

The rest of the crew's quarters stretched over Deck B, where there was also a movie theatre, a gambling room, and the Internet coffee shop and pool tables in one large lounge. There once had been a bar here, but it was torn out and replaced by soda machines. Concerning these, Captain Souri had asserted himself and convinced bin Golem to allow these products of the American beverage manufacturers, even though they were clearly the creations of the Great Satan. But he was responsible for the crew's morale, and he needed people who knew their business and could be counted on, even if they liked to drink an occasional Coke. The captain had no problem with devout Muslims, as long as they knew how to do their jobs. But their degree of dedication to Islam didn't really mean much to him.

Deck A housed the technical rooms for the many services required by the *Shiraz* and its crew. The huge central kitchen was connected to food storage, to the wine cellar, and to the workroom for the kitchen personnel. Sickbay was on this deck, as were the laundry and the fire squad. A very important room labeled "Freight Control Room" had been constructed in the center of Deck A in view of the bow. It had only one narrow window, was air-conditioned, and filled to the ceiling with advanced computer equipment.

Before the ship was rebuilt, a pump engineer had sat where this room was now, controlling the individual oil tanks. But when the *Shiraz* was reconstructed, all the crude-oil tanks were removed. There was still a pump crew onboard, but only to control the 12 giant ballast tanks of the ship.

The state-of-the-art equipment in this room would be more at home in a missile equipped destroyer. And that was fitting – because the "Freight Control Room" on Deck A of the *Shiraz* housed one of the most sophisticated launch control systems available on the international marketplace. And its job was to control the brightly polished latest-generation *Exocet* super guided missiles that lay hidden in the ship's belly.

16.

Under a multi-colored shawl that served to protect them from the sun, a pair of dark eyes followed the huge ship that slowly pulled away from the wet dock and began gliding out to the open Atlantic. The eyes belonged to a slender African woman dressed in a colorful robe decorated with large flower blossoms – and they were filled with awe and amazement at the skill of the ship's engineers.

Almost noiselessly the 600,000-ton colossus majestically set out to sea. But no one stood at the railing, waving to friends on the dock. The long window of the bridge above the superstructure shone black. There was an eerie feeling in the air as the *Shiraz* pulled away like a phantom ship.

Nowadays, huge tankers like this don't attract the attention they once did, whether leaving or arriving in port. Twenty years ago, when the first large tankers docked here, both the longshoreman and the people of Lagos would crowd the docks to gape at the giants. But very soon such sights became commonplace, part and parcel of the modern crude oil transport business – and only a few people bothered to look anymore. After the times of the oil crisis, of course, the trend shifted from supertankers to middle-sized tankers – and again these giants attracted some nostalgic attention, as when a U.S. Navy aircraft carrier anchors off Livorno in the Mediterranean.

The *Shiraz* had indeed once been such a supertanker, weighing 600,000 tons. As the dark-eyed African woman watched the black hull with its white upper deck slowly drift past her, she wondered what had become of the huge tanks in the middle part of the ship. Very light blue walls loomed up in front of the big smokestack.

She took out a small camera and started snapping pictures discretely. She had heard rumors that the hull of the *Shiraz* held secrets of some kind. Perhaps harmless ones, perhaps not.

For weeks before the ship left port, a carefully selected crew had worked on board day and night – among them many Iranian technicians and Indian computer specialists. Similarly, the portal crane worked overtime, lifting crates of heavy materials from freighters berthed alongside and lowering them into the belly of the *Shiraz*. In place of its torn-out tanks was now a gigantic cargo hold, shielded from curious eyes by a large tent.

As to what was in those crates and containers, no one knew. Strict security regulations prevented access to the wet dock. Anyone who asked about the ship and its cargo was told that the *Shiraz* was newly rigged out on behalf of an Iranian shipping company.

As a consequence, the rumor mill in the small harbormaster's building ran wild. As the *Shiraz* slid past the woman taking pictures, someone said it was just a freighter converted into a container ship. Someone else said that it had been specially prepared with gauging stations and on-board laboratories for oil prospecting off the Nigerian coast. And then a third person said it was all a big Hollywood project – and that the dark belly of the ship held a thousand black movie extras who would be brought out to sea to mimic the suffering of the slave trade in colonial times. This got a big laugh and enthusiastic shouts and applause.

The slender African woman with the camera had returned to her home country from London just a year ago. She sat in her green Honda Civic and connected the small digital camera to her laptop. In seconds she had transferred its images onto her hard drive; then she drafted a brief report and sent it along with the pictures via satellite to the Geneva office. She was employed by the multinational company Specs Inc. as an inspector, where she earned a steady income in hard cash that was transferred tax free to her bank account in Geneva. Her main job was to report on ships putting in and out of Lagos: whom they belonged to and what they carried. Occasionally she would participate in an inspection of goods, or check freight bills, or certify a ship's adherence to contractual agreements.

She turned and placed her laptop on the backseat of her car. She turned the key and the little engine caught readily – it never failed. Some of the men on the dock turned towards her – followed by suggestive laughter, some whistles and catcalls.

Well, that's the way it is at home, she thought to herself. *If you're walking, you have to put up with the macho-man's gauntlet. And if you go by car, you're a dissolute black bitch.* She shook her head in amusement. *Bushmen!*

17.

On a wonderfully warm dry morning in Los Alamos, New Mexico, Nadine Moran looked forward to her morning exercise routine. Happily singing an old hit, she left her one-bedroom apartment on the Manhattan Loop around seven, turned into Myrtle Street, and jogged downtown. The sun beat down pleasantly on her back from a deep blue cloudless sky. She noticed the shuttle flight from Albuquerque banking low over the Pueblo Canyon and descending onto the runway of the airfield just half a mile east.

Her mind ranged from the vista of the dark green mountains nearby to the horizon and then onto Europe where she was born – specifically, to France. She took deep breaths of fresh morning air. After the agitation of the last two nights, she needed to relax. As she ran she felt the adrenaline running through her body, her heart pounding. It wasn't her pace that was making her so excited this morning. Normally her run wouldn't push her heart rate up past 120. *Normally!*

And her excitement certainly wasn't caused by any thoughts of men. She sighed to herself as she turned left and jogged down Central Avenue. *Men?* There were plenty of them around here. They had tried both through polite charm and blunt passes to, as they liked to say in these parts, jump her bones.

Rather, wasn't it more a nagging desire for fatherly affection somewhere deep in her psyche? Was she feeling the lack of reliable authority that only a father, or at least a father figure, could supply? Such moments of inner anxiety reminded Nadine that a woman who has never known a father in their childhood probably carried an emotional void with her at all times – which might someday lead to either a liberating relationship or some kind of egocentric catastrophe.

What did the word father mean, anyway? If she had had as many father figures as her mother had lovers, surely she would not feel this void. She knew that since she arrived in the U.S. she always looked for signs in her dates with young men of a long-desired authority figure. On some level Nadine knew what she needed: a mature man that was her intellectual equal, someone who had experienced all the world had to offer, and who could protect her. *Hélas!* That was something that these self-important yuppies here in the American Southwest had no idea about. And besides that, as a Frenchwoman she found herself more attracted to exotic men than to blonde pretty boys or Yankee sports fans. She liked Mediterranean men; yes, Arabs with warm eyes wandered through her dreams on lonely nights. And sometimes she thought incessantly about the man who could have become her father had he not abandoned her and vanished into thin air. What did he look like? Did he have a thick beard? Kind eyes?

She picked up her pace and breathed deeply, trying to banish her lingering uneasiness. But then she remembered her meeting with Igor a couple of weeks ago, and the feeling returned. Had he thrown her off balance? No, of course not! He was just a crazy Russian with an absurd conspiracy theory. No, she said to herself, trying to calm down. No, my excitement this morning has nothing to do with men. Definitely not! *Men are the last things I need!* And she started sprinting up a gentle hill.

Two days ago, Nadine had made a breakthrough that opened up all sorts of unimagined possibilities. It was at work, where she specialized in the encrypting of software. The well-equipped laboratories of Los Alamos provided her with not only high-speed computers but also the most sophisticated encrypting equipment available in the world. Cryptography was Nadine Moran's life – which meant that her life was entwined with highly sensitive military technologies that could never fall into the wrong hands.

This afternoon her lab expected a visit from a cryptography expert from Washington. Nadine's job today was to brief their distinguished guest on a crypto-key called C-Gag or Crypto-Gag.

Nadine and her co-workers had developed Crypto-Gag to protect nuclear warheads. The software that controlled the directional maneuverability and ignition of the rockets had been given a code key. And in compliance with regulations, Nadine had also developed a kind of back door into the program, a recovery key option, that she would be officially and ceremoniously handing over to the government representative from Washington today.

The idea that, for now at least, she was the only person who had access to this recovery key brought a tiny mocking smile to her flushed features. Her development was a major step in reaching the next step in her career. There were some personnel changes coming up at the lab. Dr. Packard had been offered a prestigious chair at UCLA, which of course made the pompous ass even more intolerable. But Nadine was dying for his job as Head of Research. The odds were in her favor, and she envisioned moving to positions of even greater authority within the National Lab. She felt confident that she would get the job, with all the autonomy that went with it. Smiling as she ran, she turned into the broad avenue.

The real breakthrough, however, the one that would really make her career and reputation, was not directly connected to C-Gag at all. She had been working with her colleague Larry Johnson on the sensitive military antiballistic missile defense system known as *Aegis*. *Aegis* protected America's very vulnerable aircraft carriers from enemy missile attacks. And because the defense system was of such vital significance, it had to be protected from unauthorized access and manipulation. As a consequence, she had put a backdoor into *Aegis, a remote control device* that would be known only to the President of the United States and to his national security advisor. And of course, also to Nadine Moran!

Tinkering around with Larry on *Aegis*, Nadine had suddenly gotten lucky. By complete accident, she had comes across a Trojan Horse that had applicability to the *Aegis* system. Most Trojan Horses are relatively harmless programs that, once they find their way into a computer, open like the famous wooded horse of Troy, letting Agamemnon's warriors out to sack the city and seal its fate. If constructed by a hacker meant on doing harm, however, a Trojan Horse could show up as a virus or decrypting tool – and then track down passwords, open portals, trigger other programs, or even wipe out a hard drive completely.

The Trojan Horse that worked for *Aegis* was based on a cryptographic formula she and Larry had been working on for months without any specific applicability in mind. She liked

Larry. He was a couple of years older than she was, had a photographic memory, seemed very mellow, and knew Europe well from his time in the Navy. She felt he understood her and took her work seriously, which he backed up by loyally supporting her bold experiments with 4096-bit encoding.

Nadine remembered the night, when she realized exactly what she had with her formula. It almost took her breath away to see it implanted in the system and then suddenly watch all its hidden codes open and tumble out.

Nadine now ran in a nice steady rhythm, rolling along, breathing evenly, her thoughts miles away from her body.

What had happened? It was only the night before yesterday, and Nadine was nowhere near getting over the shock. As soon as she put her formula in (which she suddenly called *Oedipus* as she thought about it), it gained instant access into the *Aegis* operating system, opening it as if Nadine were the Commander in Chief of the Armed Forces of the United States herself. All security barriers fell before *Oedipus* like dry leaves in the autumn wind. Was it just a coincidence? Or was *Oedipus* an ingenious next generation code-breaker?

Of course she hadn't trusted her sudden success. So she did it all over again. And placed *Oedipus* into *Aegis* a second time. And again the sesame opened as if Ali Baba himself had been standing in front of the door! Thunderstruck, she had stared at the screen of her Mac G-4 at the Navy abbreviation CVN-71 and below in small letters on a blue background: *USS Theodore Roosevelt.*

Larry's aircraft carrier, the TR! She had remembered him telling her about his efforts to upgrade the Doppler radar on board to improve the identification of enemy rockets.

Her heart beat frantically as she applied *Oedipus'* new magic formula again shortly after a faint double beep had sounded over the online connection. At first nothing had happened. But the computer kept grinding as if it were at least trying to do something! She felt frustrated, and was about to go offline, when suddenly the screen blinked and began to come to life.

She couldn't believe her eyes! She stared at a chart on the screen, and slowly, almost reverentially, moved the cursor over it. Cruise missiles, high-explosive bombs, life preservers, and oxygen masks. She scrolled further down the list: condoms, basketballs, cigarettes, and dental floss. At last she got it. She had ended up in logistics, the supply department for the entire ship.

She wasn't able to go any further that night. But, at least *Oedipus* seemed to work. More out of habit than for any security reasons, she saved *Oedipus* – and since Macs had abandoned internal floppy drives, she put it on an externally mounted disk.

The next day she went over all the Navy documentation about the structure of an aircraft carrier with Larry. But she said nothing to him about *Oedipus*. She didn't have to. After all, they were working together on training programs that simulated attacks on the aircraft carrier groups for the crews who would be running *Aegis*. And of course she wanted to withhold her discovery until she was certain that she had succeeded in breaking through *Aegis* with *Oedipus*. *Oedipus?* Not for a second did it cross her mind that this name was connected with a terrible fate. Her enthusiasm for her discovery completely blocked out her knowledge of

Oedipus as the cursed prince who had murdered his father just as the oracle had predicted.

Nadine's mind wandered as she jogged. Inspirations came and went. Feelings welled up. Dreaming, she thought of last night, and suddenly realized that she had missed her turnoff to the green lake. Slightly annoyed she slapped her forehead, then turned around and ran on.

Last night, she had locked her doors, pulled down the blinds, closed the curtains, and then opened a beer and sat down in front of the computer, her heart pounding.

She downloaded *Oedipus* from the floppy disk to her hard drive, and opened it. But she immediately started working on a small adaptation to the program so it would function as a crossover. She didn't want into logistics this time; she wanted *Oedipus* to go right to the *Aegis'* central command, the core, the actual heart of the program where all actions were controlled and monitored.

As she worked on her adaptation, a sweet feeling of arousal came over her, not at all unlike the late stages of sexual foreplay. She felt hot and cold at the same time. Breathing heavily, she stared into the monitor and punched in code; and then pressed her hand between her legs and rubbed the tingling area. She felt more aroused than she ever had before, and thought she would reach a wrenching orgasm at any moment. Without even thinking or wanting to, she rubbed herself harder and faster. Then it happened – all at once. The Combat Decision System of the *USS Theodore Roosevelt* suddenly sprang up on her screen. She had entered the innermost part of the CDS, the nerve center of the defense system where computers analyzed threats, assigned priorities, and fired weapons in response. It was unbelievable! Her body shook and vibrated in total climax. Then she sank back into her chair, her eyelids half closed, with a wonderful sense of self-satisfaction.

She also felt a tremendous feeling of triumph. The aircraft carrier *USS Theodore Roosevelt* was in her hand, literally! She placed her fingertips on the keys, and wondered if she shouldn't play a trick on the ship now cruising the Mediterranean. Maybe she should fake an enemy operation? Send them a Russian MIG attacking out of Montenegro? Or maybe send them a Mickey Mouse cartoon!

She actually had one on tape – an episode called "Pluto and Mickey Mouse play blind man's bluff." It was tempting. But in the end she resisted. She closed the program, carefully saving the modified *Oedipus* back onto disk, and shut down. She had not felt this good in a long, long time.

Nadine's mind returned to her jog after reliving last night's triumph, and close to Fullers Lodge she turned down towards Ashley Pond and ran once around its light green water, imagining her forthcoming meeting later in the afternoon.

The arrogant pimp Dr. Packard would gape at her with his mouth as wide as a barn door. She would start her presentation modestly, and then lead it to a spectacular climax. "Mr. Special Representative for Cryptography, we thank you for coming all the way from Washington. Mr. Packard, or may I say *Professor* Packard, and dear colleagues. I believe it is safe for me to say that, today, the United States of America has won the race in the raging war of cryptography. I am proud to have the opportunity to pay back the hospitality that America has bestowed upon me at this fine research institute."

She left the wide and openly designed park behind her and continued her jog down Central Avenue.

Yeah, something like that. And then: *I have invented the ultimate code! The mother of all code crackers you old farts!* Well, maybe that would go too far. She burst into laughter, and a sudden car horn scared her back onto the sidewalk.

The cab driver shook his head, patronizingly pointing to the traffic light that was bright red for both pedestrians as well as joggers. She gestured apologetically and, after he pulled off, crossed the street.

But before the afternoon meeting would come there was another one this morning on the agenda – with Packard. *What do you want Packard? Is it about the second key, the recovery key? I am in total control of C-Gag!* She suddenly felt uneasy, but fought it off. *There is no way they can hold me back now!*

Her gaze wandered off to the gentle hills in the distance. Dripping with sweat, she decided to finish off with a sprint to the corner of Trinity Road. Panting when she stopped, she walked to the coffee stand and bought coffee and a croissant, which smelled wonderful to her as she leisurely strolled back to her apartment on the Manhattan Loop.

Her morning jog had been four miles long. Sweaty and feeling a bit euphoric after her workout, Nadine took a quick shower and hastily finished her lukewarm coffee. She ignored the Wall Street Journal and switched on the TV news, where jet fighters took off in a thundering roar from an aircraft carrier, on their way to attack targets in the former Yugoslavia.

A good half-hour later the beautiful French woman was ready for work, dressed in a fashionable business suit. She gazed at herself in the full-length mirror. *Los Alamos is not Paris,* she said to herself, smiling.

Americans are big boys and little girls, or little boys and big girls. Of the secret joys of vanity they know little or nothing at all. Anyway, what did maturity have to do with elegance? In the States even an inconspicuously dressed nondescript lab mouse could achieve more than the most glittering business mogul could!

Feeling quite good, she blew her reflection a kiss, and then wiggled her hips in an exaggerated parody of Marilyn Monroe. Grabbing her keys she left her apartment – in a very good mood.

18.

The feeling of uneasiness that kept creeping up on Nadine all morning had a name – but most of us don't recognize premonitions for what they are. Sometimes you get a sense that there is something in the air, but that's usually about it. And in Nadine's case, her premonition had a person attached to it: Jim Watt, *also known as Walrus*, who was lying on his bed in a hotel room not even half a mile away from her apartment on Manhattan Loop.

Watt, a CIA agent, had arrived two days ago and picked a room in the Best Western on Trinity Drive. Then he decided to wait. It was important to become familiar with his target's routine.

For two days in a row he realized that Nadine Moran stayed in shape by running every morning. Today he had left the hotel and looked just like any other jogging citizen running over to Central Avenue. And there she was, zooming by. Jim Watt had turned away from her and pulled his mustache, deep in thought; a bit later he would run into her again by the coffee stand. He sniffed the air around her; she ignored him. Her inward gazing eyes seemed to look on something in the distance, as if she were having a telepathic conversation with her guardian angel somewhere in the land of her forefathers.

Agent Watt didn't trust this Frenchwoman for a second. His bloodhound nose told him that something didn't smell right in Los Alamos. The investigations of his colleagues had strongly incriminated the beautiful young creature that jogged by him so effortlessly. These days, and with apparently good reason, the big shots at Langley and their buddies over at the FBI had an allergic reaction to resident aliens who have access to the nations' best kept encryption secrets.

And if the hot tip from an operative deep in Asia was good (wasn't 853 in Tashkent that obscure Sweeney guy?), then this saucy babe with the firm little ass was ripe for picking. And today, Watt decided, was harvest time. He would diligently perform his duties and pluck her from the tree right in the middle of the National Laboratory.

To get into the Lab was one thing; to get into it quietly and without attracting attention was quite another. Being the professional that he was, Jim covered both bases. He had called his friend John who had been with the CIA for years the day before. John was now an instructor at the Farm, where all would-be agents were trained. He had great connections to all sorts of people, big and small. And most important of all, he owed Jim Watt a big favor for keeping his mouth shut and constructing an excellent cover-up when John had nearly been caught padding his expense account.

When John got the call from Watt, he knew it was payback time. Over the secure line, he gave him the good news.

"I know the Deputy of the Security Service at the Lab. He used to work in our Research and Weapons Development. I'm sure we can arrange something."

"That's fine John," Watt said, after being told that the guard at the entrance would be carefully instructed. "But I don't only want to get in. No one there can know who I really am. I want them to think I'm with the FBI. Got it? Only the Deputy and…"

John assured him that it would be covered – and Watt

soon realized that the Deputy was still working for the Agency. The National Lab was harder to control than a can of worms – and the CIA had placed its people well.

"Do you still have that awful walrus mustache?" John asked him abruptly.

"Yeah."

"Then I'll send the picture I have to the Deputy. It'll do."

So everything was settled. Jim Watt returned to the Best Western, took a shower, had breakfast, and set off to the National Laboratory in no particular hurry.

19.

At first, Nadine had not been enthusiastic about moving to Los Alamos, which seemed to her to be the last place on earth she wanted to be. But she soon came to love its warm climate. And its unique topography: beautiful landforms with wooded plains on top of flat mountains, the edges dropping down in steep brown rock walls into dry canyons. Sometimes the green and blue hills in the distance reminded her of her native Massif Central. And the eroded rock formations pointing boldly to the sky conjured up childhood memories of old cowboy movies. The diversity of the region had come as a surprise to the Frenchwoman. Only a few miles away were the winter temptations of Pajacito's powdery ski slopes. So she began to like her life in Los Alamos, and everything took its normal not overly exciting course, until that day when the Russian called. She had been completely taken aback. *You wanna see me at the Vietnam Memorial? Why not on the moon? Who are you, Russki? Stoned with vodka, I guess? A message from whom? From a dear old man? Thierry...*

He gave her a bait. She decided to go for it. Filled with great expectations, Nadine had taken the plane to Washington D.C. over the weekend to meet with him kind of secretly. *Like an undercover agent!*

In front of the long dark building of the memorial, a broad-shouldered man with a receding hairline and two day's growth of stubble sat next to her on a bench. He put down his paper bag and opened a newspaper. After a while, he spoke.

"Awful, isn't it? They found another leak in Los Alamos. Incredible!"

"A leak in the nuclear reactor?" Nadine had answered with studied innocence.

"No, no. The Chinese are digging out nuclear secrets. You are French, right?"

Nadine didn't answer.

"I am Igor. We have an appointment," he said, smiling. His accent stirred memories from her youth.

"You are the Russian."

"Uh-huh. Stoned with vodka ..."

Nadine said nothing, staring straight ahead at a group of tourists taking pictures of each other in front of the statue of the three Vietnam soldiers.

"You've made quite a name for yourself as a computer specialist. My boss is very interested in your work," the Russian said.

"And *you* promised me a sign of life from..." She hesitated. "You know?"

Igor took a small box from the paper bag on the bench and pushed it into Nadine's hand. "Yes, from your father. He works for my boss."

Nadine looked at him astonished. *Father? Who is my father?* She mused. Reluctantly, she lifted up the box, looking inquisitively at the Russian.

"Open it. There's a necklace inside."

"Where is he? What's he doing? Who sent you?" Nadine stammered out, opening the box with shaking hands.

She cautiously touched the gold with her fingers. A

valuable amulet! She turned it over and read its finely engraved inscription.

"He's alive," she said, more to herself than to him. "Where is he? Where do you hide him?" Her hand was clenched in a fist. "Where? I demand to know!"

She jumped up and grabbed Igor by the collar with her free hand. Some Japanese tourists looked at them, smiling their standardized Japanese smile.

"When you cooperate with us, then you will meet your father. Come, we attract too much attention here."

They got up, and side-by-side walked along the Memorial Wall engraved with the names of 58,167 Americans killed in the Vietnam War.

"Don't worry, your father is alive and well," he said, handing her an envelope. "Some information on your family history, so you know we're telling you the truth. Oh, and a thousand dollars to cover your travel expenses."

As they walked and talked, he laid out the terms. More than once she stopped, vigorously shaking her head no. The Russian shrugged his shoulders, and pointed to the amulet in Nadine's hand. She pushed him away with both hands, turned her back, and marched off.

But then she stopped, turned around, and came back. They spoke animatedly to each other. Then it seemed as if everything calmed down. For a while they stood there silently, almost devoutly. An observer might have interpreted their body language as the relaxation that follows a decision of great importance. Eventually, they shook hands, turned, and went their separate ways.

20.

Nadine's short drive to work led her down a busy street lined with shops to Diamond Drive, and then across the Los Alamos Canyon to the Southern Mesa where the sprawling grounds of the National Laboratory were located. Her white '85 Corvette droned past East Jerez Road, and after a couple of hundred yards turned into a side street that led to the Computer Building where she worked. Nadine smiled and waved to the guard in his booth at the corner and then swung the Vette into her assigned parking spot.

The Computer Building was part of Technical Area 3, the heart of Los Alamos, where the research facilities and labs were housed. Even though TA3 took up only a small part of the overall complex in terms of space, it housed about half of all personnel. Inside TA3 were important facilities, like the Van de Graff accelerator, the main library, and the academic center – as well as many experimental physics labs. Every time she entered the complex Nadine was overwhelmed by the amount of scientific information available through the research libraries and databases. Further to the east there were the vast grounds of the S-site, where experiments with both nuclear weapons and conventional explosives were carried out.

Dr. Packard, the Head of Research, six feet tall in his khaki shorts, stood in his office looking down at Nadine with his arms crossed.

"Good morning," he greeted her formally, pressing his thin lips together in a frown. His long hairless legs like those of newborn mice were rooted in ridiculous brown-strapped sandals. Nadine hated his arrogance. "I have definitely decided to accept the professorship," he announced with a complacent grin.

"Congratulations," Nadine replied neutrally.

"I've decided that Jack Amelio will head the meeting this afternoon with the special commissioner."

Nadine was astonished. "And why, may I ask?"

"Because I believe this entire project belongs in *American* hands."

"But Dr. Packard, *I* was the one who made the project work. I finished it. And this afternoon I was going to…" But she didn't finish her sentence.

"Well, of course, Moran. And you did an excellent job. But I've made my decision."

A thought crossed her mind like a shooting star. *There's something else behind this!*

"Wait a second! When I started here your theoretical technology was way behind. And now we're number one." *Which is why, rat, you get the chair at the university.*

Packard stood there in his pompous pose. He didn't even ask her to sit down.

"If you don't mind, Nadine, you will leave the management of this place to me. Starting next week you will hand in daily reports to Amelio. I expect you to cooperated with him completely, and to fill him in on all of your progress and results."

Wasn't there any way to negotiate with this ass?

She took two steps back quickly and slammed the door closed.

"No way Packard! You're violating the terms of my

contract," she yelled, shaking her finger at him as she moved closer. Surprised, he shrunk back.

"Calm down Nadine!"

"No chance. I'm warning you! Don't step on my toes you creep. Who the hell is Jack Amelio anyway? What did he ever accomplish? Didn't IBM dump him here? And you're going to let him steal my work? There's no way you're going to get away with this!"

Man, are you in for a big surprise this afternoon! Then maybe I'll get a professorship myself, asshole!

"My decision is final!" Packard said, raising his voice.

"That's what you think, Packard!"

"Stop yelling!" he roared back.

Nadine stifled her tears. For months she had been slaving on this project, only now to be cheated out of her reward, her new position. And by this bag of shit, this slimy jellyfish. She summoned up her mettle and pushed back against her sense of futility.

"You are being unfair Packard. Trust me, Amelio is useless."

Packard's face was ashen. "This meeting is over."

That pushed her over the edge. Raging, she flung open the door, turned, and yelled, "Fuck you Packard!" so loud it echoed down the hallway. And then she slammed the door closed like a thunderbolt.

Red with fury, she rushed past perplexed faces to the elevator. Getting in, she took a deep breath and went down to her office. The screaming match was just the culmination of something that had been coming for a long time. There had never been any good chemistry between them. She absolutely had to talk to Larry about it.

Totally agitated, Nadine walked into her office on the fourth floor. And there with his ass on the corner of her desk was this guy with a big moustache. Was he chewing on something? Or just ruminating with his mouth open? He wore a badly tailored seersucker suit, white with blue stripes – the kind that in Europe you would see on a butcher. His presence put her on edge.

"Good morning. Can I help you?" she asked.

He didn't move, but signaled her to come closer.

"Jim Watt, FBI, from the Santa Fe office," he said by way of introduction.

"I see," she said, edging past him and reaching for the telephone.

"Don't bother," he said, lifting his hand almost as a threat. "Mister Packard in administration knows that I'm here – and why I'm here."

Nadine's corner office faced west. To the right, it offered a clear view of the Robert Oppenheimer academic center, to the left the administration building toward which Watt pointed his hairy forefinger and dirty nail. Diagonally opposite was a small nondescript building that housed the Advanced Computer Lab. This is where Nadine and Larry carried out their experiments – which she was sure, this FBI guy knew all about.

Books were scattered all over the floor. Nadine pointed to ransacked piles of paper and broken-open disk files.

"Looking for something in particular?" she asked, as calmly as possible.

"We're checking security measures," he answered, sliding a CD into his briefcase. "You're a resident alien, aren't you, Miss Moran?"

"Congratulations. I bet that took a lot of investigating."

Watt suddenly grabbed her wrist. "Don't be a smart ass. Where is your laptop?"

"Take your sticky fingers off me Watt!" she replied, with studied calm. "All our systems are networked here."

Watt seemed surprised at this, and let her wrist go.

All right, she told herself. No more screaming. But where did I leave that laptop? Her eyes searched the office in a nonchalant way. Then she remembered. *Damn! It was still in Packard's office.*

"So, you've been to Washington D.C. recently, Miss Moran?"

"Yes. So what?" she answered, shrugging her shoulders.

"And you went to Washington for what reason?"

She knit her eyebrows at him. "Shouldn't I ask for your identification?"

"You've got yourself in a whole lot of trouble," he said, reluctantly pulling out his FBI shield. "Satisfied?"

Nadine wondered whether Packard had staged all this to put more pressure on her. But then she thought of Igor and his incredible theory…

"You have given confidential material to the Russians. Bad. Very bad," Watt hissed at her as if he had read her mind.

Speechless, she spread her arms and fell back into her chair. Watt absorbed her reaction with obvious pleasure.

The young Frenchwoman opened her eyes wide and shook her head.

"You are dead wrong mister. This is complete nonsense!" She acted as indignantly as she could, but she didn't really know what else to say or do.

Agent Watt took his time. He sat there silently, rhythmically tossing a CD up in the air and catching it, over and over again. He thought it was best to handle this wildcat carefully. Maybe, if he played his cards right, he could channel her fire to his advantage – maybe even direct her heat to the right place...

Finally, he stopped playing and reached for the pictures from Washington.

21.

Watt triumphantly held up a photograph showing Nadine in Washington with a small box in her hand.

"Seems very clear to me," he said. "Handing over confidential data. Then here... and here!" Watt placed the photos on the table. They were obviously shot from a distance with a zoom lens: Nadine whispering to Igor, Nadine shaking hands, accepting an envelope.

"Why don't we go to your place right now?" Watt offered, a hint of forgiveness in his voice.

Nadine knew she had to buy some time. What should she do? Call a lawyer? She didn't know any lawyers. Call the Director of the Lab? That wouldn't help. She scratched her chin as discretely as possible, and stared at Watt critically. *Something about this stinks.*

"Let's go Miss Moran."

She had an inspiration, and said proudly, "Don't you need a search warrant?"

"Not necessarily," he answered. With your security level you should know that. Didn't they ever brief you? This is a matter of national security. You can either give me access to your apartment, or I can take you over to Santa Fe and put you in the slammer. And you can stay in jail until I get a warrant. It'll probably take a few days."

She started thinking, fast. *I need to buy some time!*

"All right sir," she said in a conciliatory way. "After all, you do represent the law, although I have to admit I always pictured justice with cleaner fingernails."

Just then a fat young man appeared at her door, filling it with his massive bulk.

"Hi Nadine, how's it going?" he asked, cheerfully unaware of what she was going through.

"Not too well Larry."

Larry Johnson stiffened, and ran his hand through his short blonde hair.

"Anything I can do for you?" he asked in his soft drawl.

Watt answered, cutting him off. "No thanks," he said, looking at Nadine as she sat there with folded hands.

"Okay, then, have a nice day," Larry answered with frowning sarcasm.

Watt waited a beat or two after Larry left, and said ominously, "There's one more thing…"

Nadine broke in to change the subject. "Would you like some coffee? I could have them bring us some from the cafeteria."

"That's a good idea. And tell them to throw in a ham sandwich for me, plenty of mustard and mayo," he grinned.

Nadine picked up her phone and ordered, hoping secretly that this FBI zombie didn't know about the second meeting that she had with the Russian later that same day. She had agreed to meet Igor once more, this time at Union Station. And from there, they had taken a cab to Arlington National Cemetery.

22.

"Why Belgrade of all places? They're being bombed every day," Nadine asked as they walked past the Iwo Jima war memorial to the entrance to Arlington National Cemetery.

The Russian shrugged his shoulders.

"We'll be at the Sudanese embassy there with potential buyers for the new Russian rockets. Thierry-Clément Moran will attend as an expert on behalf of my boss. You might privately talk to him about what we discussed. Rocket targeting programs, you know. He might ask you for specifics about the shield, okay? So be prepared."

They walked side by side, leaving the tomb of John Kennedy behind them. The sun was low in the west, bathing the lush green cemetery in golden light; the bare trunks of the poplars and sycamores looked like black, timeless memorials. The countless simple tombstones cast long shadows over the immaculate well-trimmed lawn.

Nadine stopped on the asphalt path in front of the graves of the Korean War dead.

"Hear me well, Igor. I want to make contact. I believe my... eh ... Thierry-Clément is in desperate straits and needs my help. This is not a game for me. I am deadly serious. If you are lying, trust me you will regret it."

Igor lowered his eyes from her harsh glare.

"What do you know about Thierry-Clément? Why are you so sure I'll be able to see him in Belgrade?" she asked bitterly, raising his chin with her hand. "Look at me god damn it!"

Four soldiers with rifles slung over their shoulders marched past them single-file.

"Come," Igor responded in a low voice, as behind them the changing of the guard ceremony had begun.

The Russian had emigrated to the United States decades ago, and made his money trading aircraft, spare parts, and other military accessories to trouble spots in Africa, South America, and Asia. His contacts lived in the demimonde of real and stumbled agents, arms dealers, and terrorist entrepreneurs.

"When the Russians put the new *Sunburn* on the market, I decided to move my business to Muscat," he told her in front of the gravestone of an Air Force major killed in World War II.

"So that's your registered place of business?" she mocked.

"Well, the British are always interested in new arms, and they're in Oman. Plus, Muscat controls the gateway to the Persian Gulf. Oh, I meant to ask you, is everything okay for you at your workplace?"

"Where?" She asked him in surprise.

"At the laboratory, where you slave for the Americans."

"Slave?" she asked, stopping. "What are you talking about? Of course everything is all right at work. And anyway, that's none of your business, is it?"

Igor looked at her through eyes like slits. He whispered, "Does the term 'Viper' ring a bell?"

She looked at him uncomprehendingly, her mouth slightly opened.

"Well, someone told me to pass this on to you." He

reached into his jacket pocket and groped around until he came up with a piece of paper. He held it up to her at eye level. "It is written here," he said ominously.

"*What* is written there?"

"That Packard is cherishing a viper in his bosom," he replied softly.

Nadine later remembered every detail of this part of their conversation —her arms akimbo, her transfixed look at him. When the thickset Russian returned her stare unblinking, she had turned away, stepped on the lawn, read absent-mindedly the date 1944 on a tombstone engraved with the name John Ryan. The only sounds were a faint rumbling of an airplane in the distance and the solitary tapping of a woodpecker in the peaceful silence.

She heard his shuffling steps behind her and turned to face Igor angrily.

"Spies? You mean spies in the laboratory? In Packard's department where I work? You're telling me there is a spy there?"

The Russian nodded silently. He had gotten the information from the same man who had given him the amulet – and who had told him to warn her. So he spit it out: that she was under surveillance at the lab. He told her that the warning was well meant and had come from friends in her father's circles.

"That is bullshit. Total bullshit!" She yelled so loud the woodpecker stopped its clatter and flew off. "Viper?! Of course there is competition at the lab. And there are some do-nothings who would stick a knife in your back. But treason? Espionage? I don't think so."

She shook her head in an emphatic no and clenched her lips tight.

"Our man in Afghanistan is very reliable. He's got connections to the CIA," Igor explained insistently. "Be on the lookout. And call this number if there's any trouble. You can count on us."

He pushed his business card into her hand.

CIA? Afghanistan? It must be complete nonsense. But she burst out a moment later, "And *that's* where your boss is?"

Visibly annoyed with her refusal to accept his warning, Igor shook his head – but then answered her questions.

"No… I mean yes."

"But why Afghanistan for God's sake?" she asked edgily. She held her arms against her body as if she were freezing cold.

The Russian gazed musingly off to the horizon.

"I'm sorry, I don't know all of the background. But I do know this much: after his disappearance from France, your father apparently worked in Morocco. People said he did this and that – but whatever, it's all history now. And then about five years ago he worked as a consultant to the Saudi, my boss, you know, on aircraft. Arms too. Missiles and such."

"Okay," Nadine gulped.

They silently began walking back. The new honor guards stood motionless at their posts, as if carved out of granite.

"So, how do I get to Belgrade?" she asked.

"Despite the war, there are still direct flights. There's one every day from Switzerland. Zurich to Belgrade," he offered meekly.

"Zurich," Nadine muttered back. *Not a bad idea at all!* She suddenly remembered the old general, gently circling her waist and leading her to the table like a true gentleman. His proud head held high, his eyes registering curious looks of admiration from guests at the other tables. Later Edouard Diesbach had said to her, "I promised your papa – or should I say Thierry-Clé? – that I would protect you. Although it seems to me my child that you have achieved all your goals, and that perhaps it is I who might need protection. But be that as it may, if you ever feel that I could do something for you, please, call me. Promise me that you will!" Her memory of this kind and warm moment nursed her sore aching soul.

From President Kennedy's low flat tomb, they walked like any other tourists to the famous statue of the battle of Iwo Jima. In the golden glow of the setting sun they saw the soldiers lifting the American flag – having just survived a living hell, united in triumph, pride in their eyes, strength in their exhausted bodies. Some said, of course, that the famous photograph on which this statue was based had been staged for publicity purposes. But Nadine never believed that; she was by nature drawn toward romantic affirmations. And she admired every single hero and every effort made in that most famous of Pacific battles in World War II. Frowning, she tried to remember the date of that dramatic event. It must have been somewhere between February and March of 1945, she thought.

But then she turned her eyes from the statue and looked at Igor.

"Good, then. I will go to Belgrade."

And as if the ghost of the kind general were floating

above the heads of the bronze heroes of Iwo Jima, she heard his gentle voice say "the sooner the better."

Igor nodded at her and hailed a cab.

"Good. I will provide you with more details. Do you understand?"

He reached into his breast pocket and just looked around carefully. Everything seemed normal. No one had tailed them. "Here, take this, Nadine," he whispered. "It's a map of an area we might go to, if Belgrade is cancelled. We call it plan B."

They got into a cab. As they crossed the Potomac River on their way downtown, he finally handed her his notes on the meeting's time and location.

She stared at the date. Time was running out on her.

23.

Nadine Moran snapped out of her daydream when the delivery boy from the cafeteria knocked on the doorframe of her office and put some bags on the table. Agent Watt slipped him a ten and waved him out dismissively.

Nadine took a deep breath. She had to pull herself together. Now it all made sense. Igor's words thumped in her head: *Packard is cherishing a viper.* And she was the viper! The realization made her shiver. *Be on the lookout. Our man in Afghanistan. Connections to the CIA.*

She sighed. In five days, she had to be, yes, indeed wanted to be, in Belgrade. Igor was right. She scowled hostilely at Watt. *Has he been the one watching me?*

She remembered promising the old gentleman that she would call if she needed him, at that dinner at the Kronenhalle, the fashionable Zurich restaurant with real impressionist paintings on the walls. As they sat there underneath a Picasso, she had taken the number of Corps Commander Diesbach – and kept it just in case. What the brilliant causeur had revealed to her about her father had excited her, even now when she thought about it. Suddenly she felt very close to Edouard, and to his fatherly warmth. And now the time had come to take him up on his offer. Nadine suppressed another sigh. What she hadn't been given she would get for herself. The sooner the better.

She took the coffee and ham sandwich dripping with

mayonnaise from the bag and handed them to Watt. He lowered his voice into a sort of chummy tone.

"Look Nadine, we're offering you a deal here. You hand over the results of your research and…"

"What are you out of your mind?" she interrupted. "All of my data belongs to the laboratory. It is government property."

"Miss Moran, I am the government."

"So you say. What guarantee do I have of that? I am innocent! She said, lashing out at him. "You know as well as I do that your accusations are absurd!"

"Look, you help us, and we'll help you Nadine. We want to know more about some of the encryption codes of some large French companies, like Elf Aquitaine, CC Tech, Aerospatial, and Airbus Industries," Watt explained, as calmly as if he were talking about the weather.

Nadine could not believe her ears.

"You want me to do industrial espionage?"

"Exactly. Airbus, oil, fighter aircraft, camouflage technologies, rockets, and all the rest of it."

Her voice answered him as coldly as she felt inside.

"And what if I refuse?"

"Then my dear Miss France, we will make your life a living hell. In a second the world will know you as a low-life spy – another arrogant foreign whore who would do anything for money. We'll make you look worse than those damn Chinks." His tone became totally contemptuous with this reference to the theft of nuclear secrets organized by the Chinese.

She stared at the ceiling as if expecting help from above. And then she realized how this might buy her time. She didn't let her feelings show. *Just wait, you dip shit. I'll hang your ass out to dry.*

"Think about it, carefully," Watt urged. "You don't have much time. From now on I'll be watching every move you make." And he pulled out his handcuffs and twirled them on his finger.

"Take a chill pill, eh?" she said coldly. She looked at the small digital clock on her desk. Almost noon! Larry was either sitting in the small lab in the Advanced Computer Building or sweating away some fat at the gym. She decided on the latter. "Let me think about it. If you need me, I'll be at the Wellness Center."

She got up and walked consciously slow out of her office. She felt like a torero that in the midst of his life and death struggle with the bull suddenly turned his back on it in total nonchalance. She straightened her back as she walked out, lifted her hand, and snapped her fingers three times. Her soft but piercing "Olé" left Watt behind like an exhausted defeated beast.

To get to the Wellness Center on Bikini Road, Nadine didn't have to leave the grounds of Technical Area 3. She would just have to take a quick drive down West Jerez Road and park next to the low building with the L-shaped annex where the gym and workout rooms were located.

But before she left the building, she took the elevator back up to the fifth floor. She had to consciously slow down to keep from running. Breathless and nervous, she stopped in front of Dr. Packard's office. *I'll apologize,* she decided – the smart thing to do.

The door was ajar. She knocked and tentatively pushed

it open. Empty. Her purse with the small Mac laptop was right where she had left it, leaning against the small side table next to the armchair. She embraced it affectionately as if it were a runaway kitten, and headed for the Wellness Center.

Halfway between the check-in desk and the cafeteria, Nadine saw Larry Johnson, red-faced and dripping through his sweatsuit. He could see immediately that something wasn't right.

"Nadine, what's wrong? Did you have a problem with that guy? He's a spy, right?" He ranted on. "I saw that nitwit in the small lab. He had his dirty paws on our computer. It's really a drag, isn't it?"

"Listen to me carefully Larry. They're after our programs. Today it was my turn. Tomorrow they'll be on your case. You have to delete everything, right now! I want you to wipe out my hard drive completely."

Larry stared at her and shook his head.

"That's definitely against the rules."

"No, what this jerk from the FBI is doing – *that's* what's against the rules. They're stealing our ideas, Larry. Our dream of a worldwide patent? It'll be finished – don't you get it? They're stealing our intellectual property. All of our millions flushed right down the drain."

"Is it backed up?" Larry whispered aghast.

"I saved everything on my laptop," she said, patting the purse on her arm. "Don't worry. You can delete everything in the small lab. You have access to my system. You can do it without the spy even realizing anything has happened. You will help me, won't you?" she pleaded.

"All right, I will. But I don't know anything, haven't seen anything, and the Navy doesn't have anything to do with it. Absolutely nothing. Not the Navy," he implored.

She nodded convincingly. "You have my word. You can totally trust me, Larry. But be careful. Get your files somewhere safe. But do it fast – top priority. That swine Packard is probably in on it too."

"Did you really tell him to fuck off?" he asked in disbelief.

"I did. And I'm quitting. Watch out for him. And thank you, Larry. I'll be in touch." Touching his shoulder, she added, "You're really a pal."

"You're leaving?" he asked, fearfully. "May I ask where you're going?"

She didn't answer, but rather asked a question herself.

"Tonight, this FBI guy is coming over to my place. Could you drop by? Like by accident? It would make me feel a lot better."

Johnson looked at her skeptically. It was obvious that he didn't want to get involved with the FBI. Their friendship didn't go that far. She looked down and shook her head.

"Well, all right. Forget it. It doesn't matter really. And you're right. I think I might go on a trip. Maybe even find myself a new job." She kissed his cheek lightly. "See you later, Larry," walking away and leaving him standing in the hallway perplexed.

There was something she wanted to take care of before she went home. *Home? Oh God, where is my home, really?* She was about to burn all her bridges. But there was no other way out – and certainly nothing left for her to do in this godfor-saken one-horse town.

I want to go home. Back to France. Maybe that's where my home really is.

She felt like crying. An odd assortment of feelings ran through her as she walked swiftly through the corridors of the library. Her sudden decision to leave Los Alamos had suddenly filled the place with a nostalgic halo. The well-ordered, labeled rooms, the green wall-to-wall carpeting, the desks, computers, file cabinets – all of it radiated a familiarity that suddenly made her sad. She felt like she was a visitor in her own life.

She went into the beautifully wood-paneled reading room and connected her laptop. Again her anger rose. *Packard, that bastard! He was in on it with the FBI from the start. But I'll show them all!*

She accessed the Internet, and entered Nadine@gctech.com, her old email address at GC Tech where she had worked with Jean-Philippe for many years. She attached the file of the *Oedipus* formula as well as two others containing the most often-used *Aegis* air combat simulation programs. She clicked SEND, and watched tensely as the bar graph slowly indicated the file transfer. Still a minute to go. She checked her watch. Better safe than sorry. Now at least she had her data not only on disk but also in her old mailbox at GC Tech. *And maybe Jean-Philippe has become Managing Director since I left.*

"File transfer complete" croaked a female voice from the computer. It didn't sound like Lara Croft to her! But it did relieve her and let her log off the Web.

Should she call Jean-Philippe? GC Tech had become

one of the major companies in the fast-growing cryptography market. Maybe he would have a job for her? Her escape plan was finally taking shape. But it was still nighttime in Toulouse, so she postponed her call until the next day.

There was a pay phone on the wall outside the reading room. She hesitated for a second, but then took the receiver off the hook and called information. She wrote a phone number on the back of her hand, put in a quarter, and dialed. A monotonous digital voice demanded two more quarters.

Finally, she reached the Federal Building in Santa Fe and the FBI offices it housed. When Nadine asked about an agent named Jim Watt, a friendly voice told her that there was indeed a special agent by that name. Nadine was surprised, and silent.

"Ma'am, can I help you?" the operator asked politely.

"Well, someone claiming to be Jim Watt of the FBI wants to conduct a search of my home tonight. I just wanted to..."

"One moment please!"

After a minute or two the same voice returned. "You are calling from Los Alamos, is that correct? Los Alamos is your residence?"

Nadine said yes and confirmed her address.

"Well, that is strange, ma'am... because Agent Watt is in Quantico Virginia right now. In fact, he's giving a lecture there tonight. Are you certain..."

Although the polite operator deserved at least a thank you, Nadine hung up the phone wordlessly and without hesitation. She shook her head and shoulders as if trying to wake up from a nightmare. Or perhaps loosen up her body for the fight ahead. One thing was clear now: the gloves had come off.

And it was time for another phone call. She searched her purse for the card Igor had given her at the cemetery. Fortunately she had kept it. Clutching it as if it were a lucky charm that would keep her out of harm's way, she left the building with a look of fierce determination.

24.

The black Buick moved slowly down dimly lit Myrtle Street and turned into Manhattan Loop. The green numbers of the digital clock on its futuristically shaped dashboard read 8:55.

"This is it. Park over there," the passenger said. Then he pointed to a building. "There, up ahead. In the dark there, underneath the trees."

The street was deserted, but the woman behind the wheel looked cautiously around. Out of habit, she put her hand under her jacket and made sure her gun was there: a SIG-Sauer P228, FBI standard issue, 13 nine-millimeter bullets in the clip.

She winked at her partner. "I'll go have a look." And without waiting for an answer she got out of the car.

Her partner, the older FBI agent in the passenger seat, nodded to her as she left. "Okay – but stay on and stand by."

Jim Watt heard the sound of the door slam shut. He quickly moved to the window and looked up and down the street. Just a few minutes ago he had picked the front door lock and moved into the apartment very quietly. But when he turned on the lights the place looked deserted. The air in the hallway was stale.

It hadn't taken him long to realize that Nadine Moran had taken off. He began hastily searching the room – opening closets, shaking out drawers. But after about five minutes he realized it was a lost cause. Nothing left to find. No computers. No disk.

"Bitch! You took it all, didn't you," he said to himself, gritting his teeth, when he spotted the sheet of paper. It lay on the floor next to the bookshelf and turned out to be a bad copy of a map clipping from some mountain area in Morocco. Out of pure habit he pocketed it when he heard something outside that made him start. A voice trained to speak low. Watt turned his head, his ear focusing on the source of the sound like a radar dish.

"Paul. Come to the front door. I'll check the yard," he heard the young FBI woman say into her walkie-talkie.

Watt saw a shadowy figure approach from a car parked underneath the dark trees, heading right into the front yard of Nadine's apartment. Time to split! He pulled up the blinds of the terrace door that led into the garden and peered outside. The coast seemed clear. But he was experienced, and cocked his automatic, putting a bullet into the chamber. He turned off the light, opened the door, and stepped out into the dark. He had gone about ten steps when the flashlight's beam hit him.

"Stop! FBI! Don't move! Put your hands…"

The shot came from Watt's gun, and then another. The beam of light dropped. Watt ran for the protection of the dark. He heard a moan. And then a bullet whizzed past his head. Very close.

The young FBI agent had collapsed, covered in blood. Her partner ran back to the car as soon as he heard the shots. Ripping the mike from its mount, he screamed "We need backup! Yes... Manhattan Loop!"

Ten seconds later, he was bending over his partner's body in the back yard of Nadine Moran's apartment. One of the bullets had gone straight through her heart. Her eyes were open, but she was gone. He knelt down beside her slowly, and gently touched her young forehead with three fingers. *Bye Patty,* was all he could say before he closed the lids of her lifeless eyes.

The investigation at the crime scene took all night long. At around four o'clock the next afternoon the FBI office in Santa Fe issued an APB. The fax sent to police departments nationwide showed a picture with a name printed next to it: Nadine Moran. The Frenchwoman was assumed to be armed and dangerous.

But fortunately for her, she was already sitting on a Virgin Atlantic jet on her way from Toronto to London.

25.

In the tall glass headquarters of Specs Inc., just on the out-skirts of the Genève-Cointrin airport, the consulting clerk responsible for Africa and the Middle East had just as usual printed out the pictures and report sent to him by the ana-lyst from Lagos. When he saved the transmission, certain key words were added automatically to the index of the worldwide database network of Specs Inc.

The young man re-checked the type of ship listed in the report. To do so he consulted the book of books of all the merchant navies: *Lloyd's List*. This newspaper reports today, just as it did 260 years ago, all that there is to know about global shipping, six days a week. Traditionally, or perhaps as rumor had it because Specs Chairman Joe Sorelli mistrusted everything electronic, Specs Inc. in Geneva still bound each day's pages in tall slender volumes – where they would then sit and grow moldy on the shelf.

The young consultant, however, had little use for the bound volumes of what he called wastepaper; rather, he punched up *Lloyd's List* on his 25-inch monitor from the In-ternet. The *List* cost about $760 annually, and access to Lloyd's enormous archive was another $910 a year. But the expense was well worth it. These services gave the consultant current reports as well as access to an extensive database on worldwide shipping that went back to 1991. He was also able to call up *Lloyd's Shipping Index,* which provided information on nearly every single trading ship: its owners, year of construction, ton-nage, overhauls, insurance companies, and home ports.

It also came with a search engine called "SEAsearcher," which enabled him to track the movements of 50,000 ships in 4,000 ports. He clicked on a reference that led him to another report by a Lloyd's agent, indicating that the *Shiraz* had pulled out of the Iranian port Bandar Khomeiny.

It was close to five o'clock in Geneva, and the workday was nearly done. In spirit, the young consultant was already aboard his small skiff docked at the boat basin of the Lac Léman with its famous landmark the Jet d'Eau; and he was already fantasizing about a well-shaped woman whom he might pick up as a sailing companion.

His computer listed data on the *Shiraz*, having found its way into the Specs Inc. database, where anyone interested would be able to find it under keywords such as *Shiraz*, Lagos, Bandar Khomeiny, tanker, Iran, and so forth. The clerk was in a hurry. The breeze seemed strong and promised some fine maneuvers before the wind... and perhaps some in the boat as well.

He shut down his computer, grabbed his car keys, and hurried through the open office to the elevators, where someone who fit his description as a fantasized sailing companion was waiting as well: a perky-bosomed red-headed secretary whom he had seen around the building now and then. On their way down in the elevator he stood close to her and breathed in her perfume through his wide nostrils – but discretely. Only later, as he stood next to his car, did he wonder why he hadn't asked the redhead if she liked to sail.

26.

The *Shiraz* calmly crossed the Gulf of Guinea. The breeze that had earlier whipped up sand by the Niger's river mouth to the west, making the horizon seem hazy and veiled, had died down by sunset. In the early evening light, the austere mountains along Togo's Slave Coast seemed to emerge black and threatening from the red glittering waves of the Benin Bay. Seawater had been pumped into the *Shiraz's 12* ballast tanks, which evenly pushed the ship into the water. On the bridge, Captain Souri and the first watch officer gazed into the echo sounder carefully, concentrating on the shallow bottom of the shipping lane to make sure their keel would clear it safely.

Lost in thought, bin Golem looked north to where the darkness sank over the expansive vastness of the Southwest African coast. In Nigeria, his organization controlled a network of well-functioning paramilitary units; but bin Golem hardly knew the countries they would be passing in the next five days: Ghana, and its charming coastal capital Accra; the prosperous Ivory Coast; the civil-war-ravaged Liberia, where children armed with Kalashnikovs patrolled the streets, searching for something to put holes into. *What other countries stretched further north along the coast before they would finally come to Morocco?*

The Islamic leader thought hard about it. Geography beyond the Middle East had never been one of his strengths. His interests were more along the lines of powerful nations' political forces, or their cities or airports. Military strategy fascinated him – how to use it to defeat the strength of the western governments.

If he had asked Captain Souri, he would have heard in detail the names of the nations along their route – Sierra Leone, Guinea with the Niger's headwaters that, after winding thousands of miles, emptied into the sea in Nigeria, Senegal, Mauritania, and the Western Sahara. Yet a journey by sea afforded time for such leisurely topics. Anyone who has ever stood at a ship's railing and marveled at the everchanging scenery of sky, sea, and land had added to his knowledge of geography without even realizing it.

Bin Golem, too, had time to contemplate the shoreline, and time to learn. But as he stared at the darkening ocean, his thoughts turned to bitter revenge. He saw in his vision hardship, destruction, and blood. What did a life count for if it lacked sacred purpose? What was blood worth, if shed in ignorance and the darkness of disbelief? And finally, what would become of a world that obstinately defied the sacred teachings? Allah had entrusted him with a mission. He would not disappoint him.

27.

At about the same time, the President of the United States stood on the tee of the ninth hole and took his practice swings, moving his hips just like his favorite pro Tiger Woods did. With a deep breath and a last look down the fairway, he swung his driver back – but before he completed the stroke he heard the thwapp-thwapp of an approaching helicopter. As leaves and dust swirled around him, President Jack Brenton followed through with his drive.

"Good shot!" someone called out above the roar of the engines. But it wasn't. The ball sliced sharply to the right, never getting high off the fairway, and landed limply about 150 yards from the tee.

"I kept it low, you know, so it wouldn't hit the copter," the Commander in Chief of all U.S. Armed Forces said with a good-natured grin as the fat *Chinook* helicopter settled down on the lush grass.

A man in a light-colored business suit squatted in the open doorway, ready to jump.

"Joe, do you recognize that pain in the ass?" the President asked his golfing buddy, squinting his eyes.

"Looks like CIA Chief Taylor to me," replied Joe Sorelli, Chairman of Specs Inc.

"*Right!* Christ, these people change so often you barely have time to remember their faces," President Brenton joked ironically. "Or maybe I need glasses. Or a new memory. That's it. A new memory would be wonderful."

With the slow measured stride that everyone recognized and some resented, the most powerful man in the world walked off to greet the tall, balding man who hurried across the fairway towards him. Without turning his head, Brenton shouted back to Sorelli, "Go ahead Joe. Tee off. If you hit the copter, I'll take full responsibility."

Still holding his snapped salute, Ted Taylor – the aging head of the Central Intelligence Agency – started telling his President, that a matter of utmost urgency, a national crisis, would force him to interrupt the Commander in Chief's golf game. Actually highly sensitive data had disappeared from the Nuclear Weapons Center at Los Alamos...

"Los Alamos? Not *again*, Ted!" Sorelli heard Brenton exclaim.

Taylor gestured towards two folding camp chairs that the helicopter pilot had set up in the shade of a tall birch tree.

"One thing at a time please," the President said to Taylor, as his eyes followed in admiration the strong drive that Sorelli sent over the copter and deep down the fairway.

"Nice shot Joe!" he yelled over to him.

Sorelli, whom many said it was impossible to flatter, grinned sheepishly, proving otherwise. "Off target, sir! I thought I had that *Chinook* nailed for sure!"

"C-Gag is simply the best protection we've ever had for our nuclear missiles. But the fact is we didn't develop it. It was the damned Frenchwoman."

"And who might that be?" asked the President, sliding the head of his driver through the grass and sitting in one of the chairs.

"Her name is Nadine Moran. Originally, she worked for Thomson and GC Tech in France. Then Raytheon brought her over here through some co-op program with the armaments group. First she was at Intel; then she did microelectronics and sensor technology work – I don't know what else. But it was all very high-tech stuff and all had to do with weaponry. But her real strength is encoding and encryption. And somehow the eggheads at Los Alamos heard about her, and got special permission from the Pentagon to bring her over to nuclear weapons manufacturing." Taylor paused dramatically, and took a deep breath. "And that is where she thought up C-Gag, which is ultimately a very ingenious coding system."

"*C-Gag?* It sounds like a bad joke. Sit, Ted, sit down," Brenton smiled.

"Yes sir, thank you sir," Taylor replied, but had not the slightest reason to smile back at the President as he pulled up the camp chair and maneuvered his bony ass into the sagging canvas seat. "She developed it in response to Pentagon directives that we protect our arms technologies better. You know, they realized that our most advanced technologies were getting into other countries pretty easily."

"Tell me about it," the President replied with a sigh that Taylor heard more as boredom than regret.

"Yessir. I mean, every day we run the risk of losing our lead. All our weapons manufacturers are forming alliances with overseas companies."

Silently smiling, the President watched a butterfly dance around the head of his driver in the grass, trying to land on it.

"The F-16 fighter is a good example, sir," Taylor went on. "Who do you think produces its parts?"

"Is this a quiz show Ted? Why don't you sell it to

NBC?" the President replied sarcastically, watching the butterfly move to and settle on the tip of his golf shoe.

Taylor coughed, and tried to act as if his boss's remark was very amusing.

"Yes, sir. Or maybe I'll try David Letterman. But seriously: the front of the plane is built by South Koreans, the engines are made in Taiwan, with some work done in Greece and Turkey; part of the landing gear comes from the Netherlands; the wings from Belgium, and..."

"And the pilot's watch is made in Switzerland, am I right?" the President cut off Taylor with a lift of his hand, which scared off the butterfly. "So what's the connection between globalization and C-Gag?" he asked.

"Well, given the framework of this kind of global manufacturing, it's pretty darn inevitable that sensitive ideas and new technologies move across borders all the time. And the way things are going, I think that in a couple of years a handful of manufacturing conglomerates will have a very real factual monopoly on all weapons technologies and information."

"Marx said that already, Ted." *How predictable these CIA people are,* Brenton mused. *Here I am just recovering from their amazing ability to tell me nothing about the state of things in Chechnya, and here he is again with this bullshit story about data encryption in Los Alamos, hot on the heels of his last disaster out there – the China Syndrome, which even TV talk show hosts make fun of.*

Taylor leaned forward, shooing a green fly from his forehead. "What I mean to say sir is that these mergers and alliances pose a real threat to U.S. national security."

"Uh-uh, Taylor," Brenton exulted amused. "So what

you're saying is that our secrets leave the country and we have no ability to control it?"

"Exactly. Without espionage or betrayal. The French are almost notorious for selling arms technology to rouge countries. The Germans and the Brits are in on it as well, which makes it harder and harder to control where our most state-of-the-art technologies end up. Some of it's even being sold through the Internet, where of course no one from customs can do anything about it."

"Maybe we should adjust our laws," Jack Brenton said, with a touch of impatience in his voice. The butterfly came back and danced around his head, as if the President's thick mane of graying hair was a thistle field inviting him to stop and rest.

"I don't think we can end globalization with more regulations Mr. President."

"You know Ted, you have to learn to not always take me so seriously," Brenton replied, with a deep sigh that seemed to well up from the heart of a tired old circus clown. Taylor appeared to have missed the President's subtle irony.

"That's where C-Gag comes in sir."

"C-Gag? All I hear is C-Gag."

"Yes, the code created by that Frenchwoman Moran. Actually, it could help us protect our transnational system production from undesirable access."

"Wait a second Taylor. Are you saying there's such as thing as *desirable* access?"

The head of the CIA wagged his head and smiled.

"Well, given the variety of our counter-intelligence arsenal I guess such a situation may well come up. But, to return to my point sir, C-Gag is able to decode as well as encode."

"And the military value of that is?"

"Well, it enables us to encrypt sensitive programs in nuclear warheads – and protect them from being abused."

"Please, Ted – in the Brave New World of digital communications even *I* know that," Brenton answered. Like Napoleon, he prided himself on his ability to juggle three or four situations at the same time – and now he was handling at least two: Taylor's tale of woe and watching Joe Sorelli walk around his ball out on the fairway waiting for his partner. *The stuffy old carpets of the Oval Office for just one uninterrupted round of golf!* Brenton cursed to himself.

But he answered Taylor with knowledgeable vigor. "These days, Ted, sooner or later, all codes get cracked."

"But that's the thing about C-Gag, sir. It seems to be able to outwit other coding systems no matter how sophisticated they may be. Sort of like that rabbit over there. Look Mr. President!" Taylor pointed to the small brown rabbit hopping over the lawn, sniffing the air, and then zigzagging rapidly back to its bush.

Brenton wagged his head deliberately. "What good can it do us if all the data for construction and operation of those warheads has already been passed on to the Chinese?"

"Well, that's exactly it, sir. The Chinese won't have any idea what to do with the information they stole, unless..."

"Unless what?"

"Unless they get their hands on C-Gag too."

"And that, by God, I assume we can keep them from doing? Or am I wrong?" He stood up abruptly and tightened his grip on the driver. *Always a good idea to bring God into play,* he thought. *If God can't manage it, nobody can expect me to.*

He looked down calmly at the CIA Chief, who was brushing a bee away from his head. "Do you have any more bad news for me today Ted?"

Taylor jumped to his feet. "Well, since yesterday we know that C-Gag has an even more dangerous potential."

"Ted, if I want an oracle I'll visit Delphi. What is it? Spit it out!"

"Well, C-Gag is a very ingenious program."

"You said that before."

"And this Frenchwoman, well, it seems that she has been able to modify C-Gag so that it is a code cracker as well. She apparently can invade any system with it now, and…"

"And manipulate it?" Jack Brenton asked, impressed.

"Yes, sir. It's crazy. Apparently she has experience programming combat games for the crews of the *Aegis* defense system."

"So?"

"Well, what I'm trying to say, is that we're racking our brains out over…"

"Cut to the chase Ted. What the hell is it?' *You old bastard,* he added silently, grinning to himself.

"C-Gag can break through all security barriers, in layman's terms."

"We're all layman in the face of God, Ted," Brenton added sententiously. "What does all this mean in terms of *Aegis*?"

Taylor swallowed slowly. "Well, what it means is

that this Frenchwoman is able to reprogram our *Aegis* defense system."

"Oh, right! And she simply shook this out of her skirt one day?"

"She was, after all, working at the National Laboratory on simulations for the *Aegis* crews."

"Get to the point, Ted. My partner over there is looking restless, and when he gets restless he starts to feel pressure on his bladder, and then he walks over to a tree, and then we'll all see it on the evening news tonight and in tomorrow's papers. So hurry up." And with that Brenton smiled and casually waved at Sorelli.

"In a nutshell, Mr. President, this woman has betrayed her position of trust and developed her own encryption program – and, we fear, she can simulate attacks on our aircraft carriers whenever she feels like it."

"And why would she feel like it?" *Actually,* he meditated to himself, *why wouldn't she feel like it. Murphy's law? Whatever can go wrong sooner or later will go wrong? Better get ready for the shit to hit the fan again.*

Taylor went on to explain how the Navy had commissioned the program to train carrier crews for all kinds of attack situations. Ducks quacked on the nearby pond. Behind the birches where the secret service agents were standing, a greenskeeper drove by on his lawnmower, gaping at the President.

Slowly, the magnitude of Taylor's information sank into Brenton's mind. An enemy with this Frenchwoman's program could knock out the *Aegis* defense shield with a multitude of phantom attacks while real rockets approached undetected just above the waterline, silent and deadly.

Taylor guessed the President's thoughts. "This assumes, of course, that the enemy has the means to invade our defense system from the outside."

"But that's not really possible, is it?" asked the President, hopefully.

"Unfortunately, we're not that sure, sir."

Not a muscle moved on Brenton's face, not even an eyelid. He had survived dozens of crises, and not without reason was he considered a political escape artist. Some of the friendly media people called him Houdini Brenton; others called him a lame duck. With all that had happened in his seven years as president, he considered himself more like Lazarus. And as a resurrected Lazarus, he felt certain disgust towards the world of politics.

"Actually, none of this is really my problem, Taylor," he said, switching to a more formal tone, as was his privilege. "I believe you are responsible for such screwed-up situations. See to it that *Aegis* is immunized against C-Gag. It must be possible – just like people can be immunized against a virus, no?"

"To tell you the truth, sir, I'm afraid our hands are tied," Taylor stammered.

"Are you out of your mind Ted? I didn't hear what you just said," the President exploded dramatically, which made him feel much better. He wasn't screaming or anything, but it was loud enough to let Sorelli know that they would be continuing their round in a minute.

"We've lost C-Gag," Taylor said gloomily. "The Frenchwoman has disappeared. And took every byte of the program with her. She deleted everything from the computers at Los Alamos. Everything has vanished. No copies. Nothing left behind, except a ReadMe file of the program. We're facing a potential disaster."

"You will clean this up, Taylor. Is that understood? I expect your report by tomorrow, or heads will roll. And yours will be first!"

Brenton lifted the head of his driver up to the CIA Chief's throat, almost playfully, as if he would knock his head off himself. Taylor smiled uneasily as sweat rolled down his face. This assignment was almost not feasible: mission impossible.

"The work on recovering C-Gag will be our first priority Mr. President," he stammered.

"And something else Ted," Brenton said, in a dangerously chummy tone.

"Yes sir?"

"I want to know what asshole let this Frenchwoman take off with our confidential materials, particularly right after we just barely survived the China syndrome. File a *good* report, Ted, one I'm really going to *like*. One that will explain everything, calm everyone down, and reinforce all our trust in the good old CIA and in our reliance on good old Ted Taylor. And as for C-Gag…"

Taylor's neck seemed to contract like a turtle's.

"I'm going to finish my golf game now."

"Are, are you winning, Mr. President?"

"I always win, Ted. Just make sure that you win your round, okay? After all, American dominance is at stake. We have to be number one in the world of armaments. We wouldn't want Europe to become a fortress that doesn't need us anymore, would we? Just because of a little economic globalization? You either recapture that program or destroy it, whatever it takes."

"Yes sir, Mr. President," Taylor replied. He waved to the pilot who rushed over to fold up the chairs.

Brenton answered the pilot's sharp salute with a casual swerve of his hand toward his forehead. "What's your name, airman?"

"Lieutenant Clifford Matoyan, sir!"

"Someone in the family from Armenia, Cliff?"

"My grandparents on my father's side, Mr. President."

"Thought so," replied the most powerful man in the world, dismissing the pilot with a slight nod. "Fly carefully. And keep an eye on old Taylor. We still need him for awhile."

"Will do sir!"

Again, the pilot saluted sharply and moved away, walking on air, swinging the camp chairs as if they were feathers. People could say what they wanted about Jack Brenton – but he, Clifford Matoyan, had looked him straight in the eye, man to man. With his own eyes he had seen the glacier-blue core of mortal power.

28.

Not far from Zurich I swung my old Alfa Romeo into a parking spot near the assigned meeting place, got out of the car and looked around. At least the weather was agreeable. The clouds were moving east, and to the south the sky was turning a promising shade of blue. I took a deep breath and wondered what the Head of Intelligence wanted of me. *Your uncle was a great inspiration to all of us Mr. Polinsky. To which I might reply: And how is business, Brigadier? I heard you were planning to buy a new surveillance system?*

Then I noticed her waving, with both arms, causing her bosom to surge – much as it had yesterday at Mario's store. She was standing underneath the gas station roof, wearing a bright white blouse and dark blue slacks.

"Here! Over here," she called. When I finally took my eyes off her I noticed the big black sedan being gassed up by a chubby chauffeur in gray uniform. Suddenly a station wagon pulled in behind the Chief's Mercedes. I walked over.

"Good morning, Ms. Colonel," I chirped. "How are you? You look great!"

"The Brigadier is waiting for you," she said soberly, gesturing to the back of the sedan. But the hint of a smile in her eyes gave me some encouragement – kind of an upbeat.

"Well, then, off to battle," I replied, opening the car door and slinking down into the soft black leather of the back seat.

The Chief of Intelligence was in full-dress uniform – he

shook my hand heartily, and eased my worries as I looked through the rear window at the station wagon behind us.

"Don't worry," he said, "they're just security."

We drove along the highway next to the river, through a small area of woods. The chauffeur kept exactly to the speed limit. The Chief said nothing for a while, so I opened up the military magazine I had brought along with me – but neither the article about smart weapons nor the one on ship missiles could keep my attention. We drove past a lake, and then through a mountain tunnel – and all I could think about was how my chances to come up in time with the crucial evidence of the third man in court were sinking down to a fading glimmer of hope.

In the front seat next to the driver my lovely adjutant was puffing on a cigarette and occasionally consulting a road map. The driver hit the brakes hard, and let the car roll through a village. Then he turned into a narrow street that led uphill through some pastures to a high, flat plain. Suddenly we were on a very well maintained concrete road that went into a valley that got narrower by the yard – until it seemed that we disappeared into the fir trees. Then I realized that the shadows around us were not cast by the evergreens but rather by the sheer face of a mountain.

We maneuvered past a few barriers and saw a security gate and a bulletproof glass revolving door, behind which was a reception area. Two soldiers sat on the ramp outside, smoking and talking.

Just before going in I looked up at the sheer rock face weighing down against me, at the sprawling underbrush, and at a thin waterfall rushing past.

In the reception area the Chief of Intelligence took our passes.

"So this is our hidden headquarters, Polinsky. Where at least we can do our work in peace and quiet," he explained, leading me through a vast maze of corridors, past offices and technical installations, finally stopping in front of a large room labeled Grand Auditorium.

"Who's the bald guy?" I whispered to the Chief, as the murmur in the room died down and the man I was referring to ascended the podium, glasses in hand.

"That's Professor Beinhart, Assistant Professor for Strategic Studies at the Zurich Institute of Technology."

I was impressed, and nodded back to the Chief as I studied the lecturer's angular face.

"Today's lecture is about naval warfare," he added.

"Who's the audience?" I asked.

"Security experts, Army people."

The professor began his lecture with a historical review, just as I remembered from my old university days.

"Ship cannons not only revolutionized the way ships were designed – they also had world-historical consequences," he began as he fumblingly put on his glasses. "Vasco Da Gama entered and dominated the Indian Ocean basin as early as 1502. He took Calcutta through the sheer brutality made possible by his guns, and he controlled the area with a fleet of ships – with cannons – to enforce the peace.

"Many people consider the 19th Century to be the beginning of the age of the battleship, which, say in 1850, meant a vessel displacing about 7,000 tons, in World War, however, already 60,000 tons. It was deadly to anything that came within its range. Yet, gentlemen, we must remember that this range was severely limited."

Professor Beinhart paused and projected a slide of an aircraft carrier onto the screen behind him. Clearing his throat theatrically, he went on.

"What do you think? How many battleships would it take to provide complete coverage of the entire Mediterranean Sea?"

No one spoke up, so I did.

"That's hard to say," I ventured. "But I think it would only take about two of those aircraft carriers you have behind you there to cover the job."

"Right, that's absolutely right," the professor beamed, pushing his glasses up on his nose. "Ready to be amazed? Do you know how many battleships it would take to do the job? 1,942. And do you know the one important factor that makes the difference between 1,942 battleships and two aircraft carriers?"

"Well, there never really were that many battleships," one solicitous listener suggested.

"And no country ever had a military budget big enough to build a fleet that large," suggested another.

With a smile of superiority, Professor Beinhart wagged his index finger at his audience. "No, no, gentlemen. The range of fire is the decisive factor. The range of aircraft carriers has redefined the offensive in naval warfare."

So this was Beinhart's punch line: in bringing its guns to bear a battleship must expose itself to enemy gunfire. Both fleets were forced to come into the other's range, and the result was a brawl, with victory going to the quickest and the luckiest. "The ultimate problem with the battleship," Beinhart went on, "was that it could hurl a few hundred pounds of explosives a little over a dozen miles. The problem was not that it didn't do this well. The problem was that this was all it did."

The audience mumbled amusedly, but the Chief of the Secret Service started to fidget in his chair.

"Come," he suddenly whispered, and got up. Somewhat bewildered, I followed him.

"Listen, Polinsky. We can help you. You're in pretty big trouble," he said, getting straight to the point as he led me into the men's room.

"You mean with the Corps Commander's death?"

He nodded assent, and peered around conspiratorially. When we got into the white tiled room, he went straight to the sink and turned on one tap and then another.

"We had a movement-activated camera in a house nearby," he whispered, "and self-activating *directional microphones*."

I walked into the first stall and flushed the toilet, and repeated the procedure in the three remaining ones. Then I joined him in front of the urinals, and asked thick-wittily "In *which* house?"

"Across the street from where your uncle lived, there are two old wooden... " he said, cutting off his own speech with a loud and long fart that sounded like an old Peugeot just after starting.

"And? You got some pictures?"

I gazed at the ceiling as he shook off the last drops, stuck out his ass and grinned. "You bet! We got you punching the janitor in the stomach perfectly, Polinsky. And the red file too. That wouldn't by chance be the document the District Attorney is looking for, would it?"

Squinting at the back of the Chief's head, I wondered what the next fart that came from his brain would sound like. I stood in front of the sink, rinsing my hands under the running water, and said in a friendly way: "Oh Brigadier, without the Corps Commander – may his soul rest in peace – you would be an absolute nobody. He gave you all the information you needed, all the assignments to advance your career, all the fun in your job. Isn't that true? So tell me, have you finally dug up something useful in my uncle's case?"

He pulled a paper towel from the dispenser and moved toward me. "Did your uncle leave something compromising behind?" He seemed irritated by my reproachful look, and dug out his cigarettes, nervously fingering the pack before going on. "I mean, well, you know, that damn fundraising scandal way back when."

"Ripping off the Army would be a more accurate description," I replied, going on generously: "But let's forget about all those old stories."

Keeping the sinks running, we stood under the square ceiling lamp and stared at the black and gray tile floor. A fan spun on a corner shelf.

The Chief of Intelligence lit a cigarette, somewhat fastidiously. Apparently he had regained his balance.

"You see, Polinsky, we have some pretty good shots of the guy who snuck into the building after you knocked down the janitor. And we have him rushing back out later as the upstairs windows were cracking from the heat."

"Then let me see them," I urged, a bit prematurely, as I should have realized.

"Sure. But under one condition Polinsky."

"I'm all ears."

"Corps Commander Diesbach was on to something – something that involved guided missiles," the Brigadier said, puffing on his cigarette. I just shrugged my shoulders. But he looked me straight in the eye. "It wasn't just a simple arms deal."

"So?"

"Your uncle suspected an act of catastrophic terrorism. He must have kept some notes about it."

"And you want this information in exchange for the pictures?"

He shook his head distastefully, as if I didn't get it at all.

"No, What I want is for *you* to *clear up* this case. Totally. Good old fashioned espionage, Polinsky."

"You mean with binoculars, a walkie-talkie, and invisible ink?" I asked mockingly, buying some time. If Uncle Edouard knew about something like this, it must have been something big – the old coot never dealt in trivia.

"An attack against the Yank... uh, the Americans?" I asked.

"Probably," he nodded back, dead serious.

"And which way do your leads point?"

"To start with, Oman, where the Yanks, let's say, lost an Israeli a couple of weeks ago."

"I assume the CIA knows about all this?"

"Not necessarily. They consider the murder something done by the Palestinians. They don't believe it was a planned terrorist act," the Brigadier responded, acting as if he were a close friend to the head of the CIA. "Obviously they're always getting tips about bomb threats and such."

I began to realize from this conversation that Uncle Edouard had been in possession of solid evidence about some terrorist act. My interest was suddenly aroused for more than one reason. What I smelled was a chance to get out of my current dilemma, but I might also find a way to get into other interesting areas, such as new novels, non-fiction investigative books, and big advances, fat royalty checks. Hey, this would inevitably lead my life in the direction of lavish parties with fast, hot women.

"Why not?" I told the Chief of Intelligence. "Count me in. But I'll need some time to get ready," coughing and fanning his cigarette smoke from my face. "I'll have to go through all my files. Oh, and when will I get the pictures of the third man?"

The Brigadier showed that he had not been given his position for nothing. He answered with a shrewd sense of trickiness. "Let's see, the judge gave you until a week after next Thursday. So, like almost two weeks. Right? That's enough time, isn't it? I'll give you the pictures and you find out about this terrorist act and fix it, right? That's the result we both want."

"And if I can't do it in time?"

"Well, then the film of the third man stays in the Secret Service archives. And the District Attorney suddenly comes into possession of pictures of you picking up a red file from the sidewalk," he answered cold bloodily, tilting his head to the side as if to beg indulgence for his impertinence.

Trying not to let my excitement show I told him that I would think about it. One thing was clear: the Chief was trying to rehabilitate the image of his Secret Service from its recent bad record – and he was doing it through me. I could imagine how proud he would be if he and his relatively small unit of spies could save the Americans from a deadly act of terrorism with hundreds of casualties. He might replace the St. Bernard dog as the Swiss symbol of lifesaver.

But I still wondered: Had Uncle Edouard left the answer to my questions in his notes, or had he taken it with him to the grave? I paced the hallway outside the men's room pensively, while the Chief of the Secret Service leaned against the wall and nervously sucked down another cigarette.

In his capacity as Head of the Air Force, Edouard Diesbach had stayed in close contact not only with the air forces of all friendly nations, but also with the manufacturers of aircraft and missiles. The Luftkampfbetriebe (LKB) in Emmen near Lucern was the nerve center of the brutally competitive European arms trade.

After the licensed production of the French *Mirage* expired years ago, Diesbach had arranged for new orders. In Europe and the U.S., the development of new missiles progressed rapidly. Numerous sellers courted the procurement authorities of all governments with increasingly innovative and sophisticated products. The LBK grew to be a tremendous knowledge resource. Governments from around the world sought impartial evaluations from incorruptible experts in Emmen on their planned acquisitions of competing weaponry. Working in the background, Edouard Diesbach knew how to transform questions about arms into real money. And for nailing down delicate arms deals, he had founded the Magadino SA, which flourished secretly until he died. The old fox recruited his loyal supporters, mostly women, from the Secret Service, where they were accustomed to being disciplined and secretive.

I stopped my pacing and stood in front of the Brigadier.

"Okay, I'll do it. But I need the pictures of the third man."

"You're *in*? You'll track down that terrorist?" he asked, his eyes glimmering with professional enthusiasm.

"Sure, and I'll save the world from disaster, and kill the villain whoever he may be with my bare hands in the last second," I jeered. The Brigadier showed no enthusiasm for my sense of humor.

"Okay Polinsky, it's a deal. Here are the enlargements. That's the guy. It's a good thing I had decided to keep the hidden camera installed."

He handed a dark red leather case to me. The photos were stuck tightly inside it. I had trouble getting hold of a corner to pull one out.

"This is a job for a woman with long fingernails," I said.

"Come on Polinsky, give it to me. Practical, that's what a man has to be."

"And docile the woman," I added sententiously with a grin.

With a condescending smile he pulled open the zipper I had overlooked. And the pictures tumbled out. Fast as a cat I caught them in mid-air and held them in my hands. I stared at the face with the round eyes, black like entry points of bullets, the deep-set eyes under narrow brows, the bent or perhaps once-broken nose, the full shock of black hair, and the narrow skull.

This was the guy I saw when I drove away from my uncle's house. No doubt. Just looking at him made me tense.

"You have a name for him?" I asked the Chief.

"Not yet. But we're working on it. Let's go back inside. Follow me."

The Head of Intelligence smiled contentedly to himself. He tried to figure how many birds he had killed with this one stone. Two, three perhaps even four. Well, maybe three and a half. It was this fourth bird, this bigmouth Polinsky, that the Brigadier didn't give more than a fifty-fifth chance of coming out of this mess alive.

29.

When we got back into the auditorium, Professor Beinhart was still lecturing in front of a close-up of an aircraft carrier. "The battle of Midway was a genuine naval battle and a true test of this battle machine's capability. The sons of Nippon made a fatal error during their attack on Pearl Harbor. While the first two waves of attackers had destroyed the ships and planes of the Americans who had been taken by surprise, the third wave – designed to destroy the oil tanks and dry docks – was never launched. Thus, Pearl Harbor not only remained functional – but it soon became the very center of a vast American buildup that the Japanese could not hope to match."

I was only half listening, but I was able to follow his argument.

My thoughts were really focused on the undulating bust of the beautiful adjutant, mingled with memories of other military-type women I had slept with. One thing all of these women had in common. When they climaxed in utter pleasure, they would shriek like birds of prey and yell commands as one might hear from the frontlines of battle: *get your sorry ass up and over that hill, push through that enemy line!* Well, in all honesty, maybe it was just that one British Madam Colonel, whose grandfather had ended up in Verdun – from where she probably got those juicy trench-warfare metaphors she howled whenever she came. But, thinking of her and of my adjutant, a languorous kind of puffy feeling spread through my thighs and nether regions. My dozing dormouse suddenly grew to something heavy and dangling that only needed the right kind of stimulation, say from my lovely adjutant, to reach its full potential.

Back at the podium, Beinhart described how the Japanese tried to take Midway Island to use its airfields there to attack the American ships in Pearl Harbor with long-range bombers – and to force whatever remained of the still fragile fleet to withdraw to San Diego or San Francisco. Midway was considered so important to the Japanese that the entire Imperial fleet sailed under the personal command of Admiral Yamamoto himself. The professor elaborated on the battle formation. He faded out the slide of the grim Yamamoto and spoke of the Japanese naval code, which the Americans had broken through a stroke of luck, and which allowed them to attack first – sinking Japanese carriers while losing only the *Yorktown* themselves.

"Well, gentlemen, the battleships under Yamamoto's personal command remained untouched. Yet the battle was over. Even though the major part of his fleet did not suffer a single scratch, Yamamoto broke off contact and abandoned the attack," Beinhart shouted into the audience, his eyes glowing like a kamikaze pilot.

I turned around and looked at the amazed faces, who somehow still didn't get it. Most of them stared obtusely at Beinhart. Wasn't anyone dozing off? The professor trudged on.

"Then, why did Yamamoto give up the battle?" After a rhetorical pause he answered the question himself. "At Midway, an intact, experienced, well-led surface fleet built around superb battleships simply declined to do combat with two aircraft carriers. Range of fire had redefined the correlation of forces in naval warfare."

I whispered to the Chief, scarcely hiding my impatience. "So what does this lecture boil down to?"

He scribbled something on a piece of paper and, grinning, pushed it over to me. It said: Bump, Bump, Bonk.

"Today, the entire future of the aircraft carrier and thus of the entire American naval strategy is at a crossroads," the professor declared, as if he had heard my whispering.

A Colonel, leaning back against a window, protested. "How can you say that?"

Making use of this welcome interruption, the Chief of Intelligence nudged me and pointed toward the door. We snuck out just as the professor was projecting a caricature of David and Goliath on the screen.

He asked the crowd, "What do you think I'm trying to say with this image?"

I stopped, wanting to hear his answer.

"Within its range, the battleship was powerful and deadly, just like Goliath. The aircraft carrier, not nearly as powerful, substituted range and precision by using fighter aircraft. Like David, the carrier overcame the increasingly complex defensive weapons system of the battleship with faster, more elegant technologies. And by doing that, the essence of the offensive was re-distilled. It also opened a door, just a crack, to the future revealing that the precision and range of the intelligent projectile will decisively change naval warfare. Gentlemen, the battle of the future will be between intelligent precision-guided weapons and aircraft carriers!"

With searching eyes, the professor looked through the

audience, as if he were measuring the success of his lecture. From the bank rows someone hissed the word "*Exocet!*"

So, after two hours I found myself outside again, breathing fresh mountain air. Gradually I began to get a sense of where my uncle's dying wishes would lead me. But as yet, no one had said a word about any Nadine.

My next appointment was the Corps Commander's memorial ceremony at the Fraumünster church in Zurich. So I had about three hours to come up with a plan.

Skeptic though I was, I looked up into the slice of sky that shone above the narrow valley and half jokingly wagged my finger, addressing my uncle: "See what a mess you've gotten me into now, you old lady killer."

30.

The Islamic leader had long since taken off his blue overalls, and now stood next to Captain Souri on the bridge in comfortable clothes. The *Shiraz* was traveling at full speed with full ballast tanks five degrees north of the equator – approaching the Cape Verde Islands. Two cable lengths away on portside, an antiquated coast guard boat was looking for fishing pirates, having just crossed their bow. The horizon in the distance hinted at the contours of the gold coast of Ghana. A gleaming white stripe would soon grow to be the silhouette of Accra.

Yussef bin Golem leaned on his precious walking stick of carved ebony topped with the knob of dark rhino horn. He wore a white linen jacket over a white button-down shirt and wide light brown slacks. His long bushy beard gave his head a long triangular shape, in the middle of which his hawk-like nose protruded. A white turban hid half of his suntanned forehead and set off his distinctive brows. *More than half this man's face is hiding under hair,* the Captain mused to himself as he watched his instruments.

Yussef bin Golem appeared to be very gentle, but he wielded his stick like a scepter, an unmistakable symbol of his power. Whoever defied his orders paid for the disobedience with his life. Or with something many of his freedom fighting believers considered to be far worse than the loss of life: being renounced and banished from the community of religious warriors.

Lifting his right hand almost as in blessing, bin Golem got the captain's attention immediately.

"Yes sir?"

"Where is the Frenchman working?" the Arab asked impatiently.

"Major Moran will stay in his quarters until after we pass Dakar," the captain replied.

"Any news from the *Roosevelt?*"

Riaz stepped up and said without batting an eye:

"Yes sir. She is cruising the Ionian Sea heading for Malta. She will cross the Strait of Gibraltar as scheduled."

"Is this information absolutely authentic and reliable?" bin Golem challenged his Information Officer with a menacing undertone.

"Yes, Effendi," Riaz shot back. "We have received a radio message from Colossimo's yacht. Apart from that, a crew member of the *USS Ross* has confirmed position and course of the carrier."

"We will reach Casablanca in time Captain?" the Islamic leader asked, raising his stick as if by chance to the captain's chest. "If you should fail Captain…" But he left the threat unvoiced, merely raising his eyebrows.

Shuddering inside, the captain gulped and forced himself to smile.

"Of course, sir… *Effendi.* The crew of the *Shiraz* is 200 percent reliable."

31.

The daily routine aboard the *USS Theodore Roosevelt* never varied. Every afternoon at 4 o-clock the crew gathered inside the huge hangar for its daily workout. In the wide open area the afternoon exercises looked just like they did in the barracks squares of countless bases on land. A drill sergeant stood up on a podium, shouting out the exercise routine in a fast rhythm. The salty sea air flowed into the hangar through a large open hatch, filling the seamen's lungs with oxygen as their yearning gazes wandered over the sea to the horizon. The crew got no shore leave for six months.

The *TR* is one of America's largest aircraft carriers, a perfectly self-contained war machine at sea. Everything is rigorously organized. There are five dining halls where more than 200 people work. Good food is considered the most important supply on board ship. With a crew far away from home locked aboard a steel giant, the last thing one would want to serve is dog food. Excellent cuisine was a necessary compensation, and the gigantic galley facilities of the huge carrier could compete with a four-star hotel. Every day the ship's cook, assisted by 240 hands, served the crew about 20,000 hot meals.

The lower decks of this floating war metropolis resembled a small city. Even after weeks on board, new arrivals often lost their way trying to figure out the maze-like corridors.

That afternoon, as bin Golem's mighty *Shiraz* steamed up the Atlantic heading for Gibraltar, the Captain of the *TR*, David Fisher, sat in the onboard TV studio, slowly and methodically working his way through a speech that resounded loud and clear in every corner of the steel giant. Behind his chair in the studio, the intricate gold letters *T* and *R* adorned the wall, an abbreviation of the ship's full name – a ship that, displacing 100,000 tons, was far bigger and heavier than the famed *Titanic*.

"We train the way we fight. And we fight the way we train," the young-looking commander said, speaking into the microphone with a sense of routine. He wore a khaki shirt and a dark blue peaked cap. His thin black moustache complied fully with Navy regulations, serving as a guideline for all moustaches aboard the *TR*: never wider than the mouth they sat over.

"Those were the words I spoke to you end of March, when we started our mission in the Ionian Sea. Since then, we have flown fully 25 percent of all attacks for operation *Noble Anvil*. I am proud of you all for this accomplishment. And I am also proud and happy to say that every single pilot has returned from his missions safe and sound – not a single loss on record, yet."

Day and night, 24 F-18 fighter jets took off from the *Roosevelt's* flight deck, manned by a rotating crew of 120 pilots. The other 5,000 seamen were on board to make sure these flights ran smoothly, and to take care of the maintenance duties of this naval war machine. One of the pilots, Lieutenant Morse, listened to his commander's voice as he worked out on a chest-muscle torture machine in the gym deep below deck. He was thinking about what he might consider his greatest success to date. *Coming down in one piece, that's the greatest success. And fear? Well, a little fear is good – keeps your concentration sharp. This isn't target practice. Lots of enemies out there are try-*

ing to keep me from completing my missions. I could always get hit. It's a frightening thought – and it's always there. But so far it's been okay. Not too scary – just enough.

"Operation *Noble Anvil* is coming to a close. Soon we'll be on our way back home to the States!" Captain David Fisher smiled into the camera. Like all commanders, he loved giving his people good news.

"Hey, looks like we'll be home for Christmas!" said the armory officer down on lower deck five. With a look of satisfaction he massaged his broad chest, or rather his red sweater with the black letters "Gun Boss" that left no doubt who was in charge down here. There were 3,500 tons of bombs onboard the *Roosevelt*, distributed among 46 armories whose 120 specialists, both men and women, looked after their lethal precision mechanisms.

While his commander kept talking through the closed circuit TV system about their trip home through the Strait of Gibraltar and about how he counted on everyone's all-out efforts – from the hairdressers to the flight deck co-ordinators – the gun boss worked on a 2000 pound GBU-24. A woman technician helped him, screwing on a CCG with a large wrench. The gray bomb painted with a yellow ring allowed for different heads and ignition mechanisms, depending on its mission. This one, painted red and green, had a narrow nose. When the pilot dropped the bomb, a wire pulled away from the ignition and a computer control guided it to its target. In the one they were setting up now, the narrow nose was programmed to penetrate a building and not explode until it hit the ground.

"Our mission is to bring peace to the world," the captain said in high seriousness through the many onboard screens. "We want to improve the lives of all people. We are fighting for freedom everywhere in the world, and all of you are making a valuable contribution. All of our efforts are taking us in this direction and hopefully the entire world is making progress." He nodded into the camera twice, and then closed with stage-worthy pathos: "God bless America!"

"Amen to that, captain," said the black seaman who worked in cold storage in the canteen. As he drank his tea and munched a chocolate chip cookie, he turned to the nurse from X-Ray.

"You know, I'm really here for the money, and for the training I guess. I want something better for my life. And if that means I have to fight for my country, then that's the way it has to be."

"We all do what we have to do," she replied, non-committal. She got up and walked from the cold storage area, which was as large as three tennis courts. Inside were 14,000 pounds of beef, 18,000 pounds of chicken, 400 large cases of ice cream, and pounds and pounds of fish (even lobster), and things like pizza cheese. Every Saturday was pizza night. *The day after tomorrow we're in for it again* mused the seaman, who actually preferred cheeseburgers and fries. But at least all his favorite foods were here to help ease his homesickness on the open seas – things like peanut butter, coke, and bagels...

Inside the TV studio the captain got up with a sigh of relief. "Well, that's that." An ensign handed him his cup of tea labeled "Captain" with the initials "*TR*" on the other side.

"I thought it was great, sir," perked up the young

woman who was the Head of Communications for the Public
Affairs department.

"Thanks Pamela. I'm glad at least it went smoothly.
I guess we can relax a bit until we get to Gibraltar. Then the
heat will be on again. I hate those tight passages. They always make me feel exposed."

"Oh come on, sir," Pamela said confidently. "The
boys up in the AWACS will keep their eyes open for us. I
think it's very exciting. In the old days didn't they call the
rocks on both sides of the strait the Pillars of Hercules?"

"So what are you saying Pamela? That Zeus himself
is promising us safe passage?"

She roared with laughter. "He's already done that sir.
Don't we have *Aegis*, Zeus's shield? And speaking of mythol-
ogy…"

"Yes?"

"Remember the Aegean stables? The ones Hercules
mucked out by redirecting the river through them? Maybe
we should do something like that to that hellhound Saudi
Arabian. But instead of washing him out with a river maybe
we should send him the Big Stick!"

"Bin Golem? Sure, if we only knew where he was
hiding. I'd send him a *Tomahawk* missile that would split his
head in half, Indian style. But who knows where he is? The
wimpy dog is probably hiding somewhere in Afghanistan."
Although he tried to make light of it, Captain Fisher knew
that if you couldn't locate your enemy, then everything you
had been taught in the nation's best military academies
wouldn't do you any good.

"Yes sir, you're probably right," Pamela responded in

professional seriousness, although inside she felt very cheery and excited. She knew that joining the Navy had been a bit of an odd choice: a life in uniform playing men's games. She knew she would never ascend to the rank of the decision-making Admirals, whom they received onboard from time to time with much fuss. But at least she was having an ocean-going adventure. *Who cares about bin Golem,* she thought to herself. *Now Captain Fisher, however… but, he's a faithful husband and family man. Come on, girl! Forget it!*

32.

My uncle had left arrangements for his own funeral in his will. He had chosen a funeral home with the consoling name of DivineAura Ltd. and had left specific instructions about arranging everything, so fortunately I had nothing to do but show up. Even the simple oversight duties were assigned to the fraternity of Uncle Edouard's air force buddies called Ikarus – guys who had flown Messerschmitts from '39 – '45 and who had even managed to shoot down some Swabians over northwest Switzerland.

All I had to do was enter the church on the cue word "family," and march down the aisle past the packed benches up to the front row reserved for family guests. The organ sung forth ceremoniously, and people got up to gape – and to offer their respects to the Corps Commander's family, which in this case meant myself, the well behaved Mustang (Edouard's bulldog), and the fragile sister of my uncle's unfortunate housekeeper. The sister sobbed continuously, wiping her eyes with a dainty white handkerchief – more I suspected for her sibling who never recovered from the fire than for my uncle the Corps Commander.

Behind us were seated old men with stony faces. One of them nodded at me and smiled stiffly – the Head of the Executive Federal Council. Next to him was my companion of the morning, the Chief of Intelligence, who had the only non-gray head of hair in the bunch – whether natural or dyed was another question. Our eyes met momentarily, which made me think rather heretically of his busty adjutant. But then I also noticed a very lovely looking woman with a wide-awake face and sparkling eyeglasses further back in the pews.

The organ music faded. High on the pulpit the gray head of Minister Salvisberg suddenly appeared, a witty cleric whom I knew well.

"May the Lord be with us," he started, with his youthful sounding voice. "We are gathered here together to bid Corps Commander Edouard Diesbach a final farewell."

With that Mustang jumped up on the pew, sat on his hind legs, and began howling towards the pulpit. Laughter tittered through the crowd, and the Chief leant forward and whispered in my ear "Polinsky, we have to talk. The appointment."

I noticed, even at close range, that his hair appeared to be naturally black, which didn't make any sense, given his profession. Maybe he had nerves of steel; or maybe just a first-class hairdresser.

But speaking of hair roots, the housekeeper's sister blushed all the way to hers as she hissed at Mustang and his innocent howling. The minister wisely pointed out that in his church all feelings were allowed free expression, even if or especially if one was a dog – apropos of which he muttered some quotation from the Apocalypse.

Towards the end of his sermon he praised my uncle for being an old oak braving the storm on the hilltop, one who steadfastly survived the hardships of time. Of course the women in Uncle Edouard's life were given only oblique mention at the end, when he said, "His life was giving. He gave to his country and to those who came to him and revered him. Drawing on plentiful resources, he gave much – and many can stand witness to that."

We rose to pray, and my cell phone started chirping. I tore it from my jacket and said "Amen."

"What are you, nuts?" asked Irina on the other end of the line. When I said nothing, she began to blather. "Well my friend, it's about Knosp. Remember? The conversation I overheard at the cash machine? Knosp is the name of the company. The stock price has doubled recently. But it's about to crash. The merger is off."

"So what are you going to do now?" I asked her, while Salvisberg's voice echoed from the pulpit. "There is a limit to everything. That is the way it is destined...."

"One of them said he would sell everything, millions," Irina said.

"Millions?" I asked in disbelief into the phone, to which the preacher replied, "...in the world starving."

Someone shushed me loudly from behind, which seemed more disturbing than my words. Mustang decided this would be a good time to lick my face, which caused more laughter to erupt throughout the church.

"Blessed are they who have nothing," Salvisberg continued, to which I replied into my cell phone "Sell, Irina, sell Knosp," more loudly than I had planned to. "That's what they were saying, sell it all!"

"I can't understand a word you're saying," she said, and hung up the phone.

The church was suddenly eerily silent as I put the phone back into my jacket pocket. I could feel the eyes of the mourners stabbing into my back like spears. I slowly turned around only to see the reproachful eyes of the old men of

Ikarus. They shook their heads at me in loathing as if I were Adolf's helper.

Spreading my arms I intoned with a full voice, "Blessed are they who have nothing," and sat down again.

"Amen!" came the thunderous reply from Salvisberg on the pulpit, and with that the organ struck up the funeral march. We all rose. A few faces smiled at me. Others refused to look me in the eye or just turned around and showed their pinched petit-bourgeois asses to me.

As if on cue, the Ikarus geriatrics club stepped up to the coffin draped with the Swiss flag. They stood bolt upright next to it, four on each side, and with the first blast of the trumpets lifted the coffin of their dead comrade and marched slowly towards the exit.

The Head of the Executive Federal Council pulled his cell phone out and shouted into it "Sell all Knosp stock immediately!" as he pushed his way out of the pew with a sad look on his face. Suddenly many of the mourners were doing the same thing, placing Knosp sell-orders, before lining up behind the coffin and waddling toward the exit in a laboriously dignified rush.

Suddenly I felt a heavy hand on my shoulder and turned to see the sparkling eyes of Walter Knosp himself! He was the unchallenged boss of Knosp AG, the nation's gardener, a man as hard as nails who got up every morning at a time when I was usually only coming home. Knosp, the self-made man, the economic miracle, the charming country squire. Boy, was I in for it. He looked directly at me and said with an urbane smile, "Asshole. You're finished!"

"Are you soliloquizing?" I shot back, and walked away.

Outside the church I saw two men whose faces and bearing was familiar to me, or which at least brought up unpleasant memories. They both wore light, ankle-length, beltless raincoats buttoned up to the neck and black sunglasses pushed tight against their dark skin. As I walked past them they approached me in what they probably thought was in inconspicuous manner and fell into step with me.

The taller one, with a moustache and the affectation of Mustapha the Turk, addressed me with solicitous politeness. "Dear Mr. Polinsky, may we have a quick word with you?"

The people in front of me stopped as the Corps Commander's coffin was lifted up into the hearse.

"We buy everything concerning Konkorski," the second one said, as if standing in the bazaars of Medina.

"Unfortunately, pal, you've landed in the wrong opera," I parried with a devout smile. "This is a *funeral.*"

"Exactly," Mustapha insisted, with a syrupy smile. "Your uncle has taken his secret to the grave with him."

I nodded in agreement, pointing ahead to the hearse. "He's not in the ground yet. Why don't you go and ask him?"

Both of them chewed their lips. I noticed something about the way they looked at me. And their hands? Of course! One hand in the pocket to operate the recorder. The thick sunglasses. Wait a second! Looking at Mustapha's sunglasses I noticed the tiny camera lens. Is this crap going to go on forever?

"We pay well, Polinsky! Death sings silently." The bazaar salesman looked around apprehensively. Mustapha shook his head.

Were they kidding? Death sings silently?

"You don't really want to threaten me, do you gentlemen?" I replied annoyed. "Didn't you understand the minister? Blessed are they who have nothing." And in a theatrical gesture I raised my arms to the sky, snatching Mustapha's glasses off and sending them high over the crowd. Then I heard a loud crunching sound. Someone yelled at the bazaar salesman as he walked over and bent down to pick up the remains.

The hearse pulled away. The old men of the Ikarus club got into a black stretch limo and followed the hearse. More black sedans were lined up along the sidewalk. Knosp got into one of them with the Head of the Executive Federal Council.

As his car rolled up, the Chief of Intelligence waved to me. I walked up to him with Mustang on a short leash by my side.

"I am sorry, but I won't be able to attend the reception," he said, excusing himself. Mustang growled at him. "We'll talk later," he said, diving deep into the back seat of his Mercedes.

The door slammed shut, and I saw my reflection in the darkened window. But then it slid down, revealing his pale face framed in the window. ""Will you give me the red file, Polinsky?"

I shook my head no. "Not part of the deal. No renegotiations, Brigadier. Oh, by the way, give my compliments to your tonsure designer."

"Tonsure designer?"

"Your hairdresser. In a class by himself. One suggestion, if I may. Tell him to leave just a few hairs gray over the temples. This would squelch all suspicions about its natural color."

He bit his lip and raised the window, whose blackness cut off his pleading look.

A sudden yearning for Irina overtook me. The idea of taking her into my arms seemed much more appealing than a ride to the cemetery followed by a buffet at the Zunfthaus. A seagull fluttered down from the church steeple and flew off against a cloudless blue sky. As I followed it I remembered my uncle's advice. *Life means being alive. Pleasure is the aim of all ambition.* The old man was right. I felt as if he had exempted me from further obsequies. Edouard, the clever old chap, had other plans for me.

Musing on my uncle, I bumped into another ankle-length raincoat. Only an agent or an idiot would wear such a coat on a day like this.

"Mr. Polinsky? Excuse me. Could I have a word with you?" The guy was as tall as a lamppost. He took off his sunglasses and held them out to me, grinning. "See? No camera!"

"Talking to me is expensive. $200 an hour," I said, pushing past him.

Still grinning, he limped after me. "No problem, sir."

I pointed to his bad leg. "Nam?"

"Iraq, 1997. Secret mission."

"Konkorski?" I asked haphazardly.

He nodded, and then looked around carefully, whispering, "Rumor has it you got into the old man's safe and took some very confidential material on missiles."

"Then rumor knows more than I do," I replied calmly.

"When the first Concorde appeared 30 years ago, your

uncle was closely allied with French intelligence." He pulled a CIA ID card from a hidden pocket in his coat. Central Intelligence Agency! Those good old espionage people. And where *didn't* they poke their little feelers!

"It's possible. But that was a long time ago. And since when is the CIA interested in historical research?" I looked up at the church steeple and murmured, *You, Uncle Edouard! Again?*

The CIA agent looked at me oddly, as I continued in a normal tone of voice. "So what does the Concorde have to do with *me?*"

"The Soviet equivalent of the Concorde was called the Konkorski. The Russians had stolen the plans from the French," he whispered, looking around carefully.

Of course, I knew all about this. On December 31, 1968, the prototype of a supersonic passenger airliner rolled out of the Soviet Tupolev plant and onto the runway. The resemblance to the French Concorde was so overwhelming that the international press immediately started calling it the Konkorski.

"But I don't understand what you want from me, soldier," I said eventually. "Aren't you wasting your time?"

"Well, sir, I want the material you sto… uh, acquired from the safe. As you know, we pay well, and discreetly." He was like a ventriloquist, able to speak without moving his lips as he described his terms to me.

"Well, that's easy to imagine. But there's one hitch. To be precise, I don't have the materials."

He shook his head in gentle reproach. "Think hard on it Polinsky. There's a lot at stake here."

We stood on the bridge. I looked down into the current and talked to myself. "I guess that was it, what he meant, Konkorski."

"You have to understand, Polinsky."

I waved him off. "So long, buddy."

I flagged down a cab as it rolled over the cobblestones.

The tall CIA agent handed me a card. "Call us. Just ask for Walrus, and…"

"Who is Walrus?" I asked, opening the cab door.

"Doesn't matter. A code word. You'll be instantly put through to the boss."

"I don't give a damn about your boss," I said, grunting amusedly and getting into the cab.

"It's Taylor, Director of the CIA," he whispered to me.

"Let's go!" I said to the lady cab driver, who translated her understanding of my request into a lightening start that threw me back into the seat.

"That was some nice walking away you did back there," she said to me as she eased off the accelerator.

"Don't worry, he'll be back," said another woman's voice from the seat next to me. And there she was, the lovely woman with the wide-awake intelligent face and the sparkling eyeglasses from the back pew.

"Didn't you enjoy my performance at the church?" I stammered. I must have looked like a complete idiot.

She laughed out loud. "Now everybody is dumping Knosp! But seriously, you should take better care of yourself."

I should have asked her where she came from, and what she was doing in my cab, or perhaps what I was doing in hers.

But I got the feeling there was more going on here than mere flirtation. I had to be cool.

"Take me to the Sonnenberg," I told the cab driver. "I have a dinner engagement there."

But contrary to my expectations, the woman with the glasses said nothing. She just sort of winked at me and seemed exceptionally cheerful.

"So, uh, what do we do now?" I asked her, with a gesture expressing faint frustration. "I have a date."

"So I've heard. I'll simply join you. I'm hungry anyway. And who knows? If dinner is good maybe it'll whet my appetite for a night of hot passion." And she smiled at me recklessly and took my arm.

She was certainly brazen, but I liked her at once – I guess according to the principle that some things in life are impossible to plan. *Help yourself, Polinsky! Life means being alive.* For a dozen heartbeats neither of us said anything.

"Where are you staying?" I finally asked, to break the silence and pick up where a sweet momentary trembling in my pants left off.

"At *your* place, where else?" she replied, with the most disarming smile in the world which, quite frankly, left me speechless. "By the way, my name is Nadine. Nadine Moran. And it's very important that I get to Belgrade."

Monday-Bar's bartender would have answered with his easygoing "No hay problemas." But I said nothing at first, trying not to let my feelings show.

So this was Nadine? My Uncle Edouard's Nadine? The woman he had made me promise to help in the last moments of his life? My problems seemed to multiply exponentially these days. My mind raced from Steinlin to Irina to my dead uncle and to the adjourned trial. How was I supposed to handle it all?

Well, one thing was for sure. I would definitely help this woman sitting next to me in the cab. And a sudden craving to fly suddenly took possession of me. Was I just tempted by the desire to sit behind the control lever of an airplane? Or was I filled with an inner burning to help this woman, one so strong that I simply had no other choice?

One thing was certain, though. I would have to keep a bit of distance between us. Staying together under one roof and even going to bed with her as friends, as tempting as that might seem, should probably be avoided. Mario might be able to help me with this: he kept that small attic apartment above his store. If you wanted to play successfully with a woman like this, you had to keep your cards close to your vest. But what cards did I have anyway?

My cell phone chirped, muffled in my pocket. Waldo, my publisher! I smilingly lifted my left eyebrow at Nadine and shrugged my shoulders in apology.

"Ah, Waldo. No, don't say anything. I'm not going to ask you what's happening because I don't want you to ask me what's happening so I don't have to hear a long deafening silence on your side and you don't have to hear a dirty joke reply from my side about a dream I had last night where I handed you a fat pile of paper that looked just like a completed manuscript which you took with your most beautiful smile telling me 'Polinsky you are the kind of writer I dream about'. So Waldo, let me dream on for just a little longer, okay?"

Winking at Nadine, I hung up and put away the cell

phone. Now, where were we? Ah yes, on our way to my place, and, or…

"But of course," I smiled at her. "To Belgrade. Where else?"

PART TWO

33.

Dirty gray clouds swept over an incredibly red twilight sky as our single-engine prop plane hummed along smoothly, approaching the forested hills around the provincial town of Nis in Yugoslavia. Once in a while a gust of wind shook our tail, and a few isolated raindrops splashed against the scratched-up cabin windows.

Nadine Moran sat next to me with a black and white aerial photograph held on her knees, looking for a place to land. "Do you want to land on that road over there? Or on the meadow next to it?" she asked, searching the topography with her alert golden brown eyes.

I fought against a couple of hard wind gusts, keeping the plane on a steady course for our landing approach. "We'll try the grass I think. It'll be all right."

Far below a river meandered through a narrow mountain valley like a glistening ribbon, which shrunk to a pitch-black worm, and then braided between the railroad tracks and the road that connected Nis, in southeast Serbia, to the Bulgarian capital Sofia.

As I concentrated on our approach, I wondered if I looked more like a determined mountain climber than a pilot to Nadine, as I wet my upper lip with my tongue and concentrated totally on an imaginary point on the ground ahead where I planned to bring down my plane. My sunglasses were stuck in my full head of blonde hair, and a two-day stubble adorned by determined chin.

I wondered if this woman thought of me as a daredevil trying to master my mid-life crisis with all sorts of challenges, which perhaps was not that big a stretch. After all, who but an adventure-crazed nutcase would try to infiltrate the embargoed war zone of Yugoslavia in daylight with a passenger and a shipment of arms?

Nadine bent forward and gazed into the valley below. The area appeared to be very peaceful, not unlike the valleys and canyons of Dordogne where she had spent her early youth. Perhaps the fleeting image of her mother's gentle face crossed her mind, remembering how she stood at the doorway of their house with a basket of apples, beaming an unforgettably warm smile at her daughter. *Hadn't those days been carefree?*

Below us thick forests and trench-scarred hills protected the tiny settlements glued to the valley's floor. In this diversified terrain, Nadine thought, the Serbs would be able to hold out against any invader for a long time. She felt a sour ache in her stomach, and she rubbed her belly and took a deep breath. She hated these small cramped noisy planes and couldn't help thinking about all of the crashes that occurred in single-engine aircraft.

I sensed her anxiety and gave her a reassuring paternal look, which occurred to me was not really in line with my interest in her. Or maybe it was? Whatever – now was not the time for such musings. Giving her a nod meant to comfort her as much as being in a shaking small airplane allowed, I reached for my pack of cigarettes and offered her one. She didn't take it, but just stared at me with a face so ashen I thought I might have to reach for the vomit bag under my seat, just in case. Perhaps her getting sick would improve the human element of our relationship – but I wouldn't wish that on her of course. She was a woman, who knew how to take care of herself, and reached forward and directed a stream of fresh air from the ventilating nozzle onto her clammy shining forehead. She seemed to calm herself down, realizing that up until now everything had been going incredibly smoothly. *You're doing great,* she said to herself. *Actually, you don't have any reason to worry at all.*

Our flight had started from an airfield outside Sofia, and after a quarter of an hour, we had crossed the border into the Federation of Yugoslavia. No one seemed to take any notice of us. Thus far the operation had proceeded as planned – but we had to finish quickly before anyone smelled a rat and realized what we were up to.

As we flew we could see a bluish silhouette of a mountain range to the west slowly approaching. Nadine had dug out the map from under the aerial photograph and studied the geography with an anguished expression. At nearly 6,700 feet high, the high peak of the Kopaonic Mountains was already part of the Kosovo.

Nadine fought down her sour nausea. Was it pure naked fear making her knees feel weak and pushing cold sweat through the pores of her skin? She tugged at her polo shirt as if that would solve her problem. Without realizing it she patted her chest where the disk with the *Oedipus* code – the very key to her meeting with Thierry-Clément Moran – was securely stored in a leather money purse hanging from her neck. Just feeling it there made a feeling of warmth radiate through her, helping in her battle with the nausea. Life was a big adventure. And this Polinsky character next to her, well, he seemed to fit right into her suddenly dangerous, colorful, turbulent world. Too bad that he didn't really seem to know where he belonged. Too bad...

I didn't feel like talking. Flying the plane demanded my full attention. If our luck didn't hold, the Americans would detect us with their electronic surveillance and interception systems circling over Yugoslavia in AWACS and other electronic air scouts. I had explained their crews' motto to Nadine: "We eavesdrop on everybody but God."

I had ached to ask her questions about her relationship to my uncle. On our trip to Sofia she told me bits and pieces about the role the Corps Commander had played in her life. But the real reason for his involvement with her remained a mystery to me. What had he really been? A fatherly friend and mentor? A secret admirer with an old man's longing? A business partner? *What?*

"Are there UCK rebels around Nis?" she suddenly asked, cutting into my thoughts.

"The UCK are everywhere," I growled back.

Uncle Edouard had paid for Nadine's education in Cryptography and Information Technology at the University of Toulouse. Early in her career, she had worked on a coding system for the French nuclear aircraft carrier *Charles de Gaulle* – which was a strictly confidential Navy project. The Americans had been involved with it of course, because of the data networking within the Atlantic Alliance. Even though she had been just an unproved specialist working on this conceptual integral coding, this young and talented woman had soon designed an undecipherable system. So it was no surprise that after this all the computer ants in the world were hot after her skills – as hot as red pepper in chili.

Following my own thoughts, I spoke out to her. "So don't tell me you're one of those computer wizards making millions from your Internet stock options? Like the guys from amazon.com or e-Bay?"

"No. I'm a software engineer. A more honorable profession than those Internet nerds," she answered, slightly snubbed.

"And you took the first job the Americans offered? Just like that?"

"Of course. Christ! I was 23 years old, barely out of my diapers. They treated me like a princess when I flew out to Los Alamos. Money was no object." She gave me a sneering laugh and shook her head. "That's what impresses a country girl. Look there! That must be Nis!"

She pointed to something ahead. I remembered what Uncle Edouard had said about a vast network of highly qualified informants. I could practically still hear the old master of espionage's lecture: We *had them infiltrate the French armament factories and electronics companies where they would collect technical data for us. We financed scholarships so we could train young IT and computer scientists who would later rise to high positions in the up-and-coming computer industry. And more recently we've been investing in digital cryptography – a brand new science of electronic coding and decoding. All of this has cost us a lot of money, which we've been taking from a secret fund.*

Nadine fit into this picture like thread through a nee-

dle. So, my uncle had been a kind of *control*, as the British re-
ferred to people who put spies into action and monitored them.
The old rascal had actually *bred* spies! And I suppose one example of his clandestine training operations was sitting next to
me right now – in the form of a beautiful computer whiz with
the bust measurements of a pugnacious Marianne who seemed
to have crossed my path coming straight from the barricades of
the French Revolution. *Watch it Polinsky*, I mumbled to myself. *Such busts often lead straight to the scaffold!*

34.

A long railroad bridge stretched across the Nisava in the valley beneath us. There the river widened before losing itself in the shadows of a rocky bend.

Nadine snuck a look at this Polinsky guy. *I wonder what he looks like naked? Terribly hairy like an ape, or with disgustingly pink soft skin? Who cares about fantasizing about a naked pilot anyway? He definitely seems to be well trained. He's got the thighs of a downhill skier, with those muscles tight under his jeans, and an impressive bulge down there. I wonder if he likes my looks? Is he the one who will be committed to me, the one I can trust? He is, isn't he? I mean, he's flying over a war zone for me. Who else would do such a thing? Or does he have his own reasons for doing it, which he's keeping to himself? Maybe he just wants to fuck me? Or just wants to play around? But I guess he wouldn't have to fly into a raging war zone in this bouncing soapbox just to get me into bed – after all, it's not like I project the image of a nun with a dried up date between her legs...*

Very spontaneously Nadine's thoughts went back to Los Alamos and to Larry Johnson, her friend whom she had also slept with – until the day she learned that he also liked men. That had doused the fire in her loins as thoroughly as if someone had dumped a bucketful of ice water in her lap. That queen!

For months afterwards her emotional life had seemed blocked. All her erotic feelings connected with his warmth and security suddenly disappeared. And all desire for physical contact went away as well. For the first time in her adult life she had experienced herself as a sexless creature. And it had lasted until her cryptographic breakthrough when she rediscovered the joy of self-satisfaction. She knew it was a sort of substitute sex. *Well*, she smiled to herself, *actually the substitute isn't that bad after all.*

Nadine suddenly asked me, "Did you always want to be a pilot, when you were a boy?"

Fixating on the compass, I answered hesitatingly. "No, anything but. A fisherman, a fireman, a baseball player. I grew up in Chicago. Everything my father did I wanted to do too."

"Was he with the CIA? Or did he work for the FBI?"

"Good God no! He was in the Navy for 30 years. After his retirement he bought a 40-foot yacht. He literally lived out on Lake Michigan."

"With your mother?"

"No. She died… of cancer. I came to Switzerland with her at that time. I guess she hoped…"

I turned to look into her searching eyes, and suddenly saw that we had company: a jet fighter close to our wing. Nadine followed my gaze and screamed. The black nose of the jet pushed closer in our view. It dipped its wing as if it wanted to tilt us into the abyss, as if we were nothing but a toy. It got closer, moving precisely inch by inch.

In spite of the cold temperature in our cabin, Nadine's sweat-absorbing miracle of a designer polo shirt clung to her soaking breasts like wet white veil. Her fingernails dug into my arm as the pilot started throwing bits of disjointed flier slang to me over the radio.

"He's trying to make friends with us!" I snarled subdued.

The American pilot was so close to us we could see his icy calculating eyes examining us. Was it mockery or simply the arrogance of superiority in his look?

Would the 1991 incident in the Persian Gulf repeat itself here with us? When the crew of the destroyer *Vincennes*, their nerves strained to the limit, had shot down a civilian Iranian passenger plane because it hadn't received unambiguous identification? My mind boggled at the thought that perhaps the NATO command center had heard of our little arms transport and had simply given the fighter pilot orders to shoot us down. Who in the world would care if an unidentified plane (that would be the official wording) somewhere in the remote corner of southeast Serbia failed to comply with a request to land immediately (as the explanation would continue) and somehow crashed somewhere in the desolate mountain range between the Bulgarian border and Kosovo?

But if that were the case, what was the pilot waiting for? I answered him calmly, very professionally, just as the Army had taught me, pointing to the tail of my plane repeatedly, and then transmitted an international abbreviation using the aviation alphabet – while Nadine, in mortal terror, stared at me with eyes as round as saucers. Later, she told me that it sounded as if I had never sown my wild oats anywhere but in air combat in the stratosphere... My determined gestures, so incomprehensible to her, finally yielded the desired result. Suddenly the F-15 veered off, and we saw its sooty black tail disappear into the ghastly red darkening sky.

Nadine exhaled audibly, looking over at me with a mix of admiration and doubt. I just shrugged my shoulders and smiled broadly as I reached down with my right hand to lower the landing gear of our small but powerful Bonanza. Inside I was shuddering. Needless to say, our course and destination were now known. And in a few minutes all of NATO would be well informed about our landing next to the tobacco warehouse in Nis.

We still had the most dangerous part of our operation ahead of us, so I kept quiet and concentrated. Nadine returned to fumbling around with her polo shirt to get some air, and when I pointed to the spot on the ground where I wanted to land she just nodded obligingly. But in fact I don't think she could see anything other than that the valley had widened.

We flew over the city with its blurry silhouettes of high-rise buildings sticking up into the murky haze like rotting stumps. I lowered the plane evenly, and then banked for a landing approach from the north. We could barely discern the city's buildings, its main thoroughfares, or its river in the twilight. It was impossible to make out the railroad station through the dense smog. But we could see the black river foaming against the remains of a bridge, destroyed only days ago, before it too disappeared in the black smog. The sky above glowed in seemingly poisonous colors, as if Nis were already in flames.

Nadine suddenly spoke into the quasi-apocalyptic twilight: "So, what happened back there... it wasn't a coincidence, was it?"

"You mean our friend in the jet fighter?" I asked in mock surprise.

She nodded several times. "You'd better face some facts Polinsky. Apparently, your uncle was in possession of information on the recent sale of some anti-ship rockets.

That's what *you* told me. These are third-generation guided missiles – intelligent, reliable, and also cheap weaponry that somebody wants to grab."

"You could hardly call them cheap." I argued.

"Of course you can. Something that smart, that can sink an aircraft carrier worth billions, out there on the market for less than $100,000? Don't you see the connection? Don't you realize that the mere mention of the names *Exocet* and *Sunburn* makes the guys in the U.S. Navy go into a blue funk?"

"Come on Nadine! The U.S. Navy wasn't exactly born yesterday. Guided missiles have always been a threat to their carrier fleet. The Americans call their defense shield *Aegis*, which I'm sure you know. It's one of the best defense systems ever created. No *Exocet* or *Sunburn* can penetrate it," I said, pushing the plane lower still.

I looked down again, but there wasn't much of a landing strip to see. Nadine had imagined the airfield of the tobacco company to have a nice long concrete runway, but what she saw now was just at brownish rectangle that looked to her from a distance to be much too short to land on safely. But it was really too late to worry about that. We lost altitude rapidly.

The whole area looked bleak and deserted. A gentle hill covered in small trees stretched beyond the corrugated iron roofs. Down near the olive grove by the side of the main road was an old collapsed shack with a shimmering caved in roof, which I didn't really pay attention to.

The plane's engine buzzed vigorously as I opened the throttle, correcting my course slightly. Only two days ago the bright Frenchwoman by my side didn't even know that the name Nis stood for a dreary city instead of a cute sapling.

She stretched her shoulders back, and her hard nipples strained against the wet polo shirt, almost as if they would break through it. When the plane's landing gear hit the ground and we jolted over the landing strip, she stamped her feet on the cabin floor.

"Well, that's that," I said, relieved.

"Look out for those people!" she said. I hit the breaks and then let the plane taxi slowly to a halt.

About 500 feet away from the collapsed shack on the main road was a warehouse that looked to be in much better shape. Its gate opened, and from a black gaping hole emerged the light brown hood of an old truck, slowly jerking forward until it came to a stop next to an old fashioned giant-sized green harvesting machine.

Nadine waited until the plane stopped and then opened the door and climbed out on the wing. Through the fading propeller racket she yelled back to me, "What did you say to that American up there?"

"Transport for the Red Cross," I shouted back, shrugging my shoulders in explanation.

Her mouth gaped open as she looked back at the tail and saw the Swiss national emblem shining on the rudder like a protective shield. She knew that the Americans had trouble distinguishing the Swiss Cross from the Red Cross. Hell, a white cross on a red background or a red cross on a white background – to some guy born in the depths of the Midwest at the control stick of a super jet, it probably all looked the same. I drank in the radiating look of admiration from her eyes, gleaming golden in the pale light, as the first sign of... *what?*

Pull yourself together Polinsky! There's more at stake here than an amorous adventure with a hot young French girl. Here…

35.

"That's the woman, over there!" the guy with the moustache shouted from his hideout in the collapsed shack next to the main road. Slightly disgusted by the dirty overcoat he wore to disguise him as a sharecropper, the CIA agent twirled his bushy moustache, which had earned him the nickname Walrus. "Scotty, if that's a Red Cross plane, I'm a paramedic."

His partner bent down and peered through a crack in the wall out to the airfield. He saw three gaunt men get out of the old truck and walk over to the plane.

"Who tipped us off this time?" Scotty asked, as he watched one of the men help the Frenchwoman jump down from the wing.

The question surprised Walrus. *What should he answer?* Then he remembered the briefing, and said, "Moran did it herself. The arrogant bitch thinks she's smarter than anyone else is. But the smart little cunt didn't figure that we might monitor her cell phone. Ha! She called a friend in Switzerland from Los Alamos. The rest was easy."

The nametag on the windbreaker of the man who had so gallantly extended his hand to Nadine read *Vuk*. She smiled at him, but Vuk was stone-faced. In the crook of his arm was an automatic rifle, magazine loaded. I was sort of interested in the Serbs' weapons, so I snuck up a little closer to them, hidden by the big John Deere harvester.

The ambush team in the dilapidated shack down by the road waited.

"Damn, she's pretty," said Scotty, whistling softly through his teeth. "Too bad she's not working for us."

"Skirts like her are unpredictable. And since she's French I'm sure she's a sex maniac as well. Our little Viper there is one slick, egomaniacal, power hungry chick," Walrus mumbled as he stared through his binoculars. "First she fucks your balls off, then she bites off your prick." *I've got to separate her from that pilot, and then arrest her and get her to the rendezvous.*

"Sounds like you've got a hard on for her already, just looking at her," Scotty sneered.

"Is that a fact? Don't forget, she shot an FBI woman in cold blood."

"*Her?*"

A distinct image from his memory hit Jim *Walrus* Watt. *Shit! That woman! Her flashlight! Why did she have to show up there that night – and then try to keep me from leaving? It was her or me.* He heard in memory the light barking of his silenced automatic. Soft, like a bursting pea! *Ha! Fucking workplace accident!*

"Yes, *her*," he nodded in reply.

I noticed a woman step out of the shade of the large warehouse and walk with a surging stride towards the truck, a short weapon under her arm. My guess was that it was a Heckler-Koch machinegun. And without much guessing I could imagine a luscious body suggested by the various curves under her combat shirt and cargo pants. The men respectfully stepped aside as she arrived. And the speed of all their movements increased as she threw her long black hair behind her and started barking orders at them.

No one had any idea that the CIA team was lying in wait in the dilapidated shack, ready and fully equipped as usual when it is time to move in for the kill. They were generally not accustomed to leaving anything to chance. Walrus rested his back against a wooden beam, keeping an eye on the warehouse and its wide front door. The time to attack had come. He would give the order any minute now. Timing, as usual, was the crucial factor. *Nadine Moran had to be kept in one piece so I can take her back. Might have to retire that pilot.*

"That plane was right on time, like a Swiss watch. Those Air Force guys hit it exactly," Scotty murmured, spitting on the damp ground. All of his attention was focused on his transmitter, which he held right against his face. The short antenna put him straight in touch with Washington. "Central Command, Magna Six here," he said into the transmitter.

"Magna Six from Central Command. We read you loud and clear."

"Call Director Taylor. I'll wait."

In the dim light of his lamp, Scotty examined the spider webs hanging all over the shack. The aerial war had dragged on much longer than they had expected, and the Pentagon feared they might run out of viable targets. That's why the CIA was here: to identify any remaining objectives.

Nadine had no idea that 1,000 feet away this team of agents was watching her. She gracefully jumped over two large boxes to talk to the fierce Serb. Vuk had insisted on examining the weapons we had brought. My eyes rested pensively on my hot-blooded flying companion. Nadine stood in front of the truck, raising her arms in question, seemingly helpless. She fit into this picture about as seamlessly as a nun in a nudist camp did. With her delicate frame and shining eyeglasses, she reminded me of a friend of mine from school who now studied the mating behavior of fruit flies at the Zoological Institute in Zurich. Well, if this Frenchwoman were involved, even *I* wouldn't mind having my mating behavior put to the test.

The large front wheel of the harvester was about a foot taller than me. A small ladder led to the elevated driver's cab that stuck on the front of this monster like a gunner's station. I climbed up and opened the door, sliding into the driver's seat, and from my new position commanded an excellent view. I figured they used this thing to harvest tobacco leaves. A large lever, now set in neutral, could be set for either mowing or threshing.

The Serbs hauled the boxes from the plane and loaded them into their truck. The delivery had been organized by Magadino SA and, with the help of Colossimo's men, had been delivered to Sofia as a reward for their good work in protecting Nadine Moran. It was a deal in which the efforts of the pilot, who now sat humbly in the background in the driver's seat of the thresher, were hardly worth mentioning.

36.

Standing among the beams of the collapsed roof of the shack, Walrus twirled his moustache. Other than Scotty, his team consisted of another six men. Four of them were lying disguised in the tobacco field, about 160 yards away, near the country road that led to the warehouse. Their telescopic sights were aimed at the men in front of the truck. "Delta standing by?" Walrus asked them over the radio.

"Standing by. Ready to go," came back the answer, fast and clear.

Walrus had another two men hidden in the olive grove, with clear shots at the Serbs' backs. The classic trap was set – the perfect ambush.

This time my pretty Viper won't slip through my fingers. Her eyes will pop out when she recognizes me. Should I greet her with an "Olé"? Or be hard on her so she'll scream, "Take your sticky fingers off me Watt!"

He watched the Serbs carefully – and through mere coincidence they seemed to move around to more strategically advantageous positions. These guys were battle-hardened soldiers, and they were very alert! And then there was that wild sexy looking Serbian woman with the gun under her arm; she aroused Watt, as did all women with guns and uniforms. Nadine... the Serb... all these unapproachable women called up his basic male instinct to make them submit.

Scotty had just sent his target data to Washington, automatically encrypted, via satellite. At the Central Command there the intelligence officer interpolated the data to an exact position on a map, which was then passed on to the operation leader.

"Central Command to Magna Six. Taylor speaking. Report on status!"

Not taking his eyes off the Serbs, Walrus answered: "Everything according to plan, sir!"

"Hurry up. The aerial attack will commence in approximately ten minutes," Taylor informed him.

Just at this moment the target data reached Italy. At the NATO operations center in Vincenza, the tobacco warehouse at Nis began to flash, indicating high attack priority. With an experienced eye, the young captain whose family had emigrated to the U.S. from Sicily scanned the positions of aircraft over the Adriatic, an activity he was very familiar with. "Does anybody have any idea what's in Nis?" he called out to his flight operations officer.

"Nis? Just tobacco, sir. But the target data indicates a camouflaged arsenal there now."

As they spoke a squadron of F-18s was approaching the Croatian coast from the northeast at a height of 19,000 feet. These lethal masterpieces of war could, at the flick of a cockpit switch, transform themselves from fighters into fighter-bombers, each one carrying several one-ton computer controlled bombs beneath its wings. The jets had lifted off the deck of the *Roosevelt* just minutes ago that now waited in a holding pattern on the Ionian Sea, cruising at 30 knots.

The operations leader had established clear communications with the squadron leader, and nodded satisfied when the encoded attack objective safely reached the pilots of the fighter-bombers a few seconds later.

I cast a troubled gaze up into the clearing skies and then over to the olive grove, dense and impenetrable. Even though these Serbs were well-trained fighters, there would be little they could do against a surprise attack by a squad of trigger happy UCK rebels if they came down the hill. Since they had not wanted to arouse any suspicions of their military presence in the economically crucial warehouse region, the Serbs had not brought any heavy weapons with them. The last thing they would want to do would be to provoke any kind of attack on the warehouses; it would be worse than the destruction of barracks or bridges. Cigarettes were much in demand during wartime. And crude tobacco could be exchanged for more strategic items that they desperately needed.

"Come on! Hurry up! If there are any bombers around here we've had it," shouted the Serbian woman with the beautiful flowing hair, underscoring her words with a motion of her gun. Vuk, who had experience in similar operations, looked up into the sky and nodded assent.

"Fifty micro detonators with electronic igniters, two dozen GPS receivers, 20 transmitters," one of the Serbs reeled off.

In the shack Scotty heard the inventory being counted via the directional microphones he had secretly hidden in a pile of rotted tobacco leaves.

"They're trafficking weapons! This is going to be a good catch!"

37.

In the darkened warehouse, Nadine rubbed her eyes and then put her glasses back on. She saw long rows of trestles that ran throughout the building. Tobacco bushels were hanging from taut horizontal wires like giant sleeping bats. In the middle of the passage stood a small table blackened by dust. Nadine was just about to put her bag on it when spotlights blinded her eyes. She covered her eyes with her hand as she heard a car engine outside revving up.

"You have what we brought you. What are you waiting for?" she yelled into the lights. "Bring me to the meeting point, now!"

Someone grabbed her from behind and pushed her towards a door through which she had heard the car. It was a tall, older Serb.

"I am Zvonko. We take back door. I bring you to train. You take twenty past eight train to Belgrade. Here is ticket. You stay at Hotel Metropol."

"A hotel? Isn't that a bit conspicuous?"

"Don't know more. Ranko knows," the old Serb replied, disgruntled.

"And how do I recognize Ranko?" Nadine nagged, opening the door and getting into the car. The gray seats were torn, the ashtray filled with butts, the floor mats caked with dirt.

Zvonko ignored her and lit a cigarette, inhaling deeply, starting the car, which stuttered stiffly and then caught with a jerk.

"Here, take this!" Zvonko said, offering her a piece of dried meat.

"Thanks, but no thanks,"

"Young foal. Hard to get nowadays."

"Still, I don't eat meat." She shrugged her shoulders in apology.

"We can't afford not to eat meat," the old Serb growled, taking a hearty bite. Nadine shuffled her feet over the dirty rug impatiently.

Finally, Zvonko wiped his mouth with the back of his hand and put the car in gear. The ancient Toyota slowly passed the narrow opening into a backyard and then carefully maneuvered around a rusty picking machine, and then stopped. Zvonko studied the furrowed bumpy road that disappeared among gnarled tree trunks – and they suddenly heard the barking of gunfire.

Nadine screamed. "What was that?"

Zvonko's reply was to push the accelerator to the floor. The car hesitated for a second or two and then burst forward.

38.

I was just getting ready to swing myself down from the cab of
the harvester when I saw muzzle fire from the tobacco field.
Ducking instinctively, I suddenly found myself worrying about
Nadine. *She was probably helpless, standing right in the line of
fire. Oh, forget it!* I angrily stopped thinking about her. I had
to take care of myself. *But what was I to do? Damn, what the
hell was happening here? Are we under attack? Well, then, let's
move, Polinsky!*

When he heard the gunfire in his dilapidated shack,
Walrus first thought that the Serbs had started shooting at his
men. But then, seconds later, he saw two black pickup trucks
flying down the road towards him like bloodthirsty insects.
Dense clouds of dust whirled up around them.

Shit! Those idiots are attacking the wrong guys!

He didn't need a textbook on strategy to know that
these people had the element of surprise on their side. And he
could see that they operated fast and accurately, and that their
anonymity was terrifying. Whoever the hell they were, they
obviously made no bones about shooting down anyone they
encountered – which was something Walrus wouldn't have
minded if it hadn't included Nadine Moran.

Scowling, the CIA agent realized that now he had a real
problem. And whose fault was it? *His own!* He was a professional. Why hadn't he spent more time analyzing the intelligence? Why hadn't anybody informed him of the presence of
UCK rebels in this god-forsaken hole? Why hadn't he taken

the time to ask these questions himself? Cursing his fate that he of all people could have committed this basic but so often crucial strategic sin, Walrus pulled out his transmitter.

The rebels had caught me too, as the saying goes, with my pants down. I didn't really understand what was going on fully until I had started the harvester and lifted my eyes from the dashboard. Suddenly I realized that the most important thing I had to do was protect my plane. *I had to obstruct the line of fire from the gunmen in the tobacco field, or they would blow my plane to bits!*

The good old John Deere vigorously jerked forward over the landing strip, roared, and gained speed rapidly, almost on its own. The rebels' pickup truck in front of me swerved out of my way quickly. But then its shot out tires shredded, whirling through the air.

I started shifting levers, when suddenly a gigantic stream of threshed crop – whatever it was, tobacco, weeds – shot up into the air in a wide arc. I guessed this thing had been reconstructed for tobacco harvesting, but what did I know? But I found a lever that controlled the direction of the crop stream and pointed it in the direction of the shooters, who suddenly started firing at me! A bullet hit the windshield and came through, bouncing off the metal behind me and whizzing past my right temple so close I thought I felt its draft. A surge of adrenaline went through my body, making me feel as agile as a kid. Ducking and peering through what was left of the windshield, I steered the machine up the low bumpy slope, and suddenly found myself harvesting tobacco!

The lever was set on mowing, and the machine effortlessly ate through the lush leaves, powerfully tossing the mowed and chopped stuff through the bent pipe back onto the field. Using the directional lever I hailed tons of botanical buckshot down on the startled gunmen, who instinctively recognized a greater force and took off helter-skelter. *What a great feeling! Watching these grown up hardened soldiers fall victim to the same childish panic that we all remember from the sandbox!*

To the left of the warehouse, Walrus' Delta team suddenly appeared and, taking cover behind a heap of trash, started picking off rebels quite precisely. The old truck filled with Serbs hobbled off cross-country and out of danger. Through its black exhaust I could see muzzle fire from over the rear ramp.

Scotty, in the dilapidated shack, had already buckled on his backpack. He stood in utter disbelief, watching the runaway harvester, which looked like an angry vegetable-spitting bear, chasing down his elite soldiers.

As he watched it disperse his men, he relived the countless combat drills of his specialized training. But no matter how deep he dug he couldn't find one single rule for combat against an attacking harvester. *They should supplement the Tactical Manual with a chapter about How to Fight Subversion by Farm Machinery!*

The shooting had stopped. Satisfied with my victory I hobbled the harvester back over towards the warehouse.

"Where's the Viper?" Walrus yelled from inside the shack.

"Over there. Inside the warehouse."

"Go get her!"

I saw the Serbian woman waving at me on this joke of

an airfield as I eased the John Deere close to my *Bonanza*, which fortunately was not even scratched.

"Polinsky! Wait! Stop!" she yelled.

"What's wrong?" I leapt out of the driver's cab onto the hard airstrip and found myself looking straight into the muzzle of her gun. Above it her eyes glistened in her pale and fiercely determined face. Then she pointed to the plane, undoubtedly prepared to riddle me with bullets if things didn't go her way.

"My father! He is wounded. Come on Polinsky! You've got to fly us out of here!"

I swung myself up onto the wing and helped her get the moaning Serb into the back of the cabin.

"Well, come on!" I yelled as I settled myself in the pilot's seat and started the engine. As soon as the lovely Serbian woman with her not so lovely gun dropped into the seat next to me, I accelerated.

The *Bonanza* leapt forward. Behind us, the other rebel pickup truck exploded into flames.

Twenty seconds later, we were airborne and stabilized. I had exchanged one pale wildcat for an even paler wilder cat! Whatever caused my excitement – the churning adrenaline from all the shooting down there, the vibrations of the harvester, the sweet overpowering pungent smell of tobacco, or the strong sweaty odor of the Serbian woman sitting next to me, or a mixture of all of these things – I suddenly felt a shifting and a throbbing inside my pants. From time immemorial, we human beings have been equipped with a fight or flight reflex. Maybe it was this new, far more refined variation – fight and escape – that was turning me on.

39.

"To Belgrade, Polinsky," the lovely Serbian woman commanded in her charmingly accented English. As if by chance she pointed the muzzle of her gun at the bulge in my crotch.

I gulped dryly. "To Belgrade. Okay."

She reached back to her father and took a note from his pocket, handing it to me.

"A message from our people. The Frenchwoman is in danger."

Nadine? I looked at her surprised, and put away the note. Who were her people? But I had no time to think about it. Trying to climb evenly in a bumpy headwind and navigate at the same time was taking all my attention. *Later... I'll take care of this later!*

Zvonko stopped the Toyota shortly after pulling away from the warehouse and looked back.

"Stopping is the stupidest thing you can do Zvonko!" Nadine yelled at him. She felt very jittery, with an uncomfortable feeling creeping up her neck. She stared at Zvonko impatiently, but he merely pointed to the olive grove ahead.

"That is a safe way," he growled, suddenly accelerating. With its headlights off, the old Toyota skidded off towards the trees faster than it should have. As it bounced, the chassis bottomed out.

Nadine grabbed the handle above the window and shouted, "Drive slower, will you!"

Zvonko shook his head. Whatever he did, she didn't

like it. But she had delivered the merchandise, so his people would protect her to the bitter end.

Then a crashing noise seemed to slam the Toyota into the ground like a terrible fist. A glaring bright flash of fire filled the sky. Nadine screamed again, louder and more piercing than before. Zvonko hit the brakes hard, but the shock wave just lifted the small car and threw it sideways against the gnarled trunk of an olive tree. Then the hood crashed into a pile of dirt. It slid backwards and lodged against some roots. The engine stalled, and the car was as immovable as a stubborn goat.

Nadine felt along her body, checking for broken bones. Dumbfounded, she stared at the spot where, only seconds ago, the warehouse has stood. In its place was nothing but a raging stinking inferno. Zvonko stared aghast at the blaze and suddenly let out a gargling torrent of incomprehensible curses.

"The truck! Where's the truck?" Nadine's shrill voice cut through the raging ruckus. Zvonko managed to get the engine running again and turn the car in the right direction. He accelerated just in time, as the unbearable heat from the warehouse began to ignite the trees around them, turning them into blazing torches.

"We out of here now," Zvonko shouted.

"But where's the truck?" Nadine yelled back.

"Safe. They don't get truck," Zvonko said, pointing angrily back to the flaming warehouse.

"I am so sorry," Nadine gasped, when they finally reached the main road and drove away to safety. Looking up into the flaming sky, she suddenly saw the tail of a plane almost like a mirage – the white Swiss cross on a field of red. *Polinsky's plane!* She sighed in relief as she watched the Bonanza with its inverted symbol of the Red Cross on its tail shaking in the sky but managing to climb safely among the wisps of smoke, slowly disappearing into a tiny spot in the distance. Good! At least Polinsky's safe. She caught herself worrying about the strange pilot. What's wrong with you? You need this guy like a… a… She couldn't seem to come up with a metaphor. Then all of a sudden, a sudden rush of passion spread through her body, and she opened her legs almost as if she were in a peaceful place with the man of her dreams. But in the next second she came back to earth, where reality was anything but peaceful.

Everything down here had been destroyed. She felt responsible for the bombing of the tobacco warehouse. The precision attack had probably set back the entire Nis region and any chance it had for economic development for decades.

"We dream of free democratic country, part of Europe," Zvonko railed on with a course voice as he drove away from the chaos. "Since the bombs started, my family move from air-raid shelter to air-raid shelter. Factory where I worked for years, now a wreck. We build vehicles there, not weapons like NATO say… And now the tobacco… all destroyed. I don't think Americans like us a lot." He swerved the car around the potholes angrily until they finally reached the main road.

Back at the dilapidated shack, Scotty gave his partner with the moustache a hearty pat on the back with his huge hand. "Wow! Bull's eye, Walrus! Good job, boys!" He screamed at the sky as the flames from the former warehouse turned night into day.

As far as the CIA in Langley was concerned Nadine Moran was a traitor. And traitors were hunted down mercilessly. But they also wanted to know what she was up to, and where she was going. They knew she was headed for a secret meeting in Belgrade, but with whom? Bin Golem? The Chinese? The fact that the meeting was set up at the Sudanese Embassy didn't discount either possibility.

Six of the finest hand picked agents had been dropped into Yugoslavia during a nighttime mission. No one could convince Director Taylor that a major terrorist organization wasn't involved in this set up. One woman working alone? Never! FBI psychologists and profilers in Quantico had come to the same conclusion. And that was why a squad of the best agents with state-of-the-art equipment had been waiting for her. And to top it all off, the team had heard that she had killed a FBI agent in Los Alamos. Mercy would hardly be on the agenda. Of course, none of these top-level agents had expected the attack by the UCK rebels. The local intelligence situation needed improvement, to say the least.

Operation Magna had been entrusted to the most experienced agents in the Counter-terrorism unit of the CIA. But old foxes like Walrus and Scotty knew that all such missions were risky and difficult if not impossible to control. Of course if anything went wrong heads would roll – Director Taylor's being the first. And that was why the CIA Chief had gone over every tiny detail of the operation as it approached.

Scotty remembered the conversation that finally dealt with the question of whether the Frenchwoman should be *retired*, as the Agency jargon so nicely put it.

"Well, if the Viper makes contact with one of the enemies at the Embassy building, then we'll intervene. We won't have any other choice."

"But it's an Embassy sir. We'll need some excuse."

"Why not war, gentlemen! Sounds like the ideal excuse to me!"

"Washington won't consent to that sir."

"Well, of course not. We have to find the right description for the target, you know, for the Embassy. Come up with something convincing. After all, the Sudan is one of the Islamic terrorist countries supplying the Serbs with weapons. Aren't they also supplying them with chemical weapons? Hell, that's not only an excuse, gentlemen. That's a valid *reason*."

By the time the Nis fire department reached the tobacco warehouses, they had burned down to the foundation walls. A stinking red smoke spiraled its way into the night sky.

None of the UCK rebels had survived. Like the CIA team that killed them, the fighters for independence had not scouted their attack site sufficiently. Contrary to their usual experience, they too had been taken unsuspectingly, and had walked right into the arms, or rather the telescopic gun sights, of the CIA.

40.

The crewmembers of the *Shiraz* knew the waters of the Gulf of Guinea quite well. Most of them had passed through them many times aboard tankers transporting crude oil from Iranian ports to Europe. What connected them all, though never spoken about, were the strict selection procedures they had all been put through. This meant a full testing of not only their nautical abilities but also of their political reliability. All who were allowed aboard the *Shiraz* were proven to be faithful Muslims who had sworn unconditional allegiance to their leader bin Golem. This meant not only that they had identified with his personal Fatwah and the Jihad against the Americans, but that they were also prepared to give their lives in defense of them.

However, a ship the size and complexity of the *Shiraz* could not manage entirely without disbelievers, such as technicians, engineers, electronics specialists, and communications experts who in general were not interested in having anyone tell them who or what to believe in. Brabeck, the Chief Engineer, was one such expert who did his job without complaint; but he was also a person who had been educated in London and Zurich and did not particularly care for ideologies.

After all, a 600,000-ton ship was not moved through the oceans by Allah's hand alone. It required steam turbines, control units, navigation technology, and hard-working men who knew how to operate all of the high-tech equipment.

Brabeck was in a constant bad mood ever since he had been forced to move into substantially smaller and less comfortable quarters because of the mufti who had come aboard.

In addition to this, he felt more homesick the further he moved west from his native Bahrain. And despite the plausible reassurances that the captain had given him, Brabeck also felt somehow that the journey they were on was a dark one. On some level, he didn't take bin Golem's Fatwahs seriously: he thought they were just pipe dreams. But he was very careful not to say that out loud and avoided any kind of political discussion. But despite his overall cautiousness, something today was eating at him from the inside. The humiliations that Khalid had exposed him to had started to make his usually calm blood boil. He began to really hate that man.

The echo sounder below keel used ultrasonic sounding and imaging techniques to deliver a very clear color image of the sea floor and its varying topography to the cabin above. Two sonar units had been built into the bow, which searched the dark sea in a circumference of nearly 10 miles for any underwater obstacles to their smooth progress.

High above the bridge, the radar dish revolved incessantly, detecting coastlines, islands, mountains, ships, and buoys – and then transferring this data to the large screens inside. Because of her enormous size and inertial mass, the *Shiraz* needed at least a half-hour's warning to avoid hitting something in her path. To drop from full speed to almost a standstill she needed a safety distance of about 3-4 miles.

A sort of relaxed silence hung over the bridge. The captain stood in front of the radio compass from which the ship was navigated. The navigator monitored the charts on which he marked the ship's position. Because of the ship's massive size, most communications took place over the intercom. Between the bow mast and the bridge of the *Shiraz*, there was enough space for two international competition-sized soccer fields.

Bin Golem watched the instrument positioned on an angle, over which the Captain's hand wandered and moved on. "Here you can see where we are right now. All objects that are visible on radar can be seen here. This is our present position. And this line here represents our projected course via Casablanca to Gibraltar. In addition to this we also have an electronic chart display on the screen that is controlled by GPS."

In spite of all this high-tech navigational equipment, Captain Souri still swore by the old naval academy ways. Hidden away on the bridge were many old-fashioned navigational instruments, relics from seafaring days just a few decades ago. He proudly produced a British-model sextant from a mahogany case and showed it to bin Golem.

"Cadets at the Academy are still taught how to use them," he explained to the Arab. "But soon I think they will have forgotten. You have to use a sextant once in a while and practice the calculations if it's to be any use to you."

Nodding as if interested, bin Golem turned to the First Officer.

"And you, do you like your job?"

"Oh yes sir, of course. In my mind, you feel very free in the middle of the ocean. Here, you are your own boss. I have, now, 25 men working under my command, ten more than usual." Smiling, he added, "Only the captain is above me."

"And have you taken care to see that the missiles have been stored securely?"

"Not to worry, sir. Our storage for them is state of the art. Stabilizers reduce the effect of the ship's rolling. This keeps them from swaying no matter how rough the seas are."

One screen stared at by bin Golem indicated the ship number, the international call number DXEX, as well as the depth of water beneath them. The Arab leant forward and read the present draft: almost 100 feet.

On the GPS display, he saw the electronic signature of the *Shiraz* passing south of Abidjan. *Cape Three Points* and the off shore platforms of the crude oil terminal *Espoir* showed up distinctly.

The captain toggled the display, which now showed their position in latitude and longitude next to the time that had elapsed since the ship had left Lagos. A third setting supplied weather conditions, present sea depth, and the distance to the next port – which right now showed them to be 138 miles from the deep sea port of San Pedro, east of the Sassandra-mouth, a trading port for coffee and timber.

Below on Deck A, Thierry-Clément Moran stared at a radar screen that had nothing to do with the navigation system but rather served for target detection and fire control.

Moran kept himself in shape by working out every day and by eating a healthy diet. The two young Iranians with him would not have guessed that the former fighter pilot was in his late 50s. His wiry build and taut facial features made the Frenchman look dynamic and tough. But in the greenish hue of the instruments, the years were starting to show on his anxious face.

His thoughts were on Nadine. There was a picture of

her, age three, taped onto the frame of the screen in front of him. It really hurt him to imagine how a rogue like bin Golem would bend Nadine to his will and purposes.

The way he saw it, the success of the missile attack from the secret launching pads aboard the *Shiraz* depended on three people. First of all, on Nadine, who would be able to manipulate the *Aegis* defense system; secondly, on himself, who knew how to program the missiles; and third, on the "Admiral." In an earlier stage of his career, the would-be admiral had been a quartermaster aboard the French carrier Maréchal Foch. Yet, his double chin, his broad, bald skull and his fine gold-rimmed glasses made him look more like a retired fleet commander. However, his experience in carrier operations and naval warfare in the French Navy was essential for the success of operation *Megiddo*.

And that slimy bin Golem knows this too, Moran said to himself to ease his mind. Without the ingenious trio, the Arab top sheik may as well pack his bags and go home. *My ace in the hole, and my life insurance, still is and always will be my technical knowledge. That is something these sweaty smelling camel drivers have no idea about.*

"Airplanes above us," said Ali, the younger Iranian, trained a bit in radar screens, while the rawboned one named Baba just stood behind Moran, watching him.

"Probably American AWACS," suggested Moran.

"Satan's wing," Baba corrected severely.

Moran displayed no emotion at what he considered doctrinaire nonsense, but continued in a neutral tone, "If we had infrared spectroscopy, we'd be able to clearly identify the series, model, and armament of those planes."

"I don't think we need a very precise target identification," Ali argued.

"Maybe not," replied the Frenchman, who tried to avoid disagreements whenever possible. But this time he had some objections. "And yet, those guys up there are able to identify our missiles if we put them in launching position up on deck." And that was that.

Through the porthole of his henhouse-sized cabin, Brabeck languidly stared out at the evening sea. He was missing his usual accommodations: the spaciousness of his suite on Deck D, a nice bottle of Scotch whiskey, a few action movie tapes. Instead, his right hand held bin Golem's pamphlet that one of those Islamic fanatic idiots had given him in the mess. With a sigh, Brabeck flung himself back on his bunk and began to read the summons to the Holy War in the dim light of his ceiling lamp.

… On this basis and in accordance with God's commandment, we decree the following Fatwah to all Muslims: The commandment to kill the Americans and their allies – civilian and military – is an individual duty for every Muslim. This, he is to fulfill in any country, wherever possible, in order to move the armies of the American fiend out of the Land of Islam… so that they will not longer be able to threaten any Muslim… To follow God's order and kill the Americans and plunder their money wherever and whenever they find it…

"Shit," Brabeck cursed when he heard a knock on his door.

When he opened it he saw Khalid's frowning face. "May I look around?" he asked, but came in without waiting for an answer – rummaging around the cabin, opening drawers, looking into Brabeck's suitcase.

"What are you looking for?" the Chief Engineer growled, although he had some idea what bin Golem's bodyguard wanted to find. There were no cell phones allowed on board.

"The chef is missing a rabbit," Khalid jeered. "I thought you might have hid it in your teeth glass." And he stalked out the door.

"Camel shit," the Chief Engineer hissed after he slammed the door.

41.

The breakfast room at the Metropol on Bulevar Revolucije in downtown Belgrade left Nadine with the same desolate impression as had the old limping waiter who served her coffee.

Two young men and a woman sat at a large table in the corner. The woman had a plastic ID hanging from her neck; journalists, she suspected. As they talked they kept referring to a map they had spread out among their breakfast dishes.

Light sleepy music drifted down from the speakers in the ceiling. Nadine drank her lukewarm weak coffee. She tried to figure out what was being shown on the TV-screen in the corner; a building erupted in flames, fire fighters going in with hoses, a reporter barking gravely into the microphone.

She didn't notice Ranko enter the room, but he slid down next to her as if they were old friends. She held the pack of cigarettes out to him and raised her eyebrows questioningly.

"How was the night?" she asked.

"I'd rather not talk about it," he replied. "When I tried to get back to the railroad station, they were bombing a place they thought was one of the ministries. It was a senior citizens' home."

He fumbled for a cigarette from the pack. Nadine struck a match and lit it for him. Ranko inhaled with relish, and unfolded the newspaper he had brought with him to screen off the table next to them.

"Tonight, 11:30, we go. Here's the address." He pulled a piece of paper from the breast pocket of his checkered shirt. "Our people will see to it that no one bothers you."

"And what does that mean in plain English?" Nadine asked, low but insistently.

"Our people are watching the hotel night and day."

Nadine remembered the determined eyes of the men in the lobby, convincing her that they would handle their assignments like professionals.

"Military police will escort you to the rendezvous. We'd rather not give your friends a second chance."

"Why are you doing all this?"

Ranko shrugged his shoulders. "I have my orders. Apparently you made an agreement. We Serbs are trustworthy and reliable. And…"

"Yes?"

"Well, you French are likable people."

"Thank you."

"You will go straight through the big main entrance," Ranko continued in a very business-like tone. "Your contact will await you behind the revolving door in the hall. Then just follow the instructions that will be given to you."

The old waiter dragged his feet over to their table, but Ranko had already gotten up.

"Take care of yourself," he urged, walking away in a hurry.

"One espresso, please," Nadine ordered. The old waiter slowly shook his head. She lifted her eyebrows in question.

"Isn't the machine working?"

The waiter bent down and whispered, "For a pack of cigarettes I'll make it a strong double."

"Great!" she answered, slipping him the open pack. "I'm sorry, but I don't have any more."

"Then I'll bring you a strong single," the old man growled, putting away the cigarettes.

A bit later he returned with the small steaming cup of espresso. Nadine shrugged her shoulders and sipped the hot beverage. Better than she had expected, at least with some kick. After all, Belgrade was in *Europe*! She leaned back and scanned the place. Sipped some more coffee. *Ahhh, just what I needed.*

Then she suddenly missed him. *Where is he, that lying bastard Polinsky? If only nothing happened to him... oh, come on, weeds never die. Too bad he was such a loser. Another wild romantic on his way to men's menopause... It may well be,* Nadine cautioned herself with a sunny smile, blinking at the hotel breakfast room, *but then why do I have such a nice itch when I think of him?*

42.

I don't know my way around Belgrade very well. A cab took me straight from the airport to the Swiss Embassy where a bleary-eyed chargé d'affaires scrounged up a room for me at the Intercontinental – without asking too many questions.

At least the shower had hot water; and I stayed under it a long time. In spite of the bombs the hotel tried to do business as usual, maintaining a minimum of conveniences. The phones worked trouble-free. To my amazement my belle answered on the second ring.

"You've got fan mail from London, Berlin, Amsterdam, and Tel Aviv," Irina said, bubbling. "They're all willing to help you."

Irina had sent the picture of the third man, made by the Chief of Intelligence's hidden camera, to all police precincts by email, labeling it "Wanted for Child Murder" – which perhaps was not all that inaccurate. Irina's trick was based on the assumption that a child murderer would look politically unsuspicious, while at the same time prompt even the toughest cops to feel utter contempt.

"So?" I asked.

"Specs claims to have seen him."

"Specs Inc.? The classification company?"

"Of course. They're better than the CIA. Khalid had been located by them at the Lagos Port next to a ship."

"*Khalid?*"

"Yes. Listen."

"I assume he was not going on a cruise?"

"The tub was one of those giant supertankers. It was moored at the dock for inspection."

"Anything else?"

"Maybe."

"Come on, give it up. I miss you."

"I miss you more. Are you being faithful to me?"

"Business before pleasure," I evaded her jokingly.

She gave me a dramatic sigh. "There's an obscure anti-Islamic newsletter circulating through the Jewish community of Muscat. I found it on the Internet."

"In Oman? Tell me about it!"

"Well, in that paper of all places I found a sketch of your man."

"Are you sure?"

"Pretty sure. The woman who did it does courtroom portraits for the newspapers and TV – you know, when they don't let cameras in judges, defendants – anyway, they're usually pretty accurate. And it was just a coincidence. She made the sketch of him just for practice. But when she heard about the murder, she passed the sketch onto the editor of the newsletter. The bent nose I think gives him away."

"Good. But how does that help us?"

"Well, I sent the email picture to the paper, asking them about it. Those people are more efficient than the Mossadh. They identified the man as Khalid and looked into what he does and where he went. Now listen to this: he's headed for Morocco!"

"Was he in Zurich on the crucial date?"

Suddenly my heart started to pound.

"Don't know yet. Maybe they'll find out something else for me. They think you were riddled with bullets."

"Me? What are you nuts?"

"Well, I told them my husband was Jewish and got killed in Damascus when terrorists assassinated the U.S. Ambassador. They were so sympathetic! Your death was a great help."

Smart lady, my Irina!

"What's Khalid's real name?"

"He mostly goes by the name Khalid. Some call him the executioner. He works for this guy bin Golem."

"Excellent. Any news from the FBI?"

"No, as far as I can see the FBI is on strike. They don't want to give me anything from their private data banks. They're being quite pigheaded over there."

"I know. Well, keep going. I'll call you later."

"And are you still faithful to me?"

"Just as faithful as you are to me," I laughed back and cut off the line.

43.

As she walked out of the Hotel Metropol about a half-hour before midnight, Nadine suddenly found herself surrounded by Serbian policemen in dark uniforms. Startled, she shrunk back.

"*Ne vous inquiétez pas, Madame.* Just follow me," said a young officer who moved to Nadine's right and invited her with a polite gesture to accompany him on a walk down the Boulevard.

"You speak French very well," she complimented.

"I studied in Paris, where I worked as an interpreter during the disaster of Rambouillet. Take good care of yourself, my lovely lady."

Nadine looked around as she strolled with the police. Ranko had delivered exactly what he promised. The patrol escorted her as if she were the American Secretary of State. Of course if that had been the case they would have thrown tomatoes at her instead of fleeting glances.

"They're much stupider than I expected," Walrus said, keeping his eyes on the navigation system.

Scotty stayed quiet. The luminous digits of the clock sitting on the dashboard of the old van read 23:40. Dull explosions sounded in the distance. The car holding the two CIA agents sat in the dark between two half-shattered walls of an auto repair shop. The location was perfect. Less than 200 yards away was a modern ten-story building that rose into the luridly flashing sky like a white hulk. The lens of their night camera pointed up to the seventh floor where the Embassy was housed – and then returned to street level.

"They're strolling down Balkanska like they were out shopping. Any idiot could follow our little cunt," Walrus muttered, shaking his head.

Nadine crossed the deserted street accompanied by the police, moving towards a tiny dark park that was towered over by the short side of the white building. Again, the sound of an explosion in the distance shook the quiet of the city. Then a bomb fell closer – and for a second the explosion and fire lit up the park, showing more people in front of them. Nadine ducked back instinctively.

"*Les gens de notre sécurité*," the officer assured her. "We'll go this way."

Nadine's sneakers moved silently on the fine gravel of the walkway, in contrast to the military boots of her escorts. She remembered how the old waiter at the Metropol had gaped at them as if he would consider trading her quite a few double espressos for them.

Scotty sat in the van watching the flashing red spot sent by the directional transmitter hidden in the sole of Nadine's sneaker to the monitor, and saw it deviate from the direct line to the Embassy building. He nervously bit his lower lip.

"They're walking past the park!"

Walrus felt as if blood would start to drip from his pores. *Calm down. This time she won't get away.*

"We're screening off the entrance to the building," the young officer reassured Nadine. He put his arm around her waist with modest pressure. She took the hint, looked back repeatedly, and then took several energetic steps up the stairs to

the square with the waterless fountain. A dim lamp was burning behind the glass windows of the lobby. She pushed the revolving door and entered.

Scotty exhaled loudly and nodded to Walrus who was
nervously twirling his moustache. "Want to report to ops-cen-
ter? Viper in the nest."

Walrus Watt's restlessness summoned up the lascivious
fantasy of how he'd like to wiggle *his* viper into the nest of *this*
viper.

He snapped back at Scotty, "You do the report. Can't
you see I'm busy thinking?"

44.

The warm stuffy air in the building's lobby greeted Nadine. She hurried across to where the elevators were, and suddenly she realized someone was next to her. At first she only perceived a wiry figure, but then a scowling face was right in front of her nose. At first, frightened, she recoiled. But then she realized who it was.

"Polinsky! What the hell are *you* doing here?"

I pushed her back into a dark corner and put two fingers on her lips. Had I detected a warm tone in her voice? Or was she merely scared?

"Okay, okay," she whispered, as she searched the lobby behind us with her nervous eyes. "Are we alone?"

I frisked her. When my hands swept over the insides of her thighs, she pushed them away, slowly.

"I am not armed, Monsieur," she whispered softly to me.

"Only with the weapons of a woman," I countered. We stared at each other for three heartbeats. "Or so you say," I went on. "Here's something. Shoes off please."

The tone in my voice and the small device I scanned her with made her obey at once. "Well, what do we have here? Looks like they stuck a little transmitter in the sole of your sneaker."

In the dull light I showed her the small button-like device that was stuck in the sole of her sneaker like any pebble.

"Why? Why did they do that? Who would do such a thing to me? Oh, God... the waiter in the hotel!"

"My guess is the CIA darling. They're after your secrets. And I think they'd love to catch you in the act of turning them over."

I stuffed her sneakers and their transmitter into a plastic bag and whistled softly through my teeth. Almost from nowhere a boy stepped out of the dark, looking at me filled with expectation.

"Now listen," I began, slowly and simply. "You bring this bag to the seventh floor. The seventh floor, understand? There you will see the entrance to the Embassy, the one with the cameras. Walk past it. Go down the hallway to the narrow white door – the one with the figure of a man on it. Yes, the men's room. Go in and leave the bag in the corner, and come back here as fast as you can. Do you understand? As fast as your feet will carry you. Leave the building as soon as you get down here! Immediately, do you hear? Your friend is waiting in the park for you."

The boy nodded with sparking eyes. I had slipped him two $20 bills. That was a fortune in Belgrade! Like Speedy Gonzalez he disappeared with the bag.

"So who were you supposed to meet here?" I asked Nadine.

"The people who will lead me to my father. I have to get there. You cannot stop me!" She turned away from me and began to rush towards the elevators. I grabbed her arm hard. "Let me go, I…" she hissed, trying hard to wrestle her willowy arm from my grip. *In her voice wasn't there a hint of intimacy?*

I pulled her back. "If you want to get out of here alive, you'd better come with me now!" The look on my face must have been convincing. She obeyed, grudgingly.

219

I pushed her to the back of the lobby and opened the door to the stairs. I grabbed the banister and jumped down them, Nadine hard on my heels. We raced down a dark corridor that ended in an even darker corner.

"And what *now*?" she gasped.

"A couple of really bad people are after you. More, I don't know."

I switched on my little flashlight and found the door handle, which took a bit of convincing. Then I forced open the thin metal door with my shoulder.

Outside in the van, Scotty kept up his report, speaking to Walrus who typed it into his laptop.

"Viper had reached the seventh floor. Operation proceeding as planned. She is approaching the door. Now she's stopped. Not moving anymore. In any case, she is inside. Clearly she has made contact."

Walrus hesitated for a second. He wanted, no, he *had* to check her exact position. "Why isn't she moving? Is she sitting down?"

"Keep going!" Scotty said.

"Objective clearly and positively identified," Walrus typed. And suddenly he felt a warm rush of relief in his chest. Their wonderful little substitute plan had materialized. *Our little cunt is walking into the trap like a good little mouse!* His transmitter beeped, confirming the successful receipt of the report.

The operations room of CENTCOM now registered the white building in downtown Belgrade as a central office for the procurement of arms, based on the report of the field agents. As a consequence, it suddenly assumed the highest attack priority.

For the second time that night, the message "URGENT MISSION, ATTENTION TARGET DESCRIPTION" flashed onto the large-screen display in Vincenza. Even though the target was in the heart of the city, surrounded by embassies and apartment buildings, CENTCOM in Washington was insistent: "Target description confirmed, attack immediately!"

Seconds later, the accurate-to-the-foot data sent by the two agents in the old van hidden by the bombed-out factory walls loaded itself into the target sight in the cockpit of a B-1 stealth bomber, as it hovered in a holding pattern unperceived nearly 20,000 feet above Belgrade.

Walrus stared at the blinking light indicating the transmitter in Nadine's sneaker, which now stood in a bag under the sink in the men's room on the seventh floor of the Embassy building.

"Scotty, look," Walrus said, pointing at his laptop screen. "This is it. Our guys are starting the attack."

"Well, I guess even we deserve a little success for a change," Scotty moaned.

The laptop display showed a running countdown. "Another four minutes," Walrus whispered, watching the screen in awe.

Nadine rubbed her eyes in amazement as we emerged on the other side of the steel door into a forgotten garden oasis. Slates floated on a carpet of rich moss. A 12-foot concrete wall surrounded the entire place, protected from the slate walks by a moat filled with stagnant water. A dozen beautiful cherry trees in full pink blossom filled the garden, illuminated by one surviving spotlight.

"Let's go," I told her. "We have no time to lose."

"And Polinsky, my hero, how to you propose that we get out of here?" she asked bitingly.

"We have to get up there," I said, pointing to an opening in the wall about six feet above the moat, approachable by a slate covered footbridge. "Let's go," I whispered, offering her my hand.

She refused it, but followed along, asking, "But where are we going?"

"Any place but here," I replied. "I know a safe place."

At the end of the bridge Nadine bent forward and dug her hands into the hard dry earth of the small cliff. Being in excellent shape, she climbed up the escarpment out of the garden.

In the van, 650 feet away from Nadine and Polinsky, Walrus sent another report over the ocean to Washington. "We still have the signal. Target data unaltered. Target fixed, clear, and positive."

Nadine worked her way up the dusty slope above the small cliff, using her aching naked toes to dig into the hard ground. She moved ahead slowly, until she reached a tall wire fence. She climbed it and whipped off her designer jacket, dangling it down to me. I grabbed the sleeve and immediately slipped, almost losing my footing completely. She cried out in pain as the wire fence cut her hand – but she didn't let go.

"Attack order issued," Scotty whispered into the radio. Both agents were breathless now, staring at the building that was defenseless against the coming firestorm.

Finally I gained a foothold. "Come on, now. Make it snappy!" Nadine joked, straining at her jacket with all her strength. It must have been quality workmanship – at least the seams didn't split!

"You took the wrong exit," she said as I finally joined her at the base of the fence. I struggled to catch my breath. Without another word she threw her jacket over the fence and nimbly climbed after it. Her T-shirt slipped up, and before she jumped over to the other side I got a glimpse of her sweet round breasts, blossoms that easily competed with the lovely cherries in the garden behind us. And so stimulated, I climbed the fence in a second and jumped over the top, landing next to her on the hard ground. Looking at her with poorly disguised lust in my eyes, I rose to my feet – but she was busy stuffing her shirt back into her pants and running her hands through her dark blonde hair.

On the other side of the small square outside the building, a black Mercedes sat with its motor running and its parking lights on. Above, at now 19,000 feet, the cruise missile left the fuselage of the stealth bomber, its deadly warhead racing towards the center of Belgrade.

We ran back toward the square. I stopped to straighten my shirt and pants. "Nadine, do you have the amulet with you?"

"Always. Of course. Why?"

"Your plan is down the drain. Come on, the car is waiting."

I took her arm and gripped it tightly, but she wouldn't budge. She instead pulled out the amulet and held it up in the dim light, reading her own name and next to it her birthday, followed by two groups of figures.

"Come on, girl, move it! There are patrols around here!"

She slowly pocketed the amulet, much too slowly for my taste. "And where do we go from here, my handsome hero?"

I was just about out of patience. "Who gives a shit?" I yelled, sprinting over to the car.

"Polinsky!" she gasped, clinging to my arm. I shoved her into the back of the Mercedes. She looked down at the floor, annoyed with me. But I had just about had it up to my sweaty collar. I guess it was time to let her know the score.

"What the hell is wrong with you? I thought you were this super genius from Los Alamos, but you act like the most naïve child on the planet. If you really want to self destruct why don't you wait until at least the few people who still care about you are gone."

She bit her lip and sat there, looking like a picture of complete misery. And yet I couldn't shake the feeling that this was a woman who, even in the most precarious of situations, would have no problem acting.

" Uncle Edouard knew your father," I finally said.

"What do you know about him?" she asked excitedly.

"Not much."

She held the amulet up in front of her eyes, suddenly animated. "Did you have anything to do with getting me this?"

I shook my head no. "Before the Corps Commander met his maker, he asked me not to let you out of my sight. And that is exactly what I'm doing. Now, listen up. Remember the woman at the tobacco warehouse in Nis? The one with the machine gun? Well, she knew about your meeting here in Belgrade tonight."

"So what?"

"Please, Nadine, pay attention," I scolded her. "After the firefight at the warehouse, every last jerk in town knows you are here. And every dim-witted agent and every policeman knows you've arrived for a secret meeting. You shouldn't have to be computer genius to figure this out."

"Is this what you want me to believe, Stan?" she asked angrily. "Now that I am so close?"

"You don't have to believe it if you don't want to. But you should be more careful. You are in a risky business."

She laughed mockingly. "He who avoids all risks has soon no risk to avoid."

I blew her a mock kiss and continued in a more serious tone. "You don't have to get angry at what I'm saying. But you should think about it."

"Well, what if I wanted to go back inside that building, right now? You couldn't stop me, could you?"

She looked down at the floor of the back seat. I said nothing at first. The chauffeur grunted, as if bored.

"No, you could go back in if you wanted to. But they would catch you, and rape you, from the front, from behind, and then blow your brains out. Or maybe slit your belly open before they do. But be that as it may, before you die, you'll end up telling them everything they want to hear. Believe me, *everything!*"

"What are you talking about Polinsky? Who are these people who would do such things to me?"

But before I could answer the car was hit with an ear-splitting boom, rocking the heavy Mercedes up and down as if we were in an earthquake. A bright light flashed, there was hissing and rumbling, howling and whistling. Fragments and stones rained down on the car like gunfire. The smell of phosphorous suddenly filled our nostrils. And then the earth shook, as large chunks of concrete crashed down around us. Nadine gaped open-mouthed as the building we were just talking about seemed to vanish in an ugly black cloud of smoke.

Target detection had been precise to the foot. The cruise missile hit right in the middle of the conference room in the Sudanese Embassy, and within seconds the entire seventh floor had been pulverized into a million fragments. The beautiful cherry trees we had just run through were suddenly covered in ashes and rubble. In fact, the entire garden was now just a pit filled to the rim with fallen concrete and broken glass.

I looked at Nadine and whispered, "*They* are the people who are after you. And they will stop at nothing to destroy you. So, now are you willing to come with me?"

Nadine got out of the car and stared at the burning

building and the surrounding chaos, coughing from the smoke and fumes. Standing there with her fists on her hips, she realized that for the second time in 24 hours she had escaped an air raid by the skin of her teeth.

"Come on Nadine," I hurried her. "Before the guys up there mistake us for a convoy of tanks."

Shattered, she fell back in the car and murmured something about the insanity of war. The car took off at full speed.

"I'll bring you to Casablanca, Nadine. That's the end of the line for me. I have business I have to take care of in Zurich. Do you read me?"

"Casablanca? Where'd you get that idea?" His stern face suddenly reminded her of Igor explaining her the contingency plan at Arlington National Cemetery. *If all else fails, go to Casablanca. You will find the place...*

"You've known about the figures on the amulet?"

She nodded. I squinted a bit, not at all unusual when I wasn't quite certain of something.

"Well then as you know, the figures describe latitude and longitude. Their point of intersection is very close to Casablanca. Maybe this is how your father wanted to tell you about a meeting place."

"You are good Polinsky." Her golden brown eyes looked at me in amazement and admiration, as they also seemed to size me up. Who can tell with a woman like her?

"Casablanca," she murmured, caressing the amulet as if she were a little girl and the delicate pendant the only secure thing in her turbulent life. At least that's how she played it. So was it truly a touching gesture? Or only touchingly played?

227

45.

Golden Hills Golf Club, where Jack Brenton was getting ready to tee off on eighteen, occupied a lovely remote spot eight miles from Westport in the gentle hill country of Connecticut. It was Joe Sorelli's club, and he found it to be an excellent place for casual meetings with the President. The immaculately trimmed course was set out in totally open terrain, with Highway 106 being the only entrance to the clubhouse. So the Secret Service loved the place – with very little effort they could quickly and completely control its security.

The Secret Service agents also liked the course rangers who were used to patrolling the exclusive club and knew who should be there and who shouldn't. And the other club members were accustomed to celebrities – so that when the President played golf with Joe Sorelli, hardly anyone noticed, or at least that's how they acted. The Secret Service agents who both preceded and followed the President in their golf carts were distinguishable from other golfers only by the fact that their eyes were always on that little piece of ground where their Commander in Chief was walking rather than on the flight of little white balls.

"Worried?" Sorelli asked Brenton after watching him screw up another drive.

"Hmm. Tell me, Joe, didn't you dig for Saddam's funds in Switzerland for George Bush?"

"Yes, mostly in Geneva. We found out everything. We knew where the Saddam clan hid their funds, but we couldn't get access to them."

The Saddam assignment had generated millions in fees for Sorelli's company Specs Inc. But Joe had always done well. And when Specs went public, he exercised his stock options and wound up taking in about $200 million. He had spent years building Specs' expertise and reputation. And when it came to getting the best in undercover investigations or verifying compliance with the requirements of international transactions anywhere in the world, companies and governments fought each other to get access to the experts at Specs Inc. Both the increase in global merger activity as well as the subtle infiltration of legitimate businesses by organized crime did much to increase the value of Specs' specialists.

"I guess you still have good connections in Europe," the President asked, suggesting that his mind really wasn't on his game today.

Sorelli was not tall, at five nine, and not young, at 65, but he was likeable and distinguished; and he inspired business confidence. He stopped the golf cart and turned his broad suntanned face to the President. "We have connections everywhere. What's the problem sir?"

They got off the cart. "Where's the hole?" the President asked.

"There. I'd say about another 200 yards or so." Joe lifted his hand and pointed to the red flag on the back right side of the green.

Brenton pulled a two-iron from his bag and with an expression of determination stepped up to the ball. He stared at the flag and took a practice swing. Then he hit it – perfectly. The ball came off the club straight, and rose gradually; then it fell to the ground about 20 yards short of the green and bounced three times before hitting the putting surface and rolling to within six feet of the cup.

"Wow, Jack! Great shot!" Sorelli exclaimed, clapping his hands.

"Great?" Brenton laughed his innocent country-cousin laugh. "It's great if it's holed out. And up here, I really hardly ever manage that."

By simply stressing the words up here, the most powerful man in the world seemed to give his old friend access to his innermost thoughts. Sorelli understood what Brenton was saying. *Up here* meant that *the world might consider me a bastard from the South – but you and I know me better. We both know I'm a* real *bastard from the South.*

Sorelli took his own shot, which also landed on the green, and they got back in the cart and drove on. The President gave him a brief overview of the facts, just as Taylor had presented them. Joe Sorelli listened carefully, his mind working overtime. They covered the usual topics – how the U.S. had already lost the battle to limit the exportation of high-tech devices. How the rapid development of technology created a situation where the new chip that drove a Sony Playstation III was so fast that according to current regulations it would need the approval of Washington to be exported. Sorelli told the President that he had reliable information suggesting that within the next year American computer and semiconductor manufacturers would want to market products that exceeded the government's current export limitations by at least six times, performing up to 12,300 theoretical operations per second.

"There's no way to avoid the realization that yesterday's supercomputer is today's laptop," Sorelli said, as he parked the golf cart next to the green. "And if the Chinese want our technology, all they have to do is buy a Playstation in a Hong Kong toy store. They can take that chip and simulate a landing on Taiwan. There's not a hell of a lot we can do these days to keep our high speed chips out of the hands of people who may not be particularly well disposed towards us. Now, whether they're able to really do anything with the chips, I suppose, is another question."

"Keep talking, Joe. If I like what I hear, maybe I'll let you live," Brenton said, smiling. "I mean, live well."

Sorelli nodded without really acknowledging the power joke.

"The really decisive element is for us to protect our user applications, like our aircraft carrier defense systems *Aegis*. That's why cryptography is so significant. If what Taylor said about C-Gag is true, then…"

"Listen Joe, we have to find this Frenchwoman. That's what you could do for me. *That* would be a great thing. One woman managing all on her own to outfox an entire team of CIA agents! Can you imagine that?"

They walked over the green and pulled out the pin whose flag hung limply. Sorelli was away, and he squatted near his ball, assessed the break, and stood up. He took his time, taking several practice putts. But when he hit the ball, the President could see why he enjoyed the reputation as the club's best putter. The ball slid steadily forward, broke just right over the course of its 12-foot travel, and dropped into the hole with a plunk.

"Nice putt, Joe," he said, straightening up and addressing his own 6-footer. He tried to adopt the putting stance of his golf idol and teacher Tiger Woods, who also at times had trouble putting. He remembered the young champion telling him," Caress, Mr. President, sir. You have to caress the ball," at one of their private lessons a few weeks ago. *Okay Tiger, Brenton thought, I'll caress this one for you.* He struck the ball gently and evenly, and it rolled right up to the cup, but hung on the edge, refusing to drop.

"Hell, I'd count that one," Sorelli roared.

"Well, I suppose to go all the way up to the edge is kind of an art too," Brenton smiled back at him. They shook hands.

"So that's a tie," Joe said as they walked back to the cart.

"No, I can't accept a tie, Joe. You know as well as I do that you always win when we play. Just like this time."

Sorelli knew just what the President was driving at. So he said with a broadly comic face of disappointment, "Alright sir, the ball hung up on the cup. You lose."

"Well, that too is incorrect. The President never loses, even if somebody else wins, right? But anyway, go on with your story from before."

As they got into the golf cart and headed for the clubhouse, Sorelli continued.

"When we were looking for Saddam's funds, I met a couple of good people in a Swiss company working in the same industry as mine. They're called Société Surveillance. Didn't Taylor mention a lead in Paris pointing to Switzerland? Maybe if I had a bit more information I could find out something."

"What do you need Joe?" the President asked, now all business.

"Something verifiable. A social security number, a

bank account number, the names of some contacts in Switzerland. This virtual aerial war thing, you know, if it's true, could be virtually disastrous."

"What do you mean, Joe? Don't' speak in riddles please."

"Well, I think this girl can make us look like complete idiots. Because of the work she did at Los Alamos, she has all the things she needs – the features, the software structure… she could…"

"She could do what?"

"Among other things, she could wreck the *Aegis* air defense system."

Brenton didn't reveal his emotions as this was said, as he sat there with his USA baseball cap with the gold-stitched laurels on the brim, his eyes covered with aviator sunglasses.

"Make a suggestion, Joe."

"I wish I had one to make. But I'll keep my ears open. I'm sure this Frenchwoman, what did you say her name was?"

"Moran. Nadine Moran." Brenton made no effort to pronounce her name with a French accent. So in his soft rounded drawl is sounded like Nedin Morann.

Sorelli scribbled the name down in the corner of his scorecard. "I'm sure she has some friends. I'll keep you informed. Oh and by the way, sir, has Taylor said anything to you about the bombing of the Sudanese Embassy in Belgrade?"

"In fact he has. Why do you ask?" The President seemed slightly puzzled. His mind had actually started to drift as he thought about a pension bill he was trying to get through Congress without the Republicans butchering it for their own purposes.

"Just a thought. It could have been a punitive action. The Sudanese make no secret of their support for bin Golem."

"Possible. Taylor had another plausible explanation. He said it was a CIA mistake in terms of target identification."

Joe Sorelli looked at him skeptically. Brenton could see he wanted a longer answer than that.

"Supposedly the CIA used three different maps to identify the building. None of them showed the Embassy, which was built there in I think 1996."

"They must have used a gas station map from 1947," Sorelli sneered.

Brenton pursed his lips in a kind of tortured smile. "Whatever – one thing's for sure: no more golf for the next two weeks. I have to go to Europe to visit the troops. Hey, maybe I'll put a putting green on Air Force One? Some guy's got one that sits on a gyroscopic platform. John Travolta has one and he's crazy about it. Apparently it always stays horizontal, even if the plane's banking or in turbulence – all the breaks stay the same."

Sorelli laughed. "Sounds good to me Jack. And if Travolta likes it I'm sure it works. You know I'll be flying to Europe next week too."

Brenton hit the brakes of the golf cart. "Really? Where?"

Sorelli grabbed the side support as the cart skidded to stop. "Paris. In case you need me just use that coded number I gave you. Any time, any place, you'll get right through to me."

"Okay, I will if I have to. I'm going to meet the King of Spain onboard the *Theodore Roosevelt.*

"Juan Carlos? At sea?"

"Yeah, he's nuts about flying –he'd rather sit behind the control lever of a plane than do most anything else. And he absolutely wants to visit the *TR*."

"Well, you know, rumor has it he always travels with two lady escorts…"

"Really? *Two?*"

"Very hot blooded senoritas. They interpret for him, attend to his needs, and generally act as if they are the ones at the control lever."

"You don't say? And how am I supposed to greet these chiquitas on board? With old Teddy Roosevelt's 'Speak softly and carry a big stick?' We'll see how they translate that one." Brenton's wide grin and soft laugh was contagious. He dryly added, "Maybe I'll try the expression 'Bat softly and shut up'."

"That one comes straight from JFK," Sorelli added with a laugh.

"Let's get to the point, Joe. I need a decent drink," the President said, putting his big soft right hand of power on the shoulder of his golf partner, massaging it with loving insistence. "How's about a double Scotch at the clubhouse?"

Later on they stood on the clubhouse terrace, among friendly waiters and waitresses who for some reason felt they had to stand at attention, while both men chatted with serious though statesmanlike relaxed faces.

"I think I know where Teddy Roosevelt got the idea for his famous quotation. Back in the Dark Ages there was a Jesuit general. His motto was *suaviter in modo, fortiter in re* – gentle in manner, firm in the matter."

"Well Joe, they're not just phrases, that's a way of life. And I do believe they suit you very well."

"Thanks; they're all nice mottos, especially the one with the big stick," Sorelli said, wiping his eye. He raised his glass to the American Commander in Chief. "To a safe journey over and on the sea!"

46.

"The Corps Commander told me that he owed his nickname to the Russians," I told Nadine as the Mercedes sped out of Belgrade. She watched amusedly as I took a bottle of Cognac and two brandy snifters from the small bar behind the front seat and placed them on the tiny foldaway table above it.

The driver was apparently a local and knew the area well. As soon as we hit the western suburbs of Belgrade he accelerated quickly, leaving the glowing of the fire and the ever-booming explosions behind us. The wide asphalt highway disappeared straight into the dark, and the heavy Mercedes sedan smoothly ate up the white lines that rushed toward us in the middle of the road.

As I filled the glasses with a steady hand I explained our route to Nadine. "Actually, we wanted to go north to Budapest, but the bridges crossing the Danube at Novi Sad are all destroyed. So we'll take the western route to The Croatian border and Zagreb."

Nadine took a big sip of Cognac and felt the strong drink pleasantly burn her throat. Only now were the effects of barely surviving the air raid in Belgrade getting to her. But the aged Napoleon Cognac gently calmed her quivering body. It helped her find her bearings again, slowly – and she emptied the glass of its agreeable medicine with her second sip, only to put the snifter down with a not altogether lady-like grunt. Feeling much more herself, she asked me what business the Corps Commander had had with the Russians.

"It's a long story," I smiled, hearing in memory the

voice of Uncle Edouard. "My wife was of Russian descent," he had told me, "a fact that was not likely to further my career as an officer in the Swiss Army."

I told Nadine some of the things he had confided in me, as I slowly sipped my glass of Cognac. The car droned on easily. The driver silently passed whatever other cars were on the road. Now and then the headlights of a car coming at us illuminated Nadine's classic French features. As I proceeded with my narrative, she would smile, or curl her lips in bewilderment, or simply relax. But as I watched her, my own drive heated up, aided by her lovely features and the Cognac. Surely Uncle Edouard would have appreciated my enthusiasm!

During the cold war of the 1960s, Swiss secret agents became aware of Edouard Diesbach's connection to the Russian flight pioneer Tupolev – and it raised certain suspicions. Other than my uncle, there were of course several contenders for the highly coveted position of Air Force Chief, and none of them refrained from expressing their distrust about my uncle and his connections. They even urged members of Parliament to intervene in their favor and try to keep Diesbach (with his lovely and fun-loving young Russian wife) from ever adding the stars of a general to his uniform.

Their plans would have succeeded, too, had it not been for an upcoming deal to purchase new combat planes. In the purchase evaluation process, the French *Mirage III* interceptor was up against an American jet, while the British were knocking on doors in Bern with their improved version of the *Hunter*; and even the Swedes were there, pushing the advantages of their *Viggen*.

It was a billion-dollar procurement, and the Swiss Air Force was split in two between the Americans and the French, although the larger group of flight officers favored the American jet, making the French think that their chances were over.

But then Diesbach went to work. He was a Francophile who had studied Strategy at St. Cyr – and was as fluent in French as he was familiar with the decision-making elite of the Grande Nation. And since he was an engineer as well, he had maintained close contacts with the manufacturers of the *Mirage*. So he brokered the deal behind the scenes, and the French arms lobbyists gave the Swiss an offer they couldn't refuse because it so far outstripped the American one in features and price.

Suddenly, overnight, Diesbach was a player. And in a rather turbulent procurement procedure, the Swiss Parliament ordered 57 new *Mirage III*. And when the waves subsided, the government appointed Diesbach Air Force Chief brevet Corps Commander.

He would never forget what the French had done for his career. A few years later, he discovered and informed the French that Tupolev was working on a new commercial supersonic airplane. The news hit Paris like a bombshell. The technology race of the Cold War suddenly got a dramatic boost. The designers of the British-French Concorde were baffled. How could the Russians possibly manage to design and construct such a complex aircraft so quickly?

And more bad news came quickly. Only a few months later Moscow reported on the maiden flight of the Tupolev-144, the first civilian supersonic aircraft in the world. Because of its virtually ridiculous similarity to the British-French Concorde, it was instantly dubbed Konkorski.

"I thought this was your uncle's nickname," Nadine interrupted, momentarily confused.

I shook my head vigorously and explained that insiders affectionately called my uncle Monsieur Edouard." He was a fine, almost aristocratic figure of a man, like a real count."

"So then now I am an insider," she sneered.

"You are part of the family, Nadine. The Corps Commander and your father had a very warm relationship over the years. Don't forget, Thierry-Clé was a pilot, like Edouard."

"Do you know all this from the red file?" she asked in a low voice.

I looked at her surprised. The file, actually, was in my duffel bag in the trunk of the Mercedes. But I had barely mentioned it to her. She was very alert, this Frenchwoman!

"No," I replied, shaking my head. "Uncle Edouard told me a lot about this daredevil, a very trustworthy and reliable man, apparently."

"Mmm."

"The French never forgot that the Corps Commander was the one who helped them get back at the Russians. Later, they even made him a member of their exclusive Légion d'Honneur," I continued, telling the story that never failed to thrill me. That the similarity between the Tupolev-144 and the Concorde was no coincidence was confirmed in 1977, when French counter-intelligence arrested the Russian engineer Sergej Fabiew. He was French born of Russian descent. The hint to the French that there was a Soviet agent working with them came from Edouard Diesbach in Zurich."

I gave Nadine a chance to absorb this information as I once more filled my glass and absorbed some more of the Cognac before I continued my ranting.

"It was a classic case of the kind of industrial espionage that had been systematically directed against the French from the early 60s on. Back then, the Soviet leader Khrushchev had heard of the French and British plan to develop a supersonic aircraft and had declared, as he had done earlier with Sputnik, that not only would the Soviet Union enter this race – but that they would win it too."

"And how did the Corps Commander hear about this?" Nadine asked, fascinated by the story, and wondering why this Polinsky guy was telling her all this stuff on their midnight drive through the middle of nowhere.

"Well, I guess he took that secret to the grave, Nadine," I replied honestly. "Some people speculated that his wife Natasha might have had an affair with Tupolev himself, whom she in fact knew quite well, but others…" I broke off and turned away silently.

"But hadn't the Soviets won the race with the West anyway?" Nadine argued.

Fueled by the Cognac, I gave her a grand dismissive gesture and repeated my uncle's words: "The Tu-144 wasn't destined to succeed. It crashed at the Paris Air Show on June 3, 1973. After that public humiliation, the Kremlin obviously no longer considered it a symbol of Soviet supremacy in aircraft construction. So actually the West had won the race. The Concorde went on to establish the supersonic jet market, which in the early days we all thought would be worth billions. But that euphoria didn't last. As soon as the supersonic jet went into production we knew it would be impossible to make the deafening gas-guzzler profitable – to either sell or operate."

"Tell me more about this spy story," Nadine persisted.

"Well, back in 1964 the French discovered a spy working as the Manager of the Aeroflot branch in Paris – and this discovery made them mistakenly think they had uncovered *all* the Russian spies, which lulled them into a false sense of security. So they had no idea that Fabiew was funneling the construction data on the Concorde right to Moscow. He had put together a small organization of spies, mostly true-believing communists, working-class people in France. And then of course Monsieur Edouard learned about it."

"He himself?"

Shrugging, I replied, "It's hard to say. By then the Air Force had a very reliable intelligence service of its own, fed by Diesbach through his contacts in Moscow."

"And what became of Natasha?"

"She died shortly after the Tu-144 crashed."

"Oh. Too bad."

"Well, the Konkorski was not exactly a lucky charm for your father either," I said somewhat coldly.

But she didn't bat an eyelid and asked me in complete composure, "So why did the Tu-144 crash, anyway?"

That was precisely the question I had asked Uncle Edouard a few weeks ago. I could still see him sitting in front of me, gazing at me silently, filling up our glasses with more wine.

This image was shattered by the broken English of the driver, who announced that we would soon reach the Croatian border crossing.

Nadine slouched back in her seat, totally relaxed by the Cognac. She felt that the crash of the Russian Konkorski could not have been the last chapter in the turbulent life of the man they called her father. He must be alive and up to something big. Yes, he sent her a secret message! Anyway, she had the material that would open all the doors for her. She thoughtfully caressed the moneybag with the *Oedipus* Code dangling below her breasts. And as she sat there she knew that, father or not father, Thierry Clé would lead her to a new fulfillment. But oddly enough, the longer she knew this Polinsky character, the closer she felt to him. *If only he wasn't such a fool! If only he would commit to her!* She instinctively crossed her legs. *On the other hand, this bin Golem... suddenly she felt a strange attraction to this demigod Igor was so crazy about in Washington. Yes, Yussef bin Golem must be cast in a different mold.* She suddenly had a longing to meet this man, look up to him, be his obedient servant, please him, somewhere down the road, at the end of this journey...

47.

Nadine sat there silently for a while, listening to the steady murmur of the engine. But then she said provokingly, "I am sure that the Corps Commander had a guilty conscience about my... father."

A full silvery moon broke through the heavy clouds in the west, illuminating a deserted pasture framed by dark and mighty fir trees.

I shook my head and defended my uncle. "No, I don't think so. Your father vanished without a trace over North Africa."

She raised her hands to her eyes. Did she cry? Or just pull herself together? Suddenly she cracked her window, allowing the cool air to flow over her flushed cheeks.

"I am certain he is alive. He has a mission. The amulet..." she said firmly.

"According to the Corps Commander, young Moran left in a single-engine plane headed to Algiers. But he never reached his destination."

Nadine pulled out the amulet. Holding it up, she said, "This sign of life makes that story unlikely."

"I hope you're right. On the other hand, there is no date on that amulet. Maybe it's from a time when he was still alive."

"He *is* still alive. Today. If not, why would I have gotten this?"

"Your friends must really need you."

"It *is* authentic. I *know* it," she said, evading my remark, as she stared at the engraving on her charm.

"If it is, so much the better," I said, relenting.

As the car cruised through this fierce deserted part of the country, Nadine insisted on knowing exactly what had happened. So I told her what I had learned from my uncle the old Chief of the Air Force in the course of my investigations.

The French Secret Service was infuriated by the Russian theft of the Concorde data, and the call for revenge was loud and clear. The designers of the Concorde didn't believe that the Russians would be able to successfully produce a copy of their ingenious creation, arguing that the Russian aerospace industry was much too underdeveloped. The French engineers had created a new type of material for the body and wings of the supersonic aircraft, and they did not believe the Russians would be able to manufacture it.

It was true that the Russians had the plans and the data – but the French swore that there was no way they could build the plane to spec. But suddenly there it was – the Tu-144 was coming to the Paris Air Show. But again the French refused to believe that it was not a second-rate reproduction.

"So your father's secret assignment was to get in a jet fighter and fly up to the Tu-144 right in the middle of its demo flight at the Air Show – and force the Russian pilot into taking radical avoidance maneuvers."

"And he did this?" Nadine asked breathlessly.

"Yes he did. And it was not an easy thing to do. Thierry-Clé had to fly like an ace that day. He had to stalk up on the pilot unnoticed and then fly directly at them as if he were attacking. Uncle Edouard said that your father was a daredevil, who feared neither death nor the devil.

"The Russian crew was taken completely by surprise. Suddenly this *Mirage* was coming straight at them. To avoid the collision they pulled up as hard and as fast as they could. And just as the French engineers had predicted, the inferior materials and construction couldn't cope with the stress of the maneuver. Silently, and without being seen, your father caused the crash of the Konkorski, and revenged the French."

"Wow. Unbelievably wild. But there had to be repercussions, right? I mean, thousands of people were watching."

"Well, actually, no. Nobody noticed the *Mirage*. Not until years later did a documentary discover exactly what had happened. It was all very artfully camouflaged by the French."

"That goes without saying."

"According to my uncle, all of the people involved were committed to covering up your father's mission. And they were all happy to see the Soviets pay so dearly for their espionage."

"Of course Moscow protested, right?"

"Not a word. The Kremlin was in no hurry to tell the world that their Tu-44, the great achievement of Soviet technology, had broken under a strain that the Concorde would have been able to easily withstand."

"So the French engineers were right all along?"

"Completely. And there were no loose ends to the story. Moscow backed down and shut up. And in Paris they uncorked champagne and toasted your father as a hero."

"But there were casualties, no? I mean, the people on the Russian plane…"

"Yes, 14 people died," I said, frowning.

"But you know, they called it the Cold War, but sometimes it got hot – it's basically as simple as that. Everyone involved accepted it."

"And Edouard's wife? Natasha? What about her," she asked me probingly.

I didn't answer, thinking about the same question. Had Natasha, in the end, been unmasked as a spy for the West? Where else could Diesbach have gotten his information? When I had asked my uncle about her, the old man said nothing at all. He just bit his eyetooth into his lip, and the usual composed expression vanished from his dignified face. At that point I just said to myself let the dead rest in peace.

The driver broke me out of my reverie.

"We soon at border," he announced abruptly.

Nadine ignored the message.

"I'm going to pull this off," she said animatedly, not doubting for a second that her mission would succeed.

"If I were you I'd be very careful," I urged. Your so-called friends are probably members of the *Qaeda* – and they're an operation pretty well known for fanaticism."

"*Qaeda?*"

"It's an Arab word. It means the base. They're a rather obscure bunch of extremists from all over the Islamic world. Their leader is the very well known terrorist bin Golem."

"Even better," Nadine said, not batting an eyelid. "Surely he'll be able to make some sense out of all this." The idea of meeting such a charismatic man, as this Arab was described to her, thrilled and almost aroused her. *What's wrong with you, girl?*

"I don't think you're being realistic Nadine. This man

is a terrorist entrepreneur. He's worth like $600 million. He's the leader and sponsor of a worldwide network of Islamic terrorists. And if you take up with him two things are guaranteed to happen: One, the CIA will hunt you down day and night wherever you go in the world as a terrorist sympathizer and accomplice. And two, the *Qaeda* will only help you as long as you have something you can give them in exchange. Have you promised them anything? Some kind of technological know-how in armaments?"

She nodded yes, her lips pinched.

"Whatever," I said brusquely. "But whatever you do, you shouldn't be doing it on your own. This kind of deal is really too big to be doing by yourself." But she wasn't easily put off.

"Listen to me Polinsky, and don't forget it. For me this is a matter of life and death. Do you think I'm hanging around here for my health? These people are on my side I feel it. And think of it, Polinsky: They didn't try to steal my work. They didn't try to blow me up, twice. They aren't chasing me for murdering a FBI agent. No, they were the ones who gave me the message on the amulet. They are the ones who protect me."

And with that she kissed the amulet, as if it were a priceless relic. Not, of course, that I have anything against religion. On the contrary. I could well imagine that Nadine, either after or even better before confession, might prove to be a truly otherworldly experience, in bed at least.

The Cognac was making me relaxed, and I was getting tired of arguing with her. I stretched my arms up until they hit the ceiling and my shoulders cracked.

"What makes you think that everything about that amulet is what they say it is?"

"The birthday," she whispered.

That is, according to her driver's license and passport, she was born on February 28. But in fact, she had been born on the 29th. But her parents wanted to spare her the inconveniences, real or imagined, of being born on a leap year, so they changed the date. And the only one who knew her real birthday was Thierry-Clément, and by now, maybe also Yussef bin Golem... Just thinking about that made her excited.

"I'll take any risk to get to the bottom of this mystery. Wouldn't you do the same?"

"Probably, but *I* would listen to a friend's advice. The *Qaeda* has been known to take brutal revenge."

"Oh really?" she asked sarcastically, rebelling against me. "More brutal rapes, from the front and back? More slitting of my belly?" But then she hesitated. "Okay Polinsky, what do you suggest?"

"You need protection. You need... Polinsky!" I said in all seriousness, driven I'm sure by the Cognac and by a vision of a naked Nadine confessing everything to me.

"Oh yeah. You're very convincing. I feel so much better now," she said sarcastically.

"We'll talk about it later," I said. "Better get down, we're approaching the border."

Bright floodlights lit the four corners of two low buildings connected by the flat roof of this border station. I gently pushed Nadine down onto the floor behind the front seat. I must say the situation made me think of another time when Irina had been in the same place (another car, another border), and I had to simulate a coughing fit to mask the sound of my zipper, which my hot companion had opened with teasing fingers. I had smiled at the border guard with seemingly tired eyelids while down in the dark of the backseat she served me a delicacy, for which this border guard would have shot meat once. But unfortunately, I knew that all of this was out of the question right now.

The driver lowered his window and passed a black passport to the customs officer.

"*Diplomati,*" the border guard growled, looking at his partner with the machine gun who came closer and mumbled something into his beard.

"*Svajcarci,*" said the guard, at which point we were waved through.

As soon as the border crossing sunk into the darkness behind us I pulled Nadine up from the floor.

"Being Swiss counts for something here. You can surface again."

Slightly confused, she looked at me and asked, "So what do we do now?"

"First you come here and kiss me, and then we follow our plan. We'll go to Casablanca. Some plane will fly us from Zagreb to Casablanca," and I closed my eyes and offered my face and lips for her to kiss. And I waited. Two, three, four, five breaths. Nothing. When I opened my eyes she was sitting back refilling her brandy snifter.

"Stop being so silly Polinsky," she said. What will your so-called protection really cost me? Surely more than a simple kiss. Cheers!"

"You're tough on the man, Moran, tough on the man,"

I rhymed cheerfully. "But you're right, I do want something else. I want you to help me decode the red file. If that's worth more to you than a kiss, well, then you decide which."

We suddenly sat close to each other, damn close, for a too brief moment our lips touched. And for now, for awhile anyway, we were safe. And the bottle of Cognac was still half full. I helped myself to another glass. What the hell – what did a little paperback writer like me have to lose on the way to Zagreb? Apart from his past?

"Cheers," I said, and sipped, suddenly having a very sobering image of Steinlin in my mind, who was no doubt tearing his hair out wondering where I was and what I was up to. On the slight chance that there might be a mobile antenna operating in this godforsaken wilderness, I dug up my cell phone and dialed. An eloquent hissing sound and some distant murmuring now and then interrupted by electronic beeps, proved my assessment of the situation to be correct. As I waited I poured the rest of the Cognac down my throat in one gulp and clicked my tongue.

Our driver then made some monosyllabic brutish sound that I couldn't help but relate to my rather selfish and overindulgent drinking. So I passed him the bottle, which he took without so much as a word of gratitude, and swallowed in a way that made me fear for our future. Finally he set the bottle down and croaked "Not bad, General."

I sat back in the seat surrounded by the sweet smell of Nadine.

48.

Khalid left downtown Casablanca early in the morning so he could reach the airport in time for the arrival of the overseas flights. If traffic was light, the drive from downtown Casablanca to Mohamed V international airport took about half an hour. He pulled into the large parking lot and, leaving his small Peugeot, walked single-mindedly into the one-story departure building that reflected the bright morning sun.

Khalid looked like any other businessman in his dark blue suit, white shirt, and patterned gray tie; his black duffel bag made him look like the rest of the travelers on their way to the check-in desks. But this killer wasn't planning to take the morning flight to Rabat – or anywhere else. He was here to solve a problem, hopefully within the next half-hour; he was here to figure out how to get into the restricted safe zone of the airport.

The departure area was busy this time of day, and Khalid walked past several check-in desks over to the snack bar, where he bought a cup of coffee and worked his way through the hordes of travelers pulling their luggage carts to the other side of the building. He picked up a local morning paper from the newsstand and sat in a hard plastic chair next to a heavy-set woman in a black veil. He unfolded his paper and sipped his coffee, eyes on a doorway. He did not have to wait long.

A young airport employee in blue overalls walked quickly up to the door that Khalid was watching, the one labeled *Restricted Area*. He typed a combination of digits into the little square electronic lock. Khalid moved his chair a bit to the side and waited.

The next person to approach the door was an airline pilot in a white polo shirt. Khalid bent forward to see the sequence of numbers he punched in, but the captain was security-sensitive and screened off the combination lock from view with his body.

Two airport police officers with machine guns slung over their shoulders walked near to Khalid as he tried to see around the pilot's body – so he leaned back and pretended to focus on his newspaper. Then a cleaning lady approached the door and started to push the combination numbers. Khalid stood up to get a better look. He saw three, then five…

But the two police officers turned around suddenly and pushed their way past Khalid as he stood there trying to get the last few numbers.

"Pardon me," one of them growled as he brushed past, looking at Khalid carefully, almost suspiciously. Khalid gave up looking at the cleaning lady, yawned, and sat down again.

Damn! He knew he couldn't sit there forever. He got up, with the idea of sitting closer to the lock, when suddenly a young man in a chauffeur's uniform stood in front of the restricted access door. He hesitated for a second, as if trying to remember the numbers, and then took off his cap, peered into it, and put it on again. He hit a series of numbers on the lock, but the door didn't open. Again, he took off his cap, and removed a piece of paper from the inside brim. When he tried the lock again, the green light went on and the door opened. Khalid watched the chauffeur step inside.

"Bingo!" Khalid mumbled to himself, turning and

walking away from the door. He leaned back against the espresso bar and waited. He watched the security patrol on the other side of the terminal walk away from the departure area.

Before long, the door to the restricted access area opened, and the chauffeur came out. And as if to make Khalid's job easier, he walked over the espresso bar and sat down, removing his cap and putting it on the bar. He checked his watch and ordered something.

Khalid moved closer, slowly and discretely. The bartender put a cup of coffee in front to the chauffeur and moved the sugar bowl closer to him – and Khalid turned and knocked the cap to the floor with his elbow.

"Clumsy me," he said as he bent down and picked up the cap. "I am so sorry."

"No problem," answered the chauffeur, dismissing the incident with a wave of his hand. He picked up the sandwich the bartender had placed in front of him and took a bite, chewing hardily.

With the piece of paper containing the lock code securely in his fist, Khalid wished the chauffeur a nice day and walked past the escalators to the parking lot.

49.

That same evening, the *Shiraz* cruised up the Senegalese coastline. A favorable current and the southeast trade winds helped the ship make good headway. After they crossed the 25th degree of latitude, Captain Souri had the helmsman set a northeasterly course that would take them through the Canary Islands.

Usually, large tankers chose a route further seaward of the island group, and their crews wouldn't see much of the shore. But this time the voyage of the *Shiraz,* between Tenerife and Grand Canary, offered a spectacular view of Pico del Tiede, the 12,198-foot volcano.

Navigation was somewhat more difficult between the islands, not only because of heavy shipping but also because of the shallows. Just north of Lanzarote, the sea charts showed the dangerous tip of Dacia Seamount, a marine mountain that lurked only 700 feet below the surface of the sea.

Captain Souri wasn't entirely clear why he had been ordered to take the island course. He was told there would be a rendezvous with another ship east of ten degrees longitude, just off the Moroccan coast near Casablanca. But he saw no threat to the ship's security in the plan. The ocean around Casablanca was open and deep, and, although it could often be stormy, the weather forecast called for clear skies and a moderate west wind.

The mighty ship plowed its way through the Atlantic at full speed, moving along the North African coast. The sun sank in the waters to the west, spreading a pinkish glow onto the water and sky. Darkness slowly covered the turquoise water astern, while in the distance the highest mountaintops of the Atlas Range sparkled like beacons.

Bin Golem stood on Deck A, his eyes ranging over the breadth of the sea. Captain Souri approached him quietly, carefully noting the expression of deep anxiety on his face.

"Is everything all right, sir?" he asked cautiously.

Bin Golem stared at the bow mast and said nothing. Souri was about to retreat when the Islamic leader spoke to him.

"I was thinking of my brother. Tomorrow is his birthday."

"Salim?"

Bin Golem studied the captain's face. As the sea darkened with the setting sun, its color came more and more to reflect the dreary mood of the Saudi millionaire, the most feared terrorist in the world.

Oh Salim! Painful memories came back to him. Salim's last pleading look had stabbed his heart like a knife. A bitter deadly hatred consumed the heart of bin Golem. *It was the Americans' fault!*

Captain Souri was a sensitive man and realized that the only appropriate response was silence. He knew that Allah's warrior needed someone who simply knew how to listen.

"At the time, the bombing was in all the world's media," bin Golem began. "The explosion killed 19 Americans and wounded 500 more. It was the bloodiest incident since the Gulf War and it abruptly ended the meteoric rise of the brigadier general responsible for Khobar Towers.

"Everything had started so well that night. My brother and the other soccer players had left the stadium of

Dhahran in the absolute best of spirits. The first half of the game had been a bit disappointing – too many back passes, weak defense. But in the second half there was no stopping our eleven. Two times Salim had played a hard cross, which the center forward had headed into the goal. We won three to nothing, and kept our chances for qualification. So we celebrated. We drank a lot, and toasted Salim. After awhile we got ready to go. The team left in two small buses. I followed them in a black Chevy truck."

The inconceivable happened later, on the fringe of the U.S. Air Force Base located on the Persian Gulf next to Dhahran International Airport – not far from the large bridge that stretches over to Bahrain.

"When I arrived at the scene, there was nothing I could do to stop the disaster," bin Golem muttered. Was he speaking to the captain or just communing with the sea?

The two small buses had turned off King Fahd Street when Salim ordered the driver to pull off the road.

"I have to water those guys' lawn," he said grinning as he got off the bus. He looked around and stepped up to the fence and peed though the high barbed wire onto the grounds of the U.S. Airbase Khobar Towers.

"Watch it, man, you're pissing on the Yanks!" one of the other players on the bus yelled. Three other players got off the bus and joined Salim, pissing through the fence onto the grounds like there was no tomorrow. Laughing, joking, "Look, Salim's is the biggest!"

Inside the guardhouse, Lieutenant McLane nervously watched the monitor with increasing resentment as he saw the boys pissing through the fence like dogs. *Damned camel driv-*

*ers! This is an insult to the integrity of a United States facility. It's
a damned insult!*

He stared at a memo from a security officer who had arrived that afternoon, sitting on the desk before him. It ended
with the sentence, "If a truck parks close to the fence and its
driver runs away, the building will have to be evacuated."

It was late, and nearby in their quarters more than 600
Air Force soldiers were asleep in their bunks. This fact didn't
serve to calm the Lieutenant's nerves. Only six months ago five
American soldiers had been killed in the capital Riyadh when a
200-pound bomb exploded in the barracks of the Saudi National Guard, where the Americans had been training. Since
then, anti-terrorism specialists had been analyzing the security
situations at many U.S. bases, leaving memos like the one that
sat in front of Lieutenant McLane now. He basically agreed
with it. He had told his superiors that the troop dormitories in
buildings 131 and 133 were too close to the street and should
be screened off in some way. But his warning was not heeded.
If a truck parks too close to the fence... rang through his mind.

"Look out! Here come the military police," shouted
the driver of the first small bus as he leaned over the steering
wheel. A Jeep pulled out of the complex and stopped about 60
feet from where Salim and his buddies had just finished relieving themselves. Two soldiers got out of the Jeep, their guns
held loosely in their arms.

Salim frowned at them and yelled, "Hey, what the hell
are you doing here? Go home! Get out of here!" And he took
a couple of steps toward the MPs.

"Come on Salim," his coach warned. "Leave those idiots alone. You'll just get into trouble."

But bin Golem's younger brother didn't stop. "This is my country. And I go wherever I feel like, damn it," he yelled provokingly. Then he swung a can of beer in his hand as if it were a hand grenade.

"What is that moron doing?" the alarmed Lieutenant asked the security patrol over the radio.

"He's coming straight at us. And he's carrying something in his hand."

"Chase him away from the fence. Get him and those vehicles away from the fence!"

"Yes sir."

McLane watched the monitor and saw the one Arab waving his arms and shouting at his MP unit. Then he saw more Arabs leaving the bus. *What are they up to now?*

He heard his MPs over the radio. "What should we do sir? There are seven, no, ten men here. We need reinforcements!"

"Don't do anything, no, I mean, chase them all away from the fence. Are they carrying weapons? Can't you get them away from the fence?"

"I don't see any weapons sir, not yet anyway."

When the Lieutenant saw the black pickup truck arrive, his blood froze. It pulled in behind the second small bus and parked close to the fence.

Next to the fence. Evacuate the building. Shit!

"I realized something was wrong as soon as I got out of the truck," bin Golem continued to the captain with a shaky voice. "Salim was fooling around with a military police officer. Later they told me he was discussing the rights of free passage on Saudi-Arabian territory. That would be typical of Salim. But the Yanks didn't understand him. No. They didn't *want* to understand him. I saw the taller one push his gun into Salim's belly. I walked faster. Then I saw Salim grab the barrel of the gun and push it toward the ground. I started to run to him."

All Lieutenant McLane saw was bin Golem leave the black truck and run away from it. He remembered the memo: *...close to the fence and the driver runs away...*

He pushed the alarm button and yelled into the radio, "The black truck! I thinks it's full of explosives!"

The other MP heard the screaming alarm siren and heard only the word "explosives" over the radio.

"Stop! Don't move!" he screamed at Salim who was still wrestling with the other MP over the gun.

Bin Golem went on with his narrative to the captain. "I shouted 'Don't shoot! Don't shoot. Salim, stop it! Come back here!' And all his teammates were shouting at him as well as they slowly encircled the MPs."

Lieutenant McLane shouted into the radio. "Reinforcement is on its way. Keep that mob at bay. Check those vehicles!"

The MP lifted his hand and signaled to the team members to stop. "Go back to your vehicle," he shouted.

The men only laughed at him, until he shot into the air three times. And then everyone froze.

But while everyone stood there paralyzed in shock, Salim took advantage of the confusion and punched the MP he was struggling with in the face. But the beefy MP hardly moved. He simple lifted the barrel of his machine gun and fired once; it sounded like the bark of a jackal.

Salim looked at the shooter and seemed baffled, holding his belly and slowly sinking down to his knees.

The shooter jumped into the Jeep. "Back! Get back! That truck is full of explosives!"

"Holy Shit!" his partner cursed and turned to follow him. The Jeep raced backwards to the gate. And suddenly from the PA system came words in Arabic: "You are threatening a United States Air Force facility. Return to your vehicles. If you don't return to your vehicles we will shoot – with live ammunition!"

"Salim was lying in his own blood," bin Golem told the captain. "We needed to get him help. But whenever one of us tried to approach him, Satan's brood fired warning shots over our heads."

"Return to your vehicles. We will count to ten and then begin shooting," came the message from the speakers.

The players of the national team had no choice, and they retreated back to their buses and left, honking their horns.

"But I didn't leave," bin Golem went on. "I stayed there. Salim died in my arms. A doctor from the base could have saved him. It took an hour for the ambulance from Dhahran to arrive."

The terrorist leader's grief-stricken face sunk into his hands.

On that night, May 24, in Dhahran, near the fence of the Air Force Base, bin Golem swore a solemn vow of revenge. At the very spot where his brother had died, he declared the Holy War on the Americans. A month later, buildings 131 and 133 were leveled by a car bomb. And soon after that, Yussef bin Golem left Saudi Arabia to take command of the Holy War, the *Jihad*.

Captain Souri said nothing. He was thinking of his sons, who, like Salim, were young and reckless.
Souri had no illusions about the state of affairs in the world today. The United States ruled – of that there was no doubt. In 1998 alone, 35,000 U.S. Army Special Forces troops took part in 2,600 missions in 115 countries. America used money and missiles to force the world to adopt its ideas of democracy and human rights. Over the last three years, the U.S. President ordered the launch of a cruise missile on the average of every three days.

Was the U.S.A. right just because it had military and economic superiority? Was there anyone who could defy this arrogant and presumptuous superpower? Who could dare stand up to the first real world empire since ancient Rome?

The answer was simple. Yussef bin Golem. The great freedom fighter! Long live bin Golem! Souri thought him courageous in his efforts to kick the American occupation troops out of the world of Islam. People called him a terrorist, but so what? The U.S. President launched explosive raids that killed people, and so did bin Golem. Both carried out their duties with deep conviction. Both were likable men, and neither of them were saints.

With true conviction, Captain Souri had chosen the side of Islam, like tens of thousands of his fellow Muslims – in fact, like almost everyone aboard the *Shiraz*. With of course the major exception of Chief Engineer Brabeck.

50.

At ten past seven in the morning, the American Eagle jetliner slowly rolled over the west landing strip, heading for the arrivals building of the international airport Mohamed V in Casablanca. Pale, curious faces looked out of the cabin windows as a large bus came out to meet them on the tarmac.

The 90 passengers had just completed an 11-hour flight, and they longed for a shower at the hotel, some breakfast, and maybe a few hours rest before the tour guides started pestering them about their booked tour to the mosque of Hassan II. Apart from a few travelers and businessmen in First and Business Class, most of the passengers were part of an organized tour.

The large green and white bus was ready for the passengers to depart, and the front door of the Boeing 737 opened. A stewardess stopped out onto the ramp that had been moved into place next to the plane; she waved to one of the ground crew who stood at the bottom of the stairway. One by one the passengers appeared at the doorway and said goodbye to the friendly stewardess before staggering down the stairs with their hand held luggage.

The man at the bottom of the stairs directed the exhausted passengers to the open door of the bus. They were all wearing colorful summer clothes, which fit not only the climate of their homes (most of them were from Tucson and Phoenix, Arizona), but also that of their desert destination. What most of them had in common, aside from having booked tours with Freedom travels, was that they all had jobs either directly or indirectly connected with companies that did business with the Air Force.

The very tall and husky Sam Cadwallader owned a small company that ran helicopter tours in Tucson, while his wife Susan managed the food services unit at the local Air Force base. Also on board from the base was Quintus, who was the Information Technology manager, looking much the part with his shaved head, goatee, and thick black glasses – along with his girlfriend Zoe. Xaver had been a well-respected aircraft mechanic before retiring and taking a job as fish and gamekeeper at a hunting lodge in the mountains. Snell, a former police detective, was Chief of Security at a microchip company that was a major Air Force supplier. Mark Yale, a radiologist, was also on the bus along with his 14-year-old daughter Sophie.

Before long the bus was totally packed, with people standing in the aisle. A short chubby man with a tousled shock of gray hair said "They treat us like sardines."

For a second Sam Cadwallader looked at the small friendly guy. *Wait a minute. I know this guy. That's Senator Strong!* Sam's face brightened as he looked down at the senator – but before he could say anything the senator placed his finger over his lips. Sam nodded with a conspiratorial smile.

"Man, there's no air conditioning," Quintus complained as the bus took off with a jerk.

"Yeah, and look at this lousy weather. Hot but no sunshine. I thought it was always supposed to be sunny here," Zoe added.

A few minutes later a different conversation went on in the airport control tower.

"Where the heck is that bus going?" asked the controller responsible for ground traffic as he stared down at it from high in the air.

"I haven't the slightest idea," said one of his colleagues.

"I think it's supposed to be heading for passport control, but it's going in the wrong direction."

The green and white bus picked up speed as it drove along the airstrip, moving further away from the terminal.

"For Christ's sake, where is this guy taking us?" Sam asked, ducking his cowboy hat down so he could look out the window.

"Try to relax Sam," his wife told him. Then she turned to the woman standing next to her. "Sam always has to be the one in control of things."

No one reacted to her remark. All of them were tired from their long flight – all except Sam of course. He heartily patted Quintus on the shoulders. He knew the young computer manager pretty well, since he sometimes gave his grandson boxing tips at the gym. And he especially liked his girlfriend Zoe, because she was a receptionist at the Hyatt Regency, and often sent well-heeled tourists looking for sightseeing flights his way.

"He's probably going over to hangar eight," said the controller's colleague, pointing over to the heliport.

"That's fine with me," answered the controller responsible for ground traffic. He turned his attention to the plane from Rabat that had just landed. But then he did notice that the bus had stopped in front of the small hangar where three helicopters were standing by.

Sophie, filled with teenaged energy, was memorizing the names of her fellow passengers in alphabetical order as best she could: *Quintus, Sam, Senator Strong, Snell, Sophie, Susan, Xaver, Yale, and Zoe* she recited, silently moving her lips.

"Get off bus!" roared the driver into the intercom system in heavily accented English. His orders were greeted with a flurry of questions and no movement of passengers. He opened the door and yelled again into the microphone. "Get off bus, please! All out, fast!"

"Why aren't we going to the hotel?" Sam asked in his low bass voice as he worked his way off the bus.

Khalid smiled and directed the hulky Sam to the first helicopter. *I'd better keep my eye on this one,* he thought to himself. He looked at him and said as calmly as he could, "We're flying, sir! A surprise treat from the Morocco Tourist Office."

Khalid knew that this transfer of people from the bus to the helicopters was the first critical phase in his mission. Any kind of commotion had to be avoided at all costs.

"Wow, that's great!" said one passenger. "Not bad. Look at these copters," said another. The wind and the twirling main rotors tore away a makeshift sign reading *Freedom Travel* from the first helicopter.

"They must be our helicopters," Sam called back to his group as he boarded the first one. His experienced eyes registered the starting preparations made by the pilots in the cockpit. It all looked very professional to him.

Buoyed by what seemed to be a much higher-end way to get to the hotel than the non-air-conditioned bus, the tourists quickly boarded the three helicopters.

"Whoops, my hat!" Zoe screamed as the twirling rotors sent her hat down the runway. She started to run after it, but Khalid was on her in a flash, grabbing her arm hard.

"You're running right into the tail rotor, Miss!" he screamed above the noise of the engines. "You must be careful!"

Zoe, frightened at her near mishap as well as by the force of Khalid's grip, looked at the faintly visible disk created by the whirling rotor on the helicopter's tail.

"I've never been on a helicopter before," Sophie said to her father as they climbed aboard the *Super Puma*. This is so great!"

Khalid scanned the airport grounds. *Good*, he thought. *No signs of increased activity.*

It was clear that no one had taken notice of the bus's detour to the helicopter hanger or seen it as anything unusual. But the Executioner did not dwell on their success or indulge in any illusions. He knew that the peaceful quiet of the airport Mohamed V could within seconds turn into galvanized action on the part of the police against him and his plans. He kept his guard up as he watched the Americans gradually filling up the helicopters, urging them on with quick, insistent gestures.

Finally, the third helicopter's sliding door slammed shut. Sam saw the pilot of the first one give Khalid outside the "ready for takeoff" thumbs-up sign. The Executioner acknowledged the signal by biting his lip.

In the tower, the air traffic controller responsible for ground traffic picked up the phone and within seconds had the station manager for American Eagle on the line. "Where are your passengers going today," he asked her.

"The usual," she replied, routinely. "Their bus should be showing up at passport control right about now."

"Oh really? Well, either I'm having my first hallucination of the morning or I just saw your bus load of passengers driving over to one of the helicopter hangars."

"What did you say? Helicopter hangar? Wait a second, let me find out. I'm not aware of any change of plans. I'll call you right back," she said, with some alarm in her voice. And hung up.

Finally, the helicopter was fully loaded and the hatchway closed. Drawing a deep breath, Khalid took one last look at the airport, where he suddenly saw two vehicles emerge from the shadow of the control tower. Their yellow lights were flashing, and they were accelerating in his direction. Khalid jumped into the first copter, rudely shoving a passenger out of his way, sitting right behind the pilot.

"Go! Now! Let's get out of here!" he yelled, putting a pair of earphones on.

Tremblingly, the large helicopters lifted off from the concrete field in front of the hangar signed *Royal Desert Helicopter Tours*. Simultaneously they turned their noses into the wind and tilted forward; and as soon as this little aerial ballet was completed, they thundered down the airstrip in low-level flight, heading for the coast.

"Do you have a course for those three copters?" asked the air traffic controller into the phone.

"Helicopters? What helicopters?"

This was when the controller knew that something was suddenly going very wrong at the Casablanca airport on this gray morning. He stared at the disappearing spots of helicopters as they headed into the coastal haze, and dialed the number of the airport police.

"Something's not right here," Sam said as he looked out the cabin window. Nobody but his wife heard him in the noisy helicopter, and she was used to his complaining.

"Relax, Sam. We're on vacation," she yelled back in his ear. "Isn't it wonderful?"

The ATC stood by the tower window watching the disappearing helicopters with binoculars. He finally put them down and stepped over to the radar operator.

"Where are they going? Can you give me a course? Come on Ali! Get me some information!"

"Forget the radar, Boss," Ali answered. "They're flying too low. I can't get any kind of reading at all. Nothing. They've vanished without a trace."

"Let's hope not," the controller said, shrugging his shoulders.

He wasn't overly concerned. Unauthorized flight movements were, after all, not that unusual here. Someone or something in the system had fouled up. The employees at Mohamed V had a little saying for situations like this: Enjoy *the fuck-up. A day without it would be the end of the world.*

51.

The helicopters flew very low over dry dune grass, and after no more than 15 minutes, they landed on a dusty field not far from a coastal road.

"Where are we? Do you see a hotel?" Xaver asked, looking into the cockpit where the compass revealed their flight direction.

"Didn't you know we're going to camp?" somebody joked back.

Sophie was sitting near the pilot, a dashing young guy in tight overalls who clearly attracted her attention. But her father, looking out the window at the whirling clouds of dust, pulled her closer to him.

"Stay next to me," he whispered.

"Are we getting off? Look, everybody's getting off the other helicopters," she reported.

But the hatch of theirs remained firmly fastened, and the crew showed no signs of leaving.

"I guess they're staying at another hotel?" Snell asked no one in particular as their helicopter rotors whirled faster and the cabin began to tremble. They lifted off abruptly. They saw the crews of the other two copters driving the passengers on the ground away from their machines. The bewildered tourists moved away, coughing and rubbing the dust from their eyes. Sophie noticed a gun barrel pointing out of the hatchway of one of the copters on the ground.

The confused passengers on the ground heard another armed man yell out "A bus will pick you up here. Just wait!" before he ducked back under the rotors of one of the now empty helicopters. And in just seconds, both had lifted off the ground.

From high above in the first helicopter, Sam stared at the grotesque sight. For miles around the abandoned tourists there was not a single building. The travelers stood among the dunes as if abandoned to their fate, waving their arms and shouting while the two empty helicopters disappeared along the coast with an inauspicious thumping.

Sam thought of the abandoned group with a foreboding of harm, and wondered if their fate in the one remaining helicopter would be better or worse. He looked ahead and could hardly believe his eyes. They started flying straight out over the Atlantic Ocean, very low over the surface of the sea. Only their helicopter. 30 Americans from Arizona. *Freedom Travel.*

Sam used his powers of discipline to remain calm. But he said to himself, *This smells worse than the Brenton administration! Something is wrong, very wrong!* His eyes met Mark Yale's. The doctor scowled and pressed his lips together.

Susan made a funny face and shouted something into Zoe's ear. Both of them laughed heartily. It was very loud in the cabin, so Sam made a sign to Snell to pick up the headset lying next to him. Sam put one on too. Sophie suddenly had a pair as well, and they realized that they had voice connection.

"We're flying over water," Sam said to Snell, the ex-cop. "Do you have any idea where these guys are taking us?"

"Well, not to our hotel, that's for sure," Snell answered.

"We're flying northwest out to sea," Xaver said, watching the compass and suddenly becoming vocal.

"The men in the other helicopter had guns!" Sophie said loudly. "I could see them! Terrorists! They'll kidnap us, or shoot us!"

Then they all heard the same voice through their head-sets – the voice of the man sitting next to the pilot.

"Shut up, all of you! My name is Khalid. I am also known as the Executioner. And as far as you're concerned I am the boss around here. You are in my complete control. You are prisoners of Yussef bin Golem, the great patriot of Islam, the Jihad warrior, the head of the *Qaeda*. If you do not obey my orders you will be shot, or thrown into the sea alive for the sharks to eat!"

A loud click in the headsets signaled his sign off.

Sophie stared wide-eyed into the pilot's cabin. Snell covered his eyes with his hands. *Bin Golem, of all people!*

"What is it?" Mark Yale asked, his voice drowned out by the rotors' noise. He read the answer to his question in Sam's ashen face.

At this moment, the helicopter banked steeply into an almost 90 degree curve. At the same time, the pilot pitched the machine down and opened the throttles. The 30 Americans from *Freedom Travel Tours* felt as if they might free fall into the sea. They held their stomachs, moaned, and fully realized that they were at the mercy of some of the world's most ruthless kid-nappers. Suddenly their light-hearted trip to Morocco had turned into a veritable nightmare.

52.

On the morning of their sixth day at sea, the *Shiraz* crossed the 34th degree of latitude northeast of Casablanca and moved toward the coast of Morocco at full speed.

The golden peaks of the Atlas Mountains greeted them through the morning haze. The boundless sea was colored a monochrome dark gray under the overcast skies that only here and there seemed ready to open to the sun. White crests glistened in the subdued light astern, while far in the west heavy clouds clustered in a storm that the weather forecast said would drift off to the south.

Bending over a sea chart, Captain Souri pinned the needle of a compass into the intersection point of his calculations. The imaginary point in the ocean where they would rendezvous with the helicopter would be reached in a matter of minutes, 60 miles away from Casablanca harbor.

"We're right on time," Captain Souri said to bin Golem as he walked onto the bridge.

The great patriot didn't answer the captain, but instead smiled and pointed to the television set, filled with the face of the President of the United States.

"The American is quite hot and bothered. Look, men! He has no idea how bad he looks. Have you ever seen a drunken mule? Well, that is what one looks like. And wait until he realizes where the hostages are! His jaw will drop down so far that his chin will hit the head of the whore giving him a blowjob – and she'll get a concussion!"

273

The crew on the bridge broke out into uproarious laughter.

"Well, well," the Jihad general went on, "you've got to have some fun at a funeral."

Most of the time bin Golem was a very dignified man without much sense of humor. But at times he could be as vulgar as any desert son. And whenever he allowed himself to joke, his men felt more comfortable and relieved. All of them were very tuned in to his moods.

The sound on the TV was turned down, but everyone on the bridge who, like their leader, had stayed up half the night, was either watching the picture or squatting in front of radios to hear the momentous news. They all knew why the President of the United States was addressing his nation with a very serious and sad look on his face. The attacks in Manhattan had hurled the success-crazed Americans from their height of complacent superiority right down onto the hard rocks of reality.

Suddenly the name Yussef bin Golem was on every American's lips. All over the country, border crossings, airports, and railroad stations had beefed up security. The media warned of possible further attacks by bin Golem. Military facilities both in and outside of the cities were considered to be at risk. And a call for revenge began to be heard loudly, which the President did not let go unheard.

In time, the President said, the U.S. would respond effectively to these cowardly attacks of the insidious terrorists. Just a few hours after the explosions in Manhattan, he had begun his speech with the words, "The enemy is among us," as he urgently demanded increased watchfulness from all Americans for possible terrorist activities.

"The diversion is working as planned," said the Information Officer on the bridge of the *Shiraz*.

A seaman brought a tray holding two big-bellied teapots and placed mugs on the chart table.

The leader of the Qaeda was in the best of spirits. "While they're still flapping around like headless chickens, we are already striking our second blow. And all, of course, just an overture to the main course."

Over the years, bin Golem had trained himself to be an outstanding strategist and military leader. He had been taught the trade of war in Afghanistan, where he had made a reputation for himself through successful command operations against the Russians. And then he went on to personally plan and manage 25 assaults against the Americans. Oftentimes he would remain in the background and let his executioners take care of the bloody work. But *Operation Megiddo* was different. It was itself the prelude, the first truly apocalyptic battle. And that was why he was on the bridge himself.

The two unrestrained passions that held sway over the *Qaeda* leader were power and women. "Just like the American President," bin Golem smiled to himself. Of course there were no women aboard the *Shiraz*, at least not until the hostages arrived. Yet bin Golem wasn't thinking about them. His thoughts instead revolved around the Frenchwoman. *Nadine. What a sonorous name! I will impress her I am sure. She will show her allegiance to me. Frenchwomen do not fade away in our hot climate as fast as our women do.*

He remembered an old saying from his native land,

about how a man should always bargain hard for camels and women. *She may be beautiful and hot-tempered, but still she is merchandise. First I will buy her, then I will tame her. I will make her my property. And if she refuses, well, then I'll have to teach her some manners.*

The Islamic leader knew that he was safe aboard the *Shiraz*. Even if his presence aboard the tanker were betrayed, he knew the Americans would be faced with a moral conflict – because in a few minutes the helicopter with the tourist group from Casablanca would approach, circle the giant colossal ship twice, and then cautiously land in the middle of a red-rimmed white circle, close to the bow.

53.

"The attack on the Armory is just as disastrous as the kidnapping. And the bad part is that it was probably an insider who let them know the Joint Intelligence Agency was in there," President Jack Brenton said into the wireless phone.

Joe Sorelli cleared his voice over the secure line. "Bad isn't the word for it, sir. It's a disaster." *And our good CIA had trained this bin Golem guy in Afghanistan. Now he's world's number one terrorist entrepreneur, congratulations,* he thought to himself.

"I found out a few interesting things," he added.

The President sat on the side of the bed in the White House. As he talked on the phone he played with a beige silk slipper with his foot: lifting it into the air, twirling it around, letting it fall. The bathroom door was wide open, and through it he could see the First Lady, his battle-hardened wife and partner. Happy Brenton stood in front of the sink naked, preparing herself for the mating rituals with the most powerful man in the world.

"Oh, good. You found some things out, Joe? Oh, and how is Carol?"

"Oh she's great sir, thanks for asking," the chairman of Specs Inc. replied. "But she still claims I snored at the table at your last dinner."

"Not only did you snore, but you mumbled obscene things in your dreams! But whatever, what have you got for me? Any news on this Saudi terrorist? Funny, how many of our CIA-trainees change sides."

"No, it's about C-Gag."

"Yes?"

"This Moran broad left Los Alamos real fast."

"Do we know why?"

"Well, they found a female FBI agent shot dead in her back yard."

"That's not very nice."

"I agree."

"Anything else?"

"Yes. Moran was on good terms with a radar specialist named Larry Johnson, who also worked on the *Aegis* taskforce. According to Johnson, the Frenchwoman is a born gambler, very sensitive…"

The most powerful man in the world pushed his big toe into the slipper and lifted it carefully. He could see Happy in the bathroom cleverly positioned in front of the pink marble pedestal sink so that about a third of her naked matronly pelvis was visible through the open door. Brenton remembered when this sight would prompt him to whistle through his teeth.

"So, does Johnson know what this is all about?"

"Well, he said that Nadine tweaked the *Aegis* system so you could not only activate it remotely but also control it from the outside."

The slipper slid away. *Fuck!*

"You always are the happy boy with the happy news, Joe," Brenton said. "So where is Larry Johnson spending his vacation?"

"What vacation? He's back with the Navy."

"Right," Brenton croaked jovially, reaching for the errant slipper with both feet.

In the meantime, Happy had moved over to reveal some more of her still attractive behind to him. She also turned slightly when she realized he was looking, showing him just a bit of her still blond bush. In his younger years Brenton would have clicked his tongue full of expectation at such a sight.

Sorelli went on. "Johnson asked to be transferred back to his old aircraft carrier, the *TR*. By the way, he's not that talkative a fellow. I had to promise him complete discretion."

"Does he know where Moran is now?"

"It's possible. It seems they talked on the phone recently. Johnson is working on a way to improve the radar-controlled rapid-fire cannons – you know, the ones that fire 900 20-millimeter rounds a second at incoming missiles."

"Yeah, I know about them. So where are we going to find this woman, Joe?"

"Not sure," Sorelli harrumphed. "But we have another lead you might want to look into. Concerning the Manhattan bomb attacks, it points to one of bin Golem's followers."

"You're always full of good news Joe."

"His name is Khalid, sometimes called the Executioner. And I think he's also the guy who pulled off the Casablanca kidnapping."

Why does Sorelli always know more than my secret services? If it didn't ruin my golf game I'd make him Director of the CIA.

"Well, I hear lots of rumors Joe," the President coolly offered.

"Very true, sir. We have enough parts of the puzzle I think to give us a clear picture. There was this supertanker in Lagos…"

Sorelli wanted to go on to tell the President what his contacts and experts in Geneva, London, and Teheran had put together in terms of evidence. But he didn't get very far.

"Senator Strong and about 30 Americans kidnapped in Casablanca. That doesn't sound like a joke to me," the President said with an authoritarian tone that was at least partly faked, since his eyes were following Happy who stepped into the shower without closing the frosted glass door behind her. She turned on the water and gave her usual piercing scream because it was either too hot or too cold. When she finally got the temperature right she began to lather her body in full view of her husband, one of the signs in their mating rituals that Jack was to join her.

"No, definitely not a joke, sir," Sorelli replied about the kidnapping. "Do you have any news? Do you know who the kidnappers are? Or where they took the hostages?"

The President ignored his questions. "I've talked to the Commander of the 8th Carrier Fleet in the Mediterranean."

"Isn't the *Roosevelt* the carrier you are planning to visit, Sir?"

"Yes, tomorrow. Off Gibraltar. I'll land at the Rota Base."

"But what about the hostages? Somebody's got to know something about the hostages," Sorelli tried again.

"Nothing. They vanished into thin air, Joe. Unbelievable. We can collect ice molecules on Mars, yet we're apparently incapable of tracing three helicopters."

"Three? That shouldn't be hard. To my knowledge there are no radar-safe helicopters."

"They flew too low for radar," the President replied, "and of course given the luck we're having they were invisible to our satellites because the weather over Morocco was bad. So we know nothing, absolutely nothing."

Both men were silent for a minute, and the sound of the shower from the bathroom seemed like the roar of the sea hitting the cloud-covered beach at Casablanca. Not quite sure of what to say next, Brenton was relieved of the burden as Happy turned around to face him and started to lather herself between the legs.

"Joe, stay where you are. I'll call you right back." He clicked off the phone and kicked the slipper aside. He stood up and peeled off the tailored silk pajamas and smilingly approached his wife.

"Well, my wet little cherub, what have we here" he asked, reaching out and stroking her between the legs. "I didn't know that such beautiful little angels needed so much soap to get into heaven. I thought you were all fresh and clean by nature."

Happy reacted by reaching out to the same region of his body and pulling him into the shower with her, lathering the presidential nether regions. "Umm, where is my strong little rocket so I can ride around on it? Is it going to be big and hard enough to carry all my hot wet lathered weight? Ooooo, yesss, that's it Jack...Yes... Just like that... Ooooo... Ahhhh..." she moaned and groaned as he worked his hand deeper into her and she kept stroking and stroking until he

281

himself moaned and trembled, announcing the end of their short love interlude.

"Oh, Jack... Now it's my turn..." But he had already stepped backward out of the shower and wrapped himself in a large towel. "Give me five minutes, honey," he said. "Bring your toy in when you're ready."

With the towel wrapped around his beefy hips, Brenton called Sorelli back on the secure line. He heard a snappy military "Yes sir!" from the receiver.

"Ok, Joe, where were we?"

"You said you were going aboard the *Roosevelt* in spite of the hostage crisis sir."

"You can bet your bottom dollar on that, Joe!" *I have to keep on good terms with the Navy. You never know.* "On board I'll meet with Juan Carlos. Oh, he said he wants to invite my daughter to his Lipizzaner stud farm in Andalusia. But I don't think I should let all this terror hysteria ruin my trip, should I? And anyway, once I'm on the *Roosevelt*, I'll be closer to where the action is. It'll be like a front line visit, so to speak."

Sorelli already saw the headlines in his mind's eye. *President personally intervenes in hostage drama.* He thought to himself, this guy really knows how to work the media!

The line was silent for a half a minute, while the President, as was often the case with him after orgasm, was hit with one of his brainstorms. He worked out all the details in a few seconds while the head of Specs Inc. waited respectfully on the other end of the line. Finally he cleared his throat.

"Joe?"

"Yes, Mr. President."

"Where are you right now?"

"In Washington, sir, close by."

The President looked at the old pendulum clock on the mantelpiece that had rung out the hours for many of his predecessors. The hands showed five minutes to midnight. At 00:30 a crisis meeting about the kidnapping in Morocco would begin in the Situations Room in the basement of the White House.

"You'll come to the White House in 20 minutes, Mr. Sorelli. This is an order. I need you Joe. And bring everything you have with you."

"Okay, Jack, sir. Will do."

"Good."

Hanging up, Brenton looked up to see his wife standing next to him and the bed, completely naked. She bent down and began to fumble around with the night table drawer that refused to open. Then she started rattling it. Brenton calmly watched her, accustomed to her little fits of anger.

His thoughts had moved on to John Strong, the small senator from Arizona, whom he had recently played a round of golf with in Phoenix. The preparations for freeing the hostages had gotten under way quickly. A special unit of the Navy SEALS had been put on alert that afternoon. At the same time the Commander of the 8th Carrier Fleet lying in the Mediterranean with the *USS Theodore Roosevelt* had received the orders to beef up aerial reconnaissance over Morocco in every way they could. And a report from Rabat said that crack troops of the Moroccan Army had also been mobilized.

I can't end my term with a botched hostage affair! After freeing Kosovo, and leading the NATO alliance to victory. Hell,

JFK got an airport, and USS Ronald Reagan is the name of the Navy's latest carrier." Maybe one day they'll name an aircraft carrier after me," he caught himself thinking out loud.

"Uh, they won't even name a minesweeper after you," Happy quipped, still struggling with the drawer. "This fucking thing won't open," she cursed as he stood behind her.

He put his arms around her and started to massage her dangling breasts.

"Leave them alone for a second," she said, and thrust her backside back to push him out of the way. He moved to the side quickly, but then he put both his hands, often described by the press as paws, over her more delicate hands and helped her with the drawer.

"One, two, three, hep," he counted off, and on the third try the drawer opened.

She reached in and produced her plastic friend, holding it up high in triumph. In her opinion, the device did an excellent job, whenever her husband had been too quick in coming. And it buzzed very quietly, not even loud enough to disturb his incessant phone calls, which as the President's wife she had been forced to get used to. She handed the white enamel cylinder with its soft latex head to her husband and lay back on the bed.

"And now," she said, opening her legs, "it's my turn."

"Five minutes honey, not a second more," the most powerful man in the world pouted. "I have to get to the Situations Room."

"Then off we go," Happy Brenton ordered. "I'll do it in three, no problem."

54.

A fresh strong breeze swept across the tourists' faces as they dizzily stumbled out of the helicopter onto the deck of the *Shiraz*. But they were not given time to breathe. Men masked in black, holding automatic rifles in firing position, barked orders at them that dampened any amazement they might have had at the giant ship where they now found themselves.

From the bridge, the helicopter had looked like a large ugly insect as it approached, and then like a black crouching octopus when it landed. But at the touch of a button by the Chief Engineer, the platform it was on was lowered and the helicopter disappeared into the enormous cargo hold. Khalid watched the disappearing helicopter with fascination while the hostages were hastened to the superstructure like a herd of sheep chased by vicious dogs.

The *Shiraz* was equipped with two hydraulic lifting mechanisms, one of which allowed not only the helicopter to disappear but also allowed the missile launch pads hidden inside the ship to be heaved up on deck. The shipbuilders had copied the construction from aircraft carriers that were able to move fighter jets from their hangers below to the flight deck in virtually no time at all.

On the bridge, bin Golem smiled wistfully. *Everything proceeds as planned. May Allah be praised!*
Now that the hostages had arrived, they had surrounded themselves with 30 live human shields. Human shields? He smiled in amusement. A shield like *Aegis* – and

just as effective! The thought of comparing them to the billion-dollar *Aegis* defense system protecting the *USS Theodore Roosevelt* made the gentle bin Golem erupt into coarse laughter.

55.

The cabdriver raced toward the city at breakneck speed. Casablanca, Morocco's largest city with countless coffee shops and tearooms, stirred up pleasant memories for me. As soon as we left the highway, a vibrant quarter of the city filled with small shops swallowed us. Nadine held onto the handle above the door to keep from being thrown around inside the cab as the driver searched for obscure shortcuts through the maze of narrow streets.

Our cab's departure from Airport Mohamed V had not escaped the watchful eyes of CIA agent Jim Walrus Watt. He had taken up a position in front of the rental car desk and carefully watched every passenger coming through customs into the airport terminal. As soon as he recognized Nadine he pulled the brim of his hat down and followed her outside.

He memorized the license plate number of the cab she got into, along with the man whom he recognized as the pilot in Nis. Under the circumstances, Walrus considered tailing the cab to be risky. Polinsky carried himself like he was part of the trade, not easy to be shadowed. Frowning, he dialed a number in the Moroccan underworld where he would be able to hire men for the dirty work and gave his contact precise instructions what to do.

Watt, an agent as corrupt as he was experienced, cursed his own organization as a wretched bunch of failures that produced one debacle after another. Even thought they paid his salary, he somehow felt that the CIA had lost all right to exist. His stupid director had sent him to Morocco all by himself to chase after a woman who had secrets that tomorrow would probably be available on the Internet.

Here he was, on a secret mission – a white man in a place where he stuck out like the proverbial sore thumb. No, the field agent was a dinosaur that had had its day. What really worked were the specialists in information security. People in private organizations like Specs Inc., Bloomberg, and Rand had more reliable information at their fingertips than the CIA ever had anyway. Walrus ground his teeth thinking of the local jerks he would have to make do with as his helpers. He could only make a fool of himself, at best.

We drove through a wealthier quarter of Casablanca with elaborately decorated houses and small boutiques. The buildings became ever more beautiful. A golden yellow structure was on our right. In front of it was a sidewalk made of many-colored flagstones, and its colors were echoed in a beautiful mosaic on the wall. A broad stripe of small black, brown, and dark green tiles standing on their pointed edges moved slowly past me. Then the cab got stuck behind a slow moving vegetable cart. The driver cursed and honked his horn. I elbowed Nadine and urged her to look at the opening in the beautiful wall.

A true feast for the eyes stood before us. A narrow passage with an elegant arch revealed an inner courtyard. The ground was covered with gorgeous floor tiles the same color as the flagstone sidewalk. And the front of the golden yellow wall inside was decorated with the same stripe pattern as the one outside. We saw a monk moving slowly inside the courtyard. I noticed with some astonishment that his brown-striped robe and hood fit harmoniously into the same design as the outside of the cloister, making him seem, so to speak, like a large tile.

"Do you really want to go to Moulay Hill, Monsieur?" the cabdriver asked, interrupting our amazed gaping at the beautiful courtyard.

"Yes, exactly."

"But nobody goes to Moulay Hill," he said, and as if in explanation moved the back of his hand over his throat in a slitting motion.

Moulay Ismael was the name of the sultan who united Morocco in the 17th century and gained an international reputation for his country. He was said to have tortured his slaves and pampered his camels.

When I made no reply to the cabdriver, he turned around. His immaculate teeth and white eyes shone against his black skin like the snow on the Monte Rosa.

"I will not drive there. Not me. Very dangerous for Madame," he insisted, as he turned into a broad avenue.

"Then stop over there," I commanded. He slammed on the brakes, joyfully it seemed.

"Voilà, Monsieur. As you wish."

I pushed a couple of dirhams into his hand and got out, helping Nadine up from the narrow backseat. I looked around for a fearless Portuguese cabby, which according to my friend Alaoui are among the best in Casablanca.

Nadine, with her unerring instincts, had already discovered a coffeehouse. "Let's have a café au lait over there," she suggested, and walked over to the tables sitting out on the sidewalk.

The waiter at the Palmiers du Sud Café brought us coffee and a chocolate brioche that Nadine ate ravenously. French and Arab businessmen sat next to us reading their newspapers while I contemplated our next step. The unmistakable sound of "Don't Cry for Me Argentina" drifted out over the air, lending the scene a touch of romance. No doubt the same version was dripping from the ceiling of some department store in Zurich, which made me think uneasily of my merciless deadline in court and how my time was running out. *Steinlin! No, there's no time for him now. And what could I tell him anyway? That I was drinking café au lait with a beautiful French spy in a coffee shop in Casablanca? I could just hear his nasal twang: "Impressive, Polinsky, very impressive. Why don't you jot that down and save it for your next thriller."*

Coming back from my reverie with a jolt, I mumbled to Nadine, "We should go on, as quickly as possible."

"Do you think the hill is really dangerous?" she asked in her deer-eyed innocent way.

"Quite possibly. But I thought you could hardly wait to get up there?" *There is no cure for feminine logic.*

She imitated the cabdriver's slit throat gesture and made a croaking sound. "I think beauty and hostility go hand and hand in this country," she rhapsodized philosophically.

I didn't reply, so she went on cautiously. "Maybe we should ask somebody how dangerous it really is?" And she dug back into her brioche. "Did you ... bring any ... detailed maps of the area?" she mumbled with her mouth full. Sometimes she could be disarmingly cute, for a little snake! I couldn't help but laugh at her dangerous charm.

We both knew that the crossing point of the coordinates engraved on the golden amulet was located exactly on the top of Moulay Hill, a spot northeast of Casablanca in the Atlas Mountains. I actually had a topographic map of the area from the supplies of the Royal Moroccan Army. It showed a narrow road leading to the foot of that infamous hill, on top of which was a large structure marked by black rectangles.

Tracing our route on the map I said to her, "I don't see any real difficulties. That cabdriver was probably just superstitious."

"Maybe the sultan tortured his ancestors," she countered, as I studied the steep terrain on the western side of this mysterious elevation. "We'll take the eastern approach, right?" she asked, back in the role of my co-pilot.

Looking up as if by instinct, I saw my Moroccan friend Alaoui nearby, leaning against a palm tree. He was watching us over the top of his high-end sunglasses. When our eyes met he gave a barely perceptible nod to the side and strolled away.

Alaoui was a Berber and quite familiar with the hinterlands. He had been a sergeant in the Moroccan Army, serving in an elite mountain corps – and now owned a cell-phone store in downtown Casablanca.

Nadine, in her odd mix of wanting to get on with our mission and wanting to sit and safely sip coffee all day, protested when I told her we were leaving. But I made it very clear to her that I had left everything behind in Zurich all for her – and reminded her that I was running from one crazy adventure to the next for her benefit. She snarled like a love-crazed tigress, but followed me as I walked quickly through the park to the gas station where Alaoui held the car door open.

His restless eyes scanned everything around us, reminding me of how serious our mission was.

"Anyone following us?" I asked.

He indicated that he didn't think so, and sank down into the deep English leather seat behind the steering wheel. The car was an old Jaguar 12-cylinder sedan – and I wondered how it would negotiate the winding road that, according to the map, was often unpaved and always very steep.

Alaoui read my mind. "Where we are going is all rocky slopes and narrow canyons. In the remote valleys scattered villages stick to the ledges. The Berbers have lived there for more than two thousand years."

Honking wildly, Alaoui fought his way through the crowded marketplace. He slid by an elaborately piled mountain of oranges, missing it by an inch. On a cart next to the oranges, an Arab sold spices. He and a colorfully dressed woman began walking next to us, offering their wares. She had precious woolen blankets and jackets for sale, and the two of them competed for our attention, screaming. The marketplace was an unbelievable vibrating bustle of human energy. Snake charmers, beggars, and acrobats mixed with merchants, moneychangers, and other customers in one noisy crowd. Jews, Arabs, Portuguese, Africans, Berbers, as well as the ever-present tourists mingled together. The tightly packed square was filled with bewitching scents and sounds, as well as temptingly beautiful faces.

"Here at least," Nadine marveled, "time is not yet money." She said that Morocco was always magical for her. The humming, picturesque, and not always harmless scenery had always attracted sensitive souls. Even this market, which was really just a hangout for nobodies, attracted its share of artists, writers, and singers.

Yet, in Morocco too, Islamists were not inclined to tolerance. The country's four groups of fundamentalists were often perceived not so much politically but culturally, which led to the mistaken assumption that religious radicalism was a problem of Algerians, Egyptians, and Tunisians, but not of Moroccans. In all sectors of Islamic society, however, Yussef bin Golem attracted a growing circle of adherents, for whom Morocco's long tradition of tolerance meant nothing. They formed small active cells and waited for their leader to give them an order to take action.

As the Jaguar left the market area, the city began to look terribly poor and blighted. Suddenly abject poverty was all around us. Our old and shabby but nonetheless flashy car jolted up and down over dirt roads. On both sides of us we saw primitive houses made of corrugated iron, pieces of plastic, wood picked from the garbage piles, and cardboard. I had never seen worse poverty than in these slums north of Casablanca. Nadine and I both heaved a sigh of relief when we left this depressing neighborhood, but Alaoui seemed completely untouched by the misery of his countrymen. As far as he was concerned, he was a Berber, part of a proud and independent tribe of warriors and landowners – and bore no relation to these impoverished people. As if to emphasize the contrasts of Morocco, we saw a new air-conditioned bus pulling through the same slums we had just left.

"I have talked to Brahim. I know him well. He served under me in the Western Sahara. Perhaps *he* will lead you to the hill," Alaoui said ambiguously.

"We'll take the route through the green valley, won't

we?" Nadine asked, filled with expectation. Alaoui nodded and gave me a surprised look.

The streets around us were suddenly cleaner, the houses larger. The sun was already high in the sky. Small groups of men in loose woolen caftans and djellabahs sat in front of their houses, sipping tea.

Nadine seemed more relaxed and leaned back in her seat. "Why was the cabdriver so afraid of the hill?" she asked Alaoui as we pulled out onto a broad country road and rushed north.

"The Moulay Clan controls the area," he replied before sinking into silence.

Nadine winked at me playfully. Here in the countryside, she acted more like a woman, or even a little girl. She was like a chameleon, changing her colors to suit her environment. Seemingly unconcerned about the dangerous position we were in, she suddenly appeared to be cheerful. It reminded me of our one hot kiss on the way to Zagreb. But other than that, not much had happened between us. Here and there I might feel the touch of her small hand; and once, almost coincidentally, she had patted my behind. But not much to build on. I had good instincts for self-preservation, so I guess I pretty firmly resisted what I might call the craving for Nadine Moran. But it was there, nevertheless. And that's the way it was. *Don't think of the broken eggs, Polinsky! Think of the omelet!*

56.

My cell phone rang. It was Irina, panting and rattling off her bottled-up news. "My battery is almost dead, I've got to hurry. One of the Corps Commander's last big deals before he died included the Magadino SA arranging a whole bunch of *Exocet* III missiles for a company in Oman and…"

"When?"

"About two months ago. The company in Oman was liquidated and struck off the register right after it had paid $10 million in cash."

Aside from the Russian Sunburn, the *Exocet* III was the most advanced anti-ship missile – and the one most feared by the United States.

"What happened to the missiles in Oman?" I asked her.

"As far as I could find out they never even came near the Oman coast," Irina blurted out, as if she felt she didn't have much time left.

"Taiwan?" I guessed, as the threat of Red Chinese invasion faced by that rebellious island state would make such a purchase understandable.

"Don't know," she shot back. "The bill of lading came from the print shop of a South African company that specializes in counterfeit papers. For enough dough, these people will make you any document in the world, if necessary, such as a certificate of origin for an elephant from Greenland or for Semtex explosives to be Swiss cheese…"

"Where from…?

"I've got that answer too hon. You can rely on your

lately very lonely at night friend Irina. I just thought I'd throw that in on my own behalf." She caught her breath, and I almost thought her battery had finally died, when she started to fire from all barrels. "A Norwegian freighter picked the *Exocets* up in the French La Rochelle. As you know your Uncle Edouard was on very good terms with the French Secret Service, not to mention with so many willing ladies! Anyway, a woman shipping department employee of the missile manufacturer gave him a copy of the acknowledgement of receipt."

"How do you find these things out?"

She started doing what she did best – talking really fast.

"Ifoundthescrapofpaperinthearchivesof MagadinoSA." According to this information, the Norwegian freighter *Sovereign* unloaded the missiles at the Iranian port Bandar Khomeiny. But right there, at the northernmost point of the Persian Gulf, the lead stops. It appears that the Iranians…"

"Well done Irina. Trust me, your lonely nights will soon be over," I replied, flirting shamelessly. "Do you know anything about any ship movements in Bandar Khomeiny at the time of their arrival?"

"No, I'm not big on ship movements, I like other kinds. Speaking of which, as far as my lonely nights are concerned…" but she stopped, almost as if embarrassed. "Well, just wait until I get my hands on your fly. I'll check with *Lloyd's*, access their website…"

"Check with Specs Inc. too – the Geneva office."

"Ok, I will. Oh, by the way, you know Brenton personally, don't you? Didn't you tell me that once?"

And then her battery must have run out, as the line went suddenly dead. That I knew Brenton was a little-known state secret from a long time ago, but perhaps not that long ago and not so little known. *Nobody's business*, I thought, pocketing the cell phone.

"The battery went dead," I explained to Nadine with a shrug.

"And what was the name of that battery?" Nadine asked pointedly.

"What? Oh, you mean Irina, my assistant. She helps me with research for my new book." Worth a try, but it didn't work.

"Bandar Khomeiny? Specs? Geneva? That doesn't sound like research for a book to me."

"She was just giving me updates, Nadine. Just routine stuff."

"First she updates you and then she fucks you, right? And don't you dare try to tell me she's a lesbian!"

"No no no, not a lesbian. Although, what do I know? Maybe she's a little bi? You know, nowadays, that's not all that unusual."

"Stop playing the fool Polinsky. What does that slut have to do with our plans?"

I didn't like the sound of that. Her piercing harsh tone made my stomach tense. Or maybe it was because Alaoui hit the brakes and turned suddenly. We bounced over potholes, and skidded along a furrowed gravel road.

Without a word he held up the map to me and with a meaningful nod pointed to the area ahead. I concentrated on the map and looked for contour lines and the course of a river. I guess I just let Nadine's hostility slide, hearing her harsh words pass away in the droning of the Jaguar's engine. Finally

Nadine was revealing a bit of herself through what appeared to be jealousy. Too bad we didn't have time to explore it further – but there were a few more important things on the agenda.

You know Brenton personally… Irina's words lingered.

Yes, I knew Jack Brenton.

But what was Irina suggesting? Was I, as if by chance, to call the President of the United States?

"Hey Jack, uh, listen, I've got this small problem here… it's about this girl."

"Isn't it always about some girl, Stan, with you and me? Tell me about it, or her…"

"But I think it's also involved with something going on against the Americans…"

No, Brenton would not ignore me if I called, I think. On the other hand, I didn't really have enough specifics, at least not yet. And it wouldn't make sense to feed him vague hints in front of his team, would it? I may as well call Colossimo!

So how did you become friends with the President of the United States? I remember Irina asking me that question a long time ago.

After all, there are plenty of wannabes claiming to know Jack Brenton – people who shoved past others and maybe even shook his hand. People who then never forgot his very special handshake, where he touched your elbow with his other hand and looked into your eyes so deeply that it seemed you were the only person in the world. Of course then he would go on to the next person, the next hand. It was the high art of wringing flesh, and Jack was the world's undisputed master.

But with me of course it was different, very different. Jack Brenton told me he thought I was a miracle, a part of his very soul. Maybe because our relationship involved family and blood, and near disaster. But whatever it was, it ripped open the surface of conventional pretense, and allowed the humane within him to well up.

It happened in Paris, one of those stupid receptions. Why I was there remains a mystery to me even to this day. I think I went because I wanted to do a favor for this woman talent agent whose face was lifted all the way to her eyebrows. Maybe because I thought she might be able to do me a good turn if one of my books ever reached Hollywood. But whatever, Paris is not the worst place in the world to jet off to. Spend a night at the Plaza Athénée. Something might come of it. *You never know how things will turn out. Not in a novel, not in life.*

And there were other potential perks. Sharon Stone was supposed to be there. As was Billy, the President's brother, who was in Paris promoting of all things his new record album. So I sat on the dais with the President's brother and Buzz Aldrin, the astronaut. We gave some interviews, while the photographers from Paris Match, who was paying enough money to cover the entire event including all expenses and fees, took exclusive pictures of us – why I still can't say.

Well, to make a long story short, Sharon Stone never showed up, just as Cary Grant would not have shown up if he were still alive. Depardieux, not smelling Sharon, poked his gigantic nasal organ into the place only long enough to have his picture taken. I looked around in vain for Gregory Peck or Jeanne Moreau.

But minor celebrities were everywhere. Buzz Aldrin, with the help of a very lovely model, was explaining his new rocket propulsion system to anyone that would listen – a system he guaranteed would cut NASA's costs in half if only the bureaucrats in Houston would realize the advantages of his ingenious new development.

Billy Brenton nodded, gazing out at the crowd of wannabe stars with strangely beatific eyes from a Good-Friday face. Most people said he was a pot smoker. Maybe he had moved on to harder stuff. Could the poor devil be hooked on the needle? No, the bottle was my best guess.

Later in the evening he entertained the crowd by strumming his guitar and singing a catchy tune for everyone that blared out of enormous speakers.

And as the hour got later I found myself talking to the picture editor of Paris Match, who with her beautiful body and natural blonde hair was a perfectly acceptable substitute for Sharon Stone. The later I stayed the better would be the contacts she could make for me with the American TV stations, she promised, in case I was interested in promoting my new book.

As we sat chatting on the couch in a lobby off the main room she set her snare with a "why don't you come up for a nightcap" speech. In fact, she had an even better one – a "why don't you come up and let me show you some special pictures" speech; pictures so hot she could never even print them. "Pictures almost as hot as I am," she added, lasciviously breathing in my ear.

Well, something was moving in my pants, pushing up towards my belt. And on the narrow sofa in the dim twilight, she slid over my body. Her hands were everywhere, and she was about to do on the other end of me, what after the President's testimony in front of the special DA would never ever be considered sex.

But I had another kind of pressure down below, on my bladder. *How embarrassing! Too much champagne. Whenever things get good...* I fought against my fate as long as I could, but then freed myself from her embrace. "I'll be right back sweetheart," I said as I went in search of the men's room.

But I couldn't find it, and since nature's call was imperative, I just ducked out a side door. *What the hell, it's more fun outside anyway...* With a dark alley in front of my eyes, I more or less staggered merrily into the open.

As I was relieving myself against an old chestnut tree, chosen I think because chestnuts are my favorite trees, I saw Billy being shoved out of the hotel through the revolving door. Now Billy was a regular good old boy. His room was directly across from mine and we had talked earlier in the hall. He had said that wild horses wouldn't be able to drag him out of the hotel that night, as exhausted and jet-lagged as he felt. So it seemed strange to see him being pushed through the doors by two slick Parisian bad boys. I wondered where his bodyguard was as I finished up against the tree and pulled up my fly. Something about this didn't look right.

As they approached the limos, I thought perhaps that Billy had changed his mind and wanted a fast job down in Pigalle after all. But then I saw one of the low-lifes take a hypodermic needle out of his jacket pocket. Suddenly wide-awake, I started running to their car. Before the guy could hit Billy with the needle I grabbed him by the back of the neck and pulled. The rest happened pretty much all by itself.

Between my military training and Li-Li's kung fu, I just lashed out again and again, taking out the second guy, driving the needle into the buttocks of the one who would have pushed it into Billy. He started screaming bloody murder, which got the porter's attention at last. Billy stood there kind of dumbfounded. I dragged him away from the car, dropped the needle. Finally, the hotel security guards trotted along, gaping at the car's taillights vanishing in the alley. In the broken-off needle, they later found residues of a fast-acting anesthetic that would have knocked a horse out in seconds.

Two days later Jack Brenton himself came to Paris, not only to dine in style with the French President at Alain Ducasse's as reported in the media – but also to pick up his dear brother and bring him safely back home to the States in Air Force One, where he could rest in the protective circle of their concerned family. And accompanying the President and his brother in the spacious salmon-colored cabin of America's flying command center was none other than me, Polinsky!

During the eight-hour flight we started to talk, and discovered we had a lot in common. I indulged in stories about my heroic deeds, and he told me his war stories. *Double life, double life – You are telling me, Stan?* Brenton remarked in a nostalgic tone, and once he came to understand a bit about my many tangled identities he toasted me: *To your private life, Stan!*

In that dark night outside the Plaza Athénée, I probably had derailed a plot with a sharp eye and a few well-timed punches. The President was totally convinced that I had acted in secrecy, kept my head, and looked for no reward. He was extremely grateful for the safe return of his brother, no drug affair, and no further scandal at all to give his critics any ammunition.

To your private life, Stan! Right now that toast haunted me. Down the drain, that's what my private life is. *Was it my own fault? Or had this rebellious Frenchwoman calculatingly drawn me into this delightful mess?*

Nadine Moran didn't react to my very skeptical side-long glance except perhaps by slightly pursing her beautifully curved lips. And perhaps with a deep breath that very favorably swelled the curves of her revolutionary rib cage. My Marianne! A woman of the people, who would, one day, filled with patriotism, bare her breasts. For freedom, and perhaps for Polinsky! La vraie Comédie Française!

57.

The hidden valley was far from the road. Its slopes were dry and dusty and steep. We had to cross it to reach the foot of the hill. A cool stream babbled between rocks and green meadows, and the clear mountain air made the sky so bright and steel blue that it hurt to look up into it. The sun beat down on the top of the car.

Alaoui rolled down the windows as the car left the valley bottom and meandered its way upward on a narrow road on a ledge that crossed the slope. We could see a stream glistening below us. A curve ahead of us around another ledge offered a good view of the valley behind us.

Alaoui stopped the car and we got out. I drew my cap down on my forehead and looked ahead to where the road became even narrower and crossed a long gravel slope like a dusty line. The cliff dropped off steeply, about 600 feet straight down. Then I turned around and looked back at where we had come from – and I saw clouds of dust.

"Alaoui, that doesn't look like your friend Brahim."

Alaoui already had the binoculars in his hands and stepped to the edge of the cliff. "I don't like the looks of this," he mumbled.

After a while Nadine peeled herself out of the back of the Jaguar. "I thought you guys just wanted to mark your hunting grounds," she said casually. "What's wrong?"

"Three black cars," Alaoui whispered. Because of the distance it looked as if the small convoy was driving very slowly uphill.

"Are they from the Moulay Clan do you think?" I asked him under my breath.

Alaoui shrugged his shoulders. "Hard to say," he whispered to me. Then he turned around. "Okay, let's go!"

We got back in the car and pulled out fast. The Jaguar's tires spun on the narrow strip of dirt dangerously close to the edge of the cliff.

"How far is it to Brahim's village?"

"About another half hour to the turnoff," Alaoui replied, checking the rear view mirror. "I think they're catching up to us."

He hit the accelerator hard. Rocks bounced up under the fenders. The heavy car was slipping and sliding, but thanks to the skillful maneuvers of our driver we stayed on the road, close to the rock face. When he reached the narrowest portion of the road Alaoui slowed down. We could see that further up, the road led to a small open area overgrown with brush, past which it lost itself in a tight bend.

When we reached the small elevation halfway up the slope I looked behind and shouted, "Stop!"

Alaoui, trained in military discipline, hit the brakes immediately. The heavy Jag came to a sliding halt. The view backwards was not great, as it showed the convoy of cars still pursuing us, approaching the steep slope, followed by a long cloud of dust. Alaoui and I communicated with our eyes.

"Wait behind the next bend," he said to me. Pointing behind, he made a casual gesture and put the car in reverse. I understood his intention and got out of the car with Nadine. Quite unexpectedly, she touched my arm and pointed up the hill. We could see a small stone house on top of the hill, hidden by branches. I guess she thought we would have a better view from the house, because she took off crawling up the hill towards it, waving at me encouragingly to follow her.

"Those guys are after us," I gasped, as I followed her up the hill on all fours.

Maybe it was the perspective, or maybe the sudden physical exertion stimulated my blood circulation – whatever it was, I suddenly felt that I had never seen a behind as sweet as the one seesawing in front of me on its way up the hill. *Gorgeous chassis!*

As we worked our way up the hill she asked me in disjointed fragments, "Who the hell... even knows... about us being out here... in the middle... of nowhere?"

Reaching the top just after her, I answered, "Don't forget, sweetheart, the CIA is after you, no?" I stood up straight to see if I could see Alaoui.

"Come here Polinsky!" she urged. "Look, there. It's the sign!"

Her eyes were fixed on the stone bunker-shaped structure in front of us. We could hear the droning engine noise of the convoy from the other side of the valley as well as the racing of the Jaguar's engine as Alaoui backed the car full out onto the small road, blocking it.

She held up the amulet. "Do you see the lily?" she asked, breathless, face flushed. "See, the sectional view of the blossom. And over here, on the bunker, look!"

As I stepped closer to her and the bunker an odor greeted me – actually more an emanation than a smell. Suddenly here, exhausted, sweating, excited, Nadine's body finally emitted something raw, fundamental – a sharp almost mordant odor that hit me like an animal in heat.

Doing my best to ignore it I took off my sunglasses and squinted my eyes. I saw three stylized petals on the bunker.

She held the amulet close to my face. "Exactly the same symbol. Look!"

She was right. The flower cross-section on the bunker wall looked exactly like the engraving on her amulet.

Alaoui had driven the Jag a couple of hundred yards further up the slope. Then we saw him stop and get out and start running back in our direction. Below in the background, our pursuers were unstoppably pushing ahead.

"Thierry-Clé is somewhere around here, don't you think?" she asked as we stood in front of the heavy concrete door.

I focused on the stone slab with the painted yellow lily on it. Nadine turned back and looked for Alaoui. "What is he doing with our car?"

Then I noticed an unevenness in the surface of the stone slab.

"Nadine, come here. Quickly! Help me!"

She came near me and I told her to spread her legs.

"Oh right, Polinsky."

I pointed up, and she must have understood me, because she turned her back to me and opened her legs. I pushed my head and neck between them. She wore no stockings, only a light skirt. Then I wrapped my arms around her knees and lifted her up. She sat up on my shoulders and screamed when I almost lost my balance.

Swaying on my shoulders, she stretched up, and I could feel her mound of Venus pressing on the top of my neck, firm and thick like a baby's fist. Suddenly we seemed to move in a heavy, almost dreamlike way. Time slowed down, and daylight seemed to darken like liquid honey or resin in which we became two staggering courting creatures stuck like rutting flies in amber.

I strained to keep my balance on the steep slope, and as I felt her moving on me in a certain rhythm I began to sweat profusely, especially from where her legs were wrapped around my neck. She rubbed against it, even rode it. Her muscles began to contract rhythmically, relaxed, and contracted again. She opened her thighs wider to give her hard clit contact with my neck. I obediently followed the pressure of her hands on my head and of her wetness on my neck.

Suddenly she really started to ride me, in small short jerks. Her legs were open, her knees slack, one leg on the steep slope, the other shoulder against the wall of the bunker. I helped, I guess, as much as I could, but to put it bluntly she was getting herself off. And then she came, in bucketfuls, as a crass gentleman might say. A real female ejaculation.

Nadine's hot juices mixed with my sweat as we stood there trembling. To have lent her my back like a mule so she could satisfy herself was not really my idea of good sex. And it was scarcely romantic. *At least it was safe sex* popped up in my mind.

But then I finally barked at her, "Well, if you're done now why don't you try pushing the slab up there, the one with the fucking flower on it."

She obeyed my orders without a word, as she shakily fumbled around the wall until she finally asked, "What are you looking for? Nothing is moving."

"Keep on trying," I barked, straining to keep her up there. "Try the right side!"

Just then Alaoui arrived at the bunker, breathing heavily from rushing up the hill through the brush. He stopped open mouthed when he saw us in our piggyback dance. Fortunately Nadine kept us from having to explain.

"I found it!" she called out. A slow crunching sound confirmed my suspicion as the heavy bunker door slid open slowly.

I squatted down so Nadine could get off my shoulders. We avoided eye contact. But then she looked at me as if she had just arrived from a hasty but very satisfying breakfast. *Just wait, my dear. Dinner is yet to come!*

Then she turned away and looked at the lily as if hypnotized. I wiped my neck with my hand and understood all too well. Now that I was not needed anymore I could just disappear. So what!

I turned to Alaoui and asked, "Did you know about this place?"

"Maybe she did," I heard him saying.

Startled, I looked at her questioningly.

Nadine obviously recovered from our impish pas-de-deux, just stood there, nodding slowly, lifting both hands, palms outward, and casting her eyes down in a gesture that says, *Please, not now.*

My stomach dropped. "You? Don't you dare say you have known all the time..." I panted.

"Hold it, Polinsky. I couldn't use the information... It was too vague... Not safe at all. Look, from the man who gave me the amulet I also got a map with directions how to get up here in case Belgrade wouldn't work out. But I left the map behind in my place in Los Alamos. Stupid! The only thing I knew was that it was important to get up here from the eastern side, as we did, then... "

"You better stop making excuses," I cut her off angrily, opened the first door and staggered into a dimly lit room. My heart beat faster.

Something was wrong with Nadine, though ... something didn't track in straight lines for me. Something... what was wrong here?

Alaoui quickly opened a hatch and light streamed into the room, showing us the interior of a modern command post.

"What the hell is this?" I asked.

"Please", Nadine insisted, "when we got here I suddenly remembered what the man had told me: He said, there was an army fort somewhere to control the access to the valley, so... I guess this is it." She was moving a telescope closer to the open window. I removed the protective cover from the small command console, trying to digest that the woman I naïvely thought needed my subtle guidance had just taken me on a ride, twice, in the true sense of the word. *Something was wrong... focus your thoughts somehow...* but I couldn't think in straight lines.

Looking through the telescope Nadine announced

matter-of-factly, "The Jaguar is standing right in the middle of the road."

"The perfect roadblock," I said, giving Alaoui a long look of appreciation. He grinned. Our military minds communicated silently.

"The three cars are stopping. Men are getting out of the cars. Two of them, no three of them are carrying rifles." Nadine reported from behind the telescope.

All the control lights on the console were shining bright green. The display on the monitor showed that the steep section of the road and the rubble slope were filled with mines, which would let us trigger an artificial landslide. The area was divided into three sections, with the Jag standing in section three. I found the red button with the number three on it and tore away its safety seal.

"We have to stop these people down there, haven't we?" Nadine suddenly barked at us. "Who are they anyway?"

"That is what we are about to find out," Alaoui said, pulling a heavy automatic pistol from his belt. He gave me a pathetic look that seemed to say, *man, this woman always has the last word.*

"A fourth car!" Nadine exclaimed. "A Land Rover. It's stopping!"

I moved over to the open hatch and saw a shape get out of the Rover.

"He's talking on a cell phone. I can't make out his face," she said.

CIA agent Watt alias Walrus had stopped the Land Rover a safe distance away from the three sedans. His instincts told him that something funny was going on. Not kosher at all. He didn't want to repeat the same mistake he made at Nis. His well-trained eyes saw that his men were all standing together in just about the dumbest way possible. He had to watch these guys, just as if they were raw recruits in their first week of basic training.

He pushed his hat up over his brow and got out of the Rover, groaning. He yelled into the radio transmitter, "Tell that asshole in the Jaguar to get his fucking car out of the road fast or we'll personally push him over the cliff!"

Whatever his men said to him did not add to his amusement. "Then push the goddamn thing off the road. And then head up the hill to that little rock house."

Cursing himself and his fate, Walrus stepped behind the Land Rover, opened his zipper, and pulled out his soft cock. *Damn! These local yokels are nothing but second-rate hoodlums who hire themselves out to shoot bullets into anyone they can.* Usually when he took a piss, Walrus at least had a few moments peace, which he always appreciated. But not now. His mind went back to Los Alamos, to his shallow breathing, to a flashlight moving up his chest and hitting him in the eyes – to his index finger on the trigger, to the dry bang of his gun followed by a bullet nearly grazing his head. What the fuck! Walrus' eyes nearly popped out of his head, he forgot what he was doing peeing all over his pants. He suddenly realized that he was not haunted by the nightmare of the shoot-out with the FBI-agent. There was real shooting going on here!

"Who's shooting?" I shouted in alarm and moved over to the hatch to have a look. Below I could see the four men firing frantically into the Jaguar with automatic rifles. The heavy car shook under the hail of bullets and sagged as they blew out its tires. The men kept shooting until all the windows shattered and fell out. Then they moved closer, and hesitated. And then started shooting again like madmen.

"Well, they're after us, no doubt," Nadine mumbled, frightened, as the burst of machine gun fire died away.

Walrus was squirming in frustration. The wet stripe on his pants stuck to his knee and shinbone. He really wanted to run over to those lunatics and smack them in the head. They were obvious morons. But he didn't want them to see his pants; plus something in his field experience held him back. Something wasn't right here. As he stood almost paralyzed his men flung open the door to the Jaguar. And then they shrunk back.

"Strange, the vehicle is empty, boss," a sheepish voice said over the radio.

"Just get the road cleared you idiots!" Watt raged back.

"The Moulay Clan controls all the drug trafficking around here," Alaoui said as the gangsters below started pushing his bullet riddled Jaguar out of the road. "Further north, they process kif and marijuana into hashish and sell it throughout Western Europe. They do about $2 billion worth a year."

I had systematically worked my way through the standby stages of all the explosives on the monitor screen and had been able to identify and defuse the mines in sector three where Alaoui's noble coffin of a car was. And at this moment a red triangle flashed above each sector to show how to trigger the explosions. Well, that was certainly easy to understand! My index finger itched, cautiously caressing the release.

Nadine was still looking through the telescope. *I just don't know,* she told herself. *That guy over by the Land Rover. I've met someone before who looks a lot like him... Los Alamos, Jim ... Watts, exactly. He searched my office, my apartment ... wait, could he have found the map I left behind? How else would he know the way up here...*

We stood close to each other. The animal odor about her had not entirely dissipated. Suddenly I found myself reacting now to her sexuality, not before when I had strained to keep my balance on the steep slope and allowed her a massive orgasm. But I paid no attention to my stupid hard on. Instead I looked right past Nadine down to the road, where the men were heaving and dragging and pushing the Jaguar over the low sloping side of the road. They stopped for a second, like a predator before the kill.

"Salauds," Alaoui groaned as his once proud Jaguar slowly tipped over from the final push of the thugs and gave way to the forces of gravity, noisily tumbling into the deep.

Alaoui looked at me. "Those swine probably work for Moulay. Or maybe for that stranger back by the Rover."

"For the stranger", Nadine said.

Annoyed agent Walrus got back into his Land Rover and pushed the starter. He hadn't the faintest idea that at that very second I had my finger on some buttons in the bunker and was getting ready to push them into explosive release.

The earth shook slightly. The sound of the three explosions was muffled and subdued, almost shy. The result, however, exceeded my wildest expectations. We watched amazed as about 1,000 yards of road simply disappeared into the deep. The three cars belonging to the gangsters fell down as if they were on an elevator. And the men who tried to get out of them whirled through the air, helplessly flailing their arms.

By the time Walrus looked up, the road had simply ceased to exist. Gone. The earth had swallowed both cars and men. He got out of the car and gaped, truly frightened. He stared at the destruction, not 40 feet away from him. His terrified face looked down into the yawning gash. He straightened himself up and walked swaying back to the Land Rover. A cloud of dust swirled up and obstructed his vision. Coughing, he got behind the wheel. Slowly, very slowly, he started his backward retreat.

"I'm sorry about your car, Alaoui," I said when all the rumbling faded. Nadine stood near the hatch, the amulet clutched in her fist. Her brow was pale and furrowed.

"I don't believe in coincidence," she announced.

"What else would it be, girl?" I answered gruffly, disguising my unsure feelings. *Was the lily, after all, a mysterious landmark, meant to lead us to our destination? Was Nadine keeping anything else from me?*

"Let's get out of here," said the practical-minded Alaoui as we heard the clatter of horse's hooves from outside.

Nadine, surprisingly, embraced me from behind. "We're almost there. Please, let's stay together. I am sorry I didn't tell you earlier, are you still angry with me, Stan?" she whispered in my ear, her firm breasts and nipples making my back tingle with excitement, banishing my impatience with her. I

315

pressed her hands against my belly, wishing they would move a bit further down. She owed me one, didn't she?

58.

The clopping of horse's hooves came nearer still. Alaoui hunched behind the bunker door, his gun in firing position.

My 9-millimeter is in the trunk *of the crushed Jaguar, sitting on the bottom of the valley,* I cursed to myself. Nadine sat on the cold concrete floor, holding her golden amulet to her chest. We heard a kind of growling sound from down the road, and the sound of the horses stopped. Absolute silence. Suddenly Alaoui relaxed and stood up. He looked out of the hatch and then turned back to us grinning, motioning us to follow him outside.

His friend Brahim sat straight up on a white horse, as straight as the barrel of the rifle resting in the crook of his right arm. His head was tanned from sun and wind, wrapped in a white scarf decorated with the same colorful design that adorned his horse's precious bridle. Behind him, three brown saddled horses with colorful leather bridles plucked and chewed on leaves from the underbrush.

Brahim cut a fine figure high atop his white horse, in his white anorak with the two leather belts across his chest, his suede boots, his rifle, and his proud countenance with which he acknowledged us. We cautiously started walking down to the road.

"Our luggage!" Nadine screamed, when she had caught

her breath. I was searching for some words of consolation for her and for myself (after all, the red file had been in my duffel), when I suddenly saw all of our bags neatly lined up along a small slope on the side of the road. I felt very relieved and patted my reliable friend Alaoui on the back. He gave me a short nod back while securing our bags to his horse. With some effort I heaved myself up onto the back of my animal that was apparently accustomed to inexperienced riders. My last horseback ride had been over 20 years ago.

We took off at a trot. Brahim rode in front, bolt upright and alert; Nadine followed, riding high in the saddle as if she had been born on the back of a horse. It didn't surprise me, after the ride she had just taken on my back!

Alaoui followed behind. We went a short distance around a curve, and a valley opened on the side. We turned into it, among gentle gray hills surrounded by a beautiful blue sky filled with white cumulus clouds. We rode in silence, swift and determined. For how long I couldn't say. The sun beat hot on my back, but I couldn't use it to estimate time. Just as my backside began to hurt Brahim stopped and pointed uphill with the barrel of his rifle, where a steep path wound its way up the mountain. On top of the high hill, a white wall shined against a bright blue sky. The slopes around it were covered in low thick underbrush, like fur on a bear.

Brahim and Alaoui were speaking to each other in Berber. Nadine stroked her horse's neck, and I figured I should do the same. When Alaoui dismounted and took our bags from his horse, tying them to ours, I realized that we were about to lose our escort.

"Forbidden territory," Alaoui said to me, matter-of-factly.

Suddenly a helicopter swooped over us in the knoll. Nadine's horse bucked and raised up, but Brahim was on it in a second, grabbing its reins and holding it still. My horse was as oblivious to the helicopter as it had been to everything else throughout the entire ride. The helicopter swooped high above us, banked into a loop, and headed for the hill with the white building on top. *Sure the pilot had seen us!* I thought

The thwapping of the helicopter faded as it landed on the hill.

"We're going with you!" Alaoui called out to me. Spurring his white horse into overdrive, Brahim climbed the slope to get to the path that wound its way as a light-colored lane uphill through the dull green underbrush. My horse followed his without any encouragement from me. I pressed my thighs tight against its back and leaned forward to keep from dropping out of the saddle. Behind me I heard Nadine's clear laughter. *What a moody little brat!*

Gradually but steadily we rode up the valley's slope. Cautiously, I turned around to look at Alaoui, who threw me a silent look. Forbidden territory! I shrugged my shoulders.

59.

The scenery changed abruptly when we reached the mountain pass where the path ended. Our wonder-struck eyes stared at an open gray-brown mountainous landscape. Soaked in sweat, I got off my horse to stretch my legs. My ass was definitely saddle sore.

The white building on the hilltop was invisible behind a high soaring ledge. Nadine gazed calmly at the breathtaking panorama of the Great Atlas Mountains – *A wild woman! What was she up to? Something was wrong... the man who gave her the amulet... he is around somewhere. He is on the hill!* I was almost sure, that he was on that helicopter. *No proof, premonition only.* She seemed perfectly at home here in the wilderness. To the north, the Riff Range's silhouette shimmered in the haze. In the opposite direction, the dark blue expanse was the sea.

Alaoui lent me his binoculars, which I used to study the ledge in front of us.

"This is where we go our separate ways, Polinsky," he said. "Accept this weapon as my present." A silver dagger was lying in his palm. "Strap it to your leg," he added, holding it up and revealing its beautiful sheathe with a leather strap.

The Berber was obviously not a man of many words. But his eyes spoke of loyalty and of the devotion of a true friend. With a motion of my head I pointed over to Brahim and reached for my wallet. Alaoui, embarrassed, shook his head no. "You are strangers in this country. We are Berbers! We are here to help you."

We embraced, while Nadine strapped her bag to her

back. Then I too shouldered mine, and we set off up the last stretch of the infamous Moulay Hill. I turned around after we had gone about 20 feet, and I could see our Berber friends and their horses trotting down the steep path.

"Polinsky, is there any chance we'll really make it up to that house?" She didn't really sound concerned about it, so I assumed she merely wanted to be entertained.

"Oh, we'll make it. We'll climb up along that ledge," I replied. With determination I trudged uphill. "But please, let's keep it calm this time."

"But why?" she laughed. "You were as calm as a lamb last time, weren't you?"

We stayed quiet but cheerful as we climbed up to the highest point. Gasping, we crouched behind a small head-high tower of dry clay and peeked at the white rectangular houses under flat roofs. Extending behind this cluster of rambling cubes was a longer and wider building.

"It must have been the sultan's palace," I whispered to Nadine. I crept around the small tower and instantly found an opening.

"In we go, my lady," I said, helping her.

"This is a Hamam, you know, a family bath, like a sauna," she said. And actually, the inside of the small tower did look like a sauna, decorated with limestone motifs. But most saunas didn't have a trapdoor on their floors.

"This must be a secret exit," I said, lifting the wooden boards of the trap door. The hinges creaked as if they hadn't been opened in ages, and a rat darted off. Nadine's scream went through me like a stab in the nuts.

"Hush! Don't be so prissy!" I hissed. "Come on, give me the flashlight."

With Nadine's reluctant assistance, I checked out the iron ladder leading down into the deep. We took it down and then opened a rusty door that led into a corridor free of any resident vermin. Which was good on one level and perhaps not so good on another, as Nadine's shriek had reminded me of some of the most beautiful moments in my past private life!

We moved quickly down the corridor over a thin rug. I whispered to Nadine that this must have been a secret escape route. We reached a dimly lit stairway and quietly ascended it. What we saw when we looked over the balustrade took our breath away.

We looked down into an inner courtyard covered with magnificent tiles. The room was like a large green square, made up of thousands of dark green mosaic stones interspersed with lighter colored ones with red spots. Strips of tile in the center of the floor formed an octagon, which was filled with exquisite mosaic floral designs around a small eight-pointed star made of black stones, which formed the base of a large white marble fountain.

A woman in a light damask gown with long black hair walked up to the fountain. A boy in a violet shirt hopped after her. She took him by the hand and then dipped her other hand into the fountain, washing her forehead. And then she washed her boy's face. We gazed transfixed at this cleansing ritual that had probably remained unchanged for 2000 years.

Suddenly the boy raised his eyes and looked at us. He pointed at us and said something to his mother. She looked up at us, frightened. Nadine ducked below the balustrade, but the woman's beautiful eyes captured me. I couldn't move a muscle, as if I were in a dream half wonderful half nightmare. For what seemed like an endless moment we stared at each other. Then she turned around, said something to the boy, and walked quickly away from the fountain. What could I do? It was too late. They had discovered us. The game was over.

"Come on sweetheart," I said to Nadine. "Let's go down. I could use some water."

We went down and took off our shoes at the edge of the courtyard, walking barefoot over to the fountain. I was sure somebody would show up soon. And then I would try to explain that the lady I was with had an appointment on Moulay Hill and that we would really appreciate any hospitality they could show us.

She followed me back away from the fountain, and sat on the floor tying her shoes back on. "Old Moran lives here. I can feel it, Polinsky."

That's what is wrong. She never calls him father... Old Moran!

The certainty in her voice killed any protest I thought of making.

"Well, come on then. Let's go look for him."

She pointed to a small corridor off to the side and led the way. If I had been ten years older and had a daughter like her, I would have wept with pride!

60.

The corridor led us to the narrow stairs of a stone spiral staircase. We went up and reached a mezzanine floor. Straight ahead was a red door. I approached it and pushed down the handle. It opened, and we entered a bright room.

There wasn't much in it. A bed stood next to a table. A mirror hung slightly askew on the wall. Underneath it was a comfortable modern armchair.

There was a single glass door that led out to a small balcony. Standing out there, the view was overwhelming. The balcony sat on the side of the mountain itself that, like the side of a pyramid, stretched smooth and flat right down into the deep, losing itself somewhere down in the plain.

Beyond that I could see the ocean, glistening and shimmering in the distance. I saw a freighter heading for the horizon, a small disappearing dot. The slope of the hill was covered by a reddish layer of sand, framed on either side by a rich green forest. A road went uphill in a zigzag design.

I stepped back into the room and saw Nadine sitting in the armchair absorbing the room wide-eyed. "This was his room," she said. "I can feel his presence."

"Old Moran? Thierry-Clé?" I asked pointedly and felt almost as if I were intruding. She kept quiet and I busied myself by straightening the mirror. But as soon as I touched it an envelope fell to the floor. Apparently it had been stuck between the back of the mirror and the wall. As quick as lightning Nadine picked it up and looked inside.

"Pictures," she said anxiously, pulling them out. She

motioned for me to come nearer. She quickly spread them out over the table – about a dozen old and yellowed photographs, one showing a little girl laughing. I turned that one around so I could get a better look.

"Nadine."

"Look, look at this one!" In her hand she held a picture of an airplane. I took it from her and held it up in the light. *The Concorde! Didn't I know that smiling civilian standing between those two men in uniform in front of a dark hangar?*

"Uncle Edouard," I whispered to her.

Nadine turned the photo over and read out loud, "1973." Then she looked at the yellowed picture of herself as a girl. "Papa was here. Where did he go?" Then she pulled the string around her neck and produced her moneybag. She opened it and put the photo next to the floppy disk. "Come on, we have to find him!"

"Wait, look!" I said, bending over the photo of a dashing pilot in front of his jet. "A *Mirage*," I added. Nadine peeked over my shoulder and saw the jet's nickname painted on its nose very legibly: *Tacite Cantat Mors.*

"Do you know what that means?" I asked. "*Tacite Cantat Mors?*"

"Of course," she answered instantly. "Tacite Cantat Mors means – death sings silently, or rather – The Silent Song of Death. Wait! Get me the red file. Come on, fast! Your file! I am sure that is the key. Tacite Cantat Mors. Yes!"

TCM – the three letters on my red file ... "Wait a second. How can you be so sure?" I wasn't exactly stupid, but I never would have made the connection so quickly. It's a rather sobering moment when a man realizes that the woman he is pursuing is intellectually superior to him. It's a good thing that modern psychology has invented the term emotional intelligence. Although I'm sure it was invented as a feminist answer to a male dominated world of intelligence testing – but thank God the concept is reversible and applicable in this case to a man. All tables can be turned if one wants to badly enough!

"It's Latin, Polinsky, what's wrong with you?" And in spite of my superior emotional intelligence, there was a flicker in her eyes that confused me. *Was she keeping something from me? What was wrong with her, was the question here...*

"The only thing I have to do is copy the text into my computer. The rest is child's play. Come on, help me! Pass me the red file!"

I never told her the file was red...

I thought I heard footsteps and stifled shouts, and I wanted to get going. But Nadine brushed my concerns aside with a cold hand gesture. As she worked on her slim laptop she seemed totally consumed. I had never seen her like this. She was so excited that she even forgot to put her moneybag back around her neck.

Ah, when ingenious women lose their heads... Death sings silently. Hadn't somebody said that to me recently? Yes! That Turk at the funeral! Tacite Cantat Mors. TCM? Those were the initials of Thierry-Clément Moran!

"Come on, hurry. Bring me your bag," she said, having started up her notebook. When I didn't respond quickly enough she went over to my bag herself, with a spellbound look in her eyes and shaking hands.

But suddenly she was riveted to the spot as someone kicked hard against the door, bursting the lock and flinging it open. Two tough-looking guys dressed in black rushed in, guns in their hands, fierce looks on their faces. They yelled unintelligible commands. I froze and watched. We heard more footsteps in the corridor. Respectfully one of the thugs stepped aside and a chunky man entered the room.

"Igor!" Nadine yelled. "Where have you been?"

He was a rather frail looking man, maybe 5 foot 7, dressed in brown pants and a herringbone jacket. He didn't reply to her but instead pointed at me. I was standing with my back against the table and managed to get Nadine's little moneybag stuffed into my back pocket before the guard pushed me against the wall.

"I'm not armed," I lied, lifting both my hands up high. He frisked the upper part of my body for a weapon, quickly and professionally. *Damn, this guy knows what he's doing. Better watch out, Polinsky!*

"We were waiting for you in Belgrade, Igor," I said, bluffing.

He looked at me with utter contempt and turned to Nadine. "Sorry, I was late, too late to warn you. Couldn't make it downtown Belgrade in time. Fucking air raids, you know. My Russian friends were waiting for me in Sudanese Embassy. They were all killed. Glad you made it here."

He ignored me completely, as if I didn't even exist, I thought.

The Russian stepped over to the window and pointed outside and down the mountain with a motion of his chin. "The entire Moroccan Army will soon be all over this place thanks to your ingenious demolition experiment down in the valley," he said brusquely.

"Well, maybe next time you could send us an invitation with proper directions instead of a necklace," I answered brazenly.

"Shut up Polinsky!" Nadine snapped at me. Then she turned to Igor. "Where is he? Where is Major Moran?"

"You will see him. I keep my word. But…"

"What?" she snapped again.

"Monsieur here…"

"Polinsky? He won't give us any trouble."

Not give them any trouble? Something wasn't right here…

Igor slapped his thigh. "Without this snooper, Nadine, you would have come to the Moulay Palace directly and escorted by our people."

Snooper? And she wasn't even protesting!

"Where is Moran, Igor? Answer me! This is his room, or at least it was. Where is he now?"

The Russian lifted his hand to calm her down as he started digging through my bag on the floor. He opened the side compartment and, with a triumphant gesture, produced the red leather case. Nadine watched without interest or concern. While he was fumbling around with it I tried to move a bit sideways, but immediately bumped into the watchful giant of a guard.

Of course Igor found the pictures that the Chief of Intelligence had given me in Zurich, looking at them wide-eyed. Finally, he stared at me as if I were a rare insect missing from his collection.

He knew the man in the pictures, and knew exactly what this was all about. I was in deep shit…

Igor was masterful as he played his trump card. He

took a step back and dramatically fanned out the pictures like a deck of cards. "I am afraid, Miss Nadine," he started slowly, "that your friend here didn't come all the way up on this hill because he likes your pretty face. He is spying on us, and is after this man. Look!"

Nadine looked at the pictures calmly. "Well, we know this man, don't we?" she said with a frosty smile.

"You know him? You, Nadine? No, you must be wrong," I moaned.

Igor pointed at me and said to Nadine, "This gentleman is an American agent." This time his words had an effect. Seething indignation spread over Nadine's face. "He has been leading you on," he continued. "Polinsky is after nothing or no one but Khalid. He came to Morocco looking for him." Igor's finger tapped the face of Khalid in the photo. "He is one of our best men – Khalid, the Taliban commander."

So, Khalid is the swine's name. At least, my guess was right. This looked like progress; still the situation became more uncomfortable by the minute...

Nadine stepped away from me aghast. Her facial expressions betrayed her changing emotions. Disbelief mingled with disappointment. For a second her face seemed to be pleading that this was not true. But then she seemed to be thinking and scheming. Anger flared in her eyes.

Idiot that I was, I of course had told her nothing about my past or about my search for the ominous third man who was supposed to save me from going to jail.

Moron! Now that you were so close, the mystery almost solved. Only a few more days until the hearing. And now this blow below the belt! Steinlin, Judge Righetti, Colossimo, even Mario...

all of them will consider you your rich uncle's murderer. What a triumph for the District Attorney.

'You, you deceived me!" she hissed at me. "That Irina is behind it. Just wait, you'll live to regret this!" She sent me a look that pierced me like a spear.

"Get him out of here!" Igor ordered.

The two guards grabbed me and shoved me towards the door.

"Wait," Nadine commanded. "You just don't get it, do you Polinsky? I had really hoped you were on my side. Too bad, really, too bad!"

She seemed suddenly in complete control of the situation. She took the blackjack from the belt of one of my guards and weighed it in her hand. "You won't be able to talk me out of completing my plans, Polinsky. There's much too much at stake. Much too much! You know, back home, Polinsky, we have a little saying: 'you can take the bull out of the stable, but you can't take the stable out of the bull'. Once a bull, always a bull. Once a spy always a spy. Understood?"

She was pleading so convincingly for my talents as a cop and a breeding bull that I could do nothing but stand there in a trance, nod, and grin. Then she made a slow, dance-like movement with the blackjack. And the last thing I heard was the Russian's gloating laughter as my mind exploded into a red ball of fire when she hit my head. My senses sank into abysmal blackness.

PART THREE

61.

My head was pounding as if a sledgehammer were hitting it. In front of my eyes there was nothing but flowers, blooming forget-me-nots. My aching eyes looked around, searching through the lovely flowers. But then they disappeared, and I felt soft cloth. And then someone bending over me, pulling and pushing me, trying to wake me up.

Did I smell smoke? Finally I managed to sit up and looked into the big scared eyes of the boy in the violet shirt.

"Where is your mother?" I asked, unable to forget her beautiful eyes at the fountain.

The boy just shrugged his shoulders. *Did he understand any English at all?*

I stood up, moaning and groaning.

Yes, there was the smell of smoke and fire in the air.

I asked him his name and if he knew where the other people went. I looked around the room. My bag was gone. The boy nodded and tugged my sleeve. *Was the poor boy a mute?* I collected all the pictures spread out over the table. Nadine's moneybag was still in my back pocket.

We walked from the room and worked our way out of the building through billows of smoke. I saw a soldier get out of an old Jeep and step behind a wall, probably to take a leak. I wondered if he were alone.

The boy nodded yes, as if in answer to my thoughts.

"Where did the others go?" I asked.

He shook his head and pointed a finger in the air.

"All gone?"

Nodding, he described circular movements with his index finger.

"Helicopter?"

He nodded vehemently, smiling from ear to ear.

"Let's go!"

The soldier relieving himself behind the wall had left his gun and equipment in the Jeep. We ran off, and before the poor pissing warrior of the Royal Moroccan Army realized what was happening, we were already in the car racing down the slope, engine roaring. The boy shook his clenched fists and roared with laughter as he looked back at the soldier hopping about like crazy, before he disappeared in an enormous cloud of dust whirled up by the Jeep. Above, black smoke spiraled up into the overcast skies. The palace was on fire.

After riding down the hill for about 20 minutes, the Jeep thrown side to side on the rough road, I braked hard and hid in the shelter of a clump of trees. I turned to the boy and took him by the shoulders.

"Where is the woman I came with? And the men?"

He pointed into the distance, and made a wave-like motion with his hand.

"Water? The sea?"

He nodded and formed a wedge with his hands.

"A boat? A ship? They're on a ship?"

Again the boy nodded brightly.

"And your mother? Ta mère?"

He lowered his eyes and shrugged his shoulders.

"Don't worry. We'll find her. What's your name?"

He looked around, almost as if he were looking for a piece of paper. Then he nimbly climbed out of the Jeep and bent over the dusty hood. With his finger, he slowly wrote A-L-I in the dust.

"Ali? Great! Come on kid, get in!"

But he shook his head no and wrote again. Bending forward I deciphered S-H-I-R-R-A-S.

"Shirras? What is… is that the name of the ship? The name of the ship where the men in the helicopter went? Were you listening to them, Ali? Are you sure?"

The boy couldn't stop nodding.

I turned south at the crossroads with the signpost for Casablanca and accelerated onto the asphalt road. I steered with my knees and pulled out my cell phone, typing in Alaoui's number, pressing it against my ear to try to hear anything above the roar of the open Jeep. The connection was horrible. When somebody finally answered, it was a nerve-racking tape-recorded voice – *Leave a message after the beep!*

Frustrated, I handed the phone to Ali, bent over the wheel holding it with both hands, and kicked the pedal down. Driving full speed helped us make progress. Suddenly I saw a small shack on the roadside. I hit the brakes and headed right for it. *I hope they have a phone. I need a better connection!*

The shack was actually a store that sold groceries, beverages, and other odds and ends. In the corner there was an old gray phone hanging on the wall that had probably seen its best days when Rommel marched through North Africa. But the sound was very clear, and I heard myself cursing as I got Alaoui's answering machine again. But I left him a message and my cell phone number, and called Irina. And I felt thankfully relieved when she answered as clearly as if she were standing at the counter next to me.

"Listen up my dear little Polinsky. Khalid is on a ship called the *Shiraz*, that's S-H-I-R-A-Z, get it?"

My girl was definitely on the ball. No unnecessary drivel this time. I took down everything she told me, including a web site, www.rogue.gallery.gov/quantico. *Was it a message from my past life?*

"What about it?" I asked in response to her mentioning the site.

She told me she had managed to gain access to the FBI and found out that they knew that Khalid had been seen in Zurich – on the day that my uncle died!

"Good girl," I said, trying to get off the phone.

"Don't you care where the *Shiraz* is, my hero?" she interrupted harshly. "Use your head, man. Here, write it down. According to Lloyd's, the huge tub is somewhere off the coast of Casablanca."

I took the exact positional data from her, read it all back, and said rapturously "You are a treasure, Irina! I won't forget this…"

"It's just business," she said coolly, and hung up.

There you go! Finally, a turning point. Things were beginning to look up. And high time for it. In another day or so Steinlin could appear in court with a stupid look on his face and beg the judge's permission to not only tell a fascinating story of his and his client's inability to get hold of the mysterious third man in the Diesbach case but also to give the High Court the cock-and-bull story of the hopefully temporary disappearance in the African Mediterranean of the notoriously zany and reckless bum and paperback writer Polinsky....

I threw the sales clerk a couple of bills, hastily grabbed two bottles of Coke, and ran outside. The Jeep was empty.

"Aliii!" I yelled.

Somebody poked me playfully in the ribs, and when I turned around I saw the roguish smile of the boy as he held the cell phone up to me. I took it from him. It was Alaoui! *Things really were looking up!*

"Alaoui, I need a couple of things."

He listened carefully and in the end repeated in disbelief, "A parachute?"

"Exactly. And a pony."

"Are you crazy. A pony?"

"Yes, please, do as I say. I need that pony. The best one you can find."

We arranged to meet at the port.

"Come on Ali, hurry up! Let's get cracking!"

We swallowed down the Coke as the Jeep raced towards Casablanca, guzzling its gas at a phenomenal rate. I stole a glance at my little hero.

What the boy watched up on the hill made perfect sense to me. The helicopter flew straight out on the sea to rendezvous with this tanker, that Irina reported to be nearby. The Shiraz a terrorist hideout? Nadine and Igor meeting with Khalid the Taliban Commander? A nice party to join... I decided.

On the way Alaoui called again and change the meeting point. I managed to catch the exit to the military airbase just in time, where I already saw him at the gate waving from afar, standing next to a Jaguar. *Jaguar? Hadn't I seen with my own eyes how his proud beast had fallen...*

Alaoui didn't exactly consider the parachute stunt a clever idea. Wasn't I a little old for such a thing? Not to mention that squalls had been forecasted, and not even a young, in-shape, well-trained specialist could manage to hit a moving ship in this weather by parachute.

Ok, then what was *his* idea?

He cleverly used flattery and nostalgia.

"Remember when we were training in the Riff Range? When it came to roping somebody down or even rappelling yourself down, you were the best." His argument was strong. His plan was simpler. And simply better.

"When you're right, you're right, champ! When do we start?"

"Right away."

I was about to leave when the boy reminded me he was there. He stood next to what appeared to be the Jaguar risen from the ashes. On the dusty window he had written "Ali???"

Alaoui and I whispered to each other. The first thing he told me was that the Army held the Moulay Gang responsible for detonating the mines on the roadway, and in retaliation had burned down the palace. Then he told me that Brahim had arranged for the delivery of a pony and was awaiting our instructions.

"But honestly, what do you need the pony for," he asked in desperation.

"It's for my little hero here. For Ali. My savior!"

Alaoui listened to my story with a deepening frown – about how the boy had hidden from the soldiers out in the barn, which they later set fire to.

He angrily threw his hands up into the air and stamped his foot. "Pony? Pony? He cries over the loss of a *pony*. By Allah! And what about his mother?"

"I, I don't know," I stammered.

"Ali, come!" Alaoui shouted. "My friend Brahim will take you with him. Your mother is safe. She is at Brahim's house with a group of other women."

We got into the Jaguar and drove through a gate to a small command post where Alaoui parked his new acquisition with a triumphant sweeping maneuver.

"Ok," I said, deciding to play along. "Where did you get it?"

"What? This one? This wild animal? What, are you suffering from amnesia Polinsky? I have always been driving this car. Is anybody saying anything else?"

Teaching a Berber how to steal would be like carrying coals to Newcastle, I thought, casting an admiring glance at my friend. He had that unbelievable talent of always being absolutely convinced of what he was saying. He was like the old family patriarch who, no matter what anyone else in the family said, would only believe that there was one version of the truth – *his!*

I wished I could summon that kind of confidence and become master of this art. For Alaoui, there was only one single Jaguar – *his!*

As far as I was concerned, well, today and tomorrow I am

Stan Polinsky, and maybe yesterday I was too. But when it comes to the day before yesterday, who can say for sure? Maybe my old identity was lurking. Was I Ken Custer? Major Kenneth Custer?

62.

On the flight deck of the Big Stick, the *TR*, CVN-71 *USS Theodore Roosevelt*, things were really busy. Two seamen in red jerseys were latching bombs onto two F-18 strike fighters while other crewmembers were carting cases and canisters back to the ammunition department.

Stackers and tractors were driving back and forth between boxes and cables. At first sight it all seemed rather chaotic – but the busy activities only obscured the fact that everything going on followed very tightly organized operational procedures. Every man and woman on deck had their own very specified roles, easily identified by their matching colored uniforms. The fuel crew sailors, dressed in purple, were backing away from the jet. In blue clothing were the aircraft handlers, the aircraft elevator operators, the tractor drivers, and the telecommunications people. Crewmembers on the four catapults and arresting gears all wore green jerseys. And those in red were responsible for arms and explosives or were assigned to the crash and salvage teams.

The *USS Theodore Roosevelt* was cutting the waves at full speed on a westerly course while two fighter-bombers were preparing to land on deck. Each of these gray and white F-14s was equipped with an eight-foot-long tail hook that would catch one of four steel cables stretched across the deck as it landed. Aircraft handling officers at the catapult in their bright yellow jerseys were attentively standing by, wearing safety helmets with sound dampening headphones.

In order to catch one of the four thick-as-fist steel cables stretched across the deck, the angle of the landing approach has to be exactly correct. The pilot of the first F-14 found his bearings by watching the "meatballs," a series of flashing lights that helped him line up for the landing. Although the lights were always on, the special Fresnel lenses made only one light at a time seem to glow, as the angle at which the pilot looked at the lights changed.

Right now, the lights were glowing above the green horizontal bar. He was too high. He corrected slightly downward. If the "meatballs" *under* the green bar were on, the pilot was flying too low, and if the lights flashed red it meant he was coming in much too low for a safe landing. In case the red lights on either side of the amber vertical bar were flashing, the pilot would know it was a wave off.

If the pilot caught either cable two or three – which meant his angle was close to perfect – he would earn bonus points on the ship's own internal ranking system. But even if he missed all of the cables, he could easily pull up and try again, since he hit the deck at 150 mph.

The *TR* was an aircraft carrier of the Nimitz Class, powered by two nuclear reactors through four shafts that could push it to a top speed of 33 knots or about 35 mph. From stem to stern the colossus measured nearly 1,100 feet, and it displaced almost 100,000 metric tons at full load. It was worth about $4.5 billion and carried 85 aircraft and a well-trained crew of 5,600 people, including 2,480 crewmembers in the air wing. The Officer of the Deck saw two small spots in the sky, two *Tomcats* lining up for a landing. A cable length away from the flight deck, a black *Sea Hawk* helicopter hovered over the blue waters of the calm sea, ready to spring into action if some unlucky guy should slide overboard and go for a swim.

Primary flight control was located in the control tower, where the Air Boss kept a watchful eye on the planes moving around on the flight deck as well as on those in the air getting ready to land, which he watched on the radar screen. Everything seemed normal, like a complicated but well choreographed ballet.

And all would go as scheduled.

To help the jets take off the *TR* was equipped with four steam-powered catapults that could forcefully thrust a 48,000-lb. aircraft 300 feet from zero to 165 mph in two seconds. The catapult's shuttle locked into a T-bar on each plane's nose gear and pulled it down the runway. The flight deck crews were able to launch two aircraft and land one every 37 seconds in daylight, and land one per minute at night.

The first F-14 *Tomcat* touched down on the deck with a crunching sound and smoke coming from its tires. Almost instantly the tail hook caught the cable, bringing the machine from 150 mph to a stop in just less than 320 feet. Even before his plane stopped, the pilot opened the hatch and waved to the Air Boss in the tower. Then he looked down at the plane handler who was giving him signals with her hands, directing him away from the landing strip. As soon as he had taxied to a stop in the parking position assigned to him, the second jet touched down, engines howling.

There were large cavernous hangars below deck. In seconds, each of the four deck elevators could lift two planes up to the four-and-a-half-acre flight deck. The two F-14s with their double jet engines would first be serviced on deck and then, depending on the schedule, either be restarted and sent out or lowered into the hangar.

On the bridge, the Officer of the Deck turned to glance at the elegantly shaped bow of the ship gliding beside them, the *USS Gonzalez*. This fast guided-missile cruiser, designed for multi-function missions against targets ashore or at sea, navigated side by side with the *TR*. After leaving the Mediterranean near Gibraltar, she would return to her homeport alone.

The Officer of the Deck was responsible for the safe operation of the ship, including navigation, ship handling, communications, routine tests, and inspections, as well as for carrying out the plan of the day. He reported directly to Captain Fisher. Also on the bridge with him were the helmsman, who steered the ship, and the lee helmsman, who informed the engine room about what speed to make.

At this moment Captain Fisher was visiting the pilot's briefing room, a cramped space filled with charts and screens located on the B-deck of the expansive superstructure, more or less above the officers' mess. The tall and handsome captain walked in and told the five pilots ready-for-duty who were standing to attention to take their seats. He sat down in front of a spread-out chart, coffee mug in hand.

"Well, men, orders will be issued in about an hour. But I can let you in on some of the things in store for us," Fisher said, moving the map to get a better look at it. "Here, at the intersection of 36 degrees longitude and 6 degrees latitude west, the CC will come aboard."

The five battle-hardened men in their deep green pilot uniforms showed no surprise about the visit from the

President and Commander-in-Chief of all Armed Forces. Important visitors were not all that uncommon, and it meant a mixture of nervous activity and extra bonuses, such as the kitchen crew's efforts to impress guests with opulent meals or in the case of the President the awarding of medals. Jack Brenton was not really disliked by the Navy, but he wasn't loved either. Military professionals had a hard time forgiving him for never wearing a uniform

"We'll rendezvous a couple of nautical miles south of our base in Rota," a young major said, tapping the map on the southwest part of Spain.

"Right," said Fisher. "The CC will arrive in the company of His Majesty the King of Spain."

"Ah, Don Juan."

"Yes, the Carlos guy. Did you know that he wanted to fly his own helicopter here and smash it up landing on our deck? Thank God for the old boys over at protocol – they talked him out of that crazy idea. Said it was a safety risk, there were operational constraints, you know, all those rich diplomatic phrases," the captain grinned allusively.

"So rendezvous will be just a little bit outside of the strait's critical zone, yes?" asked the F-18 pilot called Morse in a Texas drawl. A long, broad scar disfigured his cheek.

The injury, a reminder of a salvage mission, had exposed him to the mockery of his buddies. He had a problem on board they joked alluding to the vertically divided red-and-white signal flag common in shipping if an assistant pilot is required. But he was quick on his feet and said that he could send Morse code with his face: Quickly turning if from one side to

342

the other – the scarred side being the dash and the pale cheek the dot... and ever since then he had been known as Morse. "Yes," said the Captain, "exactly."

In no way had he wanted to depart from standard procedures and expose his ship to unnecessary risk. The passage of the carrier group through the Strait of Gibraltar required the utmost preparedness of all systems and the full concentration of the crew. There was no room for pranks aimed to impress superiors.

"It'll be business as usual, only more of it and better," the Captain informed them.

The pilots all nodded in agreement, concentrating on the display where a navigator had called up the strait.

"We'll be passing through the strait a little earlier than planned," the Captain said.

Like all such groups, Aircraft Carrier Group 8 was put together on a case-by-case basis according to operational needs. It was made up of the *Theodore Roosevelt*, the guided missile cruisers *Ross* and *Gonzalez*, one destroyer, a frigate for anti-submarine warfare, as well as two attack submarines and a supply ship for ammunition, oil, materials, and extra food.

According to Captain Fisher's plan, the group would begin the passage through the Strait of Gibraltar with an intense phase of aerial reconnaissance, especially over the adjacent African coastal regions but also over Spain and Portugal as well. The hills and bays were very hard to monitor and posed a constant threat of enemy ambush. And the terrain on both sides of the strait was rough, limiting the efficiency of radar reconnaissance – making them more dependent on aerial observation.

Only when everything was cleared would Captain Fisher bring the *TR* up to full speed and move past the Rock with a massive escort, heading out to sea. Nor would they tarry long at the rendezvous point south of Rota where they would pick up the President and the King of Spain. He wanted to get the *TR* out into the protective vastness of the Atlantic as soon as possible. So their famous guests would be dropped off as the carrier moved at full speed out to sea without being made aware of the high degree of alert.

"Are any special programs planned for the guests?" asked the young major, who had assumed the role of spokesman.

"We will receive them with the traditional hospitality of the Big Stick," Captain Fisher replied, with a grim smile. "Number One has put together a sightseeing tour for the King. A visit to the galley, the hangars, the control room, the flight deck for a couple of launches. The President will probably head for the wardroom to talk to the crew, and then maybe afterwards he'll chew away on a cigar on the bridge kind of like... hum... General Bradley at Omaha Beach!"

Everyone laughed at this one, which gave the Captain a good chance to withdraw with a jovial friendly nod to everyone. He didn't hear the comment "Hey, the old man's alright," as he quickly headed for the bridge up the narrow stairs.

That was nice, good. But still... still...

Something was making Fisher feel uneasy. A bad feeling in his stomach. Was he nervous because the President was coming on board? Or was it something in the air around Gibraltar? Fisher wasn't usually sensitive to such things. But he was a keen observer, and knew how to read the signs – if only there was something as clear as a sign to read. He sighed lightly as he saw Larry Johnson approaching him. *Not him again!*

"Sir!" The radar specialist saluted him smartly.

"Larry?"

"Yes sir!"

"Have you finished the prep work on your radar? Everything working?"

"Yes sir! I mean, I didn't have to fix anything. One of the systems is fully operational. But again, sir, I'd like to ask your permission to link *both* cannon batteries sir."

Fisher actually took this comment as a way to laugh in relief. The persistence of this chubby radar freak amused him. He had already allowed Johnson to connect one of their Vulcan Phalanx rapid-fire guns designed for anti-ship missile defense directly to his infamous Doppler radar system. But both? That might be going too far.

"I'm sorry, Larry, but I think I'm out on a limb already letting you hook the one gun up to your little radar project. And for us, anyway, the war is over. We're going home."

"Your decision, sir," Johnson said, a hint of disappointment in his voice but not in his sharp salute.

But suddenly Fisher realized what had been bugging him. Maybe this stubborn Larry Johnson, fixated on his radar system, was right after all. Their anti-ship missile system was probably the most delicate part of the ship's entire defense mechanism – a weak link. Especially since they would be so close to shore. *The coast of Magreb, the mountains, the hidden bays, the nests of the Islamists…*

"Wait a minute, Larry. You know, tomorrow morning we'll pass through Gibraltar. I don't think it would do any harm if you also hooked up the second gun into your radar system. But for the time being, this will stay just between you and me and the bedpost, do you read me?"

"Absolutely, sir! But we don't have much time left. I don't know if I can do it by tomorrow morning. With all due respect sir, we should've started earlier."

Captain Fisher made a casual dismissive so-what gesture and quickly walked away.

"I will do my best sir," Johnson called out after him.

Isn't that your goddamned duty, the Captain thought, shaking his head.

Recently, the captains of American warships have gotten a taste of the hidden high-tech dangers residing on close shores. After the destruction of the *USS Stark* during the Gulf War, the Navy avoided the coasts of Oman and Iran, not to mention the Strait of Hormuz, whenever possible. The Captain of the *TR* had lots of reasons for not taking the passing of the Rock of Gibraltar lightly. *Yes, those good old Brits knew what they wanted,* he thought taking the snappy salutes of seamen hurrying by. *The rugged rock faces of Gibraltar, cut out for heavy artillery, bombproofs... and monkeys.* Black thoughts and preconceptions filled his mind, all of it nonsense. *Just let them try it, these old Moors... I don't give a damn.*

All of a sudden Pamela crossed his mind – the way her snug, always freshly ironed uniform embraced what he would call a very slender, well- conditioned, high performance body. *What a gigantic waste of human resources!* With a bounce in his step and humming a ridiculous pop song from the 70s, the Captain decided to take the stairs to the bridge instead of the elevator. Time for a little exercise. *You never know what's in store for you. Isn't that right, Pam?*

63.

At the same time that Captain Fisher was bounding up the couple of hundred steps to the bridge, Yussef bin Golem onboard the *Shiraz* was looking skeptically at the "Admiral". He had called him to discuss with Captain Souri and Chief Engineer Brabeck final plans for operation *Megiddo.*

"Explain," bin Golem said harshly.

The would-be admiral was living up to his name. He bent over the spread-out sea chart in a dignified manner and waited until all of them, including the grand mufti, were giving him their complete attention. With military concision he went through his tactical plan, perfectly worked out to the last detail – a very convincing presentation, planned out to the smallest word. He explained that the ride through the channel is a potential nightmare to any aircraft carrier commander.

"You wouldn't be able to notice anything different in the captain's appearance, but inside he feels like somebody who had taken Valium walking over a bed of hot coals."

The "Admiral" straightened up and continued his lecture, making eye contact with everyone around him.

"The Strait of Gibraltar, located between the southern tip of the Iberian Peninsula and the northwestern cape of Africa formed by the Riff Atlas Mountains is nearly 38 miles long. Its western section, the shallowest area, called the Ridge, is only 54 meters deep, while the narrowest point of the passage between Gibraltar and Ceuta measures a maximum depth of 1181 meters. Gibraltar lies at the intersection of 36 degrees 8 minutes north latitude and five degrees 22 minutes west longitude. Mighty boulders flank the eastern part of the strait on both the Spanish and African sides. They are the last remaining pillars of a mountain link between Baetic Cordillera and African Atlas that collapsed in the tertiary period when a fault formed the Strait of Gibraltar."

"Enough geography," said bin Golem, cutting him short.

"But sir, it is significant," the "Admiral" went on. "The Strait of Gibraltar is only eight and three-quarter miles wide, and is a very dangerous channel. Of course the U.S. carrier groups have trained for its passage thousands of times. But going through it never ceases to make the officers on the bridge and in combat control very nervous. Nobody just relies on routine. Anyone who takes such a passage nonchalantly will generally be stripped of his duties and confined to quarters. Strict discipline, sir!"

"Which we also have here," bin Golem replied, remembering exactly how the "Admiral" had met his ruin: Women! He had been the quartermaster on the Maréchal Foch, and one evening had invited some dancers from the Moulin Rouge on board for a party. The success of his little orgy gave him the idea of permanently installing some ladies of easy virtue onboard. And for a long time his scheme worked. But eventually, as all had predicted, his floating whorehouse was discovered, and he was court-martialed. But rather than face time in jail he fled to Iran, where bin Golem recruited him. Not for women, of course, but for his nautical experience and military imagination.

"Before taking his carrier through the strait, the commander will have both coastlines carefully scouted. He will then send half of the escort vessels through before following with the carrier, also closely escorted. Once the passage is behind him, the captain will stop holding his breath. Let's see, where will it be that our captain will finally feel relaxed enough to breathe?"

Without waiting for a reply, he went on. "Here, I would say." He placed his well-worn bamboo cane on the chart, enjoying the looks of his audience. "Precisely here! At the crossing of these two lines, at the western end of the channel. We shall call this point Rota South."

"Why Rota?" bin Golem barked at him. Even disbelievers like this old womanizer understood the language of power and authority. Bin Golem knew just the tone of his voice had this aging galley boy shaking in fear.

"Sir! Rota is the American base at the western entrance to the Strait of Gibraltar. Only here, south of Cape Trafalgar, will the carrier commander feel safe again. And this is precisely where we will attack. South of Trafalgar!"

Murmurs swept through the room. The leader nodded with glowing eyes.

"Trafalgar. A fitting place, Admiral. This will be the last battle of Trafalgar. As soon as they start feeling better about having completed the passage, when everybody begins to relax, then we shall strike!" The Sheik spoke as if he had just come up with the idea himself.

The captain pointed to the spot indicated by the crossing of two lines on the chart. "An excellent place for the kill," he muttered approvingly.

"Imagine a U.S. Calvary unit back in the days of the wild west, reaching the entrance to a narrow canyon leading to the open plains," the "Admiral" began ranting. "Of course the area is filled with hostile Indians. And what will their captain do? Well, he first sends the scouts out to look for ambushes and to scale the walls to get a full overview of the place. Then he'll send a small troop through first, who will set up a base on the other side of the ravine. Then, and only then, will he take the rest of the squadron through the canyon. And this is exactly how Captain Fisher will get his floating airbase through the strait!"

Riaz came into the room. "A report from the bridge, sir. The *Roosevelt* has been sighted off Malaga."

"Earlier than expected," remarked the "Admiral", consulting the chart. *I will show them, once and for all!* In his imagination he saw future generations of naval cadets bending over sea charts studying his ingenious strategy. *I will make naval history...*

"All systems on high alert! It is now or never. Allah is with us," bin Golem exclaimed with fire in his eyes. "Remember the sequence. First we will clear away their digital antennas, then we will fire! And if all our missiles fail, we will ram them! We will break their so-called Big Stick in two, like this."

He took his own beautifully carved ebony stick in both hands and held it at shoulder height. Suddenly he brought it down on his knee where it broke in half with a loud cracking noise. Fixing all of his men with his famous deep dark gaze he said in a voice that fell almost to a whisper.

"Friends, we have but two choices. Victory, or death!"

64.

Three decks further down Nadine Moran was thrilled the same way as she had been that night in Los Alamos when she realized she had hacked her way into the *Aegis* system. *Would be nice to have a climax again right now in the middle of these pricks lusting for me...* Smiling inside, she moved a little closer to the man next to her. Looking at the monitor with the blue and white *Aegis* logo appearing gave her the same kind of peaceful sensation she had after smoking a good joint – a kind of intellectual euphoria. *No need to fancy sex anymore.* After all, she had, in fact, succeeded in manipulating the systems of the greatest naval force in the world! This gave her the real kick! *Kind of the one she experienced when she rode on Polinsky's neck... Hélas, too late to go back!*

And now she was sitting with the man who had once abandoned little Nadine. She gave him a look that could pass either for ardent admiration or intense hatred. *I never had a real father... and I still don't have one. I always wanted a strong role model to follow, like the Corps Commander, or Yussef, yes! Every girl needs a real father, Thierry. You cheated me out of that when you cheated me out of yourself! All of the coldness inside me is your fault!*

In spite of his physical proximity to Nadine, old Moran seemed strangely distant and cold to her. Was it nervous tension? Did he have any idea of what was going on in her mind? *Forget it, he's just concentrating on his job! But he never knew anything about the struggles I went through, my dreams of great adventure, my flights of fancy! And here I am at the peak of my dreams, and I'm still without a father. Who cares? You can sit there silently as long as you want to.*

Khalid stood behind her, surrounded by armed men. She despised him. He had threatened to kill her father – not only if she had refused to carry out their plans but also if anything went wrong as she did it. But what did these idiots know?

She gazed at Thierry-Clé, and for a heartbeat they looked into each other's eyes. She had been full of expectations to see him after all these years. But when she got out of the helicopter with Igor and spotted him waiting on the deck of the *Shiraz*, she didn't feel anything for him. He was a stranger to her. *He wasn't the man who showed me love, gave me a piggyback ride, threw a pillow at me,* she thought with a hint of nostalgia. The only thing that brought them together and created kind of a bond between them was their work in the *Exocet* missile control room, where they could secretly speak French. That was when she confided in him about her admiration for Yussef. He only gave her a weary smile, almost yawning...

Suddenly she felt sorry for him, for the hero abandoned by his country, the Grand Nation. But she wrenched herself away from her dreary musings. Today was the day of her greatest victory. The proud U.S. Navy, so filled with self-importance and so accustomed to winning all the time had absolutely no idea that their sophisticated defense system could be run from someone on the outside in remote mode, nor did they know that they were at the mercy of her fingertips as they flickered over the keyboard. *Wonderful!*

As with all great ideas that actually work, the principle behind her success was quite simple. Nadine would add a long string of code to the command to clear the system. Then she would select the combat simulation program that was installed on every aircraft carrier for training purposes, and start it. *Aegis* would then ask that the simulation be authenticated, and Nadine would have to feed it a full page of 4096-byte encoding known only to her. But once *Aegis* accepted this, and thus also the simulation, it was lost! Its weapons would fire hell bent for leather, the rockets of the escorting cruisers would zoom off at targets seemingly racing in from all four corners of the earth!

And invading the Navy's system required nothing but a telephone to transmit the code. The number to call, of course, was the *Aegis* system's remote server – which, for security's sake, would then call back a pre-programmed number. All of this had really been set up for the President, to give him access to the combat defense system at any time from any place.

And now I am the President, Nadine thought as she chuckled to herself like a teenaged girl from the Dordogne. She input the data. *Aegis* was at her feet.

"Are you old enough to remember the Navy's failed prototype my dear?" Old Moran's gruff voice made her start.

"What? Which one? The *Sea Shadow*? The billion-dollar disaster?" She glared at him. *What was he really trying to say?*

As far as she knew, the *Sea Shadow* project had planned to make a battleship modeled on the *Stealth* bomber, able to sail the globe without being seen by radar. But ships were not planes – they moved slower, had backwash, emitted heat, made noises. And no matter how raked the hull was, or how close to the water, it still stuck out of the sea like a sore thumb. Finally the Navy gave it up and retired the *Sea*

Shadow project honorably. But some of its technology remained and worked its way into the small low-profile warships being built for the 21ˢᵗ century.

"No, my dear, not the *Sea Shadow*. I was thinking of the new cruiser, the SC-21."

"Oh. What about it?"

"Well, when they made their trial run with it, you know, all computerized, state-of-the-art – apparently the computer operator hit a zero."

"A zero? You mean the key?" Nadine asked, distracted.

"Yes, and apparently it made the computer of the ship try to divide everything by zero, which of course yielded non-functional values – a very awkward business!"

"Just because the guy typed in a zero?"

"Yes! It crashed the entire system!"

"So what happened? Was the crew able to reset it?"

"No, it just stopped working," Thierry-Clé sneered. "The ship drifted around powerless and rudderless for awhile. Finally they had to tow it in. Very embarrassing, really!"

Nadine frowned. "Ah yes, I remember it now. But all of that was strictly confidential. How did you find out about it?"

"From the net of all nets my dear. People knew about it, and the laugh is always on the loser, in this case the system provider. News of it spread all over. 'Windows NT knocks out new warship!' So the clever boys from the competition made sure they flamed them on the Internet. Very malicious, actually."

"I see. I guess there's no such thing as 'it can't happen'."

"Exactly my point. Isn't *Aegis* just another one of

these systems? I'm sure it's no more immune to crashes or hacking than the SC-21 cruiser was. Oh yes, the Yanks have a highly sensitive computer system, enormously confidential – and with a single keystroke on zero it's all finished – just a single tiny zero!" He made his point about the incalculable susceptibility of high technology to disaster by spreading his arms high and wide.

"That's for sure," Nadine said, already lost in her own thoughts.

It occurred to her with some anguish that there was a saving code that could return the *Aegis* system to its normal operating mode – and that she had left it behind on the stupid floppy disk at Moulay Palace. But she didn't need it.

Damn shit! Who am I supposed to save? The President! Granted, powerful men like Brenton commanded her respect. But with all the scandals he had been through, he wouldn't be able to give me what I want or need. But for a man like Yussef, however, I am a gem, a trophy. With him there would be no limits, with him I could....

But of course, she had sent a backup copy of *Oedipus* to her mailbox at GC Tech. *Her well kept secret!* And it would be simple for her to download and decode it.

And speaking of decoding, the red file was safely stowed away in her luggage, decrypted and verified in plain English – *the TCM-key phrase had worked!* Once all of this was over, she would give the secret document to Yussef as a gift – a great way to maintain their friendship!

In spite of her current circumstances, or perhaps because of them, she felt a flush of heat rush through her lower body. *Men! What do they know about what goes on in a woman's mind or body? And what do we need them for anyway? A few minutes of shoving a warm hard piece of flesh into our hot ovens like an uncooked loaf of bread? And then what? My so-called father sitting here. Who knows what he or any other man conceals? What really goes on under Yussef's curtain-like beard? They all desire power. But what do they want it for? I know why: it's the power to fulfill every wish a woman like me might have. And what are my wishes? To have done whatever I want done. That is the power that we woman have over these strong... studs.*

65.

The mood of the crew on duty in the Combat Information Center aboard the *USS Ross* matched their rather dreary surroundings – dim light tinged green from the monitors, a monotonous low-level drone from the ship's engines, steadily humming computer fans.

The CIC was the nerve center of *Aegis*, the place where humans met technology; it contained 18 computer terminals, which, at times of reduced stand-by were manned only here and there. In front of the fire control consoles of the Tomahawk cruise missiles and the Harpoons the empty gray chairs swiveled slightly. No one sat in front of the four monitors handling anti-submarine operations. And according to the roster, neither the air combat coordinator nor the missile system supervisor was on duty.

The three seamen who were in the CIC were fighting the boredom as well as they could, monitoring radar images and occasionally squinting at the sonar display, keeping an eye on their own submarines. Under large electronic panels, the oversized monitor of the early warning system shined dully down on them. Now and then letters would flicker across the screen, punctuated by an occasional aerial shot. It was all very routine, and very boring.

The *Aegis* defense system was made up of three basic parts: sensors, a management system, and weapons. The sensor function, in many ways the core of *Aegis*, was largely handled by the automatic, multi-function SPY-1 radar unit, capable of detecting and tracking low-radar cross-section objects, from small missiles to stealth aircraft. SPY-1 was supplemented by another system designed to identify and track objects in an environment filled with electronic countermeasures (ECM) while it also generated ECM of its own. All information from radar and sonar sensors was fed into the Command Decision System (CDS) which helped assess threats, assigned priorities, and tasked and monitored weapons.

In fully automatic operating mode, data went straight into the CDS and then to the Weapons Control Systems (WCS), from where commands were given to individual weapons. The Operations Chief could also activate a semi-automatic mode that allowed controllers to assign priorities to certain targets – for example, if they thought backfire bombers were a greater threat than other airborne attackers in a certain instance. And when the semiautomatic mode was in use, WCS crewmembers could control weapons tasking themselves by interfacing with the automated system and exercising judgment. As a last resort there was also a casualty mode that would kick in as different systems were knocked out by enemy action, rerouting data and re-tasking weapons as appropriate.

A junior radar operator suppressing a yawn pointed at the satellite image on the monitor.

"Hey, it's the Rock of Gibraltar," the he called out. "Aren't there supposed to be enticing sea sirens or something there? Maybe I should ask for shore leave."

"You must have stayed home from school the day they gave that lesson," his senior mocked. "There's nothing but apes jumping around on Gibraltar. You want to go have a date with a pretty little monkey lady? In that case, shore leave granted!"

"Quiet!" ordered the alternate Operations Chief who monitored their connection to the *Hawkeye*, the flying "magnifying glass" of the *Aegis* system.

The E-2C *Hawkeye* circled high above the Mediterranean. It was a misshapen prop plane with high-placed wings and the number 600 written in red digits on its nose – providing early-warning and command and control functions to the carrier group regardless of the weather conditions, which it also monitored. Right now the images transmitted from the sky indicated a storm front over the Azores, approaching Spain. Atmospheric pressure was dropping rapidly and squalls measuring about eight on the Beaufort scale were detected. The E-2C *Hawkeye,* as the backbone of the *Aegis Combat System,* was also training its computerized sensors on the land and sea below, looking for potential threats to the carrier group. In case of hostile action it would control strike and interceptor operations as well as guide all search and rescue missions. *Hawkeyes* were the essential connecting link for all weapons systems employed by the carrier group.

"Ah, down there is Casablanca. I once knew an Arab beauty there... Souad was her name..." the radioman in the plane started chatting.

"Oh no, not again," said the crewman next to him. "Don't you ever have anything on your mind except women? Casablanca is culture, man. Ever heard of a movie classic with Humphrey Bogart and Ingrid Bergman?"

"And it's history too," chimed in the navigator. "In 1943 President Roosevelt and Winston Churchill met at the

Casablanca conference and argued about the second front line against the Axis powers."

"Theodore Roosevelt, like the Big Stick?"

"No, Franklin Delano, of course!"

The radioman started again. "My girlfriend used to tell me all about Casablanca. It's the largest city in Morocco, you know, more than two million people live down there, and of all two million she was the prettiest…"

"All systems operating okay," came the voice of the commanding pilot, Major Adler, as he passed on his routine report. "No unusual occurrences." The navigator repeated his words as per regulations, and pushed a button that automatically transmitted the report down to the *USS Ross*.

The alternate Operations Chief onboard the missile cruiser saw the message flicker over the screen. "Not much fun today gentlemen," he summed up. Everyone nodded. And *Aegis* hummed along in full automatic mode.

Aegis was an extremely intelligent and powerful machine, designed for an active and well-armed enemy – like the Soviet backfire bombers, or sneaky nuclear submarines, or swarms of anti-ship missiles. But when the Soviet Union collapsed, so did serious challengers to *Aegis*'s abilities. And this was basically the problem for crews of tactical warships like the *Ross* – their once powerful enemy has dissolved like a bank of fog. There really wasn't much out there to look for – militarily speaking, it was clear skies, no storms. So *Aegis* ran around the clock, pretty much for nothing. Who in their right mind would think of attacking Carrier Group 8?

The bombing runs and missile attacks from the Ionian

Sea into what was left of Yugoslavia had offered the crew some diversion. They could trace the trajectories of shot-down Tomahawks and cheer the direct hits. And the launches and landings of the fighter jets gave them something to watch on their screens. But there was nothing that even came close to being a real threat. No missiles coming at them from mysterious locations, no unidentified submarines. Nothing. And yet *Aegis* was prepared to fight off a hundred simultaneous attacks. *Was it all just useless junk because it lacked a challenge?*

Sometimes at night the young officers fresh from the naval academy would praise the *Aegis* system over their beers in the lounge – but the Gulf War vets would remain silent. With the exception of Potato. He was a master of arms in charge of security in the Weapons Department. He owed his name to his bulbous nose that looked just like a prize potato from his home state: Idaho!

"*Aegis* is nothing but a shield. And don't you forget it," he would argue to the newcomers. "Just like it was in ancient times, it's a defense weapon against blow, stab, and strike. And just like in those days, it's always possible to penetrate, or get around, or outwit, any kind of shield. It's always just a matter of time. Maybe a lucky break, or some stupid coincidence… and, boom, you get right through all the electronics, capice?"

They all loved to hear Potato's ravings – every defense shield would eventually fall, that it was the nature of defense. Trials of strength between aggressors and defenders were an age-old game as David and Goliath or the Maginot Line or even the unidentified swarm of wild geese flying against strategic targets in the heart of the U.S. in 1977. And *Aegis* was no exception. It was susceptible to electronic disruptive action. Offshore its shield narrowed, just as it had in the Gulf; the system could crash, or some other failure could flatten it or knock it out.

And when Larry Johnson was aboard visiting, he would endorse Potato's opinions. "No shield is safe from being overpowered or undermined," he would say.

"Right," Potato would agree.

"But doesn't that argument apply to all complex weapons systems?" asked one of the newly graduated cadets.

"Of course," Potato acknowledged, "but consider this. The failure of an offensive weapon doesn't do anything but thwart the attack. It doesn't result in the loss of the entire system. But the failure of defense almost always means the loss of the entire weapons system itself. Look at it this way. If one of our Tomahawks misses its target, the enemy in the target area survives and can keep fighting for a day or two. So what? But if *Aegis* blacks out, well, the failure of our defense shield could easily mean the destruction of the entire aircraft carrier group. And that's a major difference."

If Larry Johnson was around he would agree completely, and to the annoyance of his superiors he would begin to rail against the limitations placed on him and his radar system at the top of his voice. His newly developed, very compact Doppler radar could easily detect a flying insect 40 miles away from the ship. It was already being extensively employed in tornado research. Larry's version, aside from being easy to use, worked in conjunction with a high-speed database that allowed it to precisely identify the projectile coming at them. And he had installed it on one of the two rapid-fire gun systems.

"It's essential that the *Phalanx* gun systems work independent of *Aegis* as a stand-alone anti-ship missile defense system," he would urge. "And if worse came to worse, and, let's say for example, that an electromagnetic impulse from a minor plutonium bomb knocked out *Aegis*, at least the ship would have some defense against enemy missiles." He would make this argument in vain at the weekly staff meeting with the Captain and the Weapons System Chief. All they allowed him to do was hook it up to one gun – and they wouldn't even let him test it with one shot of live ammo...

"Is Larry Johnson still playing around with his Lego-kit?" the junior radar operator aboard the *USS Ross* asked?

"Well, he does love his radar," answered an electronic specialist. "And I think he's right – you know, he's able to find out miles and miles away if something is a flying dove or one of the small anti-ship missiles bearing down on us. It's crazy. I think he'd even know if it was a flying saucer coming our way."

"Man, cut it out. Your talk about radar is getting me all excited. Right. Hey look, the Yankees just won again. Well that really makes my day," the junior said, watching Sports News on a small monitor.

The alternate Ops Chief was typing in a message to the *Hawkeye*: "Request report on ship movements."

"Why bother?" asked a sonar operator.

"Commander's orders, just came in," replied the Ops Chief, shrugging his shoulders.

"Well, I guess the leopard can't change his spots. Always practicing. I guess it's in his blood."

66.

In the gym on the A-deck of the *Shiraz*, 30 hostages were sitting on the floor huddled together, when Khalid burst into the room, shouting at them unintelligibly. They jumped to their feet terrorized and moved close together.

Clad in white with the beard of a saint the Islamic leader appeared in the doorway. And like a messiah, he opened his arms wide.

"Yussef bin Golem," Khalid announced solemnly, and silence reigned.

Bin Golem sententiously let his words flow out, like a practiced preacher.

"Friends! Poverty and oppression will vanish from the world. I shall free the people of Islam from American dominance. Western exploitation destroys the soul of the true faith. By tradition I carry the sword of Islam, to keep the Lord's empire pure and powerful in the heart of Islam. If it is God's decree that blood shall be shed, then it will flow. Our war for the good and for the power of God is holy – in the state, in the family, and in every heart."

"If you are pretending to be so good and noble," Sophie bleated out loudly, to her father's horror, "then why are you killing innocent Americans all over the world?"

Bin Golem turned to the young blonde girl and looked at her benevolently.

"Your President kills people all over the world. America brings death daily to people in Baghdad, Belgrade, Novi Sad, and Tripoli. You have slaughtered thousands, no hundreds of thousands, around the world: in Kandahar, in the poppy fields of Herat. In Vietnam, you defoliated the forests with poison chemicals, and then burned entire villages with Napalm, including all the women and children. And for what? Why have your Presidents done this? For their country! Your President and your people lie, steal, and kill in the name of freedom and for the laws you have created for yourself. And you do it in the name of the God you believe in, whom you trust, as you write on your banknotes. Yes, for the dirty money of God, you're willing to die and to kill."

One of the women let out a loud sob. Sam held his head up high. Quintus was looking around the gym, squinting at the dumbbells on the floor, working on an escape plan.

"We Muslims do the same. We fight for our beliefs," the Sheik continued. "We are an ancient culture, with strong faith. We are human beings just like you, with heads and hearts and souls. I fight for these people in accordance with the laws of the Koran, which for 14 centuries has been the book of books, a precious treasure of memories that inspires the imagination, shapes the character, and gives us courage. Loyalty is no illusion for us Arabs, and the commandment of loyalty is no empty word. And as my people are loyal to me, I am loyal to my people – and because of that I fight against the evil which America represents in our countries."

"You are imperialists," Doctor Yale argued courageously, standing up for his daughter. "And always have been. The conquest and conversion of half of the Mediterranean by Islamic invaders from the Arabian Peninsula was one of the greatest predatory attacks of the Middle Ages!"

Until now the Moslem clad in white had been calm and

level-headed in his speech. But now everyone could see how anger made the veins in his forehead swell. Doctor Yale could sense the looks of reproach from the other hostages burning into the back of his neck. But bin Golem succeeded in controlling his anger. With a disarming smile he seemed to forgive the brazen words of the American doctor who already had regret written all over his face.

"Enough words! If your Navy should decide to attack our ship, all of you will die – not by the sword of Islam, but by the bombs of your own people. What is that nice term you use? Friendly fire?" And then he pointed at Dr. Yale. "Or perhaps foolish, thoughtless people like this man here will cause your death. But if any of you give us any trouble, he will be the first one we will shoot. And not in an unfriendly way, either. It is simply practical. We call it Holy Fire!"

67.

"Good God!" exclaims the senior radar operator, as the letters EAM, *Emergency Action Message*, start flashing on the wall.

"What the hell?" gasps the alternate Ops Chief as he stares at the large Combat Information Center monitor of the *Ross*. Apparently all hell is breaking loose. A siren starts to wail its combat alarm throughout the entire ship while an automatic stand-by display reads "All Weapons on SQ1."

The senior at radar jumps up. "Russian rockets, man!"

"Get the Captain!"

"The old man is over at the *TR*, What the heck...?" the Ops Chief gasps again. *Is this a fucking wake-up call? Compliments from Captain Fisher, or what?*

"High alert. Four missiles approaching fast, sir!"

"Confirm target data!"

" Deputy commander is over at the *TR* too. Who is senior onboard here and now? Where the hell are the orderlies and the phone operators?" *Nobody is in charge, complete snafu!*

In this very moment the heavy metal door to the CIC squeaks open and an officer buttoning up his uniform jacket bursts into the room. A noisy group of seamen squeezing in behind. In the dim green light of fire control the senior radar operator sees only a black face with two bright white-eye dots. He looks at the nametag: Major Black, the Security Officer.

"Is this a fucking alarm practice, or what?" Black curses.

"Negative, sir. Six missiles approaching, 5000 yards, coming in fast."

"Countermeasure initiated, sir," the alternate OC shouts.

"Good. Operation mode?"

"Automatic, sir."

Major Black nods and wipes his eyes. There's no doubt. Some lunatic is firing at the U.S. Navy. *I don't believe it! An emergency! A baptism of fire!*

"They don't realize whom they're dealing with," he says calmly.

"3000 yards! Coming closer!"

"Proceed at standard speed. Hold course," Black orders. As per regulations, the Ops Chief repeats his orders.

"I'll take over fire control!"

"Aye, aye sir, you have control!"

"Missile system ready for launch," the senior at radar reports. *We'll show these bastards.*

"Sir! It's the Commander!"

Black snatches the receiver: "Sir?" Listens, then gives his report as it's happening. "Six enemy missiles, 2000 yards and closing. Intercepting missiles launched. Contact in a few seconds. Now, sir. Direct hit, direct hit. Defense operation successful. You can see it too?" *Then why is he asking me?*

"All six missiles destroyed," reports the senior radar operator.

An earsplitting cheer rings out, and just as suddenly breaks off. All of a sudden the CIC monitor resembles a cell under a microscope surrounded by other microbes and bacteria, as killer viruses approach silently. The *Aegis* information system continuously translates the identified objects into clear text. But the senior radar operator can't keep up.

"Bomber wing, east over Macedonia, ten, no, my God, 20 missile launches from the south. And what's that? An enemy submarine on Portugal's southern tip, by Cape Saint Vincent, launching at least another dozen missiles, coming in fast. Who's declared war on us? The fucking Russians? Does anybody know what's going on?"

"ECM taken," shouts one of the operators who had rushed in.

"Let's not lose our heads, boys," roars Major Black, as if he were the manager of the New York Yankees, whom he resembles. "Get me a connection to Eagle Eyes!"

"Aye, aye sir! Connection established!" shouted the radio operator.

High above the tiny Albora Island east of Gibraltar, cruising at 20,000 feet, aboard the *Hawkeye*, the senior crewmembers Burke and Noventa look at each other thunderstruck. The high state of alarm had shaken them out of the lethargy of their routine flight like a slap in the face. All of the readings of a full scale attack that the *USS Ross* had on its screens flashed over those on their reconnaissance plane as well.

"Noventa and Burke, this is Adler," the captain said.

"Yo."

"Yo."

"Are you scanning your frequencies?"

"Noventa here. Catanzaro insists they don't have a clue what is going on."

"Burke?"

"I'm afraid, sir, it looks pretty bad."

"Burke, stay on the multifunction radar. Does anybody have an explanation for the humongous mess down there? Noventa?"

"Yo."

"Any message from the CO?"

"Negative sir. No news from the *TR*," Noventa said.

"Burke to Adler, the *Ross* and the *Gonzalez* are launching missiles, so far about 30 of them, sir."

"Noventa here. Guys, I think this is what they call war." The navigator was trembling a bit.

"But who the hell is attacking us? I can't believe it!"

"I'm afraid, sir, it looks pretty bad."

"Adler here. Quiet! Burke, have all the objects been identified?" Captain Alder's shirt is suddenly soaking wet with sweat, sticking to his skin. The plane is on autopilot, flying a steady loop.

"Gotcha. All tests for identification have been executed, sir. No doubt, they are under enemy fire, sir."

"Noventa to Adler. More missile fire, sir!"

"What??"

The display then shows a connection to the *TR*. The captain hits the switch. "Adler here!"

The commander of the *TR* informs him of the situation. A large enemy military force is attacking Carrier Group 8. Defense operations are proceeding successfully." Then the commander says something else.

"Excuse me, sir?" Captain Adler interrupts. He can't believe his ears.

"I said the Commander in Chief and the Spanish King are due aboard the *TR* shortly," the captain of the *TR* repeats.

Hearing that over the intercom, the *Hawkeye*'s crew shakes their heads in disbelief.

"Noventa to Adler. More missiles, sir!"

Lifting his hand for silence, captain Adler turns off the intercom. "All of our systems are working, sir," he tells Captain Fisher on the *TR*. "We can see what's happening. What the hell does Washington? I mean, what is the CC going to do, sir?"

"Burke to all. We have radar activity west of the strait. I've got an exact position on it! Wait a second, it looks like a supertanker."

The captain waves him off.

"Burke to Adler: It's not a civilian radar frequency, sir,"

"What?" shouts Captain Adler.

"If you ask me sir, it's target tracking radar."

For Christ's sake of course I'm asking you, boy! And you'd better be right. I don't want to be the one blamed for sinking a tanker filled with millions of gallons of oil.

"Adler to Burke. Run a close search and pass the info on to the CIC on the *Ross*!"

"Aye, aye."

A few minutes later Lieutenant Kahn, known as Morse, catapults off the deck of the *TR* and in a long curve shoots up into the gray sky. The position of the tanker identified as the *Shiraz* where the radar activity seems to be coming from flashes onto the map-up system of his fighter. Morse swings into attack course. His thoughts go into automatic mode as they adapt to the operational functions of his machine, crossing his mind in short disjointed sentences. *So, let's see where you are... Oh. There... whoever you might be...*

fire at the Big Stick! I'll show you. Scheming bastards... I'll melt your jockey shorts in a minute.

And then as he approaches he does what no one has ever seen or ever will see: He turns his scarred face from side to side furiously, sending out in Morse code his megalomaniac message of terror: "Here comes Morse the avenger, here comes Morse the avenger, here comes..."

68.

The images of the full-scale attack on the *Roosevelt* off Gibraltar flash over the monitors of Carrier Group 8. And fill the huge screens in the Tactical Air Force Command in in the Rocky Mountains of Colorado. And on the big monitor in the Situation Room of the White House, which right now resembles a beehive. Frantic adjutants buzz around, pencil pushers sharpen pencils, frenzied conversations and loud exclamations drown out the ringing of telephones as terrified looks dart from all eyes.

But it all stops as the National Security Advisor enters the room with the Head of the Joint Chiefs of Staff.

"Who knows what's going on," the five-star general thunders into the spreading silence. No one says a word. "Oookay, then, let's get a handle on this. Get me the latest reports. Now! Pronto! Let's move you lazy good-for-nothings." *At last some action,* shot through his mind. *At last something you can sink your teeth into. Finally something other than fucking paperwork!*

Not far from Catanzaro, in the hills of the Calabrian Apennines on the toe of the Italian boot, satellite dishes turn as they have for decades. The early warning system there, operated by the Americans under the auspices of NATO, controls the gateway to the Eastern Mediterranean and the Adriatic, and also keeps a watchful eye on Libya, located south of the Gulf of Sirte.

By now, Sergeant Tarranto knows the formations of

Carrier Group 8 and the *TR* by heart. Since NATO's intervention in Yugoslavia he has been following the movements of ships and aircraft in the Ionian Sea on the radar screen daily, and with increased fascination. Almost like a war correspondent, he began writing a kind of journal, counting the missile launches, tracing their trajectories, trying to deduce a tactical pattern from the constantly changing formations of the carrier group.

He also followed the group's activities on the satellite image screens, which at first looked like weather charts to him. But with the Allies' stepped-up activity he found he could also use the zoom function of the satellite images, allowing him to get pictures of the moments of impact of the cruise missiles as they hit their targets in enemy territory.

"And how is our naval war strategist today?" roared the well-meaning voice of the American Lieutenant Colonel behind him as he watched his screen, pen in hand. "La guerra è finita, caro mio!" *The war is over.*

"Hardly, sir!" the bewildered Taranto answered in contradiction, his eyes glued to the activity of the screen in front of him. "Look, sir! They're launching missiles. There, from the *Ross*! And a second ago, from the *Gonzalez*!"

Taranto rewound the data on another monitor and showed the missile cruiser on the screen.

"You're right! What in God's name? What, are those boys taking target practice right in the middle of... No, it can't be! Wait a second. Let me get on the horn and find out what this nonsense is all about."

"The missiles are exploding in mid-air," Taranto called after him.

69.

"I wish I knew what the hell was going on there," Captain Fisher moans to himself as he stands on the bridge of the *Theodore Roosevelt* and stares at the deck below as if the answer were somehow down there amid the organized chaos of air traffic.

Aegis keeps detecting enemy missiles, bombers, and submarines, and continues to automatically launch defense operations. But there are neither visual signs of air combat nor any signs of exploding missiles. And the Tactical Air Force Command insists that there is no enemy activity discernable. Are there approaching bomber wings, as *Aegis* says? The satellites can't see them at all. Is it the bad weather?

"Sir, a Russian attack submarine. Report from sonar," reports Petty Officer First Class Abrams, panting.

"What?" Fisher exclaims.

"Russian attack sub, South of Trafalgar. Lying low. No action reported."

"Sonar?"

"Sonar reports no activity. They hear nothing. No torpedo firing runs," Abrams shoots back.

"Is this real?" asks Captain Fisher. *Could somebody stage all these bloody attacks? Simulate this complete chaos? Is Hollywood involved?*

Fischer shakes his head. He has been under stress for too long. He needs a moment of quiet to think. To assess the situation.

"Is the sub confirmed?" he asks finally.

"Yessir, confirmed by *Hawkeye*," says Abrams and volunteers: "Two Russian attack submarines have been sneaking around for a while, spying on us. This one south of here is damn close, sir."

"Yeah, I know, now let's get a handle on that. Get my staff to the briefing room, immediately", roars Captain Fisher now almost determined to fire torpedoes at the Russians.

In fire control on the *Ross*, the attacks continue. Again and again new clusters of missiles descend upon them. They have never seen anything like this, not in any simulation, not in the most intense practice sessions. In the Weapons Control Room, dismay rules. They see on their screen that the defense missiles they send out trace right to their targets, by the dozens. But the AWACS keep saying that the missiles just head out into the atmosphere and vanish without hitting anything. Except for one, which apparently has hit the marina at Marbella. The men at the terminals are tearing their hair out, driven to desperation. What is going on?

"The Russian sub is moving", someone shouts.

"What about the tanker?" a calm voice asks.

"We will know soon," Major Black replies with a sigh,

Finished with his head-turning Morse-code frenzy, Lieutenant Kahn zooms over the tanker at low altitude and sees a large helicopter and a bunch of people wearing yellow life jackets and... what is that? He pulls up in a loop and decides to do a second pass, turning on the camera mounted under the *Tomcat's* fuselage, which will automatically send the images to the CIC onboard the *Ross*.

Then a screaming jolt of fear runs through him as the alarm signal in his cockpit indicates enemy locating radar. But it doesn't seem to be directed at him. Just to be safe, he unlatches a couple of luminous bodies for any missiles sent in his direction to lock on to – and comes in for his second pass.

Kahn's *Tomcat* causes some excitement on board the *Shiraz*, although the appearance of the missile cruisers had already set off their alarms. Khalid had driven the hostages onto the deck in a hurry and given them yellow life jackets to make them more easily seen, as a human shield against possible air raids.

"Now the Marines will come get us, just wait and see," Sam mumbles under his breath between his grinding teeth. Quintus makes good use of the chaos on deck to whisper the location of the lifeboats to his fellow captives. He also slips Sam, Yale, and Senator Strong a small five-pound dumbbell each, which he had hidden into his cargo pants when the F-14 had ear splittingly roared over the deck.

Morse looks down on his second pass and can see them with his naked eyes – missile launchers. No doubt. He reports in, telling them to evaluate the pictures from his camera immediately. He would love to start banging away at them right now, but he didn't want to do more harm than good. His general feeling was that if they had missiles down there, it was high time to give the bastards something to worry about.

70.

"A call from Catanzaro, sir!"

"Who in Catanzaro?"

"The early warning station in Calabria, sir!"

"Give it to me!" Captain Fisher frowns into the radio phone, his face darkening under knit eyebrows. "Target practice? Lieutenant Colonel, are you crazy? My ship is under attack! What?" He slowly shakes his head. "Are you certain? All right, please, stand by. Thank you." And he hangs up the phone.

"What shall we do, sir?" asks the Quartermaster.

Good question. Now, let's stay cool. The Russian sub is for goddam real. It's attack-class, dangerous sucker. The tanker is real. Two F-18's got in the tracking radar of three Libyan MIG attack fighters. I am not gonna take any chances. If Aegis tells me to shoot I damn shoot!

"Proceed, keep fighting off the attacks, stay on high alert," Fisher ordered. His face was screwed tight.

"Aye, aye sir!"

The Boatswain approaches, wearing a blue jersey over his combat jacket. "The President's helicopter is approaching, sir."

But Fisher seems almost not to hear him, and speaks tensely into the phone to Larry Johnson.

"What are you saying, Larry? They're killing our antennas? What the hell does that mean?"

Johnson explains to him that the enemy seems to be pushing *Aegis's* performance beyond its limits through fake

379

manipulations. And once it's completely paralyzed, without antennas so to speak, only then would real attacks come from real missiles. The Captain wants to know if he has any tangible proof for this theory. Johnson avoids answering as long as he can, but finally he says no – but then he says that his two Vulcan Phalanx guns are ready to go, adding however that only one of them is properly hooked up to the radar for *Exocet* identification.

"I can't take action based on your theories, Johnson," Fisher concludes, hanging up. The Security Officer tells him that the cruiser with the Marines and the SEALS commando unit is approaching the *Shiraz;* and suddenly, the bad news start coming in very fast. The Combat Information Center of the *USS Ross* confirms the missile launch sites on the deck of the *Shiraz*. Then a misgiving becomes reality – Senator Strong and the 30 kidnapped Americans are aboard a terrorist ship equipped with missiles!

Over the radio he hears another report from the Chief of the combined SEALS command units. "Our men are standing by, ready to storm the *Shiraz*."

"You'll have to wait," Fisher answers. "That order will have to come either from Washington or from the President himself."

To the Deck Officer next to him he shouts, "Keep *Aegis* running. Keep up all defensive combat maneuvers."

He races over to the officers' latrine on the outer wall of the bridge. He had forgotten how much stress combat pressure produced. He closes his eyes as he releases his bladder, and thinks of Pam. She is in front of him, completely naked – her tight in-shape body, her small high-set breasts, her thick pubic triangle, all in bright light – too bright light. Captain Fisher popped his eyes open. Were they hit? Was this bright light the center of an explosion? Or just pure fear? The latter. He sighed and shook off some drops. Suddenly, he smiled – there is always time to shake off, his father had once told him in his last years. *Maybe I should tell my officers at the briefing ...*

71.

With hot eyes and a warm lap, Nadine Moran stares at the mess she has created. Her air combat simulation, with more than a hundred simultaneous attacks, is way too much for *Aegis* to handle. For well over an hour now, the missile cruisers have been ceaselessly firing intercepting missiles in all directions, warding off clusters of phantom bombers and anti-ship missiles that have kept appearing chimerically on their monitors in the fire control room.

"It has to be now! Right now!" she shouts.

Bin Golem spreads his arms, his impatience apparent. Old Moran nods, hand on the launch button. With professional coldness he announces his readiness to fire systems one to six.

Her eyes on her wristwatch, Nadine gives the signal with her hand. Thierry-Clé pushes the button, announcing "Missiles one to six, firing!"

The Islamic leader stands next to the captain, his eyes fixed on the deadly missiles zooming off. "Firing, firing", he shouts holding his fists up.

On the screen of his Doppler radar, Larry Johnson sees the imminent danger very clearly. Just above the waterline the missiles race straight toward the *TR*. *These things are real! Very real!*

He immediately reports the news to Captain Fisher, without taking his eyes off the readouts from his R2D2 gun batteries. Will they fire in time?

The two *Vulcan Phalanx* guns are designed to be the last bulwark of defense to stop any missiles that might penetrate the *Aegis* defense shield. The only catch – the missiles zooming in at Mach 4 first have to be detected, identified, and distinguished from possible virtual bait that might fool the warning radar. The rapid-fire guns copied from the R2D2-robots in Star Wars can thrust an invincible wall of steel of up to 900 20-millimeter shells into the way of a deadly threat. The barrels are capable of pivoting from –25 to +85 degrees in little more than one second.

Equipped with integrated radar of their own, the R2D2 *Phalanx* guns track approaching missiles as well as its own shells. They are a kind of reinsurance or last hope, in case the heavy SM-2 anti-ship missile defense rockets of the *Gonzalez* or the *Ross* should fail to cope with the cluster of zooming in Mach 4 arrows like Exocets. The only weak spot of the *Phalanx* is its elevation angle limit of 85 degrees. If an attacking missile should fall in a direct vertical line, it could avoid the devastating circle of the Phalanx's defensive shells.

Looking into his Doppler radar display, Larry is suddenly horrified as he sees one of the approaching clearly identified *Exocets* zoom straight upward and then turn down into a vertical trajectory. *No! There is it! A 90-degree strike from above!*

The nightmare of a 90-degree strike is suddenly a reality, and Larry jumps up as if something had bitten him. *What son-of-a-bitch would know this? What ingenious hacker bastard sitting at his terminal... bastard? A man? Why should it have to be a man? I know this... it's like fingerprints... the incredible speed... the virtually perverted sleight of hand... this elegance...*

Panic was spreading throughout the control room of the *USS Ross*. No one had ever expected such a massive attack from seemingly countless missiles. The crews had never been forced to endure such unrelenting stress, even in the most challenging simulations.

"Shit, we're at the limit! More than a hundred defense operations so far. And look! Six, no, 12 missiles heading for the *TR*... one veering straight up... for vertical attack... My God!"

Like a courageous rebel in front of a firing squad, Major Black squinted his eyes into narrow slits. *Man, this thing is a ball breaker. How the hell are we going to fix this?*

Johnson runs up to the deck and puts the binoculars up to his eyes. Aghast, he looks over to the *Roosevelt. The pride of the fleet, doomed!*

At any moment now the missile will hit the deck! He boosts the magnification of the binoculars and stares into the overcast sky. *This cannot possibly be true!*

For a fragment of a second he thinks he sees the missile cutting through the clouds as a black blurry line zooming straight down. He already thinks he hears the horrible detonation. *Hit! Impact!* He instinctively hits the deck, waits for a bright flash, and closes his eyes in anticipation. But nothing happens! He blinks at the pale daylight, gets up off the deck, and sways backwards into the control room checking the monitor where any moment now the hit should be indicated. No one seems to be paying any attention to him. But then suddenly, like a distant murmur, he hears excited shouts. A telephone operator at the far end of the table waves at him. *For me? Yes, someone wants to talk to me on the phone.*

It's the crackly voice of Abrams onboard the *TR*:

"Larry Johnson? "

"Yo."

"Is the second *Phalanx* ready to fire? Don't tell me it's not."

"No chance, sir... hello! ... Sir?

"Yes?"

"You got hit, right? From above."

"No, no, there was no impact... The *TR* is fine ...Wait, yes, but only slight... The lee helmsman reports stabilizer blades sticking out from the flat roof of the... it must have been a dud! The missile didn't explode! It penetrated the roof... landed in the shithouse! The small latrine on portside next to the bridge! All it did was scare the hell out of the Captain when he was in there, that's all! Over."

Larry can't believe his ears, and their good luck. *Shithouse luck!* But his mind already understood why. *The detonation fuse blew, too steep an arrival angle! Nothing but a cold piece of shit! Can't rely on anything anymore. Why should these French frogs with their Exocets be different from anybody else?*

Aboard the *Ross* the senior radar operator moans. "Nothing is working anymore! Nothing but Johnson and his Lego-kit radar can save our asses now!"

"Another six *Exocets*," the Ops Chief replies toneless, pale as a ghost.

Transfixed, they all stare at the screen, seeing the Doppler radar's identification of the missile screaming in at zero height.

Then they see that the *Phalanxes* have spun around and shot a steel wall of millions of bullets at the approaching missiles. In the control rooms of all of the ships of the carrier group, hundreds of eyes stare at every accessible monitor.

Then every watching seaman seems to hoot at once. Every single *Exocet* has been destroyed! Every one pulverized!

"All right Larry! Hit! Boom! Larry! Great! Laa—rry! Laa—rry!" A choir of rough but ecstatic voices sings the praises of Johnson's radar. Hit! Hit! Hit! The shitty little thing is working!" The seamen in fire control are overjoyed.

"Wait a second! Is that another one coming?"

In an instant, their euphoria disappears. And the wonder weapon from Star Wars remains silent. No shots fired! Not a single one. The damn thing refuses to function! "Jam. Kaput," one whispers.

"The second R2D2 won't do it. No target identification!" Major Black's voice trembles. "If only the old man had given Johnson what he wanted."

Black's statement sums up how everyone in fire control feels. Independent of *Aegis*, the auto-adaptive controlled radar of the *Phalanx* tracks and identifies targets autonomously. Unfortunately, the Navy bureaucrats had not allowed Larry to connect both weapons systems to his Doppler radar. Which put them in a real mess now. While one gun is accurately reacting to targets instantly, firing at the limit, the second one was getting the manipulated data from *Aegis* system, remaining inactive.

The electronic alarm continues to wail aboard the *TR* as a double patrol of F-18s catapult off the deck. Desperate, Larry looks at his radar screen. No more rockets zipping away.

On the monitor next to him he sees the helicopter of the President of the United States land in front of the tower on the *TR's* deck. *Absurd! Coming aboard a sinking ship? Is Fisher out of his mind to let the President land now? Or had Brenton himself insisted on it?*

Captain Fisher is one of the few people aboard the *TR* who knows about the highly confidential saturation point of the *Aegis* defense system – and according to his rough calculations, the enemy had fired more projectiles than *Aegis* is able to handle. Who would have thought that its capacity could ever be reached? Each of the two missile cruisers was equipped with 122 SM-2 missiles with a 70-mile range... and by now, shouldn't this be the end? Apparently, someone had thwarted the billion-dollar sophisticated electronics system, *Cyberterrorists!* – either that or there had been an incredible electronic malfunction. All of this should have been anticipated a long time ago. But sweeping it under the carpet is much easier than reacting. So, *Aegis* is crippled? The invincible shield really did fail in the end?

That is exactly what it looks like, for at this very moment, a powerful tremor passes through the *Roosevelt's* hull. The colossus shakes. The sound of a violent detonation drowns out all other noises.

"We've been hit at stern sir!" yells the helmsman on the bridge.

"Damage report!" the Captain hoarsely calls out, his voice cracking.

"Rudder gear destroyed, sir. *TR* disabled!"

"Fuck, no!"

And the details come in. The tailgate, a large mobile

platform for taking on deliveries of supplies and berthing dinghies has been destroyed. Tons of water are swamping the ship.

"Bulkheads!" roars the ship's manager or CEO, even though the automatic system is sealing off the supply bay astern from the rest of the ship. "Fire fighting in progress. Unknown number of injured"

The lee helmsman reports the failure of the four drive shafts. Damages ranked as heavy to heaviest.

"The reactor?" barks the Captain, his face ashen.

"Reactor shutting down, sir!"

The CEO sums it up. "We can't maneuver, sir. Two full hits by anti-ship missiles in the stern. Rudder and drive not functioning. Water inrush under control. Fire still spreading. Injuries... hold it..."

"Casualties?"

"Unknown, sir."

Fisher says to himself, *my proud ship a lame duck in a big pond! And certainly the next deadly missile is on its way to blow us to bits.* "I underestimated those bastards," he says to no one in particular.

And then he presses his lips together as he sees the President storming up onto the bridge. *Serves him right. Why did he have to insist on landing anyway?*

"Situation, Captain," the Commander in Chief of the Armed Forces requests.

Fisher stands at attention and salutes. With a strange light feeling in his head he forces himself to give a short, matter-of-fact progress report and closes with an air of self-confidence that even to himself sounds studied.

"Permission to sink the *Shiraz*, sir!"

The President remains silent. His lips form a pale narrow line on his face, as bluish-red capillaries darken his cheeks. *Much as he looked in front of the investigating committee and the independent counsel,* Fisher thinks. A strange silence surrounds the small circle of men on the bridge, while all around them the sounds of combat raged – explosions, sirens, roaring jet engines.

"We really have no choice, Mister President. If they hit us amidships, we'll sink," the Captain urges, given new and unexpected strength by his responsibility for his 5,000 crewmen. *Not to mention the responsibility for this clown here!*

President Brenton moves his head, pensive. Despite his internal agitation as well as the chaos going around him, a smile creeps over his features. It was moments like these, of which he had seen many, that showed exactly what he was made of, and why the American people supported him as they had never supported another American president. When he smiles, everyone around him thinks that he will go to the end of the world to solve the situation, even to hell if he has to, for us.

Brenton thinks of all the relatives, friends, and acquaintances of the hostages onboard the *Shiraz* – not to mention the constituents of the very popular Senator Strong. All of them, he knows, are urging the White House to avoid doing anything that might endanger the hostages' lives. The human and ethical pressure is enormous. But there must be a way out. *Yield to the terrorists' demands? What exactly do these gangsters demand?* The President looks up and asks that simple question.

"The terrorists aren't making any demands, sir!"

But at that very moment the combat screen belies the Captain's words.

"Look! There!" the Quartermaster shouts.

On the monitor where just seconds ago they saw the trajectories of missiles and other colorful figures and circles was the image of a bearded man: Yussef bin Golem!

"Sons of Satan, we have swept away your antennas. I, Yussef bin Golem, am now in control of the *USS Roosevelt*," he says, with a gentle voice and intense, piercing eyes. As he speaks his voice is almost drowned out by the outraged protests of the men on the bridge.

President Brenton lifts his hand. "Gentlemen, please!" And instantaneously an awkward silence reigns. Brenton stares into the eyes of bin Golem on the screen, trying to assess the man. The Sheik seems calm, unperturbed. *A good actor,* Brenton judges, *and a tough opponent.*

"U-S-S! ... ha! ... The aim of the Qaeda is... unification of all Muslims... the establishment of a government in harmony with the principles of the Caliph... reach this aim only with violence... as long as the United States of America stations its troops in our countries... as long as they... warships control our ports... we will... topple Arab governments considered corrupt... liberate from the influence of the West... for the creation of a unique and unified theocracy."

"He's got a screw loose," the main boatswain groans as he stands next to the lee helmsman on the bridge.

The voices of the men on the bridge surge again. *How could this terrorist get onto their system? Madness! Espionage! Betrayal! A giant electronic fiasco, that's what it is...*

Recalling his conversation with Joe Sorelli, the President says very calmly, "The Saudi has the presidential code. Who knows anything about cryptography around here?"

Fisher stares at him as if to say *Oh great, now you're putting your two cents in!* But then the meaning of the President's words dawns on him. *Presidential code with access from outside the system. One phone call would do it...*

"Larry Johnson to the bridge!" The Captain roars. "And the Chief of Operations. And the Chief of Weapons Systems. We need all the module data for air combat. Go, go, move your asses boys!" Fisher bites his tongue, but the smile on Brenton's lips calms him down.

A new report comes over the intercom. "Reactor intact. Rudder gear still down. Tow off by oiler arranged."

Fisher shrugs his shoulders. It'll take hours for the supply vessel to arrive.

"28 people wounded, 11 killed, sir," the quartermaster practically yells at the Captain.

"That damn camel-humper won't shut up," says the officer in charge of computer maintenance as bin Golem's arrogant, humiliating, and embarrassing monologue continues on the screen:

"Before we deliver the final stroke of mercy to your ship, the symbol of your American arrogance, enjoy yourself for a bit longer. And think about this." The Arab smiles sardonically and his image disappears. But a video starts running instead.

"The hostages!" whispers the President.

A group of people all dressed in yellow life jackets is shown on the deck of the *Shiraz*. From among them steps

391

forth a distinguished, elderly man with gray hair. The camera moves in on his face.

"I am Senator Strong. There are 30 Americans with me aboard this ship. We are prepared..." But then the video clip cuts off.

The crew on the bridge gapes open mouthed at the screen, and suddenly a spotty red title appears. And then Pluto and Mickey Mouse appear, ready to play blind man's bluff.

With a gesture as friendly as it is sudden, President Brenton steers Captain Fisher to the side and puts his hand on his shoulder.

"David, I want you to know that I have absolutely no doubts regarding your handling of this situation, especially when it comes to the precautions regarding myself. Right now, we are all hostages."

Aah, so that's what this is about. You want to play hostage? Fisher seethes inwardly, as Brenton's eyes stare into his.

"Yes sir, Mr. President," is what comes from his lips, like a schoolboy in front of the principal.

"Good, Captain. Then let's proceed."

"Aye, aye, sir. Commander!"

In the middle of all this combat noise, and under all this strain, Fisher can't keep himself from thinking, *This, right here, with the President, is the real baptism by fire!*

72.

The *Sea Hawk* helicopter races low over the white, feathered waves of the stormy Atlantic.

"Do you still remember how to do it?" Alaoui screams over the noise of the engines. I shrug my shoulders as I sit in the troop cabin behind him, ready to puke, on this last morning before I was expected back in Zurich to defend myself at the court trial. If I had been flying this box myself, I'm sure I would have felt more in control and completely elated. As it was, I feel a bit jealous as the pilot turns around and then points to something in front of us. The silhouette of a ship's hull emerges from the haze.

"Ready?" Alaoui screams.

I yell my assent back to him, and grab the fist-thick rope with both hands. The hatch opens in front of me and cold wind and wet foam slap me in the face. The helicopter's skids almost touch the crests of the waves. Suddenly the black stern of the giant tanker looms ahead of us. The pilot heads straight for it – was he going to ram it? But suddenly he pulls up steeply, and as the black of the stern slips away the letters *SHIRAZ* fly by.

The pilot pushes the copter's nose up above the uppermost deck of the superstructure and shouts "Now!" over the intercom.

"Now, Polinsky!" Alaoui screams, throwing the end of the rope through the open hatch. The *Sea Hawk* hovers about ten feet above a small deck platform. I clasp the rope and leap out. The trick, of course, is to slide down fast but controlled –

something I hadn't done in years. *Where was that again? The memories crossed my mind in slow motion. Back then in Libya, was that really in Libya? As Major Custer? Or…*

I seem to be sliding fine until a squall catches me and flings me against a radio mast. I let go too soon and free fall, hitting the water. Suddenly I'm struggling to the surface, swimming – the water tastes salty. *Am I in the ocean?* I find a handle and pull myself up, coughing and spitting water. I look up, but the helicopter has vanished. Then, I try to get a grip on the situation. It could have been worse. I fell into the onboard swimming pool! Luckily I missed its hard tiled edge. Now, time was of the essence. Dripping wet, I race over to the diving tower and lean against a cabin wall. Gloves off! I slip off the thin diving suit, check the dry clothes, grope for the Glock in my belt, the explosive charges in the pockets at the thighs.

Over the rim of the pool, I squint at the large main deck of the *Shiraz*. Things were really busy there. Men were running back and forth. Cables and tarps were lying all over the planks. And in the center of all the chaos, on a mount, four sleek rockets with tail fins were aiming up into the cloudy sky. Anyone familiar with weapons wouldn't need an encyclopedia or even binoculars to identify the *Exocet III's* by their unique stabilizing wings and the three colored rings painted behind their curved warheads.

It's a miracle that those cute Frenchmen didn't paint the country's tricolors on their product!

Cocking my gun, I bolt over to the door leading into the locker room. With my back pressed against the wall I cast a quick glance around the platform with the missile launch site down on the main deck – and jump as two missiles suddenly zoom off.

I watch the fiery red tails of the *Exocets* trailing white smoke as they vanish among the clouds in the sky. Looking up in hopes of seeing their targets, I discover a large white rotating radar dish. I see a maintenance ladder leading up to a small platform and I dash towards it, climb up the stairs and fling myself to the ground underneath the good 13 feet long semi-circular dish.

I hear something below me. Turning around, I see a sailor down on the main deck gesturing toward me. I do my best to ignore him and attach an explosive charge to the dish, setting the timer for one minute. Swiftly I roll off the radar platform and land right in an open lifeboat below me – bull's eye! I get out of the boat and go through a door half-opened and rattling in the wind.

I'm in a long narrow corridor covered in wood planks; it turns off near the end, where I suspect there are some stairs. *Go!* Then I hear a hollow explosion above me, and hope that the search and warn radar serving the *Exocets* is now disabled.

I have to find out what goes on where and how on this diabolical tub. Not more than that! Just this little bit of information. The best thing to do would be to grab some crewmember that knows something about its technical facilities. In the meantime, I know that Alaoui aboard the *Sea Hawk*, is most probably passing on a situation report to his commander at the military base in Casablanca who would inform the U.S. Embassy in Rabat.

I duck my head and race around the corner – and with

the full impact of my 182 pounds I run into someone else coming around in the opposite direction. *Boom!* We bang into each other. My small world erupts in sparks. I feel like I'm being sucked into a black hole, with scary visions of rambling bones, stars shining in broad daylight, a banister turning into an ugly snake strangling me into empty black nothingness... I open my eyes in a daze and look at my sad face in the mirror rubbing my sore noggin with a frown just this side of anger. Wait a second! This isn't a mirror! What I thought at first was my own image is really the guy I ran into, rubbing his head just like me. We both sit on the floor, staring sheepishly at each other. What do I do now?

We both chuckle for a second, to cover up the embarrassment – but then my practical logical side screams *enemy*. I bounce up to my feet and pull out my gun, pointing to the cabin door behind me. The man looks me up and down for a second, and then leads the way and opens the door. Once inside, he closes the porthole and turns around.

"To make it short and sweet, I am Brabeck, the ship's engineer. And you? Some kind of American Special Forces?

I am encouraged by his British accent, but want to leave no doubts as to the seriousness of my mission and the time constraints we're under, so I grab him by the collar and press the barrel of my gun against his temple.

"You're going to give me all the detailed information I need about this ship, Brabeck, right? I need precise information. Subito!"

He wrinkles his nose. "Is your gun rotting or does your breath really smell that bad?"

I just press my Glock harder against his temple until it breaks the skin and blood trickles down his cheek.

"Okay, okay, Mister Bond. If you don't lay off that subito stuff we'll both be standing here when everything is over," Brabeck grunts.

I let him go. "I'm sorry. My name is Polinsky. What's going on aboard this ship, Brabeck?"

He quickly gives me a succinct outline of what has occurred. On a construction blueprint he marks down all the important places: the gym where the hostages are being held, the missile fire control room, the bridge, the pump house, and Khalid's quarters. "And those of the TT," he adds.

"Who's the TT?"

"The top terrorist, of course. Sheik Yussef bin Golem, himself."

In a flash of memory I see his mocking face on the newspaper in the Zurich taxi. A premonition coming true?

While explaining, he throws me a pair of crew overalls, and takes a heavy automatic from a secret drawer and pockets it. There's a knock on the door.

"Control, sir."

We communicate by hand signals. Brabeck opens the door and asks what it's all about. Two guards are panting as they come in. A helicopter was sighted, dropping off a detachment onboard and the radar broke down. From behind the door I hit one of them on the head with my gun, as the second one falls prey to Brabeck's vicious uppercut. We tie them up unconscious and take their radios and badges with magnetic keys.

"That's a good start, no?" Brabeck pants.

"Why are you helping me?" I ask as we storm down the corridor to the stairs.

"Alone, there was nothing I could do. Now we're a small army, eh?" And then he grimly adds, "I'll have a look around the deck, and let you know when..."

" No hanky-panky, Brabeck! We'll go down there together, is that clear?"

"Yes sir, boss, as you wish," he says, with a rueful expression on his face. He smiles and massages his forehead in the same place where I myself have a giant bump growing bigger. Then he adds, "With a face like yours I guess you were born to give orders!"

73

"And now, we will send them down into the deep," bin Golem says triumphantly.

"The radar, sir! It is broken down!" announces the navigator nervously.

The great patriot's neck veins swell and throb. His eyes widen, showing more white. News of the broken radar makes him both angry and calm at the same time. *Just before the coup de grâce a mishap? But not aboard the Shiraz. Surely the Frenchman is prepared for such cases. Especially with my brilliant Nadella at his side!*

Bin Golem seizes Thierry-Clé's arm as Khalid pulls a gun.

"Let him go!" Nadine screams, her eyes on fire. "I can take care of it. There's search radar built into the missiles. I can activate it manually!"

She opens the door and leaps outside, where rain has begun lashing the deck and splashing against the large windows of the bridge. Bid Golem paces back and forth, his eyes fixed on the ready to launch missiles that have been heaved on deck.

"I will transmit the target data to her over the radio, sir," Thierry-Clé whispers. "Then she'll be able to initiate the launch manually."

"Find the bastard that destroyed the radar, at once! There's probably a detachment sneaking around the ship," bin Golem says, with preternatural calm. "Radio that American Satan's brood to stop all actions at once! Kill ten hostages. Now! At once! Send a warning signal. Throw them overboard!"

Bin Golem's henchmen look at him in wonder. Khalid steps us behind the captain, pistol in hand. The beautiful cold thrill he always experiences before a kill rises in him. *Unfortunately, it doesn't last very long,* Khalid acknowledges to himself. The excitement of the prospect is almost always better than the kill. Almost always.

74.

"We're going to ram!" Brabeck yells to me from a distance on the deck.

Ram? Ram what? Baffled, I look around. There are no other ships in sight with which we could collide. Brabeck is still running towards me, out of breath. His disheveled hair hanging around his soaking wet face. The rain falls heavier, pouring down in buckets, teeming onto the deck. In the gusty wind I'm having a hard time staying on my feet. When he finally reaches me Brabeck too almost slips and falls on the dangerously wet surface.

"The Captain is dead! The *Shiraz* is heading for the *Roosevelt*! Straight towards it! The collision is inevitable. The GPS is constantly feeding the autopilot with the aircraft carrier's position data... it will force the *Shiraz* to smash into it... like a battering ram... at full speed!"

I grab his shoulders and shake him. "Damn it, Brabeck! Pull yourself together! What has happened exactly?"

"Stop engines. Full reverse engines!" he stammers.

I slap him across the face. Twice. Hard. "Brabeck! Snap out of it!"

He stares at me, dumbfounded. Rainwater runs down his cheeks as if he were crying. Finally, he comes back to reality. Shaking his head, he tells me that Captain Souri has shot himself on the bridge after being forced by Khalid to chart a ramming course for the *Shiraz*, bring her to full speed, and then block the controls. Panting heavily, he reports that even if the engines could run full speed in reverse, the ship would not be able to stop in time. There was no way to try to reverse engines, since the doors to the engine room were barricaded and the control for the turbines disconnected from the bridge.

"Brabeck, what do you know about the *Roosevelt*?" I practically yell at him.

"The American carrier... it was hit by our rockets... they said so on the bridge... it's hit... maybe it's sinking..." There is a look of despair in Brabeck's eyes.

Now, I finally got it, the scales falling from my eyes. Somewhere ahead floats the *Roosevelt*. Disabled! And Golem is going to finish it, ram it! *An easy target. Oh my God...*

"We're on a phantom ship. We can't maneuver it." He turns his head, looking around wildly. "All hands abandon ship! We have to get into the lifeboats!"

And he means it, as he gets ready to leave the ship. I barely manage to get hold of him and scream against the wind, "Man. Where are the hostages?"

He runs to a small deckhouse amidships, and I follow him, gasping. Once below deck, we run down a corridor and up some stairs. He keeps repeating "In the gym, in the gym," as if it were a life-saving mantra.

On a door in front of the next flight of stairs, however, I see a sign that reads "Pumphouse."

"Brabeck! Stop! Over here!"

He opens the locked door with his electronic access card. The fluorescent lights on the ceiling flicker on and illuminate the small control room where the gigantic ballast tanks of the *Shiraz* are monitored. An electronic board above the narrow control desk shows the tanks as illuminated areas on a diagram of the ship's hull. The displays flicker in bright green, ghostly reflecting in the smooth surface of the desk filled with red pushbuttons.

Brabeck suddenly seems calmer, more composed. He breathes regularly. Perhaps it has something to do with his being back in his familiar technical environment where professional routine carries the day over his hysterical frame of mind. He concisely explains the function of the ballast tanks to me:

"Since its reconstruction, the *Shiraz* is equipped with 12 large tanks that run from bow to stern, six on the portside and six on starboard. Because it no longer transports oil, the 12 tanks must stay filled to the brim with water in order to stabilize the ship."

"So what happens if we empty the tanks?" I ask.

"Absolute catastrophe," Brabeck says, looking at me appalled, his hands gesticulating wildly. "The ship would lose tonnage, would float on the surface like a rubber raft, completely at the mercy of the waves. Impossible!"

Despite what he says I stare at the lights evenly distributed along both sides of the long ship's body. *It should work!* Ultra-large tankers like the *Shiraz* need to be balanced accurately. If the ballast tanks at the bow and stern were filled while those amidships were empty, the ship would break in half. If the tanks on one side were emptied, the ship would capsize as if it were taking in water from just one side. *That, at least, is something to think of,* I said to myself. *It would have to work, wouldn't it?* A childhood memory flashed through my mind — naval battles in the tub, small wood ships that turned over when we loaded one side with too much ammunition... *Whoum!* Over they turned, *glubglub*... the tiny lead cannonballs sank to the bottom of the tub...

"How fast can we empty one tank, Brabeck?"

He sits there silently.

"Answer me, Brabeck!" I scream at him.

The heavy-duty pumps are constructed so that they can either flood or empty the tanks in about 20 minutes. With my head still aching from our collision I try to calculate our situation. The gym was on portside. If the ship careens to starboard...

"Brabeck! Empty all ballast tanks portside. Portside! Understood?"

"The ship will capsize, Polinsky! It will tip over towards starboard full length. We'll sink!" Naked fear makes his face white as a sheet. I realize that the only thing that will help here is blind slavish obedience.

"Do it now, Engineer Brabeck!" I bark at him. "Move it! Initiate exhaustion of all portside tanks immediately!"

My harsh drill-sergeant's voice proves effective. Brabeck gets up and moves to the control desk and starts hammering on the red buttons as if in a trance. The electronic panel above him comes alive with flickering lights. A buzzing siren starts to wail at short intervals, louder than Manhattan on a wild Saturday night. On portside the green lights representing the ballast tanks change color, slowly turning into an alarming orange, as the giant heavy-duty pumps suck out water at terrific speed.

"This is madness, Polinsky. We are lost," Brabeck groans.

"Shut up, man! Pull yourself together, will you! How long until we, uh, tip over?" My arms simulate a slanted capsizing motion.

Brabeck mumbles frantically, and then his face brightens. "The Estonia!"

"The Estonia?"

"Yes. She sank within 30 minutes. Careened to one side. The people ran for their lives... up the deck... held onto the rails... and slid down into the water! A unique situation!"

It made sense to me, and seemed our only chance. I was also hoping that the *Shiraz*, as it tilted over, would drift off its deadly ramming course and miss the disabled aircraft carrier.

"Brabeck, how can we stop the engines? We have to slow the ship down."

Suddenly the Chief Engineers exhales, as if a change is occurring within him. Slowly his tense features relax. Is this the calm before the storm I wonder?

"Brabeck, the engines!"

"Yes sir. The engines will stop automatically as soon as the ship tilts more than 30 degrees to the side," he explains calmly, keeping his eyes glued to the warning lights.

"Then let's get to the gym. To the hostages!"

Brabeck stands riveted to the spot. "I will stay here," he announces, solemnly.

A transfigured shine comes from his dewy eyes. Now he's lost his mind after all! He is, however, my only ally aboard ship. No way is he staying here! I have to bring him back to his senses. Without further hesitation I pull out my persuader and fire three shots at the electronic panel above the control desk – shattering glass and metal. The lights go out, white smoke comes from the bullet holes. Another siren begins to wail, fade, and wail again. Brabeck gapes at me as if I had shot off his hands. He needed the push!

Pointing the Glock at his open mouth, I shove him towards the door.

"Pronto, pronto Brabeck! The hostages. There are 30 innocent tourists who need your help. Now let's get going, man, or you're going to slip on your own brain."

On our way to Deck A, I ask him for the location of the lifeboats and rafts. He gives me a signal with his hand, possibly suggesting that he's understood my question. Then we reach the gym and he throws the doors open.

"Okay Brabeck, you organize the evacuation of the tourists. Don't let me down! That is, if you care what happens to your head!"

But when we look inside the gym, it is empty – not a living soul. "Up on deck!" I scream, and we charge off in the opposite direction.

As soon as we get on deck I see Nadine, struggling against the wind, fighting her way to the missile launching pad. On the portside is the gray silhouette of an American destroyer. I can just imagine the fierce faces of the Marines and SEALS waiting for their mission to begin, sitting there in their camouflage paint.

It crosses my mind that if I were their Operations Chief I would attack right now. *The point is,* my common sense and experience tell me, *that those over there don't have the slightest idea what's going on over here... that's all Brenton would need in the dusk of his spectacular career... banner headlines worldwide: U.S. President orders lethal attack on harmless tanker off Gibraltar. And printed in small letters underneath: Polish thriller writer among the victims. It would serve me right with that name!*

75

Nadine appears from behind the low deckhouse and stops, legs straddled. I was about to joke with her, *and on top of that you're late! Don't you know precision is in our Swiss genes?* But her eyes wouldn't allow any levity – nothing in them now but blind hatred flaring in those once velveteen golden brown orbs. What had happened?

"Ton père? *Your dad?*" I ask. But she just coolly walks over to the intact missile. "What are you doing?" I yell to her in a voice that even to me sounds like that of a lunatic.

"What do you think I'm doing? I'm going to launch this thing, just as planned."

"I don't think you'll do that," I stammer back, as I fumble for my Glock. But she just shouts back in a fiercely determined voice that the work has to be completed. Surely the *Roosevelt* would not survive this last hit amidships just above the waterline. She asked whether I hadn't noticed anything in our travels? And why I thought she had been so willing to follow me? Definitely not out of nostalgia for Humphrey Bogart.

"And not for your blue eyes either, Polinsky!"

She quickly typed in the numerical firing code, and nodded in satisfaction.

"For God's sake, then why?" I asked.

I watched as her right hand casually rested next to the launch button. She had typed with her left hand and would fire with her right. The right hemisphere controls the creative work of the left hand, and the left side the practical work of the right hand. It's a very tough woman from the canyons of Dordogne standing in front of me right now. The older we get the more naïve we become. I had seen in her a French Marianne, proudly exposing her naked breasts to the wind up on the barricades – *Allons enfants de la patrie, le jour de gloire...* But this was what a glorious day in the would-be revolutionary life of a wannabe Marianne looks like!

"Power, Polinsky. Power and control," she says, practically frothing at the mouth.

"You are sick, Nadine. Come to your senses. There is still time!"

"Forget it. *Megiddo*, Baby! Death sings silently!"

The silent song of death. Tacite Cantat Mors. The lily?

"And your father? Is he part of the *Qaeda* too? Where is Thierry-Clé?"

"Thierry-Clé Moran is nothing but a cuckold fake," she said, breathing hard. "My real father is dead, Polinsky. You sat at his deathbed when he passed away, Stan. No less a person than Corps Commander Diesbach was my mother's lover. For many years. He explained it all to me in Zurich. I guess he wanted to get rid of that secret before he departed this trough of mortal error for good... Bless him. I am your Uncle Edouard's daughter."

My stomach drops. Her longing gaze travels to the horizon. I swallow hard, trying to digest it all.

Nadine, my cousin?

A gust of rainy wind slaps my face.

"Edouard put me in touch with bin Golem–"

"No, no, not my uncle, never," I protest angrily.

She just laughs at me: "Edouard thought of infiltrating us into Golem's organization. You and me a team, to bring the terrorist down. Everything was carefully planned. Igor didn't have any idea that he was nothing but bait. I was almost absolutely sure that the Corps Commander had written it all down in the encrypted text of the red file. That's why I had to get it."

"So, you defected... changed side, let Edouard down, you... you knew all along that Khalid–" It took my breath away. My hand tightened on my pistol. "Why, Nadine? Why?"

"Is that even a question? Don't be ridiculous, Polinsky! Power, riches, that's what makes the world go round. We are the new counterbalance to the Americans. Well? Have you figured it out yet? Edouard is dead. I am left alone. But with Yussef by my side I will lead the triumphant advance of the *Qaeda*! We are the revolutionaries. I have all the codes. He has the freedom fighters. My life has a meaning again. Together, we are invincible!"

"The dugout with the lily? You knew about it all along?"

"What do you think? Edouard told me about the encrypted notes in the file. He even mentioned a key to decrypt it. At the time I didn't think it was important, so I ignored it. Later I remembered it was somehow related to Thierry-Clément Moran. When I saw the picture with the inscription on the *Mirage* yesterday up on Moulay Hill, the blinders fell from my eyes. Bingo. *Tacite Cantat Mors*. The key sentence. Thierry-Clé was the key! It all came back to me. It was all about luring you to Moulay Hill with the red file to make contact with Golem's people. I hoped you might join me in a great team..." She sighs. "In the file, there is all the data about the suppliers of the latest missiles – *Exocets, Sunburns, and SQ-99s.*

The names of all the go-betweens, the financiers, the politicians, the government officials. Everybody who received money from the lily. Edouard was very precise! The file is very highly charged. Whoever has it has the rulers in their grip – all the people who indirectly supply bin Golem with the most state-of-the-art weapons systems – the French government, the bigwigs of the armaments industry, even the CIA Director – the list is as long as my arm Polinsky!"

"So what you want is revenge. Your hatred is eating you up."

"So what? What's eating you, Polinsky? The Americans humiliated me. They conned me. Isn't that what they did to you? They wanted to rob me. Steal my discovery, the fruits of all my hard work. But enough babbling."

The ship starts careening hard to the right. Nadine realizes the situation.

"You will fly us out of here with the helicopter. Me and Yussef! Join us, Stan! We will enjoy life, make love... didn't you like it with me?" Not doubting my obedience for an instant, she moves toward the launching pad and puts her hand back on the switch.

"Stop, Nadine!"

I hold my gun in firing position with both hands. "This is where we go our separate ways. Your game is over!"

"You are a fool, Polinsky! You'll never get it. We are fighting for a new order of things. The power of Islam, the future..."

"And for this lunacy you're willing to sacrifice 5,000 people? Not with my help. Take your hand off that switch!"

She looks at my gun and me mockingly. Her golden

brown eyes sparkle bewitchingly. The Marianne bust, which at one point I would have loved to reveal with a quick flick of my wrist, surges provocatively.

"Come on, Stan. You can't shoot me. You'll never do it."

She sneers at me as she smiles and puts her hand on the button. *Quelle femme!* The steel of my gun is so warm it's hard to say where my hand ends and the gun begins.

"I am deadly serious, Nadine. Last warning. Step away from the switch."

She pushes the security lid to the side. I can't do it, but somehow my hand pulls the trigger. The bullet smashes into her upper arm and digs in deep, its impact hurling her against the launch pad. But even as she falls she reaches back for the button.

I don't even know where the second shot hits. But blood spurts, and she collapses. I leap toward her, and the beautiful Frenchwoman is in my arms, lifeless. The missile! I let Nadine sink to the deck, grab a thin rope and tie it around the stabilizing wing of the last *Exocet*. I find the other end and frantically search for somewhere to anchor it.

Behind me I see the silhouettes of two figures wildly rowing with their arms as they race toward me. Gasping, I pick up her body, still deceptively warm, and carry it over to the shelter of the deckhouse. Then I carefully place it on the deck. *Tacite Cantat Mors.* Or rather, *In Pace Resquiescat.* My hot-blooded gunwoman is dead. Light colored blood trickles from her stubbornly curved mouth, thickens, and clots darkly on her pale cheek.

I hear loud voices. Brabeck? The rope? Where is it? Slipped from my hand, gone. Like Nadine. Like all of us?

76.

I cling to a doorframe as the deck increasingly tilts towards starboard. Turning to look for help I see instead the muzzle of a gun. Igor holds it and grins sardonically as he grabs my arm and twists it behind my back, pushing the pistol's barrel against my neck. Then I see bin Golem trying to keep his balance as he rushes toward the missile launch pad.

"It's all over now, Golem," I yell at him. "You are old and worn-out. Today, only youth is important – and they're the realistic generation. They're programmed differently from an old ideologist like you, Golem. You're antiquated, a would-be revolutionary, just a dirty old man. Your harem pants don't count for anything anymore."

Either the Arab isn't listening to me or doesn't care what I'm saying, which makes me even angrier. "You have no idea about young people today. They're the guerillas of fun. America is not your enemy. You're a media star now aren't you? Isn't that the American dream? You may be ugly, but you're famous. I give you a year, maybe two, before you start primping yourself with dental floss and deodorant. Islam has no charms against that. Remember, Hitler had bad breath. The kids of today's media society are gentle people – they like the dental floss, and the deodorant. They're not interested in your violence. Your stupid violence is outdated, anyway, Golem. Young people today want their cell phones and their iMacs – and they want them all before their first French kiss, even in your backward Arab countries. Old freedom fighters like you are out of style and out of touch!"

Now he is close enough to me to hear everything I say. He stares at me, balefully, and speaks to me in utter contempt.

"That was your funeral address, American. I have heard better. You are a dreamer. An infatuated dreamer. And that was your last dream."

Igor presses the gun harder against my throat, so hard that I can barely breathe. Bin Golem pulls out a plastic card and steps over to the missile site where he bends over the gray box. Because radar guidance was disabled, he has to enter the target data manually, he informs me. I don't bother to tell him that Nadine had already done so. I need the time. If he was successful, I knew this last missile would sink the *Roosevelt*.

I'm seething with rage as Igor pushes the gun so hard against my throat that I nearly black out for a few seconds. Igor senses my wooziness and makes the mistake of letting my arm go, thinking the pressure of the gun barrel against my throat can control me. I instantly drop to my knees and knock the gun away with my free hand. It fires, but misses. In a flash I reach for Alaoui's knife lashed to my calf. Before Igor could regain his balance I stab him in the neck up into his mouth. I feel the metal hit his teeth from below. Pulling down I cut his jugular. Blood spurts out, and he drops the gun and staggers backwards over the slippery deck, falling and cracking his skull on a steel winch. He slowly slips down the deck and lays there, motionless.

But bin Golem jumps on me like a tiger. He is very fast and determined. I pick him up and throw him to the deck, but he is up again very nimbly and pulls a dagger from his baggy pants. The long blade glistens in the rain. I jump back and stumble over the ropes, cables, and chains used to hoist the missiles onto the deck. But he leaps over them on top of me, pressing the blade against my throat.

"She is dead, Golem. Nadine is dead!" I scream with my last ounce of strength into his sheet-white face and eyes blazing with hatred. And for a split second he eases the pressure of his dagger.

"You are lying. Nadine, Nedella, my Nedella... no she is alive..."

Amazement and doubt are struggling in his mind. His veins swell in his temples. With a last effort I throw him off me and reach out for a wrench lying between two cables. But I'm too slow! He already has the tool in his fist and hits me with it again and again. "Nobody takes... Nedella away... from me!"

The hard metal pounds the side of my head. I roll over dizzy – truly expecting the stab from his dagger that will put an end to it all. But bin Golem pauses and gets up instead. The missile launch consumes his mind. He stands before the keypad, punches in the code, spellbound by his mission. He doesn't see the heavy-duty nylon rope curling around his ankle. But he seems to feel it ... No! He kicks it away. My hands find the rope still tied to the missile's stabilizer wing. I cautiously drag the loose end toward me as the pain in my head makes everything dance before my eyes. Very gently I tie a large sliding loop in the end of the rope, and pray to God that bin Golem doesn't notice that the other end is tied to the *Exocet!*

The wind and rain whip across the slanted deck. With a triumphant gesture the Sheik presses the red button in the box.

"Ten seconds!" he shouts, apparently unaware of the world around him. I halfway straighten up and swing my improvised lasso like a cowboy in a rodeo. Could I possibly do this? Maybe he's right –I am a dreamer.

"Five, four…" bin Golem counts down, unaware that no one is watching or listening other than myself. He is fixated on the missile, his eyes glowing. It crosses my mind that this may actually be the first time he finishes his dirty work with his own two hands.

"Two…"

I twirl the lasso one more time and throw it at him. It seems to move in slow motion… much too far! But then a stronger gust of wind holds the open lasso in the air and blows it back. The noose lowers over the black-haired head of the Islamic leader in a perfect oval and slides over his shoulders. I pull my end of the rope with a jerk, tightening it around his neck just as the rocket, wailing, launches from the deck. The rope burns my hands as it zips through. At the last moment I let go and jump to the side.

The terrorist leader seems momentarily confused as the rocket blasts off, watching it as if spellbound. With tremendous acceleration the long narrow missile with its lethal explosive head roars into the sky. The rope flies after it. Bin Golem awakes from his daze, and his hands fly to the rope around his neck. But he is too late – and so powerful is the pull of the rope attached to the *Exocet* that it simply rips his suddenly gigantic looking head from his body, a dreadful sight. A jet of blood shoots up from the headless trunk of the powerful Qaeda leader. His body quivers and dances and falls on the deck, and the once proud figure is now just a lifeless mass of meat wrapped in a white winding sheet.

The headless trunk rolls against the launch pad. And

still the blood pulses from the horrible frayed hole between his shoulders, coloring the rain water on deck red. Who knows where the head is?

The powerful jerk given the *Exocet* when it decapitated bin Golem makes it spin off to the left. In an absurd corkscrew spiral, the deadly missile soars up and then tumbles down in a crazy curve, wiggling into the foaming sea.

Completely dizzy, holding my head, I struggle to my feet, totally nauseous. I lose my balance, fall to my knees, and puke my guts out, throwing up all of the disgust from my stomach and soul.

The *Shiraz* was now fearsomely listing to starboard. Breakers gushed over the railing. I bent over Igor and took his gun, stumbling around the deckhouse and then moving towards the superstructure. I noticed that the permanent soft vibration had stopped – the engines were idle. My plan had worked!

I barged into a box filled with rescue gear, lifted the lid, found flares. Unaware of naval signals, I chose one with the label "All Clear." I held it high above my head and ripped out the short fuse. A loud bang like a gunshot sounded in my ears followed by white noise. In the overcast sky I could see three bright green stars falling into the sea on three small white parachutes. The flare must have burned my hand because it looked like I had put it into the microwave – cold on the outside, numb on the inside.

77

The young wiry commander of the Navy SEALS unit aboard the nearby U.S. destroyer kept his binoculars trained on the *Shiraz* even as he delivered a lecture about its terrorist commander.

"If we judge bin Golem by his historical significance at the turn of the century, then I guess we'd have to call him a giant. I mean, to his people, he's a great reformer, trying to take them out of the dry desert to the rest of the world's fertile plains."

No one seemed to argue with him about it, so he continued.

"I mean, he uses religion, kind of like a means to an end. And with good results I'd say. In the last 100 years the Arabs have become a major power in international politics. They've become a real force. And you have to admire them for that. They're a proud people. And bin Golem cleverly exploits this pride for his own purposes. Unfortunately, like all fanatics, he doesn't have any limits as to what he'll do... Wait! Look there! It's a flare! A signal from the *Shiraz*! Ok, this is it. Let's head over there."

"Do we have orders?" a Marine sergeant asked.

The SEAL commander gave him the binoculars.

"We don't have to wait any longer, Ben. See for yourself. They're tipping over, capsizing. The *Shiraz* is definitely in distress. Let's go men!"

The wind was dying down and the overcast skies

began to clear. About 100 SEALS quickly made their way to the loading ramp.

78.

The *Shiraz* had tilted so far over to starboard that walking upright was no longer possible. Down in the ship's mess, bottles and glasses had dropped off their shelves and smashed against the floor. One of the stewards lay groaning on the dining room floor after smashing his head against a pillar. In his quarters, the drunken cook had been rolled out of his bunk.

Brabeck worked his way through the chaos of overturned racks in the ship's shopping area, crawling up a squeaking flight of metal stairs to the lifeboats on portside. Landlubber that I was, I had no idea how to leave a capsizing ship. As I staggered through corridors, leaning against the walls, I thought perhaps the best thing to do would be to slide down the hull of the ship.

I approached a stairway that was dangerously tilted to the side. Water rushed at me and gurgled into the dark depths of the ship. I couldn't think straight, and kept wondering where all the water was coming from, given that the ship's portside was rising high above the sea. I figured the best way out would be to follow the screams.

I crawled up through the first door I found, and when I opened it I looked at the quickly emptying pool where I had landed at the beginning of my brutal odyssey only, so it seemed to me, minutes ago. I avoided the river of streaming pool water as well as the floating deckchairs and made my way to the small railing of the pool deck.

The screams came from three lifeboats that were being gradually lowered over the alarmingly slanted side of the ship.

As the *Shiraz* careened still further to starboard, the American tourists in their yellow life jackets climbed over the railing. The hull of the ship was less slippery than the deck, and they went over one by one. A bright red life raft danced on the wind-whipped three-foot high waves. One of the lifeboats had capsized and was floating keel up as people clung to its side.

Two men seemed to be in charge of the evacuation. At first I thought one must be Brabeck, but then saw him nowhere. I worked my way further up. Already, two-thirds of the giant hull's russet-colored skin was rising up out of the water; on the starboard side, the deck was already deep under water.

Clinging to the brass rail, I look straight ahead over the bow. The sight was amazing. Monumental. My heart thumped so loud I could count its beats aloud – like a sledge-hammer. I couldn't move for a dozen pounding heartbeats. Less than 600 yards straight ahead was the *Roosevelt*, lying motionless, like a mighty, gray, defenseless monster. And the *Shiraz*, with the dreamer Polinsky at its railing, was headed straight for it with the tip of its bow.

Quintus helped the last ten hostages into a lifeboat and shouted something at the tall, thickset man next to him.

I saw Brabeck and wanted to warn him, but the scream stuck in my throat as I noticed Khalid, machine gun under his arm, crawl out of the large hatch of a cabin. He was roaring in anger, and he took aim at the defenseless Americans in the lifeboat. Brabeck saw him and slid quickly down a maintenance ladder. Suddenly he was not more than four feet above the executioner firing at the boat.

Brabeck threw a boathook and hit Khalid on the head,

but not hard enough to knock him out. He dropped his machine gun for a second and seemed a bit dazed, but before the engineer was able to hit him again he was back on his feet.

"Brabeck, stop!" I cried.

"That swine belongs to me!" the engineer shouted back to me. He jumped on Khalid, blocking me from a clean shot. They fought on the tilted deck, found footholds, landed blows, fell over and got back up. Khalid could take a lot, and give some too. By the time I had gotten close enough, it was too late.

"Khalid, freeze!" I screamed and fired. But I missed. And Khalid kicked Brabeck in the head. The neck broke. It cracked like a frozen branch under a boot. The engineer's heavy body went limp, and Khalid pushed his body down the slanted deck into the foaming sea.

And then the Executioner turned to me. His repulsively ugly face looked even nastier as he grinned diabolically at me. He picked up his machine gun from the pile of ropes it had fallen into.

"Ah, finally! The great Polinsky!"

He lifted his gun, not against his shoulder but at chest level. Desperate for cover I tried to move and slipped, then had to reach for something to hold on to... and my gun slipped out of my hand, rolling down the deck into the deep. Gone!

"Bad luck, Polinsky, aka Ken Custer, also known as..." Calm, almost composed, Khalid takes aim at me – as if that were even necessary from this distance. Then, suddenly, his head drops forward, his front teeth biting down into his tongue. His grin freezes into a grotesque grimace. A shiny piece of metal had come flying through the air and hit him directly in the back of the head. When he collapsed, I saw that the projectile was a dumbbell. I guessed a five-pounder. An ugly wound gaped on the back of Khalid's head. It even made him look somewhat human.

"Don't just stand there, help me!" Sam roared as he struggled to lift Khalid's unconscious body. "I don't believe in bodybuilding, but those dumbbells can sure change the look of a body! Xaver, Mr. Snell, over here!"

Two black speedboats with heavy machine guns mounted on their prows came speeding over as two Sea Hawk helicopters circled above the now nearly horizontal superstructure. In the open hatches of the copters were fierce-looking soldiers standing by. There were excited screams from the lifeboats.

"The Marines! The Marines!"

"Stop!" Sam screamed at me as I had lifted the dumbbell and was ready to smash Khalid's skull to a pulp with it.

"We want the son of a bitch alive so we can draw and quarter him and throw his body to the coyotes," he said, with an expression that seemed inclined to personally take care of the drawing and quartering. The ex-cop Snell and Xaver tied Khalid's feet and hands; and I reluctantly put the dumbbell down. But Sam was right. Khalid was more use to us alive than dead, and particularly to me. Steinlin would be insane with joy. Finally we had our third man – that was him for sure, even though he looked a bit worse for wear!

Suddenly I looked to the bow for the giant silhouette of the *Roosevelt*. And there it was… At this very moment, the aircraft carrier's Pry-Fly soared, so close you could almost touch it, above the careening *Shiraz*.

"We're going to ram! Abandon ship!"

I crept over to the ropes that had secured the lifeboats and waited for the crash that seemed terribly immanent. But then I lost my balance and my handholds, and found myself standing on the slanting side of the ship, the rough sea 60 feet below me. I could see soldiers in speedboats working frantically to pick people out of the water. My feet started to slip! Suddenly I was skipping, and then running wildly, down the outside hull of the ship, picking up speed until I couldn't stop.

Finally I dove out as far away from the ship as I could, stretching out with a concave back and trying to remember to fold and dive at the last moment. *Theory, damn theory!* The fall seemed endless. And in the middle of it a strong gust of wind turned me completely around. Rowing with my arms clumsily I crashed backwards into a black mass of waves. I hit the water so hard I passed out. I didn't even feel any pain. I only knew I was breathing water into my lungs... and black water embraced me...

When her slanted lifeboat hit the water without capsizing, Zoe tied her life jacket on tighter with trembling fingers. She pressed her legs hard against the boat's planks. The current pulled the boat quickly away from the dangerously careening *Shiraz*. In shock she looked up at the mightily towering tanker's hull. *That I had managed to get down from there!*

Then she saw a man running down the tanker's side before finally jumping and diving through the air. It almost looked like a perfect dive, but no! The wind spun him around! In an instinctive attempt to get his dive back on track, Zoe wiggled and fidgeted in rhythm with his helplessly rowing arms.

But of course it didn't help, and the body turned over, seemed to hang in mid-air indefinitely, and then finally hit the waves, back first. She screamed as if she had felt the pain herself. Somebody shouted that was him. *Who? The stranger. The one who had been up with Sam, helping them...*

Zoe didn't hesitate. She kept her balance and stepped up onto the seat and jumped into the waves. The thick life jacket impeded the progress of her strong crawl, so she peeled herself out of it and swam really fast.

The crew up on the AWAC 600 held their breath. Their bird's eye view from 3,300 feet of the breathtaking drama below was staggering: the tilted supertanker moving inevitably towards the Big Stick, almost ready to ram it. In the background loomed the dark rocks of Gibraltar.

"It's gonna be matchwood," said the weather specialist.

"No... she's veering around... She's veering round, she's gonna miss, wooh!"

A gigantic jet of foam shot up into the air as the once proud *Shiraz* fell completely onto her side and her blue superstructure splashed into the sea. As it hit the water the large black chimney that dominated her superstructure acted like a rudder and abruptly turned and slowed the *Shiraz* instantly, rotating her toward starboard.

Captain Adler aboard the *Hawkeye* thought it looked just like a boatswain had stabbed a huge oar in the water with all his might and turned the ship around. In spite of the precariousness of the circumstances, he was glad to be in position to witness this spectacle. He realized that the deviation from ramming course had literally occurred in the last minute.

Spraying foam and driving waves in front of it, the massive hull of the *Shiraz* missed the damaged stern of the *TR* by a matter of a few yards. And as it passed by, the former super tanker suddenly turned over completely, keel straight up, gliding past the aircraft carrier like a giant torpedo.

"Guys, don't tell me there's no Santa Claus!" Captain Adler groaned.

People had been holding their breath all over the world watching this near miss: onboard the AWAC 600, on the *TR* bridge and in its control room, in the CIC aboard the *Ross*, at the Situations Room in the White House, and at the Operations Center of the Strategic Air Command in Colorado. The aerial shot from the AWAC had come in crystal clear to everyone who watched as the *Shiraz*, like a giant rusty red nail nudged aside by the hand of an angel, glided past the *TR's* ravaged body. What a tremendous relief! But the crippled super tanker was still moving at an amazing rate of speed, pushing waves of foam ahead of it, sending up trails of spume that were buffeted by the wind. And within just a few minutes, the lethal danger to the crew of 5,000, including the President, had passed. Keel up, the *Shiraz* drifted towards the rocks of Gibraltar. And then suddenly, like a volcano, she burst. Jets of flame shot up from her broken hull accompanied by roaring explosions. An ugly black trail of smoke spiraled up into the slowly clearing skies over the Strait of Gibraltar. Also consumed by this fire, of course, was the red file. Burned to ashes, rejected by the fish as unworthy food. This was an outcome never expected by Edouard Diesbach, the old rake. And yet, was this the old gambler's last hand?

79.

Zoe gasps for breath as she reaches the spot where she saw the falling body drop into the sea. She takes a deep breath and dives. On her way down she does her best to remember the instructions of the lifeguard in that class so long ago!

She spots a light gleam in the dark green water and swims for it. Reaching out she feels and grabs a shirt. She sees the motionless body, and then a pale face. She swims upward with it in her grasp as fast as she can. Her lungs feel as if they are about to burst as she urges herself not to let go! Finally she surfaces, coughing, spitting, struggling for air. And then she screams for help. A large wave breaks over her head and suddenly the body slips from her grip. *Why isn't the lifeboat coming!*

Then she suddenly feels the body's hands on her legs, pulling her down into the deep. She starts to panic, but then images from her memory move through her mind in rapid succession. The swimming instructor at poolside. His hand motions about how to cope with this. The other students shouting encouragement to her. She lets the body pull her under the waves. And then she reaches down and grabs him by the hair and pulls him away from her. She slides both hands under his chin and strikes hard in an upward motion. The head with the pale face and the wide opened eyes fall back and air bubbles gurgle from his mouth. His grasp weakens. Then she pulls her knees up hard and struggles free. Even though her lungs are burning like hellfire, she reaches down and grabs his hair from behind and pulls him to the surface. Greedily she gulps down the air.

He has blacked out, and she holds his head above the waves as she floats on her back. *What now?*

A shadow darkens the water, and a massive black body sweeps over above her. She's heard of flying fish, but what is this? A flying whale?

Then she realizes it's a SEALS Sea Hawk helicopter, floating low over the surface of the waves. A diver in a rubber suit slides down a rope to her, and a second unit with a rescue basket dangles from another rope.

"Come on, man, show some life!" Zoe screams at the body. She gets Polinsky into the basket and bends forward over his open mouth. Exhaling strongly, she forces air into it.

EPILOGUE

Well, that almost would have been it – but thanks to Zoe I managed to survive my Olympic dive from the capsizing *Shiraz* into the Atlantic off Gibraltar. Fortunately the water temperature at this confluence of the Atlantic and Mediterranean was not too cold at that time of the year, which made rescuing all the hostages easier for the SEALS and the Marines, who were also supported by the *Roosevelt's* rescue teams.

I remember regaining consciousness at some time, shaking off the blankets I was wrapped in. I also remember letting a very attractive young nurse rub my aching back and numb legs – who knows, if the watchful Zoe weren't sitting next to my bed in a chair where else the Good Samaritan might have rubbed? Even in my exhausted beaten state I felt that if she kept massaging me with those strong hands for too much longer the folds of my blanket might have risen to one mighty peak. But this was definitely my kind of situation: two lovely young women paying attention to me, nice dry air, no ocean water filling my lungs. And of course nothing is as erotically energizing as success!

In the end the girls tried to get me into the uniform of a U.S Navy Commander, which might not be unfitting given what I had managed to accomplish. But I refused. More discreetly, please. Irina, Steinlin, Waldo, Mario, the dashing lady adjutant – all of them knew me as Polinsky, the very shady paperback writer. I was their kind of person – at least in some way. And that's how it was supposed to stay. So my two saving angels left me to search for less conspicuous clothes.

I was daydreaming as a very large man came into my view. His angular face melted into a warm smile.

"A message from the Captain, Mister Polinsky. The man is safely locked away behind bars on the fifth lower deck."

"Khalid?"

"Yep. He's under 24-hour guard. All the seamen are mad at the son of a b...gun."

I hoped that that would be equally true for the Grand Jury of the Supreme Court of the District of Manhattan. *Guilty. Death row...*

Sitting up halfway, I read the man's function from his uniform – he was the Ship's Chaplain. *A minister*, I thought. *Okay, I was out of the woods for sure now.*

"May God have mercy on his soul," I said. "And the sooner the better."

Nodding, the man of the cloth agreed. "Justice shall be done! And how are you feeling, my son?"

"I feel great! Body and soul in harmony, no problems." *What a great feeling! No problems, Stan!*

"That's the way it's supposed to be, my son. You are definitely blessed today. Someone was watching over you." The chaplain made a sign of benediction towards me and started limping toward the door. When he saw my questioning look, he slapped his left leg. "War injury. Nearly flew into the jaws of death. Ever since then I've been working for the Big Boss up there. That was my turn."

Smiling at me to the last, he walked out the door.

All's well that ends well! That's what Judge Righetti will have to say to Steinlin when he closes the Polinsky files. Mission accomplished, Stan. No hay problemas! This time I nearly got around to meeting the Big Boss. Good thing I had someone watching over me.

Later on I went over to the sick bay aboard the *USS Gonzalez*, which looked like a makeshift hospital – and the freed hostages were all over me with appreciation.

"Are you from Krypton?" asked Sophie the teenager, as if I were Superman. She even asked me for an autograph.

Doctor Yale was there putting Quintus' leg in a splint, while the giant Sam was sipping a mug full of hot beef tea as he sat with Senator Strong, who was sipping what looked like a Scotch. He ran his fingers through his wild mane of gray hair. As he pointed his square chin in my direction I got the impression that the two of them were talking about me. It turned out later that this clever old fox of a politician had proposed me for the Congressional Medal of Honor. Yes, I could see how he might enjoy basking in my honor! Thank God I got wind of it in time and was able to prevent it at the last moment. The Congressional Medal of Honor is a bit like the Nobel Prize for Literature – a ticket to the funeral of a normal human existence. Not that I would ever wind up on the short Nobel Prize list...

And then, well, there was this thing with the Commander in Chief of the U.S. Armed Forces. Nothing official, thank goodness. A white-haired old warhorse in civilian clothes by the name of Merritt – who looked like Sean Connery's uncle, or may even Clint Eastwood's great uncle –

showed up and politely but firmly asked me to follow him. Outside on deck it was already dark, and a stiff breeze cut mercilessly through my windbreaker. We approached the barely visible silhouette of a Chinook helicopter. Merritt pointed to the broad foldaway stairs. I tried to bounce up them as quickly as my numb legs allowed, that is to say I dragged myself up them by the handrail. In the dimly lit interior there was nobody, not even a pilot. But the door on the right was open, and then suddenly filled with a well-known figure.

"Major... I mean, Mister Polinsky," Jack Brenton smiled.

These never ending insinuations, I cursed to myself. The past should stay locked in a cellar behind me. Out of sight, out of mind. Of course, I once was Major Ken Custer, I suppose in a way I actually still was. Could I remember Philadelphia? Gstaad? Libya? Parsenn? The guys from the CIA know it, my fans know the stories... But now I am Stan Polinsky. I think you know that, don't you? So leave me alone with your hints of my over and done with forgotten past if you please!

The President grabbed my right hand and his left hand found my elbow and, moving up a bit, gave it a hearty squeeze. Brenton was as famous as he was infamous for the countless casual intimate variations in his repertoire of greetings. In spite of my stiff neck, stiff shoulders, sore back, and aching arms, I managed to produce an almost acceptable salute.

"Mister President, sir!"

"Well, Stan," he started, and came straight to the point, "what's your handicap?"

Did I look that banged up? Was I elated over his concern?

"That's a long list, sir. How much time do we have? I got pretty bounced around out there."

His smile stayed as casual and warm as it had been.

"I mean at golf, Stan."

"Oh, golf. I have no idea. I never write anything down."

He nodded at me as if this were precisely the answer he had expected.

"You see, well, Joe, I mean Joe Sorelli and I... well, we need... yes, we need a partner. An impartial partner. And so I thought..."

President Brenton's enemies often learned the hard way how deceptive his boyish southern charm could be. It was said that he would stop at nothing to get what he wanted either in politics or business – or even if he wanted you to come over for a little picnic. Like many of those poor souls, I wasn't given the time to think or to regain my composure. All I could manage was a mumbling, "Sir, I don't know..."

"Good," he grinned. "You're our man. Somebody who is really impartial *never* knows anything. Take a couple of weeks break and then call me. That's an order, Major, uh, I mean Mister Polinsky."

I barely managed to say "Yes, sir, Mr. President," and salute, before he had already turned around, acknowledging my salute in such an exaggeratedly casual way as no one but a civilian who has risen to be the most powerful man in the world could do.

And so a week later I found myself on the first tee of a fancy golf course in Zurich early in the morning of an almost stormy day all by myself, saying over and over again to myself that Uncle Edouard had never paid any attention to a golf club, even from a distance, in his entire life. Finally, I was, no, unfortunately, I was my very own boss again.

Here's something I should mention before leaving. As I was writing this entire story down, rumors had it that Polinsky was in trouble again.

But not really. I'm in the best of moods. No hay problemas, I would tell anyone who asked with a playful punch in the chest. One day, after playing golf with the President, I jokingly suggested that we make a humorous video about the last days of a lame duck. To my amazement, he thought it was a great idea and set about having it done.

The story started off well. I gave the outline and basic concept to Tony, Robin, and Deepak, and a few others – and finally they shot it and it became famous. Brenton washing his car, mowing his lawn. The press corps had fun with it, first talking about the making of it, then watching it over a dinner. And that's when my troubles started, for Robin claimed that I had stolen the idea of making the video from him – which would have been alright, but then he made the mistake of grabbing my collar and pressing his point, which was when I flattened the six foot three closet queen onto the floor... thanks to the instructions of my kung fu instructor Li-Li: learn well, do well.

Well, at least it made the President laugh to watch two very fierce-looking Marines (to keep up the appearance of a respectable dinner) escort me out the back door to the applause of the audience. And what did the papers call it the next day?

Nothing but a part of the festivities – another successful and funny interlude in a very entertaining evening.

* * *